JERI ESTES

WordSmith Productions Inc.
Studio City, CA

Stilettos and Steel

Inquiries should be addressed to:
WordSmith Productions, Inc.
12439 Magnolia Blvd., #299
Studio City, CA 91607
Tel: 800-809-6256
www.stilettosandsteel.com

ISBN: 978-0-9845173-0-5
Publisher's Cataloging-in Publication data available upon request

Printed in USA

Cover photo: Suzanne Gagnier
Cover Model: Michaela
Design: Dotti Albertine

★ ★ ★ ★ ★

**TO THE A-LIST STARS OF MY LIFE,
IN ORDER OF APPEARANCE:**

KID BROTHER ... MAX ESTES

LOVING DAUGHTER ... ELENA MERCHAND

LEADING LADY ... GISELLE NAGY

Chapter 1

WELCOME TO THE TENDERLOIN

I TURNED THE CORNER on Ellis and Powell Streets with a red rose in my hand. The chilly night air stole through my silk shirt as I made my way to the Why Not lounge. Sporting a new leather jacket and polished wing tips, I rehearsed my best clean-up lines. Carmen knew me too well for just anything to work.

At this hour, the heart of San Francisco came alive with romance and glamour. Antique fog lamps softly illuminated the sidewalks. Other suitors walked arm in arm with their girls through Union Square. Shiny black limos dropped off well-heeled travelers draped in minks, diamonds and tailored overcoats. Glowing candles on white linen peeked through the windows of the five-star restaurants. Grand facades of elegant shops and historic hotels lent the streets a Parisian grandeur.

As I neared the Tenderloin, the neighborhood lost its civility. Flower-crowned hippies, restless soldiers and glossy ladies of the night emerged from the mist. Strip joints, beer bars and panhandlers announced the opening of San Francisco's red light district. It welcomed runaways from all over, people like me who didn't fit in at home.

Only a few years ago, I was living just north of L.A. in a quiet bedroom community with my family. Predictable and secure, our middle-class suburb was like food without seasoning.

I arrived in San Francisco intoxicated by the freedom and dangers that lay before me. Enchanted by the city's opulent beauty, I'd unfortunately settled into the low-rent Tenderloin district.

I walked until I reached a large martini glass with a neon olive hanging above the sidewalk. Traveling the stem of the glass was a large sign: WHY NOT? Good and bad guys mingled after work at this favorite cop watering hole. Inside, my girlfriend was slinging drinks to San Francisco's finest, from beat heat to City Hall brass.

Dark, smoky windows filled with Budweiser and happy hour signs framed the steel front door. Stopping before the entrance of the club, I checked myself out in the hazy glass. A handsome young face and lean physique reassured me. That was good because my girl was pissed off at me again. Running my fingers through my short, wavy blond hair, I shot myself a cocky grin. I sniffed the rose in my hand and said a silent prayer.

Inside the chrome door, I stepped into the world of pigs. Smoke, booze and the sound of clicking billiard balls embraced me. I made my way to the bar, which stretched across the back of the room. The mirrored glass behind the counter was covered with racks of booze and bowling trophies.

Framed photos of fallen police officers lined a side wall. The small round tables were packed with uniformed and non-uniformed alike, drinking and swapping urban war stories. Out of the dingy smoke appeared Carmen, as radiant as a wildflower.

My girlfriend was serving drinks to two buff, pool-playing admirers. Long auburn hair fell around her beautiful face as she handed the guys their beers. She exposed enticing cleavage in a tight green blouse that matched her emerald eyes. Looking up, Carmen allowed me a reluctant smile.

I sat next to a soldier and ordered a Jack from Annie the bartender. The New York Bronx broad was a retired prison matron who could handle the rough crowd. Instantly, a Jack with a water back hit the counter.

Carmen placed her hand on my shoulder and whispered in my ear, "Give me five minutes."

The scent of her Chanel reminded me of why I was so eager tonight. I placed the red rose down on the bar. Annie stepped up and said in the voice of a whiskey sour, "How's it going, Jesse?"

Her big bosom and arms leaned in on me. Annie was hard of hearing from years of working in prison cell blocks.

"I'm good, Annie. Can you get my soldier buddy here a drink?"

The spit and shine dude ordered a German beer.

"Thanks," said the young man.

"No…thank you," I replied. "My older brother's in 'Nam right now."

He nodded in appreciation. "You San Franciscans are really friendly. Giants are kicking ass," he added, indicating the TV hung in the corner.

"I know, it's a drag," I responded. "I'm a Dodger fan. Born and raised in the San Fernando Valley."

He shot me an apologetic grin. "Can't win them all."

I went back to my drink. The young man's proud bearing reminded me of my father.

Dad was an imposing six-foot-one, handsome blond with a disciplined physique. Though he had a gentle spirit and soft blue eyes, he delivered corporeal punishment in a way that was measured, fair, and militarily precise. His commendable service in World War II as a sergeant made him someone I didn't want to mess with.

An image came to me, of him sitting at the head of the dinner table. My respectable-looking father guided us by example. He was a pleasant conversationalist with impeccable manners. Dinner was served on white linen with elegant china. He presided over the dinner table with the wit, charisma and wisdom that made him a top-notch sales manager. I admired the way he handled his gang of door-to-door salesmen. Our whole family got involved in the company social activities, making his branch office a stellar one for Electrolux Vacuums. Watching him operate, I became fascinated with the art of selling and running a business, and my dad appreciated the feisty competitive spirit which we shared.

As I took a sip of my Jack, a wave of loneliness ran through me. Running away from home, I had escaped the Valley at sixteen. I'd been living on my own ever since. Often I yearned to go home, but I knew things could never be the same.

I came out of memory lane in a big hurry. I was nearly knocked right off the barstool as Captain Clancy's huge blubbery body squeezed down next to me. By design, he blocked my view of Carmen, and all I could smell were clouds of Brut cologne. The detective's trench coat fell open, exposing the butt of his gun. On his lapel were the typical sprinkled crumbs. His big paw caressed my knee and gave it a sweet squeeze.

I glared up at Clancy's beady blue eyes and putty face. He spoke down to me in a deep voice, "Jessica, why are you dressed as a boy?"

"Because this is how I like to dress!"

A filled drink tray slammed down onto the counter next to Clancy's arm. The rattling glasses and butt-packed ashtrays arrested the detective's attention, and in that moment Carmen took me by the arm and said, "Come on, let's leave this dump. My feet are killing me."

Clancy commanded, "Take a load off your feet, cutie," as he smacked the cushioned stool next to him.

Carmen's brilliant green eyes glossed over with irritation.

"Relax, Carmen, let's all have a drink together. Jesse kinda looks cute as a faggot."

My girlfriend shot Clancy the finger with a saccharine smile. "Not tonight."

"Be a good sport. Let's share," Clancy suggested.

"You get enough of my girl's time. She's off duty, and you've got a wife at home," Carmen reminded him.

Small beads of sweat dripped from underneath Clancy's toupee as he gave up his valiant effort for the evening. The Bronx broad served a boiler maker for the captain. "Here, drink up."

"I'll catch you later, Clancy," I said as I got up to leave. I started to drop a bill on the bar, but Clancy's big hand tenderly touched mine. He winked and said, "I got it, Jesse."

That suited me just fine. He was certainly a fool with money. Putting my dollar bill away, I took Carmen by the hand. As we started to leave, a well-dressed gentleman flagged Carmen over to his table. I glanced at the distinguished man as Carmen guided me over to him.

He rose to his feet and gave us a warm smile. A chiseled face and finely tailored rags shouted power and class. His demeanor said Ivy League and Harvard Law.

"Hi, Carmen. You look lovely tonight," exclaimed the tall, prematurely gray-haired young man. He spoke with perfect diction and a refined tone.

Carmen shyly replied with a slight flush to her cheeks, "Thanks, Phillip. I'd like you to meet my girlfriend, Jesse."

I firmly shook his hand and said, "How do you do? Pleased to meet you."

"Would you ladies like to join me for a drink?"

"That's very sweet of you, but we have plans," Carmen replied.

He nodded. "I understand. Why don't you let me drive you girls wherever you have to go?"

I wanted to head off any charming, rich men interested in my girl. "It was a pleasure meeting you." I put my arm around Carmen's waist and added, "Have a nice night."

We escaped the club into the dark street. I took a deep breath of cold, misty air. We strolled down the sidewalk in silence that was not altogether comfortable.

Under any other circumstances, I would have been arrested for impersonating the opposite sex. Luckily, the best perk of having the captain of homicide as my john was a lot less busts. To make money, I would pop on a long blond wig, throw on a dress and hit the side-walk hookin'. After work, I would shower and dress in my best men's clothes. Looking like a pretty boy, I'd hook up with my girl.

I fought off a twinge of jealousy as I asked Carmen, "Who was that rich asshole?"

"He's only the district attorney, Phillip Princeton III."

"Great, a trust fund baby playing civil servant, how cute," I replied.

Feeling possessive, I reached over to kiss my girl. She turned away slightly, resisting me. I flashed my prettiest smile and offered her the rose. Carmen ignored my gesture and continued walking. I wasn't being forgiven so easily. I asked, "Is something wrong, baby doll?"

Carmen shot me a skeptical glance. Last night I had stood her up for dinner. Carmen and her mother labored for hours over a sim-mering pot of meat sauce. They prepared an old family secret recipe for spaghetti and sausage. I was unable to come because Clancy had demanded an unexpected date.

"I can't say no to Clancy. I didn't know I would have to stay late."

"You could have at least called. I'm getting sick of this, Jesse."

I couldn't believe this was a problem for her. "What are you get-ting sick of? Are you trying to say you don't like my line of work?"

"Jesse, I don't care if you hook. Every lesbian in the Tenderloin hooks. I just don't like to disappoint my mother."

I held out my hands in innocence. "Honey, I like buying you nice things, and I enjoy taking your mother out."

Carmen abruptly stopped walking. That fire in her eyes would be attractive if she wasn't about to lay into me. "You just don't get it, do you, Jesse? I feel like you care more about things than me. Money is not why I'm with you."

I stood quietly and studied her for the right opening. Lowering my head, I attempted to give her the rose again with a sweet smile. As if in a confessional, I whispered, "Forgive me, I have sinned." I added a sincere mea culpa. "I fucked up. I promise I won't put work first again. You know I can't stand Clancy."

Carmen's red lips started to smile as her eyes softened. She took the rose from my hand, cuddled close and kissed me on the cheek. We lingered under the fog lamp as I gave her a long kiss. I felt her warm body press against mine.

"Jessica! Oh, Jessica!" Clancy's bellowing voice destroyed my moment of romantic intoxication.

"Come here, baby! I gotta talk to you!" Clancy hollered as Carmen released me.

"Dammit!" I said. "I'll be right back, just give me a minute."

"Ignore him! Just tell him to go fuck himself!"

"I better deal with him now before I go to L.A. tomorrow," I said, exasperated. "I want to enjoy my kid brother's birthday."

Carmen appeared even more irritated. "Suit yourself."

Carmen was not happy with my travel plans. She knew I had made arrangements to stay with my old buddy Speedy, and she knew what that meant. His name had been derived from his affection for methedrine and excessive partying.

I couldn't solve that problem right now. Instead, I walked back to head off Clancy. He was lumbering down the sidewalk with outstretched arms, like a sloppy drunk.

"Why won't you be my mistress? Tricking is no good for you," he slurred.

"Clancy, I don't have time to go over this again. You know you're my favorite john. Let's just leave it at that." Hurriedly I reassured him, "I'll visit you soon in a hot, sexy dress, but I gotta go now."

A shiny black Cadillac pulled up. The handsome district attorney lowered his electric window. He leaned forward and politely inquired, "Jesse, is everything okay?"

Clancy roared at him, "We're having a private conversation here!"

Flinching at the cop's manners, the D.A. nodded at me and drove off.

Clancy continued, teary-eyed and maudlin, "I'm just trying to get you off the streets."

"I know, Clancy, that's very considerate of you. Can we talk about this later?"

I turned around and saw the black Cadillac stop next to Carmen. Panicking, I sprinted toward the Caddy as she hopped into the front seat.

"Carmen!" I yelled. "Wait a minute!"

Carmen slammed the door.

"Damn it! Carmen!"

I watched as the taillights faded into the fog.

Chapter 2

RUNAWAY BLUES

L.**A. SUNLIGHT BURST THROUGH** the open Venetian blinds. Fighting off the morning, I turned my face to the wall. I wanted to drift back to sleep.

The sound of a barking dog tugged apart my slumber. I tried to gather my senses as I lay on the couch. Slowly, I opened my eyes. Staring down at me were the big black eyes and large shaggy head of Speedy's sheep dog, Grady. His hot panting breath blasted my face.

"Go away."

The dog was standing by my forearm, which I noticed was the color of a banana and swollen to the size of a baseball bat. My head was killing me, and I could taste last night's party souvenirs: stale peyote-laced hash and Red Mountain wine.

Grady flumped down beside me on the floor, and in a few moments he was sound asleep.

I lowered my head back onto the soft, worn cushions and reflected on how my life had gone from bad to worse lately. Before I ran away from home, I had been a typical middle-class teenager. That seemed like a lifetime ago. In a way, it was. The sordid way I was now living had aged me more than the three years I'd been gone.

For the past few months I'd been crashing at my friend Speedy's pad in East L.A. Speedy was a scrawny, wired white dude who dressed like Jimi Hendrix and shot speed like Janis Joplin downed Jack. A nickel-and-dime street rat, he dealt grass at the Whiskey-A-Go-Go. He worked Sunset Boulevard's dance clubs, where he catered to the soldiers on leave from Vietnam.

My brother Max and I had celebrated his birthday with Speedy at Gazzarri's Nightclub on the Sunset Strip. Afterward, we went with Speedy's friends to a party. The hippies lived in Venice Beach where the debris meets the sea. That night whiskey and weed persuaded me to travel on the mainline express. Speedy shot meth and I fixed Sweet Georgia Brown heroin for the first time. Max went back home to Woodland Hills, and I woke up in the East L.A. projects. A few weeks later, my one-night stand with the seductress of escape had turned into a bad marriage.

I wanted to get back home to San Francisco. First though, I had to get off this couch. I'd passed out last night fully dressed in a white wife-beater t-shirt and a pair of Levi's. My Saint Christopher medal dangled around my neck, showing off under my unbuttoned baby blue shirt.

Struggling to get my head together, I forced myself to sit up. Violent pain radiated up my arm. I studied the sore on the back of my hand next to a distended red vein. Judging from the look of the recent track mark, it was infected. Gingerly, I lifted my tender hand and rested it on my chest. I wanted a shot of whisky to numb the pain. That meant I needed to get to the bar over on Alvarado Street.

I could hear Speedy and his mother Dolores talking in the kitchen while she prepared breakfast. Dolores was a soft-hearted, silver-haired old lady who doted on her only child. Social Security checks and memories of more glorious days sustained her.

My temples pounded. Outside, Mexican children played in the streets. The strong aroma of greasy pork sausages from the kitchen assaulted my senses. Why did Delores have to pick this morning of all mornings to cook chorizo and eggs?

I sat up on the couch and stared vaguely at the braided area rug under my feet. My head spun and my stomach churned as my eyes followed each shade of green in the oval rug. I prayed aloud, "God, please let me make it to the bathroom." On the coffee table I spotted the joint I had left there last night next to my silver Playboy Zippo lighter. The Playboy rabbit's black perky face greeted me. Reaching down slowly with my good arm, I picked them both up.

Like a seasick sailor with his eyes on the horizon, I focused on the hall archway. My land in sight was the bathroom. I put my bomber and lighter down on the toilet tank cover. Courageously, I peered into the mirror. Much to my relief, the rest of me wasn't yellow like my arm. I smiled at my reflection.

"My arm might be ugly, but I'm still cute," I thought. Leaning against the stained white porcelain sink, I checked myself out. My brown bedroom eyes danced in the rays of the morning sunlight. Their hazel flecks sparkled and coupled nicely with my sun-lightened hair. Luscious, wavy locks, cropped in a boyish cut, fell around my soft, tanned feminine face. My eyes, lined with thick dark lashes, were arched by well-shaped brows; soft full lips accented my slightly cleft chin.

I thought I resembled Kookie, the sexy television star in the hit series *77 Sunset Strip*. He played a cool valet who was always combing his hair before he parked a car. Imitating Kookie, I grabbed the comb from my back pocket and ran it through my hair with a cocky smile. How funny it was that I now looked like Kookie and was living in East Los Angeles.

Back home in the Valley, I'd been a regular Gidget: cheerful and clean-cut, with my long blond hair styled in a girly flip. At Taft High School, I wore sweaters and skirts that would have made Doris Day proud. Like any proper young lady, my social wardrobe consisted of basic black, white pearls and good leather pumps.

When I was fifteen and fell in love with my best friend, my life completely changed. I was terrified that someone would find out, including her. That dread suffocated my soul. More and more, I felt like a lonely imposter living in a straight world.

Then I heard rumors that the queers had formed a colony in Hollywood, and I decided to run away. Fleeing shame, I abandoned my friends, family and beautiful home. My journey of liberation began in Hollywood and later led me to the Tenderloin.

Turning away from the mirror, I shook off the runaway blues and looked forward to getting down to the bar. Maybe I could pick up a trick and make a little cash. I could at least have a few drinks and talk shit with the sissy drag queens. Maybe one of them would buy me a drink.

Putting the joint in my mouth, I clicked open my Zippo and stroked my thumb against the wheel rapidly a few times. I heard that beautiful "click" just before the flame lit the grass. I took a deep drag and listened to the pot crackle. While putting my Zippo in my pocket, I found a wadded dollar bill and some loose change.

Tucking away the lighter in the little pocket within a pocket, I tripped for a second on how awesome it was. It's like Levi Strauss knew it would make a perfect little house for my lighter.

Feeling much better, I ventured out into the living room. I could see the crown of Speedy's little bald head as he leaned over, talking to Grady. Poor Speedy was only in his early thirties, but he already looked like an old man. His rotten buckteeth protruded over a thick bottom lip, exposing vampire-like side teeth. They'd become sharp and pointed from all the years of grinding.

Today he was wearing his favorite watermelon-seed necklace. The huge black peace sign on it hung over his hippie fringed leather vest and his tie-dyed long-sleeved shirt. Around his balding head was a bright yellow headband with a large white, wilted daisy hanging from it, drooping over his eye.

Speedy grinned, then noticed my swollen forearm.

"Holy shit, your arm looks awful. Hey man, you okay?"

"Yeah, I'm okay, but my arm is fucked up. It's killing me. I'm heading down to the Open Door. You wanna come with me? Maybe some old whore there can fix me up. If they can give themselves abortions, they can help me with my arm."

Speedy nodded his head and methodically stroked his stringy, gray, Fu Manchu. Grinding his teeth, he had a pained expression, as if he was in deep thought. His dilated pupils stared off into la-la land.

Speedy finally replied, "I'm too tired to go to the club. I think I'll stay home with my mom."

"Great," I said. "I'm stuck without a car in East L.A. To get to the State Street bus stop, I'll have to walk through the middle of the projects. I'll be lucky to get past the gang members that line the streets."

"Jesse, it's early, they're not up yet," Speedy said reassuringly. "Anyway, it's cool. Manuel's got your back."

Manuel was my homeboy and the leader of the Ese Gang. He offered me protection because he knew my grandmother was Spanish. He had nicknamed me "SFV Ese" because I was a Valley girl. Hoping that my passport stamped with Manuel's protection would suffice; I headed out the front door and walked down the hill through the beige brick buildings that made up the project compound.

I was amazed how peaceful this little neighborhood of welfare recipients looked. I started to sweat, but it wasn't from the hot July sun. This benign-looking housing crackled with violence, exploding at unexpected moments.

Finally, I reached the bottom of the hill and exited through the main gate of the projects onto State Street. I saw the bus stop on the corner. It was a relief to be able to sit down on the little bench in the shaded shelter.

Seeing a large display poster for The Mamas & The Papas concert at the Greek Theatre, I couldn't help but notice how fat Mama Cass was now. I heard the group in my head, singing "California Dreamin'." Those hippies singing about L.A. didn't know this part of town, that's for sure, or they'd be happy to stay Back East.

My thoughts were interrupted by the approaching bus. It was the L.A. Express that would take me down to Alvarado.

"Thank God!" I said aloud.

The bus door opened, revealing an Afro-headed gigantic-breasted black bus driver. She smiled down at me and said, "Hey, baby, come on in. Where you going, sugar?"

"Eighth and Alvarado," I smiled back.

Cheerfully, with the big steering wheel in her hands, she said, "Put your quarter in the meter and go sit down. We don't have all day." Chuckling, she added, "Get a move on! This is the L.A. Express, child!"

I put my money in the meter and walked down the aisle to find a seat in the back. I passed Mexican maids, busboys and the L.A. poor, careful not to look at the curious faces. Walking with my head down was a habit I had gotten into for my own protection. It was a shielding maneuver I used in the straight world. I also knew better than to talk much, since my voice was not as deep as a young man's. No sense in giving myself away. The last thing I wanted was to get busted for impersonating the opposite sex.

By mistake I stumbled on the shopping bag of an old Mexican woman. As I apologized, the woman's black eyes bore into mine for a few seconds. I saw in them pity and contempt. Dismissing me, she grabbed the child sitting next to her protectively.

After settling into my seat, I thought about her dirty look. I didn't know if my arm grossed her out or if she just hated queers. Whatever it was, she could go fuck herself!

The stink of diesel fuel wafted through the open windows as we rolled by small wooden houses, countless billboards covered with graffiti and assorted taco stands. Our bus lumbered alongside low-riding *Vatos* in their dice-adorned Chevy Impalas. Gang members cruised by old pickup trucks, loaded with lawnmowers and laborers. Overweight women pushed shopping carts down the littered side-walks with little children in tow. Groups of Mexican men dressed in cowboy hats and boots lingered outside the liquor stores.

I closed my eyes to shut out the ugly streets. The hot sun beat through the bus window onto my face and I felt homesick for San Francisco. I could be myself in the gay ghetto. Amid the rhythm of the city, I mingled with friends and freely walked the sidewalks lined with gay bars and restaurants. The girls were crazy about me. I had been making good money and it wasn't going into my arm.

The vision of Carmen's beautiful face and long auburn hair kept me company on the lonely bus ride. My lady could put up with my philandering but drew the line when it came to hard drugs. I could never let Carmen see me in this condition. To top it off, the vein in my hand looked like freakin' Frankenstein.

My arm was killing me. It felt frozen and stuck to my chest. Each time the bus stopped or jerked my arm would throb. Much to my relief, I finally heard the bus driver say, "Eighth and Alvarado!" The announcement of the dirty streets that queers and dope fiends roamed sounded like heaven. I grabbed the rail with my good arm, pulled myself up and started to leave.

As I passed the Mexican bitch with pity in her eyes, I stopped and said, "Have a nice day." I was a polite Californian and a nice Valley girl. I was not going to give up my good manners for any rude Ranchero.

Long, busy Alvarado Street was flanked with small shops, liquor stores, restaurants and bars. It also hosted two of the oldest lesbian bars in the country, the Open Door and the If Club. Straight-laced square homos avoided them like the plague. What separated these particular cocktail lounges from your average queer hangouts was their commerce of human flesh. They were meat markets for heterosexuals with a taste for lesbian prostitutes.

A good portion of my L.A. business came from straight housewives. They wanted sex with a butch and liked my youthful looks and soft appearance. With any luck, one of those lustful suburban perverts would be in the bar today.

I caressed my Saint Christopher, the good luck charm I always wore around my neck. The cold medal would startle the lady lying underneath me as it touched her pussy. I would make a mental notch of her face. I felt as cool as one of the cowboys I used to watch on TV when I was a kid. Bang! One down!

As I walked, I recognized a tall, thin, black-haired butch named Dino sitting on a stool at the Chicken Shack. Dino was a good-looking gangster pimp who frequented the If Club. She sat in the hot sun dressed like a full-fledged high-roller eating a piece of fried chicken.

Dino sported a fedora-style white hat and a lavender sharkskin suit which I knew hid her silver plated .45. Dino was a gun totin', Tiparillo smokin', no shit takin' New Yorker. Her most recent claim to fame was that she had shot a john right in the ass. Dino was hiding under the bed while her bitch turned a trick with a rough john. As soon as the john got a little too forceful, Dino fired away, almost taking out her whore.

I had been raised to be a perfect young lady. My parents' goal in life was not for me to end up on Alvarado Street. We had planned for me to go to Julliard in New York to study Theatre Arts. Years of

private drama lessons were an investment designed to enhance my sophisticated demeanor. Instead, my sorority sisters were characters that Sergeant Joe Friday in "*Dragnet*" would have liked to put away.

The Open Door was dark and cool inside, a welcome refuge from the L.A. heat and smog. As my eyes adjusted, I looked for someone to help me with my arm. I noticed there was not one old whore in the place. Not even a fucking trick.

My situation looked bleak, especially since I had only a dollar and forty-five cents to my name. At least someone had fed the jukebox. One of my favorite songs was playing and I tripped on the lyrics: "I'm your puppet, I'm hanging on a string, I'll do anything." Right now, I definitely was in need of a puppet master.

The only other person in the joint was Bunny, a beautiful, petite femme playing bartender. It really surprised me to see her tending bar. God knows she didn't need the money. Bunny was the biggest moneymaking hooker on Alvarado Street. I didn't know it then, but she would turn some of that money my way. She was about to give me the opportunity to become the most infamous female pimp in San Francisco's history.

Chapter 3

OPEN DOOR

I LINGERED BY THE JUKEBOX, mesmerized by the steamy femme. Bunny was a glamorous lady of the night, wrapped in designer fashions. I was intimidated by this goddess of femininity who exuded pure sexuality.

Usually Peaches, a girly-girl friend of Bunny's, served me here. She was a drop-dead gorgeous lesbian prostitute, a high-yellow fox who worked the bar as a way to meet new tricks. The two femmes were a team of money-making barracudas that devoured their johns.

Bunny's butch girlfriend, Tattoo Jean, kept her on a short leash. The tattooed pimp dyke made the Worldwide Wrestling Heavyweight Champion, "The Destroyer," look meek and mild.

I glanced sideways and noticed Bunny was eyeballing me as she wiped down the large wooden bar. Her cleavage inspired me to swagger, and I did my version of a rich pimp daddy's strut to mask my desperation.

The familiar voice of shame tapped at my spirit. "That beautiful femme doesn't want to serve your lowlife ass. Bunny is a top-notch professional girl with the eye of a financial expert. She knows you don't have any money."

I decided to check out the jukebox to bide some time. Maybe someone would come in and buy me a drink. Then that cute little femme wouldn't have to see how broke I was. As sick as I felt, I straightened my shoulders and held my head up high in my finest finishing school walk as I crossed the room.

My grandmother Nani Lou had taught me how to walk with books on my head. She used to say to me, "All wealthy people walk with elegance and ease. Always move with your head held high and steady, as you gracefully glide to your destination."

Despite my outward calm, my heart started to race. I was totally broke and alone. I knew the hooker standing behind the bar could see right through me and was not fooled by my cool, debonair stride.

I leaned against the glowing red and blue jukebox, trying to focus on the flip boards holding the song titles. Just then a Ray Charles song came on. He was happily singing, "Hit the Road, Jack." I realized I had to do something. I had to either sit up at the bar and face my embarrassment with the sharp-looking femme or go across the street to the If Club. My mind was made up. I was going to go sit at the bar and order a beer. That snobby bitch was going to have to serve me whether she wanted to or not.

Turning around, I focused on the enticing red stool with silver legs. I put my leg over the soft round cushion, and sat down in front of Bunny. I had never really seen her up close before. Usually she was all dolled up, but I couldn't get over how plain-Jane she looked today. With her shoulder-length brown hair styled in a pageboy right out of the 1950s, Bunny looked like a conservative young secretary. Underneath her tight little white cashmere sweater was a pair of huge firm tits accented by a simple strand of white pearls.

Hypnotically, I watched the round mounds slightly rise and fall with each breath she took. I saw the quickness in her baby blue eyes as she studied me. Leaning forward, resting my good arm on the bar, I looked up at Bunny and nonchalantly said, "I'd like a draft, please."

She stood across the bar from me and said, "Sure, Jesse."

Stunned that she knew my name, I gathered my composure and smiled at her. Bunny's tone was sexy, soft and caring, like Marilyn Monroe's. It occurred to me that her freshly fucked, out-of-breath voice was why she made so much money.

I had to fight the urge to throw my head between those soft pink breasts and cry like a baby. All I yearned to do was fuck this clean-cut little girl and have her hold me until I forgot my pain.

As she turned to fill my glass, I admired her tight ass wrapped in a black miniskirt. Bunny set the mug on the bar in front of me. I detected a hint of a smile as I said, "Thanks for the beer."

I raised the frosted glass to my lips and took a sip, enjoying the cold damp feeling on my fingers. Never had a cheap draft beer tasted so good. I swallowed the cold amber liquid and felt it go down my throat. As I licked the foam off my upper lip from the head of the beer, the tension started to leave me. Booze and being in a gay club often had that effect on me. I was now safe in a cocoon of darkness, protected from the outside straight world.

I lit up a Pall Mall with my good hand, careful to keep my other hand hidden under the bar. Yet she had already noticed. "Hey Jesse, you okay? Is there something wrong with your arm? Why don't you want me to see it?"

Realizing I was busted, I put my burning and now nearly immobile closed fist on the smooth surface of the bar. As she studied my gross-looking hand, I cockily explained to her what had happened. "It's nothing, man. I just missed a vein when I was fixing some cooked-up Red Devils, and I got an abscess."

"Don't people usually drop Reds? They're sleeping pills, aren't they?"

"Yeah, but Seconals beat heroin. I'm trying to lose the taste for smack," I confessed honestly, surprising myself.

Bunny leaned close and said in a soft, sexy, caring voice, "Your hand looks pretty bad. I think you should have it looked at."

"I was hoping one of those old street whores would be here today to play doctor on me. They're pretty good when it comes to first aid stuff," I replied with macho bravado.

Bunny looked at me like I was crazy. "I understand, Jesse, but that sounds a little risky."

She then gave it to me straight, "Jesse, I've been watching you run up and down Alvarado with your speed freak buddy Speedy and that dog of his, selling his cut liquid meth. It is obvious you're down and out and broke. You walk in here like you own the place, putting your last dime in the jukebox. I must admit you have a lot of chutzpah. Why don't you let me help you?"

She really got my attention. I hadn't been spoken to like that since I'd left home. I was confused as I wondered what her motives were. Who was this girl standing in front of me and what did she want?

My experience had taught me you never get something for nothing. Everybody wanted something: your money, your body or your booze. I looked into her inquisitive eyes, and it suddenly occurred to me that maybe she wanted me to fuck her.

I flashed Bunny a cocky smile, exposing my pearly white teeth. I answered in a suave, lust-laden tone, "It's nice of you to offer. I may need help, but if I go see a doctor, I'll get busted for tracks."

Unimpressed, Bunny grabbed my good wrist, holding it down. "Don't worry, Jesse. I have a john who's a doctor. His clinic is right down the street."

Bunny gently turned my injured hand over, exposing my wrist and the small red line going up towards my elbow. "See that red line going up your arm? Jesse, you have blood poisoning. It can travel to your heart and kill you. We need to go now," she said briskly. "I'll handle it. Don't worry. You'll be safe—he won't call the heat."

I wasn't sure I wanted to be seen with Bunny. "I'd rather have the red line kill me than have your big old fucking butch, Tattoo Jean, do me in."

Bunny's whole face lit up and she laughed. "Don't you worry about her either. I'll handle Jean. Peaches is in the back room. Let me get her up here to cover for me. I'm taking you to Dr. Li."

As Bunny started toward the back room, she called over her shoulder, "Meet me out back by my Caddy. It's the pink convertible."

I walked out into the bright sunlight. The smog and suffocating heat of the day stung my eyes. Squinting, I walked around to the back of the club and spotted the long, elegant convertible. The Cadillac looked like a pink aircraft carrier with white tuck-and-roll leather seats. The wide whitewall tires shouted to the world, "Now, this is a car!"

As I reached the Caddy, the back door of the club slammed. In daylight I was able to get a good look at Bunny. She really was pretty in a fresh, simple, clean-cut way. Short like my mother, she was a stacked bombshell with radiant skin and a dynamite hourglass figure. The simplicity of her clothes and hairdo allowed an observer to focus on the main attraction—her sensuous and voluptuous tits.

Bunny walked to the passenger door and opened it for me. The gallant gesture was not typical for a femme. I normally hated it if a femme opened a door for me, but I let it slide. I gratefully got into the car, willing to risk my life for this newfound feeling of power and strength that the hot little femme ignited in me.

As we roared down the alley, I nodded my head sagely. I could get used to this.

Chapter 4

SOO HAPPY

*T*HE BREEZE HIT MY FACE and I experienced a sudden burst of joy, a real L.A. moment. Leaning my head back and feeling the heat of the sun, I closed my eyes and fantasized that we were driving down the Pacific Coast Highway in Malibu. Of course, we were really going down a rancid alley behind Alvarado Street, but the little mental trip helped ease my worry about going to a strange doctor.

After several blocks, Bunny pulled up to a large green Dipsy Dumpster and parked. She quickly got out of the car and walked toward the building with a familiarity that let me know she had come here frequently. Meekly, I followed her to a side door and waited as she pounded on the glass door inscribed with the lettering, "Jin Li, M.D."

In a few moments the door opened. An enormously fat Chinese nurse stood in the doorway smiling at Bunny. I was taken aback by her size, for I had never seen such a fat Chinese. When the Chinese nurse opened her mouth, I had to stop myself from laughing so I wouldn't embarrass Bunny or the nurse. In the thickest coolie accent imaginable, she said, "Oh soo happy, soo happy to see you. Dr. Jin Li, he soo happy, too. Come, come, I take you in back."

As we entered the air-conditioned building, the smell of alcohol and disinfectant was overpowering. I got a little paranoid and wondered if this guy really had a medical license or if he had bought some dead guy's. We followed the colossal nurse down a long, dimly lit hallway toward a bright examination room.

Her huge ass was squeezed into a tent of a dress. The nurse's hips were so massive that as they swayed, they brushed against the dingy walls. She looked like a celestial body eclipsing the doorway.

She motioned for us to come in and cheerfully said to Bunny, "You sit now and relax." Then she turned to me and aggressively slapped the white tissue paper on the examination table. "You get on table and wait." I quickly climbed up on the table and stared down at my feet. The nurse then left, leaving Bunny and I alone in the cold, small room.

Bunny sat below me on a short silver-legged stool. We both waited in silence, listening to the sound of the crinkling tissue paper beneath me as I restlessly tapped my leg.

A thin middle-aged Asian man in a white jacket and a stethoscope around his neck entered the room. Recognizing Bunny, his favorite "patient," his face lit up. He joyously said to her, "Good to see you. I soo, soo happy. What's up, Bunny?"

Once again I had to fight the urge to laugh. Why were they always soo, soo happy?

I was shocked into composure when Bunny hugged the doctor tight. I thought it odd to hug a trick.

In her out-of-breath voice, Bunny said, "Well, doc, my friend here has a problem with her arm. Will you take care of her, baby? I'll take care of you, like I always do."

She looked at him with such admiration, as if she truly adored the doctor. Watching this pro, it occurred to me that Marilyn had nothing on her.

The cheerful physician's face broke into a smile, which quickly faded as he came over to me and picked up my hand. He carefully studied it. The doctor's expression curdled like he was examining a diseased piece of meat. Excruciating pain shot through me as he probed my fingers.

Dr. Li finally let go of my arm. He became extremely animated, throwing his arms like a conductor at the philharmonic. "Most terrible! Pwobabwy staff infection and bwood poisoning! Very dangerous!" Then he stopped shouting and calmly said, "I going to fix your arm right now."

Opening a drawer, he pulled out a syringe and grabbed a small vial of clear liquid. He stuck the needle into my swollen hand, right between my thumb and forefinger. It hurt like hell, but in a second it was completely numb. The doctor told me firmly, "Don't move one bit! Don't look! I going to lance the abscess, okay?"

Eyeing him suspiciously as he picked up a shiny scalpel, I gave him a defiant glare. "Fine, Doc. but I'm lookin'." Obviously, he didn't know I grew up watching John Wayne and knew that only chickens didn't look.

He took the blade and made a fast, deep cut right over my swollen vein. Immediately, blood and pus started dripping from the sore. Dr. Li efficiently proceeded to soak up the poison. He kept muttering under his breath, "Very lucky you here. Infection goes to heart. You die. You soooo lucky."

Once he was done, he proceeded to stitch me up. After pulling each suture through my open wound, he looked at Bunny with a hunger in his eyes for approval. When he was finished, he announced to Bunny proudly, "Your friend, she going to live."

Watching the dynamics between them was fascinating. The lust-struck doc looked like a puppy begging for a crumb of approval.

Bunny rewarded Dr. Li by reaching over and kissing him on the cheek. It was shocking. This whore in front of me was breaking every cardinal rule of tricking. She hugged and kissed a john, all within one day! What kind of a hooker was she? Obviously she was a very good one because after the kiss, Dr. Li spoke a lot better English.

"Bring her back in three days. I'll take the stitches out," he said sweetly. "Okay, honey Bunny?"

"Yes, Doctor," Bunny said submissively.

The doctor then bandaged my hand and put my arm in a sling.

"You need antibiotics. Stand up and lower your pants. I give you shot!" Dr. Li snapped.

He came toward me with a damn massive syringe. Attentively, Bunny got up, walked over and helped me unbuckle my pants. Bunny lowered my zipper with the expertise and efficiency of a woman experienced in undoing pants.

Dr. Li injected the syringe into my buttocks. With a short, sharp sting, it was all over. The doctor then rubbed the spot vigorously with a cotton swab soaked in alcohol.

Bunny carefully raised my pants for me and started to slowly slide my zipper up. With her head bent down directly beneath my nose as she focused on dressing me, I could smell her hair. I inhaled her clean, fresh scent, like jasmine in springtime. When Bunny finished adjusting my Levi's and tucking my shirt into my pants, she stepped back to admire her work. Like an attentive mother, she looked me up and down with a critical eye.

Like a devoted wife, she said, "Okay, let's go, honey."

I don't know when I got promoted to "honey." Maybe it was when I bravely watched while the doctor was cutting me. Whatever the reason, I liked how it sounded. The intimacy in her voice made me feel like a respectable husband. She took physical ownership of me by telling the doctor, "I'll bring Jesse back in a few days." Slowly thrusting her tits up like facial expressions, she added, "I'll come visit real soon. What would I do without you?"

Walking out of the clinic felt a lot better than walking in. I was genuinely happy to see the pink chariot waiting for us.

Once in the car, I told my new friend, "Thanks, Bunny, for taking me to the doctor. I'll pay you back in a few days."

Bunny, looking straight ahead down the alley, with her tiny hands lightly gripping the large white steering wheel, didn't reply. Once again, I nervously told her, "Don't worry, I'm good for it."

This time she took her hand off the wheel and laid it on my leg. She tenderly patted my inner thigh. "Jesse, don't worry about it. Really, think of it as a gift. You need to rest, so I'm going to get you a room."

Bunny kept her eyes on her driving, not on me. Intuitively, I felt she was trying to protect my pride by not witnessing my confusion. Not knowing what to say, I watched the bums in McArthur Park as we cruised past them. I fought the urge to sink down in the seat. I feared that Tattoo Jean or someone else might spot us together.

"I need to stop and pick up a few things at the store," Bunny said, pulling into a Ralph's Market.

When she got out of the car, she asked, "What would you like to drink?"

Bravely, I answered, "Schlitz, Jack Daniel's, whatever you like." Less enthusiastically, I added, "Even Red Mountain wine is fine… whatever."

"Red Mountain wine?" asked Bunny, amused, as she gave me a warm smile. "Plus, you need to eat something."

"I'm not really hungry. But maybe you could get me some Hostess Cupcakes."

"Stay here, I'll be right back," the friendly hooker said as she opened the car door and stepped out. "We'll shoot over to Edward's Steak House and get a bite later."

I shrugged my shoulders. "Nah, I'm cool."

Bunny studied my face intently. "Sure you're not hungry?"

I looked away, wounded by her gentleness. "No, its okay, I'm fine."

Bunny left and walked into the market.

Kicking back on the luxurious leather seat, I checked out the car's interior. The dashboard was lined with chrome that glinted in the sunlight. "Cadillac" was proudly displayed in handwriting in the center of the console. I pushed in the cigarette lighter, pulled out a Pall Mall and lit up.

Feeling like I had just hit the jackpot, I relaxed and blew small round smoke rings. Suddenly, it hit me that I was sitting in Tattoo Jean's ride by myself in plain sight. To make matters worse, her old lady was in the market buying me booze.

My survival instincts kicked in, and I wanted to get out of the car and run like hell. I started thinking about Bunny suggesting Edward's Steak House. What a great idea! I'll just go over there with Bunny, sit in a big booth in front of everyone and order my last meal.

After a few minutes, Bunny returned with a large bag in her arms and a big smile on her face. She placed the bag on the back seat, hopped in and turned the key. We floated down the street.

Along the intersection of Sunset and Western, newspaper stands and magazine racks fed the hunger of visiting tourists for scandal and stardom. A guy sat in a chair beside a board offering maps to stars' homes. Neon stardust trailed a brilliant gold star advertising the Starlight Motel. The pink Cadillac drove through its stucco arch.

Towering royal palm trees hinted at the glamour Hollywood once knew. We docked the boat in a stall reserved for guest check-in. Bunny grabbed her purse and refreshed her lipstick.

"Wait here." With that command, she proceeded into the motel office to check us in.

Again, I obediently said, "Okay." I sat there, lit up a Pall Mall and scoped out my surroundings.

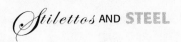

It occurred to me that she was smart to leave me outside. No reason to let the motel clerk see us together. That way, if Tattoo Jean showed up, she wouldn't be able to beat the information out of him. What he didn't know wouldn't hurt him.

In my mind's eye, I saw Tattoo Jean whip out her .45, push it up against the clerk's head, and yell, "Where the fuck is Bunny and that dyke? What room are they in? Speak up, before I blow your fucking brains out!"

I took a deep drag, shook my head and cancelled that vision. I remembered clearly the first time I saw Tattoo Jean and Bunny together, at the If Club. I couldn't get my head around the fact that they were a couple. Bunny was petite and adorable. Tattoo Jean, on the other hand, was a walking human refrigerator. She looked like something out of a carnival act.

Jean's white shirt sleeves were rolled up, exposing red, black and blue painted arms. Because she was so heavy, she looked sloppy even though her clothes appeared expensive. Her shirt was wrinkled and ill-fitting over bulging layers of flesh. I was both amazed and appalled at her gargantuan biceps that reminded me of Rosie the Riveter.

I reflected on the sparkle I had seen in Bunny's eyes as she hugged that animal of a person. The six-foot dyke leaned her three hundred and fifty pounds of undisciplined flesh against the wooden bar. She rested one of her big boots on top of the foot rail. Glued to Jean's back with her arms snugly around her waist was this petite, pretty femme. Bunny's manicured hands were clasped together tightly in front of Jean's mammoth stomach.

Jean's colorful flesh brought to mind the night my father first saw my tattoo. He had tracked me down to the Camelot Hotel in San Francisco. Unannounced, he knocked on my door and I swung it open. I was wearing a wife-beater t-shirt that exposed a recently inked tattoo on my right arm that said "Jesse." He saw my tattoo and burst into tears.

In between sobs he cried, "How could you have done this to your body! It is so low class. This is going to kill your mother. How are you going to be able to go to the pool at the country club? What if you have children? You have got to be kidding...who the hell is Jesse anyway?"

Judging by my father's reaction, my inked skin seemed to have endangered all of my family's dead ancestors.

Once my father stopped shouting, he pleaded, "When are you going to give up this insanity and come home?"

Eventually, my parents accepted that I was gay. They were grateful that I was at least alive. It was awkward for them, but they realized they couldn't force me to change or come back home. But I vividly remembered the guilt and shame I felt seeing the pain I had caused my father.

Bunny appeared and jolted me from my daydream. "Come on Jesse, I got you a room."

"Don't worry about it! I really don't need a room," I said, panic-stricken. Bunny didn't look so adorable anymore. "I've thought about it. Maybe you can get your money back."

Bunny looked at me with confusion. "What do you mean, you don't need a room? You must be exhausted. Come on, you've got to rest."

"N-n-no," I replied.

Bunny finally realized the cause of my fear. "Don't worry about Tattoo Jean! She has no idea where I am. Besides, I know how to deal with her. Let's get you into your room, okay?"

So I followed behind her, muttering a prayer. "Dear God, please don't let me get into anything that we can't get me out of."

Bunny just chuckled.

While she was opening the motel room door, I thought, "Now its payback time." I figured I'd probably have to pay with my body for her kindness and generosity. I wondered, "Did she want me to fuck her the minute we got into the room?" It struck me that I wasn't prepared. I had left my dildo under Speedy's mom's couch. I hoped Grady didn't find it.

As we entered the room, I was beginning to feel performance anxiety. The pain in my arm was back. I was exhausted and dreaded the thought of having sex.

Bunny went to the king-sized bed and pulled back the clean white sheets. I stood awkwardly by the foot of the bed. She went to the sink in the bathroom and took the paper cover off the glass on the counter. She struggled to twist the cap off the bottle of Jack with her delicate fingers. I heard a quick snap.

"Damn, I broke a nail!"

She managed to pour me a drink, which she handed over with two Darvocets. "Take these. They'll help you relax."

"Okay," I answered gratefully. I popped the pills into my mouth and washed them down with a big swig. Mentally preparing myself to perform, I went to the bed, sat down and reached to unbuckle my pants. Bunny's hand stopped me as she began to undress me again. My stomach quivered as she touched my lower abdomen.

The busty bombshell looked into my eyes and said, "I'm going to go home now. I want you to sleep and not worry about Jean. I'll come by in the morning." Bunny opened her purse and pulled out a bill from a wad of cash. "Here's a twenty in case you get hungry. If you need anything else, just call the desk, all right?"

I looked up at her, bewildered, and wondered, "What kind of whore is this?" Bunny gently kissed me on the forehead and whispered, "I'll see you tomorrow."

She closed the thick drapes over the Venetian blinds, turned off the lights and walked out of the room. As she closed the door softly behind her, I lay back on the clean sheets and rested my head on the soft, fresh-smelling pillows.

The Jack and the Darvocets kicked in. Yet even as my body unclenched, my mind tried to figure out: Why was Bunny being so nice to me?

Chapter 5

TITS 'N PEARL GIRL

THE WARMTH OF THE MORNING SUN tickled my eyelids. I slowly came back to life. It felt strange to have a crisp, clean sheet under my naked legs. I couldn't believe all the space I had in the soft king-size bed. Like a camper arriving back to civilization, the luxury of creature comforts intoxicated me.

Flexing my fingers, I felt the gauze on the palm of my left hand and gently touched each finger, measuring their size. Pleasantly surprised, I realized they weren't as swollen as yesterday.

I sat up and looked down at my blue-and-white checkered boxer shorts. It occurred to me that I didn't have to fuck anybody last night for anything. This was so unusual, I shook my head in disbelief.

I spotted my lighter on the end table and immediately remembered the roach still in the little pocket of my jeans. Looking around the room, I searched for my Levi's. I had just spotted them on the floor when I heard a timid-sounding knock at the door.

"Who is it?" I asked groggily.

"It's me, Bunny!" she replied with a spring in her voice.

"Are you alone?"

"Of course, Jesse," she responded brightly. "Let me in!"

In my wife-beater and boxers, looking cool like Stanley Kowalski in *A Streetcar Named Desire*, I strutted across the orange shag carpet. I opened the door cautiously, still fearful of an encounter with a human refrigerator.

On the other side of the screen was a femme on a mission. Bunny's petite feet arched in white high-heeled "fuck me" pumps. They showed off her beautifully defined calves. Her pink capri pants outlined her young, superb ass. Slung over her bare shoulder, Bunny carried a matching white leather purse on a strap which appeared soft and expensive. It reminded me of the white tuck-and-roll leather seats in the Cadillac.

Bunny had a carton of Pall Malls under her arm, and in her petite hand was a Bullocks Wilshire shopping bag. Encircling her pretty little wrist was a diamond tennis bracelet, the only jewelry she had on besides a simple strand of white pearls around her neck. Her low-cut, snug-fitting white blouse was the perfect showcase for her tits.

"Come on in," I said to the tits n' pearl girl. Bunny looked up at me sweetly and I instantly felt that strange masculine power well up inside me. The alluring femme sauntered into the room. Her tight ass under the pink capris made me want to bend her over the side of the sofa and fuck her from behind.

This thought startled me, because I hadn't made love with anyone since Carmen. Sex was just a job for me. To desire this pretty young woman caught me off-guard. Bunny turned around, smiling brightly, and asked me in her naughty breathless voice, "Are you hungry, honey?"

Unexpectedly, glorious warmth radiated through my chest. Her addressing me as "honey" had a profound effect on me. I stood before her, trying to comprehend this odd feeling. I finally realized this strange sensation was hope. I was starting to trust this chick. In a quiet voice I responded, "I was thinking of having a Hostess Cupcake and a beer."

Bunny's response was a warm and tender smile. She came closer and said, "Jesse, look at me." I reluctantly raised my head and looked her in the eye. She asked me straight out, "Jesse, do you think I want something from you?"

That question made me feel back in control. After all, I could understand somebody wanting something from me. With an arrogant grin, I replied, "Yeah."

She smiled back at me and asked, "What do you have?"

I had to laugh as I thought, "What did I have?" I realized that all I had was a staph infection, no money, a pair of jeans, a t-shirt, a Zippo lighter and my Saint Christopher medal. As I laughed, Bunny laughed with me. We just stood for a few moments giggling like children, celebrating the blissful joy of connection.

"Jesse, let me run you a nice bath so you can clean up and get dressed," offered Bunny. "I thought we could go over to Edward's for steak and eggs. I'm hungry!"

"Okay," I replied as I followed her into the spacious bathroom. Bunny turned the faucet handles and water gushed into the tub. Pulling back the shower curtain, she said, "Test the temperature."

"I like it pretty hot, being half-Castilian Spaniard," I said, using my best Rico Suave Latin lover act. My roots offered me the best combination: Spanish for passion and English for class. I was hoping she could sense the lustful impetuosity in my romantic blood.

"I'll help you take your shirt off," said Bunny, appearing unimpressed with my Latin playboy act.

Self-consciously, I avoided her proposal.

"I've seen them before," said Bunny matter-of-factly.

"Okay, but look the other way," I said, unaccountably shy.

Bunny removed my sling and gently held my sore arm as she pulled my shirt over my head. I felt the warmth of her fingers as they touched my back while she skillfully removed the safety pin securing my binder. Her hands brushed across my breasts as she unraveled my device of deception.

She neatly folded the Ace bandage as I stood before her in my boxers with my good arm covering my breasts. She just smiled at me, turned and walked out of the bathroom, softly closing the door behind her.

I double-checked the water, which was actually too hot, even for a Latin lover. After a solid shot of cold water, it felt soothing and the solitude was very peaceful. I relaxed, thinking it was so nice to have someone run a bath for me. What I missed most about Carmen was the thoughtful little things she did for me.

I kept my bandaged hand dry and rested it on the side of the tub. I was relieved to see that the red line of blood poisoning up my wrist was gone.

I heard a tentative tap-tap on the door. I pulled the shower curtain open just a little, exposing my head. Bunny stood there holding a glass of my favorite amber liquid. In her other hand were two Darvocets, my lighter and a nice big fat joint.

My whole face lit up. "Damn, girl, I think I've died and gone to heaven! Are you sure you're not an angel of mercy? Good God, Florence Nightingale has nothing on you, girl."

I was pleasantly surprised that I sounded like my old self. In fact, I sounded better: as cool and charming as the sweet-talking mac daddies charming their whores at the bar, spoonfeeding them flattery, so they would go to bed with people they wouldn't have lunch with.

Bunny handed me the pills. I popped them in my mouth and washed them down with the booze. She put the joint in her mouth, fired it up, and handed it to me without taking a hit.

I felt like a king with my huge balls floating in the warm tub. In a gallant, cavalier voice, I said to my angel of mercy as I motioned toward the toilet seat, "My fair young maiden, please sit down on this lovely throne, here in my luxurious chambers, and smoke a joint with me."

Bunny smiled at me, amused. "Maybe later, baby. I don't smoke grass before work. I'm going to make a few business calls, and when you're finished taking a bath, we'll go eat."

A while later, Bunny tapped on the door, slightly opened it and said, "By the way, I picked up a new shirt, underwear and socks for you."

"Cool. Just put them on the toilet," I replied, impressed.

Bunny entered the bathroom and hung a beautiful silk navy blue-and-white paneled short-sleeved shirt on a hook. She laid the boxers, t-shirt and socks on the toilet seat.

As she left the bathroom, she casually added, "Call me if you need help getting dressed, okay?"

"Okay, thanks," I called after her.

I checked out the groovy bad boy shirt and said, "Far out."

Soaking in the tub with a glass of Jack in one hand and a joint in the other, I wondered if Carmen was taking a bath right now with a butch waiting on her. After all, I did go AWOL. Dampening my mood quicker than the cooling water was the thought of her with another lover. Quickly, I shook myself free of that fucking bummer and thought of more pleasant things.

I was starting to find Bunny's softness very attractive. In some ways, she reminded me of Carmen. She had a determination in her walk and a calm, take-charge attitude. Yet she didn't come across as being bossy. I heard a tap on the door again.

"How're you doing in there?"

I replied in a mellow voice, "I'll be out in a minute, thanks." I stood up with water dripping from my young lean body. I quickly toweled myself dry. I got dressed but left the sling off and looked in the mirror. The expensive shirt was cut just right and fit my shoulders perfectly.

I struggled with my shoes though. Coming in, Bunny kneeled down in front of me and carefully slipped them on. Trying not to betray my attraction, I casually remarked, "Hey, Bunny, thanks for the shirt. It's really nice. You know, I'm surprised you even knew who I was when I came into the bar yesterday."

She continued putting on the second shoe. "Silly, I see you come in the Open Door all the time. I've even poured you drinks a couple of times. I think you were too wasted to notice." She tied the laces with firm, definite strokes. "It's always Jack, straight up with a water back. It's usually the old queens buying shots for you, I've noticed."

I sheepishly answered, "Yeah, they're cool. Uh, I've had a rough couple of months."

After she tied my shoes, Bunny got up and said, "Let's go, I'm famished."

"What about the Jack and the cupcakes? We just can't leave 'em."

Bunny expressed her first sign of exasperation as she answered, "Honey, I rented the room for a week. It's yours, and it'll be here when you get back." She turned around and left.

I stopped at the door, cautiously poked my head out, looked to the right and left and quickly inspected the parking lot. Directly beneath the balcony I could see the pink convertible. Satisfied that Tattoo Jean was not around, I walked behind Bunny to the car.

Her hips swayed from side to side with her white leather purse. Staring at her ass in the hot pink capris, I tripped on a little music in my head, and with each swing of her hips, I heard a rhythmic, "ba-boom, ba-boom..." Shaking my head to stop the silly trip I was on, I casually asked her, "Where is Jean, by the way?"

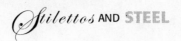

Without skipping a beat in the sway of her hips, she replied, "I left her."

I lost my composure for a moment. "Oh, wow, man. What's up with that?"

The pretty femme turned and faced me square-on. "I'll fill you in more at the restaurant. Let's just say, I need a partner that can seize a prime opportunity." She tapped me firmly on the chest. "Like you."

Chapter 6

PIMP 101

I SWEPT OPEN THE HEAVY WOODEN DOOR to Edward's Steak House, letting Bunny pass through the entrance in front of me. The welcome coolness of air conditioning and aroma of juicy steaks greeted us. Looking up at the round wooden-framed clock on the wall, I realized it was much later than I had thought.

It wasn't busy due to the late afternoon hour. A fat, balding man was sitting by himself in the corner booth at the back of the room. Wearing a cheap blue blazer and a loosened wide-striped tie, the disheveled gentleman was nursing a cup of coffee and eating a piece of apple pie. He smiled broadly as we entered and shouted, "Hi Bunny!"

She smiled back. "Hi, Bob. Nice seeing you. I'd like you to meet my girlfriend, Jesse."

"It's very nice to meet you, Bob." My mother and father had always taught me to be polite. Good manners were a must in my household, and being polite was second nature to me. Bob sized me up, trying to figure out what kind of girlfriend I was. We sat down in the worn red leather booth right next to his. A boisterous elderly woman came to our table and sang out in a warm deep southern accent, "Hi girls, welcome to Edward's. Isn't it a beautiful day? Bunny honey, you look just lovely." She drawled the word "lovely" as if it was a mile long.

Bunny responded with warmth. "My, Miss Alabam, you certainly are cheerful today."

"Well honey, I believe in having an attitude of gratitude."

Bunny laughed and said, "It shows in your twinkling eyes."

Alabam grabbed a small pad and pencil from her pocket, asking, "You ladies know what you want yet?"

Bunny cheerfully asked me, "What are you going to have?"

Quickly, shame dampened my good mood. "I'm not really hungry."

Actually, I was starving. I was also sick of living perpetually broke. I thought about the twenty in my pocket which Bunny had given me. I decided it was best not to eat anything so I could hang onto the money.

"You have to eat something," Bunny encouraged.

"Nah, I'm not that hungry. It's cool."

"Come on, Jesse. You can take me out next time."

"All right." With my old swagger, I placed my order. "I'll have a T-bone steak, scrambled eggs with sliced tomatoes, sourdough bread, a little strawberry jelly, and if you don't mind, I would like a Hostess Cupcake for dessert."

"I'll have the same," Bunny added, smiling, "but you can hold the cupcake."

Amused by my burst of confidence, Bunny looked at me intently. "So, did you grow up in Los Angeles, Jesse?"

"No, I grew up in the Valley. For the past few years, I've been living in the Tenderloin."

"I love the TL. I've done a lot of business up there."

"Yeah, I love it up there too. I can't wait to get back. I just came down to L.A. to visit my kid brother, but I got kinda hung up here."

Bunny daintily wiped the corner of her mouth with a white linen napkin, giving me an all-knowing glance. Graciously, she avoided the subject of my getting "hung up" and asked, "How'd you end up in the Tenderloin?"

Like a true butch, I said in a macho tone, "I hitchhiked."

Bunny was pleased by my adventurous spirit. "That's brave. It's quite a trip from the Valley."

"It has been quite a trip!" I laughed.

"Do you always hitchhike? It can be dangerous, especially if they find out you're a girl," she reprimanded me softly, showing a hint of cautious feminine wisdom.

I nodded casually. "The first time I hitchhiked was when I ran away from home to Hollywood. I had picked a bullshit fight with my mother. I ran out of the house, declaring that I wanted my freedom."

"Is that a pattern of yours, Jesse?" Bunny inquired coyly.

"Femmes, always the detectives," I quipped back with a teasing grin.

"Actually, I just needed an excuse to leave home. The week before, when my girlfriends and I had been out dancing at Gazzarri's, I was befriended by an exotic Hollywood girl named Angel, and she loved my Valley girl clothes. She had told me that if I was ever in Hollywood, I should look her up and we could party together."

That special time of my first taste of freedom came back to me all in a rush.

"The magic word was 'party'. The next week, after the fight with my mom, I went to Hollywood looking for her. I showed up on Angel's doorstep and told her I had run away. Angel took me in and we partied all over Hollywood, hitting all the clubs, having a blast. My biggest concern was that she might find out that I liked women instead of boys and kick me out. I lived with her for two weeks before I realized that 'she' was a 'he'!

"I threw my hands in the air. I ran around Angel's apartment shouting, 'Free at last, free at last, thank God almighty, I'm free at last!'"

Bunny started laughing hard for the first time since I'd met her. Her laughter was as happy as mine was the night I found out that my roommate was a faggot.

"Well," I continued, "Angel worked at the Queen Mary on Ventura Boulevard in Studio City. She was Diana Ross of the Supremes in the nightclub's drag show. Her sequin-gowned sissy backup singers were Miss Zada and Miss Penny."

I told Bunny how great it was being openly gay and having queer friends. My only concern was getting caught by my family and being forced to go back home. So when Miss Zada and Miss Penny said they were going to San Francisco, I jumped at the chance to join them. The three of us put flowers in our hair and hitchhiked along Pacific Coast Highway to San Francisco.

Miss Zada and Miss Penny were dressed in adorable miniskirts, long black wigs and stiletto heels. They looked like two hot black chicks with a little too-large Adam's apples. I was wearing the latest in runaway fashion, a guy's shirt that I had bought from a five-and-dime store and, under my men's Levi's, knee-high boots with spiked heels, which were the rage at Taft High School.

Between rides in Santa Barbara, we were stranded on the side of the freeway with no food and no transportation. A Highway Patrol officer pulled up, got out of his car and asked, "Who are you?" He screwed up his face. "What are you? And what are you doing here?"

"We're going to San Francisco, sir, with flowers in our hair, like everyone else," Miss Zada replied as she seductively touched the gardenia adorning her long, glossy Cher-like locks.

Unimpressed, the officer curtly answered, "You're going to jail with flowers in your hair if you don't get out of town in fifteen minutes."

Miss Zada tried hiking her skirt up, but the gentleman was not amused. So I quickly replied, "We were just visiting Santa Barbara, officer, and we'll be happy to be leaving."

Disgusted, the cop jumped back in his cruiser, and before slamming the door, he shouted, "You all better be off this road when I come back or you're going to jail! It's illegal to impersonate the opposite sex, assholes!"

As the dust from his spinning tires flew into our faces, we stuck our thumbs out in a big show. While waiting for our next ride, we smoked a few joints and got the munchies. In a few minutes, as if sent by angels, a Helms Donut truck pulled up. The nice old bakery man asked us if we needed a lift. We jumped into the back alongside the jelly donuts and headed toward the city by the bay.

With tears of laughter in her eyes, Bunny said, "Oh, my God, Jesse, I think that's the funniest story I've ever heard."

She pulled a gold cigarette case from her purse and removed a filtered Kool. I quickly flipped open my Zippo and gave her a light.

"Will that be all, girls?" Alabam inquired, approaching our table. "Sorry, young lady, we're fresh out of cupcakes."

"I'll have a beer," I said.

"Hmm…a drink sounds good. I'll join you with a glass of Chardonnay," requested Bunny.

"Sure thing, girls. Be right back," Alabam said, cheerful as a sunbeam.

"My story is not as entertaining as yours," Bunny said modestly.

She had left home shortly after meeting Jean. The hulking dyke was like no one Bunny had ever met, to say the least. Jean was getting a tattoo on the boardwalk in Atlantic City, and Bunny couldn't believe a woman was getting inked. She stopped to chat with her about it and the next thing she knew, they were in bed.

Bunny's mom was infuriated over Jean. She cut off Bunny's trust fund allowance. Bunny had a simple choice: hell in New Jersey or freedom and love in California.

"I'm really sorry," I said. "Are you okay with your mom now?"

"We've made up. She realizes that she can't change me. In fact, recently my stepfather has been very generous to me. Go figure," Bunny said.

"Why are you hooking now, then? If you don't mind me asking."

"I love the power and the cash," said Bunny with a shrewd grin. "It's one hell of a business. Hooking is just acting laced with lust."

"I've never thought of it that way," I replied. "But you're absolutely right. Last year I had my own pad at the Camelot Hotel."

"Everybody's stayed at the Camelot," she exclaimed. "I used to work Turk Street. That's a rough beat."

"No kidding," I commented. "I've made a lot of money on Turk."

Bunny took a drag of her cigarette and exhaled slowly. I noticed the small pink lipstick mark on her Kool as she set it in the ashtray. She looked up at me with calculating baby blue eyes. "I admire a butch who's willing to turn her own tricks. Real butches can't get a decent job. They're lucky to make minimum wage in drag." She pointed at my new shirt. "Jesse, you don't look like a minimum-wage kind of girl. I have to admit you look very handsome in drag."

I felt a slight blush come to my cheeks and heat to my loins. "Thanks."

"Here you go girls, enjoy," Alabam happily said as she placed our drinks down and shuffled off.

My fingers played down the side of the cold glass, avoiding Bunny's gaze.

"Jesse, you know why I broke up with Jean? I wasn't in love with her anymore. I was also very uncomfortable with how lazy she had become. I'm looking for a new pimp to work with." She paused to take a sip of her wine. "I have this neighborhood pretty well sewn up, but my plans are to get out of Los Angeles. A john of mine is a cop, and he told me Alvarado Street is going to get real hot. Mayor Yorty is hellbent on cleaning up vice before the elections. So last year I bought a house in San Francisco."

"It's very cool to have a cop for a trick," I said, thinking of Captain Clancy. "That can be more dangerous than hitchhiking."

Bunny acknowledged my comment with a sexy smile. "Jesse, I'm moving up north."

"Wow! Is Jean okay with that?" I asked, stunned.

"No, she's not. I fronted her some money to get on her feet. I own everything, Jesse." Seeing my surprise, she said, "You'll find that I'm a little different than most whores. I believe in saving money and looking toward retirement. If Jean hassles me too much, she knows I'll use force if I have to. Rampart Randy is in love with me."

My head shot up. "Oh shit, Rampart Randy is your john? I heard he shoots street people for target practice," I said, alarmed.

"Oh, he's a teddy bear next to Deadly Chang the Chink," Bunny said nonchalantly.

Visions of decapitated heads at the hands of Deadly Chang the Chink's ninja crew made me tense up. Like all street people, I was aware of the San Francisco Chinatown mobster. I nervously blurted out, "Cool."

"The boys told me that if I ever needed a favor to just ask. I'm sure Randy and Chang would do anything for me." She gave me a shared look of women's wisdom. "It's amazing what they'll do for a little head. I really don't think Jean will fuck with me."

The way Bunny said "fuck with me" made my skin crawl. A new edge under-pinned that hushed and helpless voice of hers: an edge of pure cold steel.

"Besides my hookin' money, which isn't exactly chump change, my stepfather has contributed quite a bit," she continued. "The house in San Francisco is a beautiful old Victorian right in the heart of Chinatown. I've turned it into a bordello for some of the ladies that I've recruited."

The more I heard, the more impressed I was. "That sounds like a great investment, Bunny. I miss San Francisco. I used to work North Beach and sometimes Chinatown."

"So you know the city well?"

"Of course," I answered. "I still have a good book of business in San Francisco. I've got a lot of steady johns, all the way from Columbus to Turk. I've made a fortune from tricks sent to me by Alex, a Filipino guy who owns a classy men's hair salon on Powell Street." I frowned momentarily. "My clients have been neglected lately, but I know I can still work 'em once I get back to the TL."

"Jesse, I want to talk with you about a business proposition. You know, I have plenty of cash. I might be interested in buying your book of business from you while allowing you to retain a percentage of what your johns bring in."

"I'm listening."

"If you're open to taking on a new position, you won't have to turn your own tricks anymore. How would you like to be promoted to management?"

Her words were like an angel's voice trumpeting from heaven. I listened very carefully as Bunny went on.

"Jesse, I like you and I can see in you the makings of a great pimp, if you stay off heroin," she said pointedly. "All you need is a good femme to back your play. With a little help you could back up that cocky attitude of yours with genuine confidence. Your sexy, arrogant stride and soft, classy good looks packaged right could make you a real femme magnet."

I was feeling better and better, but she wasn't trying to butter me up. She had an agenda.

"The same game you play walking into the Open Door, acting like the head rooster in the yard, is the same front a whore needs in a good partner. I think you have the looks and class to get johns on a higher level than Jean ever could. The way you carry yourself and your charming softness could help fill my books with wealthy clients. The fact that you've worked the streets yourself is a big plus. You really understand what prostitutes have to go through."

I nodded my head in rapid agreement. Yet concern filled Bunny's eyes.

"Jesse, look at me and be honest with me. How hooked are you?"

As she spoke, all I could do was look at her glossy moist lips. Instantly, my mind was racing to tell an acceptable lie to avoid answering.

"Jesse?" she asked softly, touching the back of my arm as she waited for a reply.

Instead of telling a story filled with elaborate excuses, I heard myself say, "I'm pathetic." Discouraged by the past few months, I laid it out on the line. "I'm so broke; I don't have enough money to support a real habit. I'm just a chippie. But smack has fucked me up. I have a girlfriend back in the TL and I haven't been able to go back because I just can't let her see me like this," I confessed with a quiet sob.

Bunny opened her purse and pulled out a fresh handkerchief. She reached over and handed it to me. Her soft fingers lifted my chin. She looked me in the eyes, forcing me to hold her gaze. "Jesse, you just need someone to believe in you. Dr. Li and I can help you clean up."

Grateful for her offer of help, I said, "I haven't known what to do. I've been hanging out here with Speedy and his damn dog Grady. Well, I guess Grady's not too bad."

She withdrew her hand and sat back in the booth. "Jesse, I can teach you the art of pimping. My instincts tell me you have what it takes to do a man's job. Trust me, pimping will be your way up and out!"

I heard the strength in Bunny's words and stopped crying. The heat of shame that had enveloped me faded as I wiped away the tears.

"Jesse, we're street people. We don't look at prostitution like normal people do. We've got an understanding. Johns are just a job. We're women. We have a special kind of love for each other. Tricks don't count, because they're just business. Our body is a commodity, sex is our currency and every day we fight for survival. Honey, it's time we went into mass production."

I was caught up in a wave of excitement. "Salesmanship is in my blood. My father taught me everything he knows," I replied. Bunny's confidence reminded me that I had potential. I confidently told her, "We'll make a hell of a team, Bunny."

"Jesse, I believe we will." She cocked her finger like a gun. "I want you to come with me downtown and I'll buy you a new wardrobe. You're gonna need a new front. I want you to return to San Francisco in style."

"I'm up for that," I responded. "Thanks, that's very generous of you, Bunny."

"Today you start 'Pimp 101.' The first lesson is: It's all about the front. Rich rags and flowery rap, backed with a badass attitude. I think you'll be a natural."

"That works," I said. "Pimping is simply marketing and sales management. I learned from the best. My father could sell ice cream to an Eskimo and charge interest. I'll teach the girls everything I know and treat them well."

She took a long sip of her Chardonnay. Sparkles danced in her eyes.

"You'll love the house in Chinatown. It's an elegant place, with a wonderful Old World charm. The house is perfectly located, close to North Beach and five minutes from the Tenderloin district."

North Beach reminded me of the Sunset Strip with its abundance of nightclubs, restaurants and tourists. It was an upscale Little Italy and party section of San Francisco. The neighborhood was flooded with restaurants, coffeehouses and topless clubs. Though it didn't have the red-light ambiance of the Tenderloin, North Beach had plenty of hookers. They just looked classier than most of the TL girls.

"I already have many talented ladies in my stable," Bunny chatted on, "and I know a lot of first-class prostitutes that want to work for me. But I need help in managing them."

"What do you mean?"

"Most gay women work better for a pimp whom they're emotionally involved with. I'm a woman who can share my butch sexually, as long as I know she has my best interests at heart."

I boldly announced, "I'm a very good lover."

Bunny laughed. "We'll see."

I grinned and asked, "When would you like to find out?"

Bunny ignored my pass and told me, "First things first. You need to stay off of smack and remember to eat. Every day you need to have at least one good meal with protein in it."

"That's an old street rule. Miss Zada used to always say the same thing."

I was flattered that this beautiful, talented woman had seen what I had to offer. I made a commitment to myself, right then and there,

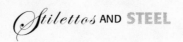

that I was going to stay off heroin and become the best business partner this woman ever had.

Bunny slowly took another sip of the golden wine and sweetly said, "Your eyes are beautiful when you cry, but honey, never let anyone see you cry again. To cry is to look weak on the streets. Please keep your tears inside of you, okay?"

"I promise," I replied.

"We'll head up to San Francisco in a few days," she said in her familiar freshly fucked voice.

I reached across the table and shook my new partner's sweet pretty hand. We were in business.

Chapter 7

VENTURA HIGHWAY

*V*ENTURA HIGHWAY SPUN OUT BEFORE US as we zoomed down
the fast lane toward San Francisco. The Caddy was packed
and topless, showing off its pretty passengers. Bunny and I reveled
in the California sunshine that bathed our tanned bodies. My ambi-
tious chauffeur had insisted that I recover on the shores of Malibu
before starting my new position.

We passed through Woodland Hills, where I had grown up. As
we drove to the peak of Chalk Hill, I could see my family's home
from the vista. The wind blew strongly, ruffling my newly highlighted hair. Bunny, who collected Barbie dolls, had me dressed like
her own personal Ken.

Taft High School hugged the side of the freeway. I was glad my
dark sunglasses and hard drag shielded me in anonymity. I pointed
toward a large ranch style home on top of a hill and said, "That's
where I used to live."

"It's lovely, Jesse. Looks like you had a nice view."

"Yes, you can see the entire west end of the Valley.

"Do you keep in touch with any of your old friends?" Bunny
asked sweetly.

"Nah, and I won't be attending any high school reunions. That's
for sure. This part of my life is over," I answered resignedly.

"I understand, Jesse," Bunny replied as she took my hand. "I actually enjoyed getting dressed for my prom," she added with a girlish giggle.

"I didn't go to mine. I broke my quarterback boyfriend's heart when I ran away from home."

"I'm sure you did."

"I thought it was best to split before anyone found out I was gay. Suburban parents can be vicious, you know. My best friend Renee went to bed with a Mexican boy. When her parents found out, they shipped her to Israel to live in a kibbutz. The next morning she found herself picking oranges and being shot at by Arabs."

I lit up a cigarette to Bunny's laughter.

"When I found out what the medical treatment was for lesbians," I continued, "I thought Renee got off easy. Middle-class girls like me received the best of care: private mental asylums, shock treatments and lobotomies."

Bunny shivered at that notion. "I can't wait to hit the TL."

I took a deep drag and looked at the side mirror. We passed the sprawling Warner's Horse Ranch.

"It's so green and open here, Jesse. I can't get over how pretty it is."

"Yeah, but not for long. I heard that ranch was sold. They're planning on building a huge mall and hospital here. When I'm old, I can tell people I lived in the Valley when it was nice."

As we silently drove through the rolling hills, I had a sudden vision of playing army in the fields of my youth. The only war I knew back then was the big one, the war we won because we were good and the Nazis and Japs were bad.

The best thing about World War II as far as I was concerned, was my father's army shovel. It was just the right size. It had a small V-shaped blade and a short handle, a perfect tool for a ten-year-old tomboy. I would crawl on my belly quietly and quickly, with my shovel strapped over my back and my army canteen hooked on my belt. I loved my canteen. The cap was attached with a small chain to the round silver canister that fit snugly into an army green canvas case. It was so butch, so very cool the way you could open it and take a sip.

Behind me, my troops would be making progress crawling though the high grass in the field down the block from my house. My "troops" consisted of my younger brother Max and my best friend, Ronnie Hickenbotten. I figured that any soldier who had survived being named Hickenbotten and who had "Okies" for a mom and dad could handle any German.

The rest of my loyal troops usually included my cousin Suzanne, a five-year-old little girl with unruly, black curly hair. I would see her at the end of the line trailing behind her older skinny sister, Christine (when she was willing to join in the game), with her small helmeted head bobbing up and down just above the tall grass.

Suzanne was always the straggler and because of this, she would often fall into enemy hands. More than once we had to rescue her.

After sneaking up on the enemy's camp, I would whisper to my men, "Get prepared to attack and don't shoot until you see the whites of their eyes." I'd adjust my helmet over my ponytail, grip my rifle firmly, rise to my feet already running and yell at the top of my lungs, "CHARGE!" That powerful command would unleash a furious full-fledged assault, and the battle would begin.

"Rat-a-tat-tat, rat-a-tat-tat."

"You're dead, lie down!"

"Give up you lousy kraut!"

"Put your hands up!"

"Stop crying, you sissy!"

In the heat of battle, above the noise and clamor of war, I would hear that dreaded sound in the distance coming from my front porch: "Jessica, Max, come on in for dinner!" It was my mother calling us, telling us to stop playing. She would yell at the top of her lungs, joining the chorus of other young mothers whose voices sang out through the warm summer night air.

Despite what I'd told Bunny, I allowed myself to linger in the vision of my childhood. I could picture my mother so well, standing on the front porch. She looked out of place in comparison to the other mothers. She was beautiful, always immaculately dressed and usually wore a simple black dress with white pearls. Her nails were done and her face made up just enough to emphasize her pretty features. My mother was a proud first-generation Californian and a descendant of the great Lopez Portillo family of Spain.

Like a classic fifties TV mom, standing tall at her full height of four-foot-eleven, poised, her hand resting on the front porch railing, she looked more like a model doing an impression of Donna Reed than a housewife. She was a mysterious and glamorous sight in our neighborhood.

Stella Hickenbotten, my friend Ronnie's mom, would yell for her boys while planted next to the old Chevy pickup parked in front of a small camping trailer in their driveway. Stella would be wearing her favorite muumuu, looking like a white Aunt Jemima.

Bunny's sexy voice pulled me out of yesterday. Squeezing my hand, she excitedly said, "Oh, Jesse, I can't wait to get to Chinatown! Today Macy's is delivering my king-sized Simmons Beautyrest!"

"Hookers, money, booze and a pillow top bed. Hit the gas, bitch!"

Chapter 8

CITY BY THE BAY

UNNY HELD MY ARM AS WE WALKED past my old haunts in the Tenderloin. The chilly fog broke like faint clouds as we briskly stepped side-by-side past the strip joints and beer bars. The civilized San Franciscans were asleep, but the street people of the TL were just getting started.

Bunny's fur coat pressed up next to my new camel-hair overcoat that protected my custom-made gray gabardine pinstripe suit. We had just finished a late dinner at Original Joe's Italian restaurant and were heading toward the Hilton Hotel.

Bunny was meeting a high-rolling Easterner. The gentleman wanted a taste of New Jersey while visiting the city by the bay.

As we ducked around the corner toward the brightly lit high-rise hotel, Bunny said, "Jesse honey, why don't you go to the bar for a drink and wait for me?"

"I don't know, baby. I think I'll check on a few of our ladies walking Turk. I'll come over to your place later tonight."

She pulled me into a doorway. "If you promise, I'll let you go take care of business."

Her sparkling baby blues looked up at mine with yearning. "I want to take you grocery shopping in the morning to fill up that empty fridge in your lonely little bachelor pad." She grabbed hold of my lapel. "At least let me make it homey for you, since you insist on living there."

"I'll get a nice apartment soon. I just haven't had a chance to look. I've been building our stable, in case you haven't noticed." She nodded, knowing I'd been busy. "We'll go apartment hunting for me tomorrow instead of grocery shopping. Okay?"

She wrapped her arms around my waist and said, "I probably won't see you until tomorrow, knowing you."

"Maybe," I said as I felt her breasts push up to mine. I held her in my arms and gave her a long kiss in the shadow of the doorway. At last I pulled myself away from her warmth. "I'll catch you later."

Bunny headed toward the entrance of the Hilton in her unbuttoned luscious knee-length mink. Perfect breasts pushed up in a tight black dress dazzled onlookers. Valets and bellhops watched Bunny's breasts bounce with each step she took up the stairs toward the lobby. Her defined calves caught my eye as her stiletto-dressed feet marched toward her date.

When Bunny was out of sight, my mind returned to the obsession which had plagued me since our arrival in San Francisco. Would I run into Carmen tonight?

I decided to head over to the Why Not to look for her. Hopefully I wouldn't witness her flirting with the rich, Ivy League dude. My TL buddies had informed me she'd been sitting at his table recently. This concerned me.

Carmen's older sister Phyllis, a beautiful and talented lady of the night, had been the D.A.'s favorite pastime for years. Gossip had it however, that Phillip was secretly in love with Carmen. Besides these rumors, I was clueless on how Carmen was feeling toward me or what she was up to.

Feeling gloomy, I hiked toward the Why Not. Carmen had been giving me the cold shoulder, not returning my calls. I was sure that she had heard about my new position as a pimp. The currents of gossip flowed through the Tenderloin like sewage to the ocean.

The olive was glowing in the neon martini as I arrived. Hesitantly I checked myself out in the smoky glass. My elegant wise guy attire gave me confidence as I adjusted my charcoal-gray fedora. Bravely I cracked the heavy door open and peered into the smoky dungeon of pigs. Much to my dismay, Carmen was nowhere in sight.

I did spot Clancy though, holding court with a group of rookies at a table filled with glass steins of beer. At the sight of my old suitor, I quickly ducked back out the door. If a simple pair of slacks had upset Clancy, my new suit would give him a coronary.

Disappointed at not finding Carmen, I turned my mind back on my favorite pastime: business. Passing Compton's, I turned the corner of Turk and Taylor, the crossroads of the Tenderloin. Half-undressed hookers, door-lingering hustlers and wandering johns decorated the neighborhood. Pan-handling, folk-singing hippies strummed their guitars at the curb.

I decided to cut across the alley behind Eddy Street to see if any of our girls were flaking off. The ten-and twenty-dollar street walkers we employed had a tendency to get distracted; shooting up behind dumpsters or taking extended doobie breaks. Playing heavy-handed pimp was not my style, but letting my girls know that I was watching was just good management.

The long alley was empty and dark. Up ahead, I saw the silhouette of a girl walking by a row of large trash bins. I could see flowing black hair down a light colored coat.

Headlights of an approaching car highlighted her thin frame. She screamed as two black dudes suddenly jumped out of the car in front of her.

One of them rushed up and said, "Now we got you bitch!"

In the headlights, I could clearly see the men. It was Giuseppe, an old running buddy of mine from my early days in the TL, and his brother Prince. The beautiful Asian hooker stood stark still. They moved in on her with a sadistic glee on their dark faces.

Prince was a six-foot-five, horse-faced pimp who ran the Fillmore district's crew of psycho punks. The Fillmore boys were a gang of pimps who beat, tortured and starved their bitches if they didn't produce enough. I was not happy to see them in our territory.

Giuseppe, Prince's kid brother, was a pockmarked crank-head who flaunted his convict, iron-pumping physique in tight, black silk shirts. His massive chest was covered with gold chains that caught the headlights.

Giuseppe stood next to their prey grinning. His oily, bald head glistened as he spoke with exaggerated facial expressions. "Run for it, bitch!"

He grabbed the Asian girl's hair as she started to flee.

Terror shot through me as I heard my own breath coming fast. Sanity told me not to move as I watched. I was no match for an ex-con. The Asian girl's face showed the fear I was feeling as she got kicked in the ass by Prince's large foot while his brother grasped her hair.

"Get walking, bitch. You're supposed to be sucking dick, not strolling through the alley!" Prince shouted.

She answered back pleadingly, "I had to pee. I was taking a powder break."

That comment caused Giuseppe to drag her towards the open car door. She fell and tried to hold onto the bumper as he pulled her over the asphalt.

Prince bent down in front of her as he grabbed her foot. Giuseppe pulled her hair as Prince held her. She kicked with her free leg and screamed, "Let me go. I'll not do it again!"

I held my breath as I saw the flash of a six-inch blade shoot out from a switchblade Prince pulled from his pocket. He pushed the tip of the knife against her pelvis as Giuseppe laughed, twisting her hair in his large fist.

Desperation and terror filled the girl's face as she eyed the knife. Prince cackled and said, "Maybe I'll pop a hole in your bladder, then you can piss right here, bitch!"

Giuseppe joined in the fun. "Let's throw this lazy-ass bitch in the trunk. Maybe we'll swing by the dump."

They started laughing in unison.

I didn't have a piece. I was a lover, not a fighter. I knew if I intervened, they would cut my throat. Giuseppe looked completely wired. His eyes bulged out as he grinned, showing his excitement. The more she squirmed, the happier he got.

With a disgusted grunt, Prince let go of her foot, and she stumbled trying to get up. Giuseppe yanked the screaming whore to the rear of the car. I heard the trunk slam and the front door close. In a moment, a large purple El Dorado passed in front of me as I hid in the darkness.

The fear etched on the young whore's face lingered like heavy fog. I remembered my own countless nights of degradation as a streetwalker. I said a silent prayer for the girl in the trunk.

Pimping was the ultimate power play. My most powerful tools of persuasion however, were charm and sex. Humiliation was a barbaric technique that I vowed I would never resort to. Yet tonight had shown me one thing: I had to protect my turf. I couldn't cower behind a garbage can like a frightened little girl. I decided to head over to the bordello and tell my old friend Marie about the Fillmore boys moving into our territory. I was curious to hear her take on it.

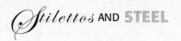

I hurried out of the alley and hailed a cab. The scruffy-bearded driver asked, "Where to?"

Jumping into the back, I requested, "Take me to the big yellow Victorian on Bell Street in Chinatown."

The driver spun away from the curb. I sat back, thinking about what I'd seen. I needed protection, and I needed the kind of badasses who could provide it.

Chapter 9

MARIE

I GAZED UP AT THE GRAND YELLOW VICTORIAN HOUSE. The stately wrought iron fence surrounding it was dotted with large red roses. As I inhaled their sweet scent, I felt like I was coming home. I unlocked the heavy ornate gate, pulled it open, and ventured up the brick pathway to the bordello.

The wooden steps creaked under my weight as I stepped onto the charming and spacious veranda. Red geraniums greeted me, potted in their freshly painted planters. Beside the front door was a white wicker porch swing. Its plush, rose-patterned cushions offered southern comfort. The large varnished oak door had an elegant brass plate engraved in romantic cursive script: *Tara of the West*.

I knocked: three short fast raps. The heavy peephole cover squeaked as it was opened. I looked directly into the eye of my friend Marie. She was a streetwise hooker with the looks of Liz Taylor and the brains of a Wall Street stockbroker.

"Who's there?"

Aggravated, I replied, "It's Jesse." I appreciated her precautions, but I was in no mood for them tonight.

"What's the code?"

"Twelve, twelve. Give me a break, Marie. It's freezing out here!"

She replied in a pleasant southern voice, "Hold your horses, honey."

The heavy deadbolt turned and the large door opened. I greeted Marie with a quick nod, feeling really annoyed for having to stand out in the cold.

As she bolted the door behind me, the large rock on her finger caught the light from the foyer chandelier. I felt the soft plush Persian rug compress beneath the soles of my shoes. Like the johns that came here, I was soothed in style.

Marie smiled, her velvet blue eyes delivering a hint of divine rapture. Large diamond stud earrings sparkled against her curly black hair.

Reluctantly, I smiled back at my friend. "I gotta talk a little business with you, but let's have a drink first, okay?"

Marie indicated an adjoining room. "I'm completing 'The Madonna' and it'd be nice to have some company."

Marie was a passionate artist, and she loved to show her latest pieces of work. She displayed them in her own personal studio which doubled as the dining room. A devout Catholic, she volunteered her talents by painting the saints for the local parish. Mary Magdalene was her favorite.

Marie gave me a hug, softly kissed me on the cheek and said, "Let's go in the dining room, honey. I want to show you my latest. I'll fix you a drink."

I followed Marie through the large house, passing the luxurious parlor. Rich leather chairs sat across from each other in front of an open fireplace. Between them stretched an ivory-white polar bear rug. On the marble mantel, sterling silver frames showcased the ladies of the house. An elegant gold baroque chaise lounge and sofa surrounded an antique mahogany coffee table. The beautiful bay windows were framed with long, green, velvet drapes.

We entered the large formal dining room and I took a seat in the ornate high-backed mahogany chair at the head of the table. Feeling like King Arthur in his court, I waited for my Genevieve to fix my drink.

Carefully, I placed my cigarettes apart from the open containers of turpentine and paint-smeared rags on the newspapers covering the table. I shared the table space in front of me with a foot-and-a-half, partially-painted statue of the Virgin Mary, tubes of paint, a painter's palette and a variety of brushes.

"Jesse, are you hungry?"

"I'm just a little hungry, what do you have?" I replied like a tired husband to a doting wife after a hard day's work. I knew exactly what the menu was. It had been the same for years, but there was no harm in asking.

Marie announced, "I just happen to have some southern fried chicken and some fried green tomatoes. I only used a little batter, because I know you're a Californian and you like healthy foods."

I gave Marie the same reply that I always did. "Yes, dear. That's just fine."

Even though our romantic interest in each other had been short-lived, we always acted like an old married couple. She liked to serve, and I liked to be served, so it worked out just great.

Marie left the dining room like a faithful wife rushing to fulfill her duty of feeding me. She would return in a minute with fried chicken and fried green tomatoes on a large rose-patterned English porcelain platter.

I looked over at "The Madonna" and said a silent prayer, "God help me eat this fried chicken and green tomatoes once more."

I heard Wolfman Jack announcing one of my favorite tunes from the radio in the kitchen, "Cherry Pie." I closed my eyes, envisioning a large piece of freshly baked hot cherry pie. I would have preferred a slice of that instead of chicken again.

I heard the scuffling of shoes on the hardwood floors and opened my eyes to see Marie carrying the traditional platter with her "love offering."

"What would you like to drink, honey?"

"Jack and water."

I saw the familiar expression of shock on Marie's face as she replied, "Oh Jesse, don't be silly. I know you love Southern Comfort, and that's what you're gonna get."

Marie headed over to the Tiffany decanter set on the antique butler's table. Her elegant fingers, adorned with a six-carat diamond ring, removed the crystal top and slowly poured the rich dark amber lifeblood of the south over ice.

Peace and comfort enveloped me as I gazed up at the crystal chandelier. "Good God, Marie. How did we ever end up rich?"

Marie shrugged and let out a little laugh. "We sold a lot of ass, baby!"

I laughed and slowly ate my food. She picked up her paintbrush and applied light blue to the Madonna's robe.

Marie had a toughness that lay beneath her southern belle act. When Marie first entered the life, she'd had to turn cheap five-and ten-dollar tricks on the streets of Hollywood. Her patience and motherly instincts toward the girls in the house surpassed all under-standing. I believe that's what made her such a great madam. I had instinctively chosen powerful women to encircle my life as business partners and the smartest thing Bunny and I ever did was to hire Marie to baby-sit our stable. Bunny and I had zero tolerance for the daily ins-and-outs of running a bordello.

I enjoyed watching Marie methodically paint her statue. Her

paint-smeared fingers meticulously applied the final touches to the Madonna's robe with a long brush. While she worked, I reflected on the first time I saw Marie at a funky San Francisco hippie bar called, The Nest.

Marie was slouched on the large pillows of an old sofa in a corner of the smoke-filled poolroom. She was wearing a midnight blue t-shirt with small mirrored sequins and faded denim bell bottoms. Her pretty bare feet with hot-pink toenails dangled over the armrest. Marie's full attention was devoted to a *Vogue* magazine she was reading. When I entered, she looked up at me and blew perfect smoke rings. I was stunned by her dark blue eyes and long beautiful black hair. She was a mysterious young woman with chiseled features, softened by full lips, and her beauty captivated me then as it did now.

I watched her paint with the brush in one hand and a Kool in the other. It was mesmerizing watching my friend get lost in her art. I felt a deep satisfaction knowing that Marie would never have to turn a trick again and that she could indulge herself in her greatest passion; painting Catholic art.

I interrupted my friend's concentration by asking, "Marie, have you heard any news about the Fillmore boys recently?"

Marie carefully set her paint brush down on one of the open jars of turpentine and turned to me with a concerned expression. "No. Is something wrong?"

"Prince and Giuseppe got pretty ugly with one of their girls in the alley behind Eddy Street tonight. They threw her in the trunk and took off. I don't even know if she's still alive."

She looked pained but said, "Don't worry, Jesse. No pimp in his right mind kills a money-making whore. Maybe they were catching a stray."

"Yeah, most likely," I replied, still uneasy. "It's probably just a fluke."

"I would mention tonight's episode to Bunny though. You're lucky they didn't rob you."

I bristled at that comment. "I know how to take care of myself. I've been walking these streets for years."

"That's before your shoes cost more than most people's rent," she pointed out.

Solemnly, I pondered Marie's admonishment as she put away her paints and tools.

"Jesse, you need to get yourself a piece," she went on. "I think it's time you got a bodyguard too."

"I'm a lover, not a fighter, girl," I said, though I'd had the same thought.

"I remember, honey," she said with a worried smile. "I'm going upstairs to get you a little something. I'll be right back."

I watched as Marie left the room. She was wearing faded denim overalls, but she could quickly change into a sexy dress and look like a million bucks when it came time to greet a john. She had voluptuous breasts which she would expose like greeting cards in low-cut décolletage.

She would always place her soft hand on a john's chest as he entered the foyer to stop him for a moment. She demurely looked up at him with an expression of complete adoration. She would give the standard greeting, "Welcome to Tara of the West. Come on in and stay a while…we guarantee you'll leave with a smile."

Her eyes told the john, "You're so handsome, you're so tall, you're so smart, and you're so strong. I know you'd be truly happy with your cock in my mouth."

Her seductive, husky voice entranced the trick. She knew that each hushed word she spoke allowed her to hike up the price as the john became harder and harder.

Marie returned with a gun in her hand. She placed the pearl-handled snub-nose .38 on the table in front of me.

"Take this, baby. Careful, she's loaded. This beauty's got me out of more than one trick-gone-bad."

I picked up the gun and studied it, feeling its surprising weight in my hands. Reluctantly, I put it into my pocket, knowing she was right.

Marie slotted her paints into the wooden case on the table. She looked at me and recited an old street saying, "The nicer the nice, the higher the price."

"You got that right," I replied.

Our moment was jolted by a loud knocking at the front door. Marie walked over to the kitchen doorway and called out in a musical voice, "Ju Ju, Jujubees, would you come in here, please? I need you for a minute."

The flamboyant Filipino houseboy stepped into the dining room. His white Eisenhower jacket emphasized his svelte waist and firm ass. Jujubees was both as sweet and as obnoxious as the candy that gets stuck in your teeth. The only time the young man moved with any urgency was when he wanted to show his vexation at being treated like a houseboy.

In an annoyed tone he asked, "What is it, Miss Marie?"

"It's the door, Jujubees," she said in an exasperated tone.

"It's probably that Puerto Rican floozy." Jujubees did a Barbara Stanwyck turn and sauntered away.

There was another loud knock as Jujubees called through the door, "What's your code?"

"Two, four, six and I'm not a trick," answered Little Rosie in a thick Latina accent. "Open the door, you fruit! My nipples have frostbite!"

Marie looked at me and smiled, "Looks like Little Rosie caught your scent."

Sassy Jujubees let in a foxy Puerto Rican in four-inch heels.

"I smell Aramis. Where's Jesse?" Rosie demanded.

"She's having a drink with Marie in the dining room."

The sound of clicking stiletto heels grew louder as Little Rosie made a beeline to me. Rosie was a hooker who moonlighted as a topless dancer. She had the hots for me and was the first lady to join my stable.

"Hi, my pretty little chi-chi mama, looks like you got off work early," I said.

"I never stop working. Don't be silly, *papi*," she said as she snapped her fingers.

Rosie's intoxicating brown body was poured into a low-cut leopard dress, revealing a bodacious bosom that made her a fortune. Rosie's stylish bouffant hairdo towered above gigantic gold earrings. Her bright brown eyes playfully challenged me. "Don't you give your baby girl a kiss when she comes home from work?"

Her well-shaped face and strong nose were softened by round cheeks. Full lips painted in bright pink lipstick seemed frozen in a perpetual little girl pout.

"Mellow out, Rosie. Join us for a drink and a joint," Marie put in.

Rosie shot me a teasing glare and said, "Chat, chat, chat, smoking dope, just sitting and a-chatting…when you could be upstairs in my bed." Rosie gave me a big wink. She slowly turned around, bent over and stuck out her behind. The playful Puerto Rican slapped her sexy ass and said, "Just think. You could have this instead."

Marie and I burst into laughter. I had to admit, she had a point.

Rosie was the first femme who showed me the ropes in the art of making love as a baby butch. The passion we experienced years ago after a quick pickup at Maud's bar still burned intermittently.

Rosie seductively took off her shawl and flung it over her shoulder. She moved to hug me and said, "Jesse, I need to slip into a hot bubble bath. Come join me. I have a hidden stash of Jack."

Rosie was familiar and fun, like a taste of home. Guilt gnawed at my conscience a little. My heart was reserved for Carmen, and I couldn't let anyone else in. Tonight though, I could use a little light entertainment. "I think I'll take you up on it, foxy lady," I answered as I got up and followed her toward the stairway.

"That'll be nice if you two spend a little time together," Marie called after us. "Maybe Rosie will be sweeter to Jujubees tomorrow."

As we reached the top landing, Marie called up, "Oh, Jesse, I have someone in mind for that henchman job. We'll discuss it on the veranda in the morning."

Chapter 10

RAT-A-TAT-TAT, JESSE'S BACK

I STRUTTED DOWN THE CROWDED SIDEWALK of my old neighborhood in the Tenderloin. The fading afternoon sun caressed my face and a cool breeze carried mingled sounds of the city as I made my way toward Compton's Cafeteria.

I maneuvered through the familiar, violent underbelly of strip joints, bars, cheap hotels and liquor stores. Colorful queens peppered the neighborhood, dressed to the nines in high heels and high hair. Lesbians dressed like men boldly walked in public, holding hands with their femme girlfriends.

The Tenderloin was different from most red-light districts because it was a Camelot for homos. It offered freedom to dress in drag, which was against the law. That freedom was regulated by the dirty cops. The "Tax Squad" allowed the queers to prostitute as long as they stayed in the gay ghetto. Of course, when the mood struck them, the pigs cracked a lot of heads and made big bucks shaking down the homos, hustlers, hookers and dealers. Like the cops said, "Clubs were trump." Legend had it that the Tenderloin's name came from the prime cut of meat which the dirty cops could afford to eat after collecting all of their bribes.

I passed my old home at the Camelot Hotel. It was a seedy joint next door to a Turkish bathhouse. Sweaty, smiling gay boys exited the baths as johns of every variety cruised down Turk Street. The procession of "bargain shoppers" reminded me of my streetwalking days before I met Bunny.

I thought about how far I'd come since my grand entrance back into the city. I had paraded through the streets of the Tenderloin chauffeured by Bunny in her pink Caddy convertible. Proudly, I displayed my recently awarded rank of gangster pimp.

Like a top-notch head hunter, I'd gone to work implementing my new employee recruitment plan. I offered bonuses and perks that were irresistible to any prostitute. My new girls encouraged their friends to follow. Like hair stylists, the hookers brought their clients along, too.

To secure my position as a thriving gangster, I was in need of a henchman. Today, I had an appointment to meet Diana at Compton's. She was a young lady from Oakland who was interested in the shield position. Diana's street handle was "Junior" and she had come highly recommended by Marie.

"Jesse, look for a Latin butch dressed in black, carrying a briefcase," Marie had told me.

The cafeteria on Turk and Taylor Street was my favorite place to rendezvous. It was a convenient meeting spot in the heart of the Tenderloin. Any time was a good time, since it was open twenty-four, seven. The corner was a mecca for every variety of street people, including the young runaways who panhandled in front of the restaurant.

Compton's had large windows that ran the full length of the cafeteria, which made it an ideal location to check out the street action. The cooks and servers were immune to the hard drag butches, dolled-up femmes, flamboyant queens and army of hippies and bikers that lingered inside over cups of coffee. Besides the folks talking shit into the wee hours of the morning were the tricks who scurried in and out before going next door to the conveniently located Camelot

Hotel. The employees and patrons nonchalantly watched the endless transactions of the commerce of sex and drugs that took place in the brightly lit eatery.

I spotted two hippies working the front entrance. I recognized one of them, an old acquaintance and occasional party buddy named Two Bits. Her wild blond frizzy hair shot out around her head like a tumbleweed. Bursting gold stars danced across her psychedelic hip-hugging bell-bottoms. Two Bits' big belly protruded under her faded blue Timothy Leary t-shirt that advertised "Turn On, Tune In, Drop Out."

This sweet-spirited acid head was a fixture of the Tenderloin. She flashed the crack in her plump ass as she bent down to pick up a dime that a military-looking dude tossed at her from a passing car. Two Bits shot the dude a peace sign, and her turquoise and silver bracelets jangled down her arm. Strands of glittering love beads bounced off her big tits as she shouted, "Peace, man!"

On the other side of the entrance stood a sad-eyed barefoot girl with long flowing red hair. The tattered hem of her long white dress, which was embroidered in pink peace symbols, fell down around her filthy bare feet. The hippie's wafer-thin waist was wrapped in a thick rope belt that gathered the loose-fitting garment. The girl held a few colorful flowers by her side.

She was Two Bits' partner in crime and boldly broke the law by asking a passerby, "Can you spare a dime for a flower?" Two Bits kept an eye out for the pigs. She stood in fringed, blue-beaded Indian moccasins next to a coffee can filled with wilted flowers. The can held up a small sign which read, "STOP THE WAR!"

I caught Two Bits' attention with a greeting of, "Hey, man… got a dime?"

Two Bits' large acid-dilated eyes lit up in surprise. "Hey, Jesse! Man, is that you?"

Giving a small bow and tipping my Stetson, I replied, "You got that right."

Two Bits' face broke into a wide smile. "How cool to see you, Jesse!"

"Nice to see you again, man. Glad to be home."

Two Bits shot me her traditional peace sign. "Let's all come together right now!" Excitedly, she started rapping, "You're the talk of the TL, Jesse. I heard you're all rich now and you got your own big stable."

Playfully, I held an invisible Tommy gun, grinned like a gangster and said, "Rat-a-tat-tat, Jesse's back!"

Two Bits laughed gleefully. She motioned with her thumb toward the young girl. "This is my crash bitch, Tulip."

Politely I tipped my hat and said, "I'm pleased to meet you, Tulip."

The wafer-thin chick shyly held out a small beaded red hemp change purse. With hollow blue eyes she implored, "Can you spare a dime for a flower, Jesse?"

Two Bits smiled at me apologetically. "Sorry Jesse, she's hungry."

"It's cool, Two Bits," I replied, pulling out my gold money clip pregnant with big bills.

I handed Two Bits a ten spot and said to the amiable street urchin, "Please buy your pretty lady a nice dinner. Catch ya guys later. And Two Bits, I may have a job for you soon. I need a runner for messages and errands."

Stuffing the bill into her jeans pocket, the cheerful dyke blurted out, "Far out! I'm up for that, boss."

The heavy glass doors surrendered and I entered the all-night diner. Through the large plate glass windows I caught a glimpse of Two Bits and Tulip scampering down the sidewalk.

The welcoming aroma of sizzling burgers, French fries and fresh coffee met me. Happily chatting customers sat in red-cushioned chrome chairs at Formica tables. In the background, the Everly Brothers'"Cathy's Clown," softly played. Behind a stool-lined counter, two burly cooks in tall white chef hats busily filled orders. Uniformed fast-moving waitresses, holding heavy trays above their heads, glided down the shiny black-and-white checkered tile runway.

Karen, a spunky Asian waitress, greeted me. She smiled, exposing a wide gap in the middle of her teeth. "Hi Jesse, your table's open." Her long, wispy hair was pinned with a small pink waitress hat. Displayed on her crisp white polyester uniform's breast pocket was her embroidered name, under a neatly folded pink handkerchief. She escorted me to an open table.

"Hey Jesse, guess who I just saw walking past?" Karen asked as if she held the answer to the $64,000 question.

"I don't know, Karen ... Janis Joplin?" I shot back.

"I'll give you a clue: feisty femmes!"

"The feistiest femme I know is Carmen," I commented casually.

Karen's eyes lit up. "You got it!" She poured my coffee, pleased to be the bearer of good news. "She was strolling down the street with her sister Phyllis a few minutes before you came in."

A light suddenly went on. "Man, she must be circling me. How cool," I said. "There're no secrets in the Tenderloin. They must know I've been hanging out here."

Smiling, Karen said, "Jesse, as you would say, you got that right."

My mood brightened up a thousand watts. "Cool, I'll have the usual. I'm kinda hungry."

"Coming right up, Jesse." She scribbled my order on a pad and winked a dark almond eye at me.

I pulled out my trusted Zippo, comforted by its weight, and lit a cigarette. I sighed with relief, knowing my girl was close by. Carmen and Phyllis could have walked down any other street. But Carmen always knew how to get my attention.

Karen came back with a dish of lukewarm ravioli and a stale French roll. She refilled my coffee and whisked away, off to put out other fires.

I saw a patron dressed in black seated at the counter. She rested a dark leather briefcase against her polished square-toed boots. Sensing my attention as I approached, the young woman turned around.

I was taken aback by her stunning good looks. Her thin, straight nose and sensuous full lips were exotically Spanish. Her light olive-skinned face was framed by short black curly hair.

"Junior?" I inquired.

"Yes. It's nice to meet you, Jesse," she said. A warm smile pushed deep dimples into her cheeks. Junior's broad shoulders and trim waist were packaged neatly in a silk shirt and creased slacks. She was strikingly handsome with refined pretty-boy features.

"Hi, Junior, I'm Jesse Rawlson. Pleased to meet you," I said, warmly introducing myself.

Junior took my extended hand, giving me a firm handshake.

"Grab your coffee. Let's go to my table so we can chat," I said.

"Okay," Junior replied. She pulled out a fifty-cent piece, placing it on the counter. Grabbing her briefcase, the neatly dressed butch followed me. We sat down across from each other.

"Why don't you get something to eat, Junior?

"No, thanks."

Pulling a pack of Pall Malls from my jacket pocket, I offered Junior a cigarette. She took it and said, "Thanks, man."

After lighting up, I slid Junior my coveted lighter. "Marie's spoken very highly of you."

"That was nice of her," Junior replied. Perfectly white straight teeth appeared magically from behind her stoic expression.

Junior lit her smoke and took a drag. She clicked my Zippo shut. Politely, she placed it atop the red cigarette pack.

I continued to study my potential new employee. Junior's hands looked refined yet strong. Her short fingernails were manicured with clear polish. As she puffed, wisps of smoke drifted past her face.

"Marie said that you're a hard worker with street smarts."

Karen approached with a large metal coffee pot. She poured the steaming liquid into our cups and buzzed away.

"I am a hard worker, Jesse. I hear you are too. Word on the street is you're gonna be the biggest boss in the TL."

"Well Junior, I've had a jump-start most bosses don't get. Bunny had bordello girls before I hooked up with her. I brought in top-of-the-line call girls for our escort service. And we also run a group of street-walkin' Turk Street bitches. I make a percentage off everything our stable brings in."

"Marie brags that you're a very sophisticated pimp. She said everything you touch turns to gold." Junior spoke in a matter-of-fact tone and I didn't get the impression that she was trying to flatter me with bullshit.

"Marie's a good friend of mine. We were lovers for a hot five minutes when I first hit the TL. Marie's always liked a lot of diamonds, and I've always liked a lot of girls. With that combination, we're better off as friends."

We laughed, and I went on.

"Junior, to make big bucks, you gotta learn from the best. I implement corporate strategies. When I hire a hooker, I give her a sign-up bonus. Every good whore insists on getting paid first."

Junior chuckled as I continued to give her a thumbnail sketch of the business.

"Bunny is a true hooker at heart. 'More' is that girl's middle name, man! The bitch is rich, but she still personally services her V.I.P johns."

"Smart," Junior replied. "She keeps an eye on her money."

"She has a client in every trade. John the banker is an Ivy League, old money man. He's a creative dude when it comes to banking matters. Her big gun is Deadly Chang the Chink. He's a mob boss that makes Capone look like an altar boy. What he can do for Bunny, we don't want to talk about. You understand this?" I asked.

"Respect. Respect, man." Junior voiced the ultimate street accolade. "You got some heavy players in your pocket." Her face showed little expression as she continued. "Jesse. I grew up in the Oakland projects. My mom had to work two jobs to keep a roof over our heads. I raised my younger brothers and sisters by myself."

Junior's proud bearing was softened by a natural refinement. Her body language and small hand gestures revealed calmness. Junior seemed to possess the strength of a Mexican Indian and the elegance of a Spaniard.

She took a pull from her cigarette and spoke reflectively. "I fought every day of my life till no one would fuck with us."

"I'm impressed," I commented. "My henchman will need to be a good bodyguard. Sounds like you got that part of the job down."

She nodded, casual but tough underneath, I could see.

"I know how rough Oakland is. I grew up in the San Fernando Valley. You ever been there?"

"No, I've never left the Bay Area. Marie told me you were from the country."

I laughed to myself. Marie's adopted snobbish West L.A. attitude toward the Valley was very funny considering she was originally from Georgia.

"Junior, the San Fernando Valley is beautiful. It's suburbia, with rows of tract homes, surrounded by miles of open fields, orange and walnut groves and horse ranches. Everyone who lives there looks like they stepped out of *Ozzie and Harriet* or *Father Knows Best*. It's filled with nice middle-class families with good wholesome values, including mine."

"Sounds really nice," Junior said. "You must miss it."

I shrugged. "I do. But I don't miss acting straight. I lived a sheltered existence in an all-white neighborhood. I never even saw a real hobo or met a black person. The only blacks I ever saw were on the *Amos and Andy* show. We definitely didn't have queers or gangsters."

"We didn't have any whites in my neighborhood," said Junior. "We do have some queers in Oakland. We keep it to ourselves so as not to get killed."

"Sounds pretty fucked," I said commiserating. "I've been in the TL for over three years. Let me tell you something, Junior. Turning tricks for even six months in the TL is like doing two tours in 'Nam. You get hard in a hurry. Now that I'm in management, it's a lot nicer but even more dangerous."

Then I turned the subject to why we were meeting in the first place.

"So, are you any good with a gun?"

"Yeah, I pack a .38," Junior answered assuredly.

"Cool, I have a snub-nose .38 myself," I said, moving onto my next question. "Do you have an old lady, Junior? 'Cause you'll be married to this gig."

Junior answered, "I can be your shadow twenty-four, seven. I don't have time for a girlfriend." A nervous tinge entered her voice. "I wanna be totally honest with you. I tried to go straight a couple of years ago and ended up pregnant. I have a little girl. My mom is raising my daughter for now…I guess its best… But she's constantly threatening to report me to social services for being a homosexual."

"That's a drag about your mom, but having a kid is cool with me, Junior. Marie mentioned it. If you end up on my crew, needless to say, you'll make good money. What's minimum wage now? A buck an hour? When your mom sees cash, she'll get liberal real quick."

Junior smiled, appearing more relaxed. She took a long drag off her cigarette and snubbed it out.

I put my hand over my cup as Karen approached with a fresh pot of coffee, "No thanks, Karen. Just bring me the check, please."

She pulled the check from her apron pocket. As Karen held it toward me, she gave me a mock wink and said, "See you later, Jesse."

"Just give me the check, bitch," I said playfully as I snatched it from her fingers.

Karen laughed, "Just kidding." She made an about-face and left our table.

"Let's go, Junior," I said standing up. "I gotta get over to the Grapevine bar and pick up some cash. Little Rosie, one of my best whores, dances there. She's a Puerto Rican pistol that makes a jalapeño seem mild."

Junior smiled, took a last sip of water and grabbed her briefcase. I dropped three bills on the table.

Junior and I walked through the crowded restaurant toward the exit.

We passed a table packed with trash-talking queens, eating French fries and sipping Coca-Colas. The TL mommas' dazzling earrings flung about with each flamboyant head toss and bejeweled gesture.

I tilted my Stetson and sweetly said, "Good afternoon, ladies. Don't let Miss America see ya, or she'll die of envy."

I was smiling at their giggles when, like a red light, I stopped in my tracks at the sight of Carmen coming through the front door. The sexy femme approached like a queen strolling before her court. She politely paused her walk as she held my stare. Her body let me know she was happy to see me as she slightly bumped the table next to her.

I smiled and said, "Baby doll! You look great!"

Carmen halted in front of me, glanced over at Junior and said, "Thank you, Jesse. You look nice…like you've had some help picking your wardrobe."

Obviously, she'd heard about my involvement with Bunny.

"Carmen, I'd like you to meet a potential business associate of mine. Junior say hello to Carmen."

Junior said, "Hello."

Carmen and I stayed fixed on each other, like boxers in a ring, not too close out of mutual respect. I led with my chin. "Would you like to get together for a drink? I mean, if you got a moment."

Carmen's auburn hair fell loosely around her elegant neck. It was adorned with a new single diamond stud on a thin gold chain. She did not deign to reply.

"How about a cup of coffee right now?" I pleaded.

With that last request Junior flinched, seeing how Carmen's look of indifference wounded me. Carmen's eyes showed a slight sign of warmth at my pain.

"I have plans for today," she replied.

Pride fanned breath into my wounded ego as I nonchalantly said, "So do I today, come to think of it. Let's keep in touch." I tipped my hat to the lady as I headed toward the door.

Chapter 11

THE HENCHMAN

*A*S WE STEPPED OUT ONTO THE SIDEWALK, a nippy breeze announced another chilly night ahead.

"What a fucking fox!" Junior blurted out.

"Yeah, she's my fucking fox. That's Carmen, my old lady, she's just pissed at me."

"Oh, damn! That's *your* Carmen. Marie told me all about you guys. I'm so sorry!"

"Forget about it." I had a gangster moment and tapped her on the shoulder. "Let's go, *Vato*."

Junior and I, looking like two executives after a hard day's work, sauntered up Taylor Street toward the Grapevine. We passed a couple of men lingering around the sidewalk newsstand.

Tommy, a stocky bomber-jacket clad newsstand man, shouted out as he sold papers, "Hey Jesse, can you drop by later tonight?"

"You got it, Tommy," I shouted back. Turning to Junior, I said, "Tommy's one of our tricks. He probably wants to arrange a date at the house."

Tommy was selling a paper to Johnny Fuck-Fuck, a small-time pimp. The wannabe whore master was wearing an ugly mustard yellow suit and a white fedora. Cheap fake gold chains ran down his open golden lamé shirt. White patent leather shoes hadn't helped his recruiting efforts.

Johnny shot me a dirty glare. Standing next to Johnny was a tall dude dressed in denim. The pasty-faced guy had long red hair and full mutton chop sideburns with a thick mustache. The mutton chop chump yelled, "Hey, pussy pimp! Who's the cunt with the briefcase… your secretary?"

Johnny Fuck-Fuck broke into a loud laugh. Puckering his lips, he made a loud kissing sound and grabbed his crotch. "Come on, girls, its big enough for the both of you!"

I said in an undertone to Junior, "Let it slide, man. Johnny Fuck-Fuck's chump change."

"Which asshole is Johnny Fuck-Fuck?" Junior inquired in a very irritated tone.

"He's the one in love with his cock. I don't know that mutton chop punk."

Junior laughed as we turned the corner. Her height nearly matched mine, allowing us a comfortable stride.

"What's their fuckin' problem?" asked Junior.

"Well, I noticed lately some of the straight guys don't like that I'm making so much money," I replied.

That didn't surprise her. "Why is that dude called Johnny Fuck-Fuck?"

"He's a chump-change pimp that has a couple of skanky old whores. Sometimes they lose their way from Fillmore and end up on Turk Street. He shoots pool at the hall over on Market Street," I said jabbing a thumb in that direction. "The dude has Tourette's. Every time he misses a shot he yells, "Fuck! Fuck!""

Junior laughed.

Out of nowhere, Mutton Chop shot past us. In a flash he grabbed Junior's briefcase and raced off.

Her olive cheeks reddened with rage. "Hey, come back here!"

Junior and I burst into a full sprint after him. The mugger weaved in and out of the foot traffic. Furious, we pursued the denim-jacketed freak, tracking his flying hair above the crowd. At the corner, the towering thief darted into the alley.

Trash-filled dumpsters were parked under fire escape ladders which ran down the old hotel buildings. Water-filled potholes slowed my feet.

They slowed down our target too. Junior lunged forward, flying through the air and landed on the winded chump. She anchored her hands into the back of his long mane and the dude's head violently jerked back. Junior slammed him hard against the fire escape. She smashed the bandit's face on the dumpster. The sound of cracking bones filled the alley as his nose broke. "I'll kill you, pussy bitch!" he shouted. Blood spurted, spraying onto the dumpster as he struggled to get away.

My determined comrade wrapped her arms around his bloody head. Like a champion bronco buster, Junior locked her legs around his waist and hung on for dear life. "Drop my briefcase, shit head!" She yelled at the top of her lungs.

"Fuck you! You man-wannabe cunt!" he raged.

The chump kept trying to fling her off, but Junior wouldn't let up. Like a dirty street fighter, she gouged her fingers into his eye sockets with no mercy. He screamed through his blood-filled mouth, "Get off me, bitch!"

She spat through gritted teeth, "Fuck you!"

Junior rammed his head into the metal bin again and the dude finally collapsed to the asphalt. As he hit the ground hard, blood gushed from his broken nose and gashed forehead.

"Lezzie bitch!" he yelled as he unsuccessfully tried to rise to his feet.

Like a Rockette, she kicked him squarely in the head. He went sprawling.

Junior pulled her gun out of an ankle holster in one swift motion.

The deadly sound of the .38's hammer cocking filled the alley. Junior put her foot firmly on his chest while leaning over him. She jammed the steel barrel tip up his nostril. The dude's eyes flew open. He stared cross-eyed down past his shattered nose to the cocked gun.

She demanded in a hard, calm voice, "Show some respect."

I glanced up and down the alley, checking for the heat.

The sweating scumbag stared up at Junior and pleaded, "Don't kill me, man."

Instead, Junior whacked him with the butt of the gun and knocked him out cold. Stepping off him, the street warrior neatly wiped the blood on her gun's barrel on the dude's jacket.

"Junior, let's go, man, before the pigs get here."

Junior tucked the piece back in her ankle holster and dusted off her pant leg.

"Okay, Jesse," she answered, picking up her briefcase.

Junior's slacks were dirty and torn at the leg. She limped for a second before picking up the pace as we hurried to the end of the alley. When we hit the sidewalk, we started walking slowly as if enjoying a twilight stroll after a hard day's work.

"It's not all roses, Junior." I joked, still catching my breath. "If it was easy to get to the top, everybody would be there. Next time, handcuff your briefcase to yourself."

Junior, also winded, replied, "That bastard was *loco*."

"He's a jealous prick." I pointed down at her leg. "The son of a bitch ripped your slacks." I pulled out my money clip and handed Junior a Benny. "Take it."

"No, Jesse, it's cool, I'm fine," Junior answered as she raised her hand in protest.

"I want you to get yourself some nice slacks," I said firmly. "When people hang around me, they gotta look good."

Seeing my point, Junior shrugged.

"You know what I like hearing from my employees?" I light-heartedly asked.

"What?"

"'Yes, boss,' and that's about it."

She smiled good-naturedly and took the Benny.

Chapter 12

LITTLE ROSIE

*T*HE SOUND OF THE MOTOWN MASTER, Marvin Gaye, carried through the black velvet curtains hanging in the doorway. Pushing them aside, I was greeted by the perfume of the Tenderloin: stale booze and tobacco smoke. Tables lined the base of the stage of the poor man's North Beach Topless Club. Here, the patrons downed cocktails and watched Rosie's bouncing brown boobs.

As we lingered by the entrance, Little Rosie dominated the spotlight, dancing down the runway in the center of the stage. She moved enthusiastically, each boob jiggling to the beat as she jerked her arms up and down. Beneath Rosie's bouffant hairdo, her large glittering gold-hoop earrings swayed as fast as her miniskirt-clad ass.

I was pleased to see my girl hard at work. Junior and I stood watching her as she dramatically pointed her finger at the audience and sang along, "I heard it through the grapevine."

"Hey Junior, that's Rosie up there shaking her little Latin ass. She loves dancing." I waved a hand, indicating the crowd. "If the girls are happy, it reduces turnover and saves us the cost of training new ones. A gig like this provides us with a steady flow of new clients."

Junior nodded and said, "That makes a lot of sense."

We walked to the bar and sat on the tall barstools. Stacked bottles of booze sat on glass racks in front of the mirrored wall behind the bar. Black-and-gold labels dressed my companions in escape; like old friends they greeted me. The tall wild turkey and bold red-dressed English beefeater rubbed shoulders with a grinning pirate whose booted foot pinned down a keg of rum.

The silver-haired bartender, Larry Tuttle, wiped down the mahogany counter. His bushy eyebrows rose above his sparkling blue eyes as he gave me a warm smile with all three of his teeth. The old man was neatly dressed in a white shirt and black bowtie.

"Hey Jesse," called Tuttle, "lookin' good!"

Tuttle prepared my usual: two shots of Jack with a water back. He opened the cash register, removing a fat envelope from under the cash drawer. Deftly, he placed the envelope down in front of me." "Jesse, Bunny left this for you."

"Thanks," I said, casually putting away my week's take into my jacket's inner breast pocket. "Hey Tuttle, this is Junior, a friend of mine."

Tuttle's wise old eyes sized her up. "Nice to meet you, Junior. What's your poison?"

"I'll have a draft beer," Junior answered.

"Have a real drink, Junior," I urged. "After your Cassius Clay act back there, it's on me, man."

"I'll have a scotch and soda, Mr. Tuttle."

Tuttle smiled as he mixed her drink. Over his shoulder, I studied my reflection below the booze bottles and adjusted my hat. I studied the crowd from my perch like a Las Vegas pit boss, counting tricks like cards.

Little Rosie danced to the beat, pointing her finger accusingly toward me as she mouthed the words, "How much longer would you be mine?" The smile in her eyes let me know she didn't believe them. I downed the shot of Jack and tossed her a grin and a wink.

I tapped my finger on the wooden bar and said, "Hit me!" As I finished off the second shot, the warmth of the whiskey slowly spread through my chest like a river of lava. I lit a cigarette and inhaled the calming smoke.

"How the hell did you learn how to run like that, Junior? You're fuckin' fast!"

"I have a Mexican mother with old-time Catholic values who can really handle a tree switch."

Chuckling, I replied, "I'm Catholic too, but my mom only had to give us the warning, 'Wait till your father comes home.'"

Junior sipped her Scotch and soda. "You're pretty fast on your feet too, Jesse."

"I have an older brother who thought I was a punching bag." I took a long drag off my cigarette. "In fact, I thought my name was "bitch" until I was sixteen."

We exchanged a smile of understanding.

"Junior, I want to explain my business structure to you," I said matter-of-factly.

"Okay," she responded, alert with interest.

"Although your job will not require selling per se, it's good that you understand how we operate."

Junior said, "I don't know of any big-time women pimps. The only ones I've heard of have just a few girls. There was a Fillmore dyke that was a pretty big player. Only problem was, she was found last month with her hands tied behind her back and a bullet in her head. They shot her execution-style and dumped her body behind the Turkish bathhouse. I guess they think queers belong in the TL."

"Yeah, I remember hearing about that—another dyke killed for pissing off the boys. Recently, a few of the Fillmore players have been spotted in our neighborhood. Why do you think I wanna hire you?"

Junior chuckled, "*Cabrons*."

"Poverty is safe. You're anonymous, invisible, not a threat to anyone. The more money I make, the more muscle I need." That made sense to her, and I expanded the scope of the talk. "It's simple. Prostitution is like the restaurant business. We have three streams of income generated by three categories of hookers. Our McDonald's, fast-and-cheap, are the Turk Street bitches. Lawry's Prime Rib, fine dining in a nice atmosphere: the bordello ladies. Fairmont Hotel's five-star cuisine: our top-of- the-line call girls."

Junior's eyes widened. "You get johns from Turk Street to North Beach!"

"That's right, Junior. We have a hooker to suit every man's wallet."

Junior approved mightily. "Fuckin-A."

"As women, we have to outthink, outfight and outrun every male motherfucker. We gotta keep a tougher game face than the chump-change pimp wannabe players in this fuckin' ghetto. See all these men? Sex is entertainment and it sells like popcorn. By the way," I asked nodding toward the stage, "what do you think of Little Rosie?"

"I can see why she makes you a lot of money," Junior said with genuine admiration.

"Rosie's a sweetheart, as long as she's the star of the moment," I said with a good-natured grin.

The spotlight followed Little Rosie's glistening brown flesh. Her firm, full tits spun the black sequin pasties around and around, hypnotizing her johns' dicks like a master snake charmer. Pinning the crowd with her lust-filled stares, Rosie's mouth formed a perfectly seductive O as her wet tongue circled her glossy lips just before she blew them a kiss. Little Rosie's bright eyes mischievously sparkled like her brilliant costume jewelry. She bent low, snatching up money from the dollar-wielding patrons. As the vamp left the stage, she rhythmically ground her hips to the fading beat of the music, blew them a final kiss and danced off stage.

Within a few moments, the sound of clicking stiletto heels approached us. "This bitch is tired! Aren't you going to get your baby girl a drink?"

A snap of Rosie's fingers rang in my ears as she kissed me on the cheek and said, "Hi Jesse, baby."

Her Windsong perfume pleasantly seduced my nostrils.

Rosie placed a book of matches nonchalantly next to my drink on the bar. This was standard protocol for how I collected the revenue. It usually hid several tightly folded Bennies. I picked up the matchbook and smoothly tucked it into my jacket's inner breast pocket near my gun.

Junior's eyes widened, picking up on the subtle maneuver.

Rosie started up, "Hey, who's your butch buddy?" She gave Junior a disinterested glance as she grabbed my arm and pulled herself up onto the stool next to mine.

"Rosie, this is Junior. She's interested in joining our crew."

Little Rosie tossed her head and raised a thin black eyebrow as she grabbed one of my smokes. She placed the unfiltered Pall Mall between her shimmering lips.

Addressing Junior, she said, "So you wanna be a fucking henchman?"

Junior met the pretty lady's suspicious eyes and politely replied, "That's right. You're a very good dancer, Rosie."

She leaned seductively forward for me to light her cig and put her hand firmly by my crotch. "Thanks. I took lessons at Arthur Murray's dance studio in San Juan."

Junior nodded and said, "Cool," as Tuttle set a rum and Coke in front of Rosie. In almost the same motion he picked up an ashtray and dumped it in the trash can behind the bar. Elvis Presley's voice serenaded us as we all chatted for a few minutes.

"We have sales contests for the girls," I informed Junior. "The whore that makes the most money wins a prize. That's how Rosie won those earrings."

Rosie laughed, sipping her rum and Coke. "We Latinos know how to work it." Rosie proudly leaned forward toward Junior, pressing her hand deep into my thigh. She enjoyed showing off her large fourteen carat gold hoops and firm tits. As Rosie bent across me, I caught a glimpse of the Derringer concealed under her opened leopard print blouse. The mother-of-pearl handle on her mini-piece rested between her breasts in a tight black bustier that acted as her holster.

She placed her hand on my shoulder, smiled at Junior and said, "That's what makes Jesse sexy: brains, money and power, baby."

Little Rosie shot down her rum and Coke. "Not only that, but Bunny's step-dad dropped dead and left Bunny a bundle. He was a rich pervert, baby." Rosie cackled in delight. "We're going shopping tomorrow with the dead bastard's cash."

Junior gave me an inquisitive glance.

"That's right, Junior," I said. "Bunny's step-dad was a freak. He was a bit too affectionate with Bunny. To keep the peace and keep his wife in the dark, he bought his way out of it. Now Rosie gets to go shopping, Bunny doesn't have to deal with the pervert, and you got a job. Looks like we all have something to celebrate. Tonight, I hire my first henchman!"

I patted Junior on the back and asked, "Well, *Vato*, how about joining my crew?"

Her face lit up like a light in a window on a dark night. "I would be honored to be your soldier. Thank you very much. I pledge my loyalty, boss."

"Junior, I'd like you to start right now," I stated seriously.

"You got it, boss!"

"Good. You'll spend the night at the house. Rosie will take you over there. Tomorrow evening we'll meet at Pasquel's Men's Shop."

"Yes, boss," she answered.

"His stuff is top of the line. Just so you know, Pasquel is one of our clients as well as a good bird dog. He sends us a lot of business. Be there at seven."

"I'll be there," Junior replied quickly.

"If Pasquel is busy, his new apprentice will take care of you. He just hired some Brit named Austin who's right off the boat. I haven't met him yet, but I'm sure he's an excellent tailor also. The shop's on Market Street, a few doors past Powell."

Junior was very happy with this news. "Thanks. You've got some badass rags, boss."

I put a twenty on the bar and watched Tuttle move with the speed of a much younger man. His blue eyes sparkled through the hazy light of the bar as he folded the bill into his pocket and said, "Thanks, Jesse."

"Tuttle, line em up! We're celebrating." Proudly, I informed our paternal confidant, "Meet my new right hand."

"Congratulations," Tuttle responded with a smile. He set out three shot glasses and poured.

Rosie wrapped her arm around mine as she seductively asked, "Jesse baby, are you going to spend the night with me over at Marie's?"

"Not tonight," I said brusquely, "I got business to take care of."

Junior gave me an admiring glance.

"I got quality problems, man. One too many ladies and not enough time. It goes with the territory."

Proposing a toast, I said, "*Viva la numero uno henchman!*"

We clinked glasses and downed our shots.

Chapter 13

MONEY TALKS

*R*OSIE, JUNIOR AND I STEPPED THROUGH the black velvet curtains of the topless club out into the dark foggy night. The streets glowed with neon signs. The Tenderloin pulsed with the music escaping from the doorways of countless cocktail lounges. Street hustlers, drag queens and winos meandered through the neighborhood, soliciting passersby and scanning for cops.

I said to Rosie and Junior, "I'll catch you guys tomorrow." They flagged down a passing cab.

Carmen and I used to rendezvous nightly at Compton's. I still showed up every night, hoping she would pick up our old routine. As I headed back to Compton's on foot, a cloud of steam floated up from a manhole. I put my hand in my trouser pocket, shielding it from the chilly air. Holding my Stetson on my head, I fought the wind.

After a short walk, I passed an older lesbian couple. The butch, dressed like a dapper old man, held her lady friend's hand as they walked down the sidewalk of our ghetto. I felt empowered by the freedom to be myself here. The Tenderloin was the only place where I felt truly alive. At night, with booze, drugs and wishful thinking, the Tenderloin transformed into my own Wonderland.

I turned the corner of Turk and Taylor with a bounce in my step. A row of parked Harleys, manned by shit-talkin' boisterous bikers fortified the side of Compton's restaurant. I entered through the glass doors. Glossy tile and bright lights illuminated the way to my table by the window.

Karen shot me a smile hello, exposing the famous gap between her teeth.

I sat looking out the window, disappointed that Carmen probably would not show up again. As I stared blankly, memories of her flashed by like frames in a film. By stages, I settled into a pleasant memory of the night I first met Carmen at Lettermen's.

I could still picture how the white stripes of the psychedelic strobe lights danced on the couples grinding on the dark, crowded dance floor. A small black femme held her arms around her full-figured black girlfriend's neck, hanging on for dear life. The chubby dyke's oversized hands cradled the tiny femme's little leopard-skinned ass. I watched the short girl wobble in her shoes to the beat of the Four Tops. Her small feet moved in slightly too-large black stiletto heels with each thrust of her lover's pelvis. The sexy black fox pressed against her linebacker girlfriend's chest.

Surveying the dance floor like a radar scanner, I searched for a live bleep on the screen. My outfit—a new dark blue silk shirt and black trousers—was completed with classic Bostonian wingtips. My hunting companions and I stood together in a small circle. Bobby, Chip and I cruised Lettermen's with drinks in hand and talking shit. The three of us were posing, knowing we were handsome butches.

With a cocky smile, I pointed to the cute chick in leopard skin. "Which one of you is willing to take my bet? For a hundred bucks, I can pick that bitch up tonight."

"Oh, yeah?" replied plump-faced Bobby. Behind her Buddy Holly black-framed glasses, her blue eyes danced with astonishment.

"Sure, Jesse, just walk up to the sweet little black mama hanging on King Kong and ask her out."

Chip piped up with the enthusiasm of a cheerleader. "Go for it, Jesse! You can do it! If it goes to blows, we'll lasso King Kong. I'll hogtie her for you."

"No, seriously, I can pick that bitch up," I challenged my friends again, asking, "Who will take me up on it?"

Bobby jumped in, "I'll bet you a beer."

"You got it!" I replied.

I turned to ask Chip if she was in on the bet when suddenly my words were slapped out of me. My cheek stung with heat. My mind raced to comprehend what the hell had hit me.

Directly in front of me stood my assailant, a young girl with fire in her eyes.

Frozen in surprise, I looked directly into two beautiful emerald green eyes. They had specks of gold in them, as if sparks of anger flew out toward me. The eyes belonged to an exquisite auburn-haired young woman in stilettos and a short red dress, one hand on her hip.

I was in a trance. Her luscious red lips seemed to move in slow motion. "Who the hell do you think you are? That's my friend over there that you're talking about. She's a lady, not a piece of meat!"

The three of us stood stunned.

But her striking beauty acted like smelling salts.

She looked me in the eye. "I have seen you walking through the Tenderloin like some king rooster. You think you're a real player— every lady's dream, come here from L.A. to give us San Francisco girls a treat. But the number one player in the TL is my buddy, Carrie Mickens. She has enough class and good looks that she doesn't have to brag about the girls she gets. She loves us femmes. You think we're just sport."

I noticed Bobby and Chip's faces went from astonishment to agreement as the lady read me the riot act. My cheeks started to turn red with the Carrie Mickens remarks. She was my secret idol in the TL. She was tall, dark and handsome, with large blue eyes and an adorable soft spirit. I put my hand in my pocket and felt her Playboy Zippo lighter in the palm of my hand. It was a gift that Carrie's lover had given me the night I picked her up at Maud's bar, took her home and made love to her. I felt the cool, rounded edges of the lighter. Confidence flooded over me as I thought about how I had seduced Carrie's girlfriend and acquired her lighter.

"I know Carrie Mickens," I replied. "She's a wonderful girl and you're right about her and me."

Her glare faded and confusion clouded her eyes. They were protected by the thickest, most luscious long lashes I had ever seen. In seconds, she blinked away the look of bewilderment and replaced it with a sarcastic expression.

I raised my right hand and put it over my heart like I was about to say the pledge of allegiance. I had managed to save my drink through the assault and held it in my other hand. Speaking over the background music of "Do Right Woman" by Aretha Franklin—it was as if the DJ heard my cue—I said, "I am wrong and very sorry if I upset you or showed any disrespect to your friend. My name is Jessica Rawlson. My friends call me Jesse. I am the new kid on the block, and I am probably trying too hard to prove myself. I hope you'll forgive my adolescent behavior."

I watched her eyes calculate whether I was being sincere. After a moment, she replied with a hint of disgust, "Words are cheap."

I thought, "Oh shit…strike two."

Again I pleaded my case, with less servitude and contriteness. "You're right, words are cheap, but you're not, nor are your friends.

Please let me buy you a drink and we can discuss this further. You are helping me by calling me on my poor behavior. I can learn from your insight." I then quoted my mother, hoping that the young girl would realize I respected women. "My mother Ophelia always told me that I should give people the benefit of the doubt. Please extend me that courtesy. Please, let me buy you a drink."

"Oh yeah, right, I am helping you."

Realizing I had met my match, I pressed harder. "How about having just one drink with me and talking this over? Fair enough?"

Finally, she relented. "Okay, I'll have a drink on you."

Chip chimed in, "That sounds great. I'm Chip from Montana and this is Bobby from New York. It appears you've already met my friend Jesse, the Valley girl from Woodland Hills."

The reference Chip made about my being from the Valley seemed to amuse the pretty girl. A hint of pity sparked in her eyes as she laughed with my friends.

I good-naturedly said, "I know I'm a Valley girl, so way down deep I'm shallow."

"I'm Carmen from Oakland," she said with a wink. "Jesse, I'll have a Tom Collins."

With the first softness in her voice, I fell in love.

Out of the gloaming, I saw Carmen's sister, Phyllis enter the haze under the street lamps. Her determined stride was distinctly like that of Carmen's. Her long black hair blew in the cold, damp wind. She moved her long legs like a lioness on a hunt.

The older sister walked through the glass doors of the restaurant, bringing the wind in with her as she came up to my table. I rose to my feet like a gentleman and tipped my Stetson before I removed it in the presence of the pretty lady.

Phyllis was very striking and somewhat harder in appearance

than her sister Carmen. The Sicilian really came out in Phyllis, whereas Carmen had lighter Irish traits.

The older sister glanced at my new hat. "Hi Jesse, nice hat. Did the Bunny bitch with the platinum ovaries buy it for you?"

I found it hard to keep a straight face, since I admired the way she drew first blood. Phyllis deserved my respect because of her fierce loyalty to her younger sister. I calmly replied, "Nice to see you, Phyllis."

I watched her pull out the chair hurriedly, not allowing me to pull it out for her. She dropped her large black leather purse on an empty chair at the table. Phyllis shrugged out of her long leather coat and matching gloves that she casually lay over the back of the chair.

Karen appeared at the table with a cup of coffee for Phyllis. I asked, "Would you like something to eat?"

"I'm not hungry. I'm here on business," she said crisply. "Carmen wants to know what's up with the pimp act. If you want to see her, you gotta drop the midget with the cash. With or without money, Carmen loves you. So, bottom line, what's up?"

"Please tell Carmen that I love her too and the Bunny thing is just business," I assured her. "And, speaking of business, I have a proposition for you."

"Oh?" she said. "I am always up for talkin' business. Let's hear it big shot."

"My business partner and I run a brothel in Chinatown. It's perfectly located and has high-class clientele. We also have a great madam who manages the girls." I leaned forward. "Phyllis, I can offer serious protection. You can make a lot more money than you're making now. Plus, you'll be a hell of a lot safer working as one of my high-priced escorts."

Phyllis kept her regal cool. "Sounds good, Jesse. Are the profits going to go up your arm?"

"No, I kicked that shit!" I cried. "I am all about taking care of business now."

"I always prefer working referrals," Phyllis conceded. "They are safer. And you do look like you got your shit together." She was liking the idea the more she thought about it. "It might be cool working with you. Let me run it past Carmen first."

"That's cool. Let me know."

Phyllis picked up my pack of Pall Malls from the table and helped herself to one. I immediately lit it for her with my Zippo. I watched Phyllis smoke, sip her coffee and study me cautiously. My mind scrambled to get a game plan together. I didn't want to blow my shot at impressing Carmen.

My profits from last week's take! "Phyllis, by the way, I have some cash for you. Split the cash in this envelope with your sister. Consider your half a sign-up bonus and previews of coming attractions."

I pushed the fat envelope toward Phyllis and said, "Please deliver my gift to Carmen."

Phyllis felt the thickness of the envelope. A subtle grin replaced the hard glare as she stuffed the heavy envelope inside her black bag.

"Jesse, Carmen quit her job at the Why Not. She had enough of groping, cheap-tipping guys," Phyllis said. "Now Carmen wants to make real money. She asked me to help her out, so I turned her on to a few of my johns." Phyllis took a long drag off the Pall Mall. Her large brown eyes showed no emotion. She flicked the ashes from her cigarette nonchalantly into the ashtray as she glanced out the window.

"Cop tricks may not be the best training wheels," I said with a raised eyebrow.

"I put her uptown, in City Hall. Phillip is a gentleman and I personally trained him."

"Phillip the D.A.?" I said, trying to hide my jealousy.

"Money talks, Jesse."

Lighting up a smoke, I took in the news. I thought about Carmen being a whore. After years on the streets, I had adopted the lesbian gangster codes and values. Carmen's turning tricks wouldn't influence our relationship, because hookin' was just a way of life in the Tenderloin.

"That worries me, Phyllis. We both know how dangerous it is."

"You know Carmen, Jesse. She's very determined and competitive."

"Yeah, you got that right," I said in resignation, understanding that johns don't count. Sex is just business. I knew that my girl would never kiss a trick; that would be intimate.

"If she's gonna work, it might as well be with you. I know you'll do your best to keep her safe," Phyllis said.

"Thanks. I will. Whatever she decides, it's cool with me," I said sincerely. "All I know is I love her and I miss her."

Phyllis took a deep drag of her cigarette as she started to stand up, this time waiting long enough for me. I pulled her chair back and held her coat as she slipped into it.

I spoke softly over the shoulder of her sexy, slick coat. "Tell Carmen the cash is a gift. She can buy herself a pretty dress. Make sure you tell your sister I'm off heroin and I'm waiting for her. I'm staying at the Queen's Arms, apartment 212."

"Don't worry, Jesse, I'll clean this up for you." Phyllis turned and hugged me, pressing her breasts against mine just a little too tight and a little too long. "By the way, you look good in a pimp suit."

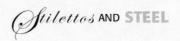

As Phyllis strutted toward the door, she paused and seductively looked back, holding my gaze for a second and said, "Respect."

"Respect, Phyllis. Respect to you and your family."

Phyllis walked out the door of Compton's back into the cold windy night that had carried her in. As I watched her disappear down the foggy street, I realized I had just crossed a line. I knew that this night had been a major crossroad in my life.

Chapter 14

RESPECT

*C*IVILIANS FLOODED THE SIDEWALK LIKE ANTS carrying brief-cases and purses packed with the rewards of their daily toil. Overhead, seagulls and pigeons watched the rush-hour pedestrians in hopes of crumbs left behind. Walking through the masses of respectability like a boyish shadow, I made my way undetected to my tailor.

A large blue awning hung above the display windows featuring male manikins dressed in Italian and British suits. Protecting this exclusive world of fine fabrics and imported leather was an ornate door with a small distinguished sign on it. A crest consisting of a top hat crossed by two long-stemmed red roses appeared above small gold letters which announced, "Est. 1948." Arched above the crest was the name: Pasquel's Men's Shop.

I entered the small, elegant clothing boutique. Ornate mahogany display tables presented neatly folded cashmere sweaters. Rows of polished Italian men's dress shoes and sporty brown and black jackets lined the wall, filling the air with the pleasant scent of new leather. Hollow eyes of well-dressed manikins stared down at thick stacks of fine dress shirts and ties. At the back of the shop, dressing rooms with long gray curtains lined the tailor's work area. An undressed manikin with a measuring tape hanging over its shoulder stood beside a large full-length mirror with a small wooden platform in front of it, ready for the next tailoring job.

Not being greeted by Pasquel or hearing the customary pipes of Dean Martin crooning, I wondered if I had missed everyone. Had Junior not shown up? Loud and out of place, the Beatles' "We Can Work It Out," bounced around the empty store.

Abruptly, I was startled by a strange male voice with a British accent screeching, "It's a bird! It's a bird!" Suddenly, the dangling gray dressing room curtain burst to life.

Jumping back, I instinctively grabbed my gun from its shoulder holster. The thick British accent bellowed from behind the curtain like the great Oz, "Good God, ol' chap, you're a fucking bird!"

Tumbling through the curtains, Austin, the lanky store clerk, fell backward to the floor. Junior fell after him, tripping onto his chest, pinning the Brit to the floor. Scrambling to get up, they grabbed the curtains and tore them from their hooks.

Junior's Ace bandage, wrapped around her chest, loosened. A lone tit popped out. The young man's pale English complexion turned stone white as he saw Junior's big breast hanging above him.

Looking like she was doing the Mexican hat dance, Junior stumbled over him, trying to regain her balance. In the process her unbuttoned trousers fell to her ankles. As the Brit frantically sat up, he came face to face with Junior's huge dildo loosely dangling before him in her red silk boxers. He shrieked madly, "Ahhh! Good God!"

Mortified, Junior quickly used one arm to cover her tit and the other hand to cover her dong.

Austin moved his mouth back and forth like a feeding goldfish. "I'm sorry, ma'am, so terribly sorry," he said in a discombobulated state.

"Step away from the Brit!" I yelled out to Junior like a pig on a raid.

Junior, surprised at my presence, turned beet red and said, "He called me a fucking bird!"

"Junior man, it's cool. Bird means 'woman' where he comes from. He didn't mean any disrespect."

Looking confused but calmer, Junior replied, "Okay, boss." She regained her composure and re-entered the fitting room to get dressed.

The young man rose to his feet staring at my .38. I calmly put it back in my holster and asked the dude, "You must be Austin? I'm Jesse. I'm pleased to meet you."

I shook his trembling hand.

"Oh my God, you're Jesse the pimp!" he said, relieved. "Pasquel told me about you. It is a pleasure to make your acquaintance. I'm so very sorry for this misunderstanding. I had no idea..."

"Don't worry about it, man. We'll keep this to ourselves." I helped him regain his feet. "Next time Junior comes in here, hook her up a full wardrobe. She's my new personal assistant. By the way, did you get her measurements?"

He professionally replied, "Yes, I did, and that's how I unfortunately disturbed the young lady's breast. I assumed she was a young man who had injured himself in a sporting accident. You can imagine my surprise when I found my hand firmly around her boob!"

I fought back a bubbling spurt of laughter as I pulled out my money clip and handed him three Benjamins and a Jackson. I set him at ease with a warm smile and asked, "What part of England are you from?"

"I'm from Matlock," said Austin proudly as he began to tidy up the area.

Junior stepped out of the dressing room in a spiffy pair of black trousers, an expensive burgundy silk shirt and new black leather wingtips.

"You did well," I commented. "Very stylish, Junior."

"Thanks," Junior replied, abashed. She was in no mood for small talk.

With a stiff bow Austin handed Junior a Pasquel's Men's Shop bag stuffed with her old clothes.

As we left the store I told him, "Put the three hundred down on Junior's wardrobe and keep the twenty for your troubles."

That cheered him up considerably. "Thank you so very much. Good evening…ladies!" he cried.

I stepped back into the world of respectability with Junior by my side. As we headed down Market Street, I said to my brooding companion, "Don't worry about it, man. It's kind of funny when you think about it. At least now your tailor knows your measurements."

Junior shot me a weary look.

"One thing, though," I said with a chuckle, "The pigs will beat your ass worse for packing a dick than packing a piece. I better give you more bribe money."

Junior gave a faint smile as I continued.

"Know what, Junior? I have a theory. I think our asses were born with too much testosterone."

Junior looked at me with curiosity. "I never thought about that, boss."

"The first boy I ever beat up got his ass whipped because he asked me to be the wife when we were playing house in the back-yard. I didn't want to be a dumb woman who did all the housework and didn't get paid shit. I wanted to be like the guys who got to do everything and have all the fun."

"Yeah man," she chimed in, "back home I hated dressing like a girl, especially when I had to wear a frilly first communion dress."

"Damn, Junior, you had to wear that thing too? My aunt and mom would always try to stick me in a dress with lacey socks and patent leather shoes."

"How awful!" We both laughed loudly, startling a pair of prim and proper suburban matrons as they passed.

We made our way to the Turk Street night scene. I viewed the familiar bustle of street walkers, drag queens, hippies and other regulars. A stream of daring taxis and slow-moving cars lit the street as a cool wind blew on us.

"Dykes!" An angry voice assaulted my senses from behind us. Junior and I realized that we were the object of the verbal attack. We turned our attention to a white guy who stuck his blond head out of the car's driver-side window.

A deep purple El Dorado stopped beside us. Sitting shotgun, a pale Asian girl with long straight hair turned her gaze on us. She was the hooker Prince and Giuseppe had worked over in the alley. Their captive's right eye was filled with blood.

I offered the girl a smile, glad to see that she had survived. Her hollow stare and expressionless face ignored my silent gesture.

The handsome young driver jumped out of the car. He rushed around the front of the Caddy and came toward me and Junior. He sneered scornfully at us and spat, "Fucking lezzies."

Realizing this was an attempt at insulting us, I replied, "Thanks!"

I now recognized the dude. Blondie the Swede was well built, quick of wit and impressive-looking, like a Hollywood movie star. The image was blown the moment he spoke with his thick South Central L.A. accent.

Momentarily slapped to silence by my reply, he continued, "Listen up, dyke ho, Prince wants a word with-cha."

The darkened backseat window slowly went down. Behind the sinking glass was a black man with a large Afro. Contemptuous eyes studied us from head to foot. He sneered, disgusted and amused, and his pockmarked horse face broke into a sinister smile. He exposed one gold tooth surrounded by large yellowed ones. He pointed his bony finger at me. The curly manicured nail reminded me of a hawk's talon as it extended from his purple velvet sleeve. A heavy gold-and-diamond bracelet hung from his wrist.

"I'm the Prince of the bitches," he hissed. "I want a word with you."

The rear door flew open. Out of the back seat unfolded a six-foot-five pissed-off pimp. Prince pulled his leather jacket aside. The butt of a silver-plated .45 caught my attention as the bastard put his huge hand on the piece.

Glancing at Junior, I saw she had problems of her own. Blondie held his bulging arm around her waist, like she was his girlfriend.

Junior stood stark still as a stiletto was pressed against her side. Blondie grinned and said to Junior, "Where's your briefcase, bitch?"

Prince bent down and got in my face. I could smell his foul booze breath as he raged. "Pussy pimp!" he growled. "Think you're somebody, motherfuckah? You and that pink Caddy cunt! Tryin' to show my ass up! You better watch your motherfuckin' backs!"

Fear rose through me, though I forced myself not to react. I stared him in the eye. Showers of spit hit my face as he shouted, "You're a fuckin' pussy! Act like one! Don't be poundin' on my fuckin' crew!"

I calmly replied, "I think we can have this conversation later."

Prince pulled back, surprised at my calm response. I motioned my head toward the corner. We all glanced over at a beat cop strolling our way.

Blondie the Swede slipped his blade away as quickly as he had pulled it out. Prince gave up a big grin for the heat as he rose up. I smiled back at him and said, "Respect. It's been nice chatting with you."

He gave me a withering look. "I'm watching you," he whispered.

Prince slinked back into his car. The electric window rolled up and they drove off. A shiver slithered up my spine. Junior searched my eyes.

I merely grinned and remarked, "Never thought I'd be so happy to see a pig."

Chapter 15

NATURAL WOMAN

*M*Y APARTMENT ACTED AS A COMFORTABLE HAT RACK until I could find a nicer place. It was as empty as my refrigerator, which contained a few bottles of Schlitz and tonic water. The starkness of my crash pad with its simple couch and coffee table matched my mood. The stillness engulfed me as I put my keys away in the kitchen drawer next to my buck knife.

The shiny black and silver knife had been a sweet sixteen gift from my brother, Max. My kid brother had always recognized and accepted the twelve-year-old boy in me. Tonight, his affection and loyalty gave me small solace.

On the white-tiled counter sat a bottle of Jack and a carton of cigarettes next to a small dish rack filled with a few glasses and dinner plates. The narrow stove bumped up against a small white refrigerator in the corner of the compact kitchen. Atop the back burner was a silver coffee percolator that had never been used due to my deficiency in domestic skills.

I pulled open the fridge and cracked a cold Schlitz to keep me company, prepared for another lonely night. Despite taking occasional refuge in Bunny or Rosie's arms, a nagging void haunted me. My yearning for Carmen had turned into an obsession. Phyllis had reminded me of the energy of her sister last night, temporarily satisfying my longing. I thought about Phyllis and her promise to help me as I despondently sipped my beer.

I slammed the refrigerator shut and slung my hat onto the couch. On the empty queen-size bed in the open alcove attached to the living room, a simple white comforter covered the bed. I tossed my jacket aside and lay down, exhausted. My gun rested on my shoulder in its leather holster. Its heaviness made me feel safe.

A knock on the door startled me and I jumped up, cocking my .38. I went to the door and said in a deep voice, "Who's there?" I heard no verbal response, just another tap on the door.

Peering through the peephole, I saw Carmen. She was standing on my doorstep. Quickly, I put my gun back into its holster. My heart fluttered with weird spikes of nervousness. I wanted to rush into the other room and throw on my new suit jacket, comb my hair, brush my teeth and put on cologne all at the same time. Instead, I just took a deep breath to slow the flurry of unnamed emotions running through me.

I ran my fingers through my hair and tucked my shirt into my trousers. I calmly opened the door.

Carmen simply said, "There's something you want to tell me?"

Her radiant green eyes challenged me to answer as I awkwardly stood before her. My voice rose higher than its normal range and undercut my self-assured response. "Hi, baby doll. Come on in, it's good to see you."

"I bet!"

Yet Carmen's mouth betrayed her, showing a hint of warmth as she walked arrogantly into the living room. I was captivated by the shine of the thick auburn hair which fell down her back. Her slender frame was accentuated by a stylish white rabbit coat. Her well-defined calves were raised by soft blue satin high heels.

Carmen reached into her shoulder bag and pulled the envelope out that I had given to Phyllis. As she turned to face me, I forced myself not to grab my unexpected visitor and kiss her on the spot. My senses were alive with anticipation and the need to read her mood.

Carmen's beautiful face reddened as her cheeks flushed in anger. She violently slung the cash-fat envelope onto the coffee table. Her moist red mouth twisted in a sarcastic sneer. "Is that the best you could come up with? Whatever happened to flowers and a phone call?"

I fought back tears as a feeling of shame filled me. I did not have the courage to risk being rejected by her. My big shot gesture of cash to win my prize had just been thrown back in my face.

We stood gazing at each other, motionless. Carmen's finely shaped features—the small cleft in her chin, the way she held her long, elegant neck—made her look like a glamorous 1940s movie star. It always amazed me how flawless and clear her skin was. Her eyes had a fire in them and underneath resided a wild animal alertness.

She began to unbutton her coat as she continued to stare into my eyes. She slid it off her shoulders and casually placed the fur on the sofa with her purse. An overwhelming passion possessed me. All I wanted to do was fuck away her aloofness.

I went from looking at her mesmerizing eyes to tracing her sexy body. Her firm breasts stood at attention in a strapless powder blue dress. My vision rested for a moment on her inviting cleavage as I mentally started to undress her. Interrupting my lust-inspired trance, Carmen said, "I want to work for you, Jesse."

"What did you say?" I asked, stunned.

"Jesse, I'm not new to the world of hooking," she said casually. "I've been coming to the TL before you arrived here. My sister and every other lesbian brave enough to live here pays with her body. What's the big deal?" She shrugged, calling my attention to her bare shoulders. "I had to act straight slinging drinks at the Why Not eight hours a day," she went on. "I've done my time getting groped by crude men for cheap tips. I've decided I'd rather close my eyes for a few minutes and make a fortune."

"Carmen, are you here on business?" I asked, confused.

She just held my stare.

"Why did you give me back the cash?" I asked. "I gave you the money as a gift. The money I gave Phyllis is different. That's business. Did you think I was actually trying to buy you?"

"I am your woman," she said softly. "You can't buy what already belongs to you."

Grabbing her hand, I took her in my arms and kissed her hard. Heat rushed up my spine, spreading all over my body. Carmen's arms wrapped around me as my tongue danced with hers.

We stumbled backward into the bedroom, entangled in lust, kissing desperately. My fingers brushed the back of her long hair as they made their way down and unzipped her dress. I caressed the soft skin of her warm back. The satin garment floated off her body to the floor around her stiletto-clad feet. She kicked the dress to the side and stepped out of her shoes.

She slipped my gun off my shoulder like an old friend, comfortable and unaffected by it. The scent of Chanel flooded my senses as her hands effortlessly removed my shirt and undid my binder. The cool air danced on my bare skin while her hot tongue encircled my nipples. My back tingled as her fingers brushed lower. She quickly undid my belt, fell to her knees and lowered my pants. I saw the crown of her head at my naked waist. I closed my eyes and allowed her to go to the core of me.

Pulling Carmen to her feet, we kissed and lay down together on my bed. Intoxicated with desire, my senses transported me into a realm of ecstasy as we made love. Carmen's nude body fit perfectly under mine as our most intimate parts reunited. She pressed hungrily against me. Love's stream of pleasure dripped from Carmen as my tongue awakened her heart. Afterward, I rested into Carmen and the peace that surrounded us.

I cradled her in my arms while she lightly stroked my back. "Jesse, remind me baby to pick you up the 'World's Best Lover' trophy," she whispered contentedly.

I covered her mouth with kisses and smiled. "That's what they tell me," I heard myself stupidly say, sounding like an indifferent player.

Carmen laughed and punched me in the side. "Maybe the girls you've been with have all been virgins," she said mischievously.

"Yeah right," I whispered back, disarmed.

"Jesse, you can't fool me. I know who you are. I can see your beautiful soul, honey." Carmen's words melted my shielded heart. "You can drop your player act with me."

We spoke as young lovers in sacred, hushed tones. The warmth of her young body soothed me as we held each other close. Carmen gazed into my eyes, captivating me. She whispered, "I understand the need to keep up a front, Jesse. In the Tenderloin, it's all about who's left standing. I'll back your play, baby." She kissed me on the cheek, sealing her promise.

After a while, Carmen got up, slipped on my unbuttoned white men's dress shirt and went to the kitchen to fix us both a drink. I turned on the radio. Dusty Springfield was singing "Son of a Preacher Man." I pulled on my boxers and grabbed a wife-beater t-shirt. From the cigar box in the top dresser drawer, I removed a fat bomber. Back on the bed I fired up the joint with my Zippo.

My girl poured us both a short drink of Jack in two water glasses. I heard her call out from the kitchen, "My, I guess you're not Betty

Crocker. There's not even an old bagel in your fridge. Now I know you're not into any other bitch."

I chuckled and took another hit of the weed. "Femmes! If a girl gets in your refrigerator, then I guess it's love, huh?" I called. "No one fills my fridge but you, babe."

Carmen returned with our drinks. Her sexy nude body glistened under the white shirt, and her deliciously messy hair fell around her glowing face. She handed me the drink and we clinked our glasses. I shot my lady a quick smile and jumped into a James Cagney routine. "Jesse, that dirty, dirty rat is happy to be back."

Carmen laughed as she took the joint out of my hand and took a hit. She exhaled and naughtily popped on my Stetson. Pulling the brim low over her forehead, she acted like a tough guy and pointed her finger at me like a make-believe gun. Playfully, she growled like Humphrey Bogart. "You were a dirty rat!"

After another sip of her drink she lay next to me. She was quiet for a moment. "Where the fuck have you been?" she asked at length.

I could see concern in her eyes and it made me feel as if she could see right through me.

"I'm sorry," I softly replied. "I've missed you every day but I just couldn't tell you the truth. My body's ached for you. I didn't want you to see me when I was so down and out. I always want to be my best self for you."

She kissed me softly. "Jesse, we can all get lost. Next time, just be honest with me. Someday you'll understand that you don't need to keep up your front with me. All I want is truth. Don't you think it was hard for me to tell you that I've been tricking?"

"Yeah. But honestly, I'm surprised you lasted so long working that square gig." I reflected on that statement and added, "I'm also surprised I've lasted so long on the streets not getting hooked on the hard shit. What's a few months on a chump change run? Believe me, I've learned my lesson."

"I'm glad I didn't have to see you fixing, Jesse. That way I didn't have to kill you," she said frowning at the idea of shooting up. "Although, God knows, I can understand just wanting to nod out. Since I've been working with Phyllis, I can imagine what you went through working Turk."

I instantly protested that idea. "Carmen, you don't need to turn cheap dates. Your sister is beautiful like you are and has a lot better johns than most Tenderloin girls. You're gorgeous and maybe you don't even have to hook. I could hire you as an assistant. Damn, I'm doin' so well that I just hired my first henchman. What do you think, girl?"

She wasn't impressed. "I'm sure you have plenty of cash, but I'm not taking Miss Big Tit's money. I can make my own. Let's get real, Jesse. You're just getting started. I've always known I would end up in the life. It's the price we all pay to live free in the Tenderloin. Your L.A. bitch has nothing on Phyllis and me but road time and a little extra cash."

I smiled at the catty swipe about Bunny's age. Bunny was in her mid-twenties, but on the streets, that's middle-aged. I asked sincerely, "Why were you afraid to tell me you were hooking? You don't have any other surprises in your life, do you?"

"Like another butch?" Carmen coyly smiled back.

"Don't fuck with me, girl," I said, my temper flaring. "I can dish it out but I can't take it. It's different with us pimp butches. Ladies come with the job. You know you were my first real girlfriend and you'll be my last. Now answer me, girl, before I have to kill you," I playfully said.

Bracing myself for her answer, I took a big swig of Jack.

Carmen took the joint out of my hand and took her time before taking a drag. I didn't breathe as I waited for her reply. Seductively, she wrapped her leg over mine, placed the Stetson on my head, exhaled and said, "Baby, you're the only daddy in the family."

Carmen wrapped her arms around me, pressing her semi-nude body close to mine. Smokey Robinson & the Miracles' song "Ooh Baby Baby" filled the air. Burying my face in the softness of her hair, I felt the sting of trapped tears behind my closed eyes. Overwhelmed with unexpressed emotions, I clung to my girl.

Carmen held me tight and softly pleaded, "Please never leave me again."

"Never, girl," I whispered as I kissed her.

Carmen leaned back, searched my eyes and said, "Seriously, Jesse, no more running away."

I whispered into her ear, "I got it."

Chapter 16

SUGAR AND VICE

*C*ARMEN'S TOES PLAYED WITH MINE as we lay together in bed eating chop suey. The late afternoon sun was setting, and our marathon of sex had come to an end. Carmen had to get ready for her date with the D.A. As for me, I had rounds to make.

Carmen propped herself up against my headboard, wearing nothing but my shirt and a smile. She closed the little Cantonese cardboard containers on the nightstand, placed our chopsticks neatly on top of the boxes and said, "I'm gonna hop in the shower and get ready."

I flippantly told my girl, "This better have been a preview of coming attractions."

Carmen giggled and pointed archly towards me, "Only if you're as good as you were this time."

I watched Carmen slip out of my shirt and walk nude into the bathroom.

Brenda Lee's heartfelt voice soothed my contented soul as I listened to Carmen humming along with the music from the shower. Finally I jumped out of bed and joined her in the bathroom. I slowly pulled the shower curtain back and asked, "Want company?"

Carmen slapped my face with a wet washcloth. "Let me get ready," she said, gently pushing me aside.

She slipped on a simple basic black dress delivered by Phyllis earlier. The wise older sister wanted to make sure Carmen would be ready for her date. As I watched Carmen apply her makeup, I put on my wife beater and boxers.

"How's your mom?" I asked.

"She's going to AA now."

"Really?" I was shocked, since both of Carmen's parents were real guzzlers. Her dad was a part-time truck driver and her mom worked at the post office. "How's your dad feel about her being sober?"

"Oh, I don't think he's noticed yet," Carmen answered darkly.

"Very funny. Does she rag on you now about partying?"

"Jesse, you know my mom, she's cool."

That was the truth. Both of Carmen's parents accepted our relationship. They were the most understanding straight people I had ever met.

"Jesse, my mom told me, 'You can lead a horse to water but he might prefer whiskey.'"

I chuckled as I slipped on my slacks. "Want another beer?" I inquired as I headed for the refrigerator.

"No I'm fine. I want to act like a lady tonight."

"That's right… a lady hooker," I called from the kitchen. "That's how you make the big bucks," I added, speaking from experience.

Carmen giggled from the bathroom. "I knew all those finishing-school lessons you gave me would pay off one day."

"Yeah," I said, not liking the reference, "I just didn't think it would be like this."

Carmen, who had always been ashamed of her parents' drunken poverty, coveted sophistication. Her hunger for refinement was one of the things that attracted her to me. Our Tenderloin romance had been filled with ghetto getaways. We took field trips to museums, art galleries, operas, and fine restaurants. Our budding romance included playacting like Professor Higgins and Eliza Doolittle. Her transformation from an impoverished Oakland girl to a stylish young woman was as stunning as her beauty.

"Open up! Police!" A familiar bear of a voice bellowed through the door.

"Oh, fuck!" I said as I sprinted to my piece. "Carmen. It's fucking Captain Clancy!" I grabbed the fake philodendron by the front door and stashed my gun in the pot.

In a girlish voice, I cried back through the door, "Just a second, Clancy, I gotta get dressed!" I grabbed the weed and flushed it. Carmen rushed into the living room with me and stood by my side. I opened the door.

Filling the door frame from head to toe stood the immense pig. His Brillo-pad toupee scraped the top of the doorframe as his soft putty face smiled at me.

"How nice to see you again, Jesse. Good afternoon, Carmen. Aren't you ladies going to invite me in?" he asked as he entered, pushing us back to the couch. Instinctively, we sat down.

The tower of trench coat looked down at us. His badge was sloppily pinned on his lapel, next to a few crumbs. His holstered gun protruded from his left breast like a suppressed tit.

Clancy had conducted numerous raids on gay clubs when he was a young beat cop. Just seeing the same sex dancing together had been a legitimate excuse for him to crack a few heads. He was an oddity among the corrupt cops who ruled the TL since he wouldn't accept bribes.

"Hey, Jesse," he began, "so, you're a high-rollin' parasite now, huh? Congratulations." He gave Carmen a fatherly reprimand. "Miss you at the Why Not. Heard you're goin' for the bigger tips now. I thought you were a smarter broad than your older sister." He shook his head.

Masking my irritation, I remembered my manners and asked Clancy, "Would you care for something to drink? Do you wanna sit down for a minute?"

"I'm here on business, smartass."

He pulled a Polaroid picture out of his coat pocket and stuck it in our faces. The blank stare of a dead black girl, with a huge bullet hole in her blood-crusted forehead, loomed before us.

"Jesse, did you know this dead dyke?" he demanded.

"No, I never met her," I replied, shocked into honesty.

"You fuckin' lezzies all know each other," he said suspiciously. "Where the hell were you last month?"

"I was in L.A., like you already know. What do you want, Clancy?"

A slight flush of color crossed his face. His gaze rested on my young firm breasts that stood erect in my wife beater t-shirt.

Clancy cleared his throat. "A new witness came forward. She said she saw you with the lady pimp the night before she was killed."

"Well it's awfully hard for a person to be in two places at once. I was in L.A., under treatment for a badly infected arm. I'm sure Dr. Li would be glad to verify that I was under his care at that time."

His face grew harder at my retort. "I like that about you, Jesse. A queer hoodlum that always manages to sidestep shit."

"It's nice to have an admirer," I said with a hint of seduction, just to fuck with him.

"In case we need you for a lineup don't go anywhere."

"Glad to know you still like having me around."

"Well, maybe... it's nice to see you again," he replied gruffly, taking a step closer.

Carmen reached over protectively and took my hand. Clancy's neck turned red and his jugular vein began pulsating. The smoldering rage which he held on a short leash was about to snap.

In response, Carmen cuddled up next to me on the couch. She wore a defiant fire in her emerald eyes, glaring at the sexually deprived Clancy. Everyone knew that he went home to a frigid muumuu mama. He'd told me his bonbon-eating wife's love life consisted of watching the daily soaps.

Clancy said, "Hooker and pimp. How sweet. You'll be sucking a lot of dicks to dress Jesse's pretty-boy face!"

"I thought you boys shop on Turk," Carmen snapped.

We were too quick for him and he was getting flustered.

"I can't figure you fuckin' lezzies out. You don't even look like a whore, Carmen."

I quickly shot back, "I'm sure your wife doesn't either!"

Enraged, Clancy pulled out his revolver. Clancy leveled the gun in front of my face. My heart started pounding like an oil derrick.

"Don't push me, Jesse!" Clancy rammed his piece back into its holster. His anger subsided, and he added like a kind father, "Jesse, you should let Carmen go. With a man, she could have a good life."

He turned his massive body toward the front door and called, "See you in the neighborhood, ladies."

He saw himself out.

Trembling, Carmen and I walked silently to the kitchen. We each took a large shot of Jack straight from the bottle. I held my girl as she rested her face on my shoulder. "I always get into trouble with my bad boy," she sighed. "I'm happy nothing's changed."

"That son-of-a-bitch is right, though. Maybe I'm no good for you, Carmen," I replied, suddenly filled with shame.

"He's just pissed that he can't get you in bed," Carmen said, irritated. Finished with the conversation, she snapped, "Fuck him and the horse he rode in on!"

Carmen picked up her purse, opened it, and applied dark red lipstick. I threw my clothes on quickly, grabbing my keys and gun as we left the apartment.

We walked through the TL in gloomy silence. Clancy's words resonated in my mind and I reflected on the first time I had heard that word, "lezzy."

I was twelve years old and spending the summer vacation with my grandmother, Nani Lou. My father's mother was a charming woman who I adored. She dressed beautifully, wore her age well and spoke with finishing school diction. I enjoyed staying at the elegantly decorated apartment in the building she managed in North Hollywood.

One day she rushed through the living room interrupting the television show that I was watching, *American Bandstand*. Nani Lou was, as a rule, a calm, soft-spoken, kind woman. But on this day she was irate. She raced into the kitchen and started excitedly talking with the property owner on the telephone.

"Yes, Mr. Andrews, I evicted those two lesbians faster than God made little green apples! I would have never rented to them if I had known that they were lezzies. Judy told me they flirted with her in the laundry room! She's only sixteen. It's just awful!"

As my grandmother expressed her rage, I thought to myself, "That Judy's a slut."

Judy and I had often talked at night out by the pool while she was sneaking a smoke. She always bragged to me about how she could seduce every male in the building. I really didn't know what a lesbian was, but I knew it was bad. It certainly was enough to get evicted for.

When my grandmother hung up the phone, I asked inquisitively, "Nani Lou, what's a lezzy?"

Embarrassed by my question, she snapped, "Its way too disgusting to talk about, Jessica. You're too young to know."

Carmen pulled me out of my reverie with a kiss. She grabbed my hand and said, "I have to go soon, Jesse."

We hit the outer border of the TL at Van Ness Street and ducked into an alley. Parked up ahead was a new black Cadillac. Carmen and I walked over to the district attorney's car.

The D.A. gave me a polite nod and took Carmen from my hand. He gallantly opened the passenger door and kissed Carmen on the cheek. Jealousy joined my sadness as he closed the door behind her.

Phillip said, "Good night Jesse."

Living on the edge, we never knew how long anything would last. Happiness had finally come back to me, but now it was stolen away again. Watching the car's taillights, I had a premonition of disaster. I shook it off, though, being sensible. I had work to do.

Chapter 17

CHINATOWN

UNIOR AND I LEAFED THROUGH A PLAYBOY MAGAZINE in front of Tommy's newspaper stand. A horn honked and we turned to see Bunny's pink Caddy convertible pull up alongside us. The car was filled with three hot babes. Fresh out of the beauty parlor, Bunny's hair was now a striking platinum blond. Her new hairdo matched her furry white mink. She smiled at Junior and me from behind her rose-tinted rhinestone cat eye glasses.

Little Rosie sat shotgun with a lavender scarf tied under her chin, protecting her beehive from the wind. In the back seat sat Asian Pearl, an experienced hooker with china-doll features. Pearl's red silk mandarin dress shimmered under the street lamp. Her slender shoulders were wrapped in a white cashmere wool shawl.

A veil of detached annoyance cloaked Pearl's demeanor as Little Rosie exuberantly shouted, "Hi Jesse, baby! Hop in and bring your badass bad boy with you! We're going to Chinatown!"

Rosie jumped out of the front seat excitedly. Her tight, short black dress showed off her dancer's legs, and her exposed cleavage spoke up under her opened black wannabe mink coat. Pulling the seat forward, I said to Junior, "Get in."

Junior jumped into the back of the large cruiser with Little Rosie following behind. I hopped into the front seat and grabbed the Saks

Fifth Avenue bags out from under the dash. I tossed them all to Junior, who caught the packages and piled them onto her lap.

As I settled into the front seat, I admired Bunny's bright white hair and exclaimed, "Wow! Girl, you might have to put the top up! Your hair is so gorgeous it could cause a riot!"

"Oh, do you like it?" Bunny asked coquettishly, brushing her windblown hair off her forehead. "I've heard you have a fondness for auburn hair too lately."

I ignored the swipe about Carmen. She had obviously heard about us getting back together.

Junior awkwardly kept her arms tucked around the bags, close by her sides, careful not to have her elbows graze the breasts of her traveling companions.

"Junior," I said, directing my gaze toward our stylish chauffeur, "this is Bunny, my sweet benefactor and too-hot-for-words girl."

Bunny smiled and put the car in gear. Wheeling away from the curb into the fast lane, she breathlessly said over her shoulder, "Hi, Junior. Welcome aboard."

"This is Pearl," I said, motioning toward the Asian beauty in the back seat. "Pearl has a lot of street wisdom and fabulous looks, as you can see."

Pearl turned her gaze to Junior and gave her a weary nod of acknowledgment.

I reached over the seat and gave Little Rosie's hand a squeeze. I playfully said to Junior, "How lucky can a pimp be: a hot Puerto Rican fox, a gem from the Far East, and a Jersey 'tits n' pearl' girl."

As we cruised down the street, bobbing in and out of traffic, I viewed Junior through the visor mirror. She appeared afraid to look to either side of her.

"Junior, Asian Pearl will show you around North Beach. That's her territory."

Asian Pearl slightly inclined her head toward Junior. Her foot-high lacquered lovelocks were perpetually dressed with long chopsticks embossed with fiery white dragons. The tips, hidden in her hair, were razor-sharp steel. Pearl's thin black eyebrows were permanently painted in a severe arch. One eyebrow raised skeptically above her heavily painted jade eye shadow. Her thick black eyeliner enhanced the cold, dramatic look in her hard gaze. "Move over, you're squishing me," demanded the leering Asian bitch.

Junior fumbled with the large packages on her lap as she inched toward Rosie. Junior returned the gaze, not flinching from Pearl's harsh demeanor. "Nice to meet you, Pearl," she said.

Pulling out my Pall Malls, I pushed in the silver car lighter. Bunny's windblown platinum hair wisped around her baby blues as she glanced at me before turning back to the traffic. The lighter popped out and I lit my smoke.

"Jesse, the girls and I have been shopping all day," Bunny informed me. "You're going to love the shirts and the boxers I picked up for you."

I leaned over and nibbled on Bunny's ear, causing her to giggle as I whispered, "You're the best."

Bunny replied, "Sit still. I can't concentrate. I am trying to get us to Chinatown." She kept her eyes on the road as she added, "I'm excited to show you the new jewelry store I just bought."

"Wow! That'll work," I responded, surprised.

Bunny proudly explained, "It's a great way to launder money. I learned about finances from my father. He was a CPA."

Rosie piped up, "I've always wanted a ruby tiara."

Asian Pearl sarcastically said from the back, "A white girl playing retail in Chinatown, this should be entertaining!"

We ignored the geisha wannabe, realizing her need for negative attention.

Bunny countered, "Girls, Mr. Chang's cousin is managing the store for me."

"*Aye aye aye*," Rosie said. "Deadly Chang gives me the creeps. You know he keeps sharks for pets? They never find his enemies." She quickly crossed herself. "That's right, child."

I fought off the cold shiver that ran down my back at the thought of Bunny doing business with the mob boss. I realized that we were already in Chinatown as I was violently jolted by the vision of a naked duck hanging by its neck in a shop window. Soon, we pulled up in front of a small jewelry store next to a Chinese restaurant.

Bunny requested, "Rosie and Junior, would you be sweet enough to wait in the car? Pearl, come with us, I may need you to translate."

I watched the hard-edged beauty come to life. Pearl's high cheekbones and pretty lips revealed a small blossom of excitement. "I want diamond-studded hair combs."

"Diamonds! You wish, Pearl!" I shot back. "Win next month's sales contest."

A large painted marquise diamond on the glass door advertised, "Chang's Fine Jewelry." The jingling bell above the entrance announced our presence. Inside, Nag Champa incense sweetened the air. Across the room, a few red and gold Chinese teacups and bright oranges rested at the feet of a smiling Buddha. The spiritual teacher sat lotus-style above a large glass case which displayed colorful jewelry. A brilliant blue Oriental rug softened our footsteps.

Bunny waltzed up to a Chinese couple attending the shop. Both were dressed in rich purple Mandarin silk jackets and black pajama-style bottoms.

"Hello, Mr. and Mrs. Chow," Bunny greeted them. "Mr. Chang said you'd have my keys ready for me. I'd like to show Jesse the office."

Mr. Chow, a radiant Chinese man with slick polished hair parted at the side, broke into a broad grin. At his side, a solemn-faced Mrs. Chow stood stiffly as her fingers rubbed prayer beads. Her features were set in disapproval. Ceremoniously, the pair bowed in unison.

Mr. Chow said, "We are happy to see you, Miss Bunny."

Bunny proudly took me by the elbow and nudged me forward. "Jesse, this is John Chow and his wife, Helena. They will continue on as our store managers because they do such an excellent job."

"John, it's nice to meet you," I said politely with a bow of my head.

"It is my pleasure, Jesse." Mr. Chow returned a small bow.

Mr. Chow led Bunny and me to a room at the back of the shop. A teak Oriental chair was tucked under a matching table. A telephone sat on the table next to a tall filing cabinet in the corner of the room.

Mr. Chow reached into his jacket pocket and pulled out a set of gold-colored keys, attached to a small jade cat. He presented them to Bunny. "Here are your keys."

"Thank you, John," Bunny replied and placed the keys in her purse.

"I'll leave you two alone. If you have questions, I'll be up front." He left the room, closing the door behind him.

Bunny turned to me and smiled. "You know, Jesse, this room would make a wonderful office for you. It's a great location. You can walk over to Marie's whenever you want to check out the business at the house."

Bunny reached out and took my hands.

"Jesse, I'd like to call my banker and have you added to the deed."

Not sure where this was all coming from, I studied this new woman in my life.

"Bunny," I replied, "my father always told me that there's no such thing as a free lunch. That's a generous offer, but I think I should decline. This doesn't have anything to do with me seeing Carmen again, does it?"

Bunny pulled back in surprise. "Of course not. It was a given when I met you that you'd see her again. You're already with both of us, so why not enjoy the best of both worlds?"

I couldn't read her reaction. Was Bunny playing me, or was she for real? I said suspiciously, "I can see how this could benefit me, but I don't see how it will help you."

Bunny playfully grasped my trouser pockets and pulled me to her. "Jesse, I'm a woman who knows how to protect my assets. The more money you make, the harder you'll work. We'll have a joint venture as equal partners, preventing future resentments." With a sparkle in her eyes, she went on. "We could have so much fun building a small empire together, Jesse. The way for us to make really big bucks is by running a high-priced escort service. This little room could make us a fortune, baby."

"So you're sure this has nothing to do with Carmen, huh babe?"

Her baby blues locked on mine. "I don't care how many girls you have in your life. I'm a woman; I can handle a little competition."

I remembered another complication and I voiced it. "I don't know about this, Bunny. The mortgage could be pricey and I don't feel comfortable being this close to Chang... hope you don't mind."

Bunny wrapped her arms around my waist and pulled me close. Sweet perfume drifted up from her as she softly said, "Don't be silly. I'll make the payments reasonable for you. I'll be your business partner, not Chang."

Deadly Chang the Chink must have been pussy-whipped when it came to Bunny. That was the only scenario that made sense. Her filthy rich sugar daddy was the most terrifying Chinatown mob boss on the West Coast. I just hoped he never fell out of lust.

JERI ESTES

"What if I can't make my mortgage payments?" I asked hesitantly.

Bunny pushed her breasts against me, rested her head on my chest and sweetly said, "Rumor has it you're pretty good at paying out on trade."

I laughed at my seductive landlord. "Okay Bunny, I'm sold."

"Great! I'll call the banker and have him draw up the paperwork."

We walked into the showroom to find Mrs. Chow standing over a jewelry case like a gargoyle with both eyes on Pearl.

"John, I'll have to rely on your expertise," I said, "because I just became co-owner of the shop. I know nothing about the jewelry business. In fact, I'm concerned. I may have too much on my plate to run more than one business."

"Why only one business?" he asked with the solemnity of a Buddhist monk, his question phrased like a philosophical inquiry.

"It might be hard for me to concentrate on this and my other endeavors."

Mr. Chow replied in a tone of complete calm and awareness. "I will teach you how to have a disciplined mind. You will learn to cultivate your Buddha nature."

His stoic mate flushed with anger. She nudged him and curtly barked something in Chinese.

Mr. Chow responded to his wife with a few harsh words himself. He then turned to us and politely continued, "Please allow me to give you jade prayer beads on authority of Mr. Chang. He wants us to respectfully welcome our new boss."

Mrs. Chow was also all sweetness and light. "Yes, dear." She deftly opened a display case behind her. An array of beautiful jade bead bracelets with bright red strings running through them glimmered under the lighted glass counter. With slender fingers the merchant's wife delicately pulled out two bracelets and carefully laid them on the counter in front of us.

Mr. Chow picked up a bracelet and held one of the little round stones between his thumb and forefinger. "*Na mor bun schi da zi zai wan fo.*" He then moved onto the next stone and repeated the same words. Bunny and I watched until he finished. Mr. Chow held the bracelet toward Bunny and gently slipped it over her hand.

Bunny responded, "They're beautiful! I will wear them with pride. Thank you, John."

"Now, what is it you just said?" I asked Mr. Chow as he held the other bracelet up toward me. Bunny watched as Mr. Chow took my hand and placed the beads on my wrist. The rich green stones rested under my white French-cuffed shirt, dressing up the gold tone in my cuff links.

"Miss Jesse, this is a Buddhist prayer. It is called the 'Nine Word Prayer.' It means, 'I take refuge in Buddha nature and follow the original wisdom of all Buddhas and bodhisattvas.'"

"That is very spiritual sounding, John," I said. "I'm sure I'll grasp the meaning later." Maybe a lifetime later.

I took Bunny by the hand and said to Mr. and Mrs. Chow, "It was a pleasure to meet you, Mr. and Mrs. Chow, but we've got to get going."

As my girls and I reached the sidewalk, I turned to Pearl and curiously inquired, "What were Mr. and Mrs. Chow arguing about in there?"

"Mrs. Chow reprimanded Mr. Chow for revealing the sacred Nine Word Prayer to a gangster. Mr. Chow replied, 'Who needs it more?'"

I smiled and said, "Wow, that Zen dude's enlightened."

Chapter 18

POST & POWELL

*M*Y ELABORATE OFFICE IN THE JEWELRY STORE was filled with expensive European furniture that echoed the grandeur of old San Francisco. Hot babe Bunny sat across from me in the large Italian leather guest chair. Her black lace blouse and soft platinum curls accented her stunning figure. The exotic scent of Jungle Gardenia perfume wafted over me as she swung her petite foot back and forth and methodically applied red lipstick. My eyes traced the outline of her calf up to the slit in her black silk skirt.

It was our late Friday afternoon meeting. Like the Prime Minister visiting the Queen, we honored our tradition. During the past few months every stone in our castle of success had been planned in meetings like this one. Strategizing, brainstorming and implementing our goals were the aphrodisiacs of our relationship. The leather placemat protecting my mahogany antique desk displayed my itinerary for today's meeting.

"Jesse, why don't we get out of here and talk business over an early dinner?" asked Bunny.

"Not tonight, Bunny. Carmen and I are going out," I said nervously.

"That's nice. Are you going anywhere special?" Bunny asked, feigning interest.

"Not too special. We're just gonna catch dinner at the Drake. Carmen wanted me to take her to the opera."

"Since when has Carmen been into the opera?" Bunny asked, her feathers slightly more ruffled.

Ignoring her comment, I switched to a business topic. "Baby, I have to tell you I'm impressed with that corn-fed whore you recruited. She's been bringing in top-dollar johns. What's her name again, Melinda?"

"Her name is Linda. Linda from Missouri," Bunny responded, her thoughts still on socializing. "I hope you haven't forgotten, we're supposed to go with Chang to dinner and the opera this weekend. It's an important social event that I don't want us to miss."

"Yes of course, Bunny. I haven't forgotten," I said, just as determined to stay on track. "Linda, huh? Linda from Missouri. She's so wholesome-looking Bunny. Where the hell did you find her?"

"Oh, the poor thing. She was a manicurist at my salon on Post. The pretty girl was so distraught one day; she couldn't focus on my nails. Her husband left her high and dry. He took everything including all of her cash. She couldn't even pay her rent." Bunny gestured with her bejeweled hand and said, "By the way, Jesse, these rocks are the greatest recruiting tools ever."

"You got that right," I replied, enjoying the congratulations. "Linda seems so sweet."

"Yes, Linda looked like an innocent angel, but as we started chatting I realized she had been around the block a few times," Bunny continued. "I'm happy she's been working out well. Linda is one of the prime girls in our escort service. Pearl did a great job teaching her the ropes."

"Pearl's the best," I commented. "Do you think Linda's old man will be a problem? When husbands smell cash, they have a tendency to pop up."

"Yeah, especially when they're named Calvert Lee Tucker," Bunny said with a chuckle. "He sounds like a dreamboat. We should be all right, though. Linda thinks he's in jail for some assault beef."

"That's good," I replied, checking my watch. "Carmen should be here any minute."

Bunny smoothly got up, walked around the desk and stood behind me. Her soft fingers played with my hair and caressed the back of my neck. Leaning forward, her warm breast pressed against my cheek as she pretended to study the itinerary on my desk. Bunny softly kissed my ear and whispered, "I love studying your itinerary."

Hearing the longing in Bunny's voice, I placed my hand between her thighs and caressed her.

The oak door to my office opened slowly. Carmen, draped in a full-length black mink, entered.

She ignored Bunny, who respectfully straightened up.

"Hi, Jesse. Hope you're done with your work," she commented with a subtle glance toward Bunny.

"Hi, baby doll. Good timing," I said as I got up to go grab my Stetson and camel hair overcoat.

My girl intercepted me with a hug. Hands on my shoulders, she gave me a long kiss on the lips. Strands of beautiful pearls lay over her black cocktail dress. Carmen's luscious auburn hair was up in a French twist. Her delicate ears wore the finest iridescent mother of pearls, plucked from the sea.

Bunny greeted Carmen with a sigh of admiration. "Oh, my God, Carmen, that coat is just gorgeous."

"Glad you like it, Bunny," replied Carmen. "Jesse picked it up for me."

"Oh, how nice," Bunny said, shooting me a look. "Jesse was sweet enough to give me one just like it. Mine may be a little longer, though."

"I would imagine most of your clothes fit you a little long," Carmen replied, looking down at her.

Bunny swiped right back, "My breasts usually lift up my coats a few inches, so I'm glad for the additional length. At least then my clothes don't look like they're just hanging on me."

Bunny was quick, but she didn't know who she was dealing with here.

"You might have a point there, Bunny. My mother's breasts have also gotten larger as she's grown older."

Rage crept across Bunny's cheeks as she stepped closer to Carmen. "I think," she bit off each word, "I'll wear the mink Jesse gave me when she takes me to the opera this weekend." Skillfully delivering her coup de grace, Bunny smugly smiled.

I decided to end the proceedings before the fur started to fly. "Well, ladies, it's time we got out of here." Quickly, I slipped on my coat. Putting on my hat, I tilted the brim slightly over my eyes.

Noticing Bunny struggling to put on her mink, I came to her rescue and lifted it over her shoulders. Bunny and Carmen both gave me weak smiles. Before exiting, I kissed Bunny on the cheek goodbye. I opened the door, allowing the girls to walk out in front of me.

As we left, I said good night to Mr. and Mrs. Chow and exited the front door that now displayed the sign, "Rawlson's Fine Jewelry."

From the sidewalk we saw Nick, my cabbie, parked at the end of the block waiting for us. Bunny headed toward the Cadillac in her long, flowing snow white mink.

"Have a good time, Jesse! Bye, Carmen!" Bunny shouted as she got into her pink chariot.

Carmen gave an indifferent wave goodbye. "Jesse," she said, turning to me, "I feel a need for a vacation. Why don't we escape to L.A. for a few days? I want you to take me to the opera in a new coat. We can go shopping in Beverly Hills for something original," Carmen said pointedly.

"Baby doll, there's no opera in L.A., just singing waiters." I grabbed Carmen, kissed her on the lips and flagged Nick. "I'll take you to the opera in Milan."

Nick's yellow bomber screeched abruptly to a halt in front of us. Through the windshield I saw a small statue of Jesus on the taxi's dashboard and smiled. We hopped into the backseat. I said to Nick, "Shit, I would hate to see how you drive without Jesus as your co-pilot! Hell, man, you damn near jumped the curb!"

The cheerful Greek chuckled. He adjusted his worn cabbie cap over his salt-and-pepper curls. "Wow, you girls look hot tonight. What's your pleasure, Jesse?"

"Take us to the Drake," I said.

"You got it, boss!" Nick always performed his religious rituals before he took off. He rubbed the Saint Christopher medal that dangled from his rearview mirror, patted Jesus on the head and then threw down the meter arm and slammed on the gas.

Nick was one of my best birddogs. He would send busloads of Japs over to the house. Japs and Greeks seemed to know how to make money and find good pussy.

Carmen rested her warm soft hand over mine. We sat nestled in the back of the cab, content in each other's company.

"It's nice to have a little alone time with you." I took her hand and kissed her fingers lightly. "Sorry I've been working like a maniac. I'll make it up to you."

She caressed my cheek with her palm and warm breath as she leaned close, kissing me passionately. "You can start tonight, Jesse."

I slipped my hand between her legs as the lights of Chinatown blurred from view.

In a few minutes, the sights and sounds of Post and Powell greeted our cab as we entered Union Square. I rolled my window down for some fresh air. Rows of elegant stores, fine restaurants and historical landmark hotels lined the world-famous shopping district. The trolley car jingled with an upbeat clank, heralding the excitement of San Francisco's heart. Like town criers, conductors yelled, "All aboard!"

Hotels bearing the names of ancient knights shone in bright neon above the crowded sidewalks. Windows exposed the elegance and grandeur of opulent wealth, advertising escape from mediocrity. Gold-framed menus stood regally in front of establishments of fine dining and spirits. Shuffling the expensive luggage, smiling bellmen verified the importance of the guests entering the Sir Francis Drake Hotel.

Instantly, our car's rear door was flung open by a greeter of the elite dressed in a billowing red beefeater costume. He saluted us with a cheerful grin.

Leaning forward with a ready twenty, I told my jovial jockey, "Have a nice night, Nick."

With Carmen at my side, I stepped out of the cab and onto the red carpet. "Welcome to the Sir Francis Drake. Do you have any bags?" asked the silver-haired imitation beefeater.

"No, we're just having dinner. Thanks," I replied as I handed the gentleman a bill.

With Carmen in tow, we walked into the realm of the dignified for a bite to eat. Soft jazz notes twinkled from ebony and ivory keys. The gazes of elegantly dressed men and women lingered on the auburn-haired beauty by my side as we strolled through the lobby. Cathedral ceilings hung heavy in crystal rose above the gold-veined marble at our feet. Brilliant, massive bouquets sprang from elegant vases.

I caught the reflections of Carmen and me in the beveled mirrors. My brown slacks complemented the rich gold-toned camel hair overcoat. Topping my expensive garment was a chocolate brown

Stetson with a cream-colored feather in its band. Carmen's luscious black mink and classic hairdo barred anyone from questioning her occupation or sexuality.

As we passed through the lobby, we looked to the unsuspecting eye like a glamorous straight couple. Carmen and I flew under the radar. Our fellow diners had no idea that we were the king and queen of the Tenderloin queers.

Near several marble columns sat Asian Pearl and Linda from Missouri on silk Baroque furniture. The ladies were holding court with a few black-tied debonair gentlemen. My jewel from the east and the farmer's daughter looked like fashion models on the cover of *Vogue*.

We walked past my working girls with a quick nod. A leather-padded lectern with a tiny lit desk lamp stopped our entrance into the fine dining room. We dropped our coats at the small wooden coat check. Luis the maître d' saluted us with his pearly whites. "Nice to see you, Jesse, Carmen."

His manicured fingers ran over the guest book. "I see your reservation, Jesse. Please follow me." His lacquered pencil-thin mustache matched his French accent. We followed him to the white linen-draped round table in the romantic back corner of the restaurant. Candles and silver sat prepared for our meal.

We were greeted by our favorite waiter, Daniel. The handsome young gay boy, working his way through college, was thrilled to see us.

"Jesse, Carmen, great to see you two here. What's the occasion?"

"Romance. I'm taking out my special lady," I replied.

"Really?" he said with a raised eyebrow. He knew I'd brought other ladies to the Drake. "That is so sweet."

"So, Daniel, how's school going?" I asked.

"It's going great! I am *finally* almost finished. I cannot wait to be done."

"Don't finish too soon. You don't want to get your ass drafted," I said.

"That's for sure. Don't worry; I've got a 'get-out-of-Saigon-free card!'" He gestured with an exaggerated fey limp wrist and we all laughed.

"What can I get you two to drink?" asked Daniel.

"Let's start with a bottle of Dom Perignon," I said.

"Oh, Jesse!" exclaimed Carmen.

"Very good, coming right up," Daniel said as he flitted away.

We toasted our love with pricey champagne and enjoyed a sumptuous meal. As the last plates were taken away, Carmen rubbed the top of her foot up my calf. "This moment with you is paradise. I don't want it to end."

Daniel stopped by our table and inquired, "Jesse, will that be all for tonight?"

I told the cute waiter, "Yes, Daniel. Thanks for everything."

He placed his check portfolio on the table. "Have a great night."

Glancing at my watch, I told Carmen, "Damn... I gotta get back to work. I'm supposed to hook up with Junior."

As she took a sip of champagne, I detected sadness in her beautiful green eyes.

"Carmen, why don't you come with me to Compton's? I have to make the rounds and meet up with Junior."

"Sure, Jesse, that would be cool," Carmen said as she sat up, elated.

I put a couple of Bennies in the check holder and we got up to retrieve our coats. We dressed for the night and walked through the mammoth lobby. In the corner of my eye, I caught a glimpse of the distinguished-looking district attorney, with his devoted wife by his side at the lobby bar. He held a rolled-up playbill from the Geary Theater. His eyes spotted Carmen just as we noticed him. His glance lingered on her. She seemed to welcome his admiration as I detected a small smile cross her lips. I reassured myself that her reaction was strictly business. His Nob Hill wife, completely oblivious to the moment, missed her husband's flushed face and lustful stare.

We quickly left the Drake, walked into the chilly night and made our way up Post to the TL. I held Carmen's hand when we hit Taylor and strolled toward Turk. Hookers replaced well-coiffed ladies. Neon signs, hanging from cheap hotels and topless joints, lit the way as we entered our ghetto home. Working queens competed with their ovary-packing hooking sisters for cruising johns. Irritated, the queens purse-slapped loitering hobos; shoving them off their sidewalk.

Rows of Harley hogs lined the outside of Compton's large picture windows next to shit-talking bikers enjoying the night. As Carmen and I approached, we saw Junior on the corner talking to Animal, my biker dude. Animal was on my payroll to provide muscle and baby-sit our hookers. Six-foot-three, with long flowing hair down to his waist, he had refined good looks that appeared almost effeminate against his heavy leather and chain jacket.

Junior, tabbed back and looking slick in her three-piece Italian men's suit, happily called out, "Good to see you, boss. Carmen, you look great!"

"Thanks, Junior," Carmen replied. "I'll be joining you bad daddies on your rounds tonight."

"What's up?" I asked Junior and Animal.

"Same old, same old, boss. Threw a couple of rowdy tricks out of the Camelot tonight," replied Animal.

"What's up with that, Animal? Maybe the girls aren't properly qualifying their johns. They're not taking any young ones, are they?"

"There've been a lot of soldiers on the streets. The girls feel sorry for them," confessed Animal gruffly.

"Yeah, I can understand that," I said sarcastically. "They're also cash-heavy while on leave. I'll talk with the girls about this. I'm glad to hear they're so patriotic."

"Been crackin' the whip a little," bragged Animal. "Had a couple of lazy hookers taking too long breaks smoking in the doorways. Got it all under control now, boss."

"Good job, Animal. Keep up the good work."

Animal turned around and got on his big hog. He kick-started the candy-apple red Harley. His long hair flowed in the wind as he roared away down Turk Street.

The three of us ventured on to Chuckkers down in the Mission district. The streets got darker as the area got poorer and poorer. The lonely sidewalks on Taylor echoed our footsteps as we made our way onto Mission Street.

Suddenly, like a brick wall from nowhere, an army of men sprang out of a parked purple El Dorado. Prince towered in front of me with his kid brother Giuseppe at his side. Blondie the Swede stood next to another lowlife I recognized from the past, the redheaded mutton chop chump who had tried to steal Junior's briefcase. The odor of booze and smoke fouled the air.

Instinctually, Carmen, Junior and I halted. Like hikers in the wilderness coming face-to-face with grizzlies, we stood our ground and showed no fear.

"Gentlemen, nice to see you all again," I said. Carmen's hand tightened like a boa constrictor around my arm as she indifferently looked the other way.

"Gimmie your money, bitch!" Prince demanded. "Enough is enough, cunt lover. It's tax time, bitch!"

Prince's three flunkies, dressed in loud vulgar pimpwear, stood by his side, but they didn't faze me. I'd been building my empire for months, and they hadn't shown their faces once.

Prince's giant hands swayed through the darkness in a chuckin' and jivin' manner. "Pimpin's a man's trade. You fuckin' stud daddies are snatchin' up my johns. You're spoiling your bitches and giving my girls ideas. I ain't losing a john or a fuckin' whore to a woman. Pussies aren't gangsters, you motherfucker!"

I replied to Prince in an extremely calm and cool voice, though enraged that the son-of-a-bitch would have the audacity to speak to me like that. I was aware of the subtle movement by Junior as she reached for the gun in her belt. Carmen was prepared to pull out her small silver mother-of-pearl handled .22 pistol. It was a handy snub-nosed hooker's special that she always carried in her coat pocket. I coolly raised my hand as I watched Prince's henchmen also reach for their pieces.

"Cool it, gentlemen. Prince and I got business to talk," I said confidently.

The henchmen hesitated, awaiting Prince's reaction. He looked surprised as he waited to hear what I had to say. I noticed a large gold Star of David hanging around Prince's neck.

Pointing to the jewelry, I said, "I'm surprised, Prince, that a brother who's a Jew, and knows the sting of persecution, would hassle me. Why would you be prejudiced toward a sister who's in the same boat you're in? After all, we're both minorities."

Prince was shocked and actually embarrassed because he knew he was no Jew but couldn't admit that he didn't realize he had a loud-ass Star of David hanging around his neck.

Realizing he looked foolish, he tried to regroup like every street person does when they're confused. "It's cool, it's cool. I ain't gonna give you no fuckin' disrespect. Stop servicing my johns, dyke. If one of my bitches comes to see you, you send her ass back to me quick and in hurry or you're dead, motherfucker. Take this as a warning, bitch."

I felt the tension drain out of the air as I nodded and said, "We got an understanding. Respect, man, respect."

We both shrugged and laughed a little. I said to him, "Prince, drop by my jewelry shop in Chinatown. Tell my guy, John Chow, that you want a diamond put right in the middle of that beautiful star of yours. It's on me, man. Giuseppe, you pick out something for yourself too. For old time's sake, my friend."

"You're fucking-A stylin' now motherfucker," Giuseppe said, not sure how to take my generosity. "You're not sleeping on the floor anymore now are you?"

"No, Giuseppe, I'm not. But I'll never forget your hospitality when I first landed in the TL."

Everyone's faces showed confusion as they tried to figure out Giuseppe's and my connection. Addressing the audience like a Shakespearean actor with grand gestures, I started to give a summation of our history.

"Giuseppe is a stand-up dude—"

"Jesse, no…its okay," said Giuseppe, trying to cut me off. "You don't need to run it down now. It's all cool, Jesse."

"Miss Zada, Miss Penny and I crashed at his pad when we were between residences," I reported. "He was a complete gentleman. He never took advantage of me or wanted anything for his generosity. Giuseppe is a class act all the way."

"What? You took in queers?" Prince asked Giuseppe and then

slapped him upside the head. "Ain't you got no sense?" He knew his intimidation play had fallen flat. "Come on, let's get out of here, before I find out my brother's a cocksucker."

Prince and his crew jumped into the El Dorado with Giuseppe defending himself. "I had no idea those sweet chocolate bitches had cocks!" he said. "I swear I didn't!"

When their taillights finally faded from view, we roared with laughter.

"Jesse, that was fuckin' slick!" complimented Carmen.

"Whew, that was a close one. I thought we were all dead," said Junior sincerely. "Did you see that briefcase stealin' chump's nose though? It's still fucked up," she added proudly.

"I never thought I'd see him again," I said. "He is dressing better these days."

"Yeah, he is," said Junior.

"But Giuseppe…what's up with that tomato red suit?" I jeered. "Now that's really tacky!"

"You got that right," Carmen said, playfully mimicking my favorite phrase.

We all laughed in agreement.

"I gotta tell you, I hate violence," I said, reflecting on the near-ugly confrontation. "I'm grateful for what a little fast-talking can do."

"Yeah, talk isn't always cheap, Jesse. If word ever got out that you allowed anyone to disrespect you, we would all be dead," Carmen pointed out.

"Yeah right, that includes you, baby doll," I reprimanded her.

As we headed to our camp at Chuckkers, though, I wasn't feeling so cheery inside. My turf was spreading, and next time I might not be so lucky. It was time to find more reinforcements.

Chapter 19

A JOHN NAMED JOHN

*T*HE CHARACTERS, TONY CURTIS AND DAVID NIVEN, playing in the movie I was watching, were living my dream. They were gigolos romping through Europe on an adventure with gorgeous women paying for the pleasure of their company. After all, I had wealth and a sophisticated lifestyle like the cads on the tube. All I had to do is look down at the expensive black-and-white checkered slacks I was wearing and my classy "pimp" socks. The black, pin-striped knee-highs cost more than the old shirts I used to buy at the five-and dime-store, that's for sure.

Sipping my Jack, I relaxed on the couch in our tricking pad. The apartment was used by all of our hookers. Bunny had carefully picked a corner unit on the fourth floor with a fire escape. Many of the neighbors were seniors and, fortunately, hard of hearing.

The girls would get each john in and out within fifteen minutes. They never booked a young trick. The last thing they wanted was a lover with stamina.

With my sleeves rolled up and my feet on the coffee table, I took a joint break. We had plans to go out with Chang later tonight. Bunny wanted me to finally meet her favorite sugar daddy. She was excited that I had agreed to go out with him socially. Chang was taking us to dinner and the opera.

I tripped on the gigolos on television while Bunny turned a date in the bedroom with a john named John. The cads were hysterically funny as they discussed their seduction strategies and, with each hit of my joint, they got funnier. My hilarity was suddenly jolted, however by loud pounding on the door. A deep voice forcefully yelled, "Open up, it's the police!"

"Oh shit!" I thought. "You've gotta be kidding!" I yelled back.

I immediately put the roach out in my drink and gulped down the nasty- tasting shit. I yelled over my shoulder as I hurried towards the bedroom, "Just a minute, I'll be right there!"

In the bedroom, Bunny was stark raving nude sitting on the john named John's dick. He sat up as best as he could with a whore on his hard-on. Through his horn-rimmed glasses, his eyes looked terrified. I hurdled over Bunny and the banker as I lunged for the top dresser drawer.

"It's the fucking heat!"

Standing on the end of the mattress, doing a balancing act, I opened a dresser drawer and pulled out the shoebox full of grass. I threw in the Zig Zags and couple of old whites. Tucking the box under my arm, I ran like hell to the bathroom. I avoided stumbling over Bunny and the john as they frantically tried to get dressed. The trick's glasses were falling off his balding head as he fumbled for his pants to cover his now limp willy.

Very calm and cool, Bunny said to me, "I'll handle this," as she deftly put on her skirt.

I had no time to listen. I darted through the kitchen like a running back with the shoebox under my arm, determined to make it to safety before the door came crashing in. I could hear the cops trying to break down the heavy wooden door as I flew by. I made a beeline toward the bathroom window to toss the shit out, so it could fall and scatter on the cement below us. Pulling back the shower curtain,

I stepped up onto the side of the tub, ready to sling the contents through the open window. I found myself looking right into the barrel of a cocked .45.

"Drop it, you motherfucking dyke!" yelled Clancy. His toupee bobbed up and down as he repeated, "Drop it, you fucking dyke!"

I looked directly into the barrel of his gun, the hammer held open by his thumb, ready to blow my brains out.

"Fuck you!" I yelled and dropped to the floor. The next instant, I was violently jerked from behind, picked up and thrown through the air. I landed on the same couch where I had just been peacefully tripping a few minutes earlier.

Bunny and the john stood handcuffed in front of me. I looked up from my crash landing at a two hundred and fifty pound pissed off black cop. Then Clancy ran into the living room behind him waving his gun. Red-faced, he yelled at me, "You stupid fucking dyke, I almost blew your motherfucking head off!"

Like criminals on the eleven o'clock news, we were escorted out of the building in handcuffs. Greeting us was a polished black Town Car, pulling up. I heard Bunny gasp, "Shit, it's Chang."

Three lean Asian killing machines piled out of the car. Like Secret Service agents, they scanned their surroundings. A tall soldier opened the rear door. Out stepped a petite man wearing a brown derby. Chang was the exact same height as Bunny. His handsome features were accented by a graying Vandyke beard. Clenched between his lips was a fat cigar. He held an orchid corsage in his hand.

Bunny gave Chang a weak smile. His dark eyes softened as he smiled back at her. His gaze then landed on Clancy. Through his slanted glare I saw smoldering fury. Chang and his gang stood silently as we passed. Somebody was going to pay for this outrage.

The next thing I knew, the three of us were sitting together in the back seat of a squad car. We bounced up and down as Clancy zoomed through the streets toward the station. Slowing on Market Street, he stuck his fist out the window and yelled at a ragged group picketing in front of an army surplus store, "You motherfucking hippies!"

Poor John, sitting next to me, got whiter and whiter with each bump of the car. Bunny whispered under her breath, "Don't worry, I have a trick lawyer." She nudged him to make sure he understood. "Don't say anything, okay? They'll separate us."

The enraged captain turned around, spitting as he screamed, "Shut up, you fucking lezzies!" Clancy was apparently furious with me for refusing to be his mistress. Either that or he was putting on a show to impress his partner.

We pulled up behind the station and violently jerked to a stop. The john's glasses fell off again and the black cop turned around and compassionately put them back on his sweating, bald head. He helped the old banker and Bunny out of the car.

Clancy turned around from the front seat and said to me enticingly, "You know I can make all these charges disappear."

I had nothing to say. I was not amused by my treatment. He got out of the car and yanked me out of the back seat.

Once we were inside the station, we were treated like VIPs. Bunny and I went directly to booking and were told we would be held in the felony tank. They charged me with pimping and pandering. It's amazing how much more attention you receive when you get busted for a felony instead of a misdemeanor.

We were turned over to a massive matron who politely introduced herself. "Hi, I'm Deto. I'm going to have to strip-search you ladies."

Pale and wide-eyed, I asked Bunny, "Is there any way you can get us out of this?"

Bunny replied in a foreign-sounding voice, four octaves higher than usual, "I don't think so."

Reassuringly, Deto said, "It will be over in just a few minutes. Relax. I've seen it all before. You may want to keep your eyes closed, however, when they spray you for lice." Deto was obviously a veteran servant of the state.

A few minutes later, as Bunny and I left the search room, thanking the polite matron for such a pleasurable and harmless humiliating experience, we were separated. Deto had informed me that I would be going to the "Daddy Tank," in Cell Block 5000 down in the basement. Bunny would be housed with the general prison population.

I had my own personal escort, Lakesha, a young hip gum-smacking Afro-headed hot black mama, who sashayed through the corridors with an air of complete indifference.

"Welcome to the Daddy Tank," she said. "If I was you—as pretty and young as you are—I'd sleep with one eye open tonight."

When we got to my cell, she turned the key, opened the door and I stepped in. As she walked away, leaving me alone, I heard the dreaded sound of my cell door slamming shut behind me. Before she left the cell block, Lakesha called back, "Good night, daddy."

The cell door slamming was like the jaws of a trap snapping on its prey. Feeling hopeless, I became aware of how completely alone I was. There was a small solitary bed at the rear of the cell. Its gray coarse wool blanket was tightly tucked under the thin single mattress. It looked like a monk's bunk.

I took a deep breath. "I'm definitely not at the Hilton. There's no little chocolate mint on my pillow tonight," I thought. Instead, laid out neatly on the dirty beige, frayed pillowcase was a pair of folded dark green jailhouse pajamas. They were hideous. I wondered,

"Whatever happened to basic-black jailhouse stripes like Elvis wore in *Jailhouse Rock?*"

On the bed was a small bar of soap, a rough white cotton towel and a single black comb. In the center of my cell, against the back wall, a low coverless porcelain toilet protruded from the floor. It stood in plain view of the guards and inmates. Nearby, a graffiti-etched, battered steel mirror hung above a matching sink.

I studied myself in the mirror and was shocked at my reflection. I looked ridiculous in the low-cut, boxy green rag. My head stuck out like a fat eraser on a thin pencil. My short boyish haircut now looked completely out of place.

There was an old street saying, "You can do easy time or hard time." I lay on my bunk and tried to do easy time.

My lighter was doing time in the property room along with my Saint Christopher medal and roughly three grand in cash. I lit up a smoke with a wooden matchstick from the box Lakesha had given me. I realized that I was lucky I hadn't been shot earlier, but my pimping and pandering charges carried a fifteen-year minimum. That wasn't exactly chump change.

Tears welled up in my eyes, but I was determined to never appear weak. I quieted the panic. The months I had practiced acting like a badass were beginning to pay off. I put on my game face, acted cool, and convinced myself not to worry.

After the remark Lakesha had made about sleeping with one eye open, I was grateful that the other inmates were all asleep. I was in a cell block full of hardass horndogs. Not a safe place for a pretty baby butch. Some bubba-dyke might try to make me her punk. "Good luck!" I muttered under my breath.

When I thought about it, fucking bull dykes were the least of my problems. I knew Bunny must be pissed at me. She was probably blaming me for getting us busted. She had expressed her irritation regarding Clancy often: "Jesse honey, he's beginning to interfere with our business. Our girls are getting arrested more frequently. Just sleep with him once in a while. He'll calm down." Now Bunny had missed her date with big bucks Chang.

I unfolded the property slip that the cop had given me and read it. Typed clearly on the yellow blue-lined paper was a large dollar sign next to 3,041 dollars and thirty-one cents. I refolded it and stuck it in the toe of my black shoe, relieved at knowing the money would buy me protection.

I rested my head on the flat hard pillow, stared at the bars in front of me and said my prayers. The occasional cough and rhythmic sound of snoring coming from adjacent cells gradually put me to sleep.

I must have been exhausted, because I was jolted violently out of my slumber by loud clanking and a coarse deep woman's voice yelling, "Rise and shine ladies, roll call!"

I fumbled out of bed in my bare ass, having been unwilling to sleep in the tacky pajamas or the gross green dress. The floor was cold under my bare feet as I threw on the dumb green smock and stumbled out of my cell.

Immediately after roll call, the matron ordered, "Okay, ladies, hit the showers."

Panic hit me like a body blow. "Oh God," I thought, "I have to take my clothes off again, and this time I'm going to have company."

I marched toward the showers following a lanky Afro-headed, six-foot-tall black dyke. I cautiously turned around to see what was trailing me. A powerful-looking ugly Mexican woman was huffing, puffing and snorting directly behind me. I felt like a walking red cape in a bullring of bull dykes. I said a silent prayer to the Virgin Mary.

First thing I did was a few pull-ups from the shower bar, showing off my strength. I didn't want any misunderstandings with my cellmates. It was a relief to be dismissed from the showers and go into the day room for breakfast.

Finding a seat on a bench, I put down my tray. I sat near a white girl who looked familiar. Looking at my plain oatmeal in the cheap cereal bowl, I took a bite of the dry white toast and washed it down with the bitter coffee, careful not to burn my fingers on the hot tin mug.

Politely, I said, "Good morning" to the blond stocky girl sitting across the table.

I was pleasantly surprised by her exuberant reply.

"I know you. You're Bunny's pimp!" she exclaimed. "I've seen you at Chuckker's. Respect, man!"

My notoriety along with this girl's friendly tone of voice made me feel better immediately. I replied, "Yeah, Bunny's my old lady."

"Far-fucking out, I've heard about your operation," said the friendly inmate.

"My name's Jesse Rawlson," I said, extending my hand.

I shook hands with the stranger.

"I'm Little Bastard. Pleased to meet you," said the tough dyke.

"Likewise, man."

Little Bastard pointed her thumb over her shoulder at a dark-haired woman who looked like a gentle giant, "Jesse, this is my running partner, Rascal."

As she introduced me to three hundred and fifty pounds of solid muscle sitting on the bench, I noticed that Little Bastard appeared perfectly comfortable next to this gigantic life form. With a demeanor similar to that of an older brother, Little Bastard had a protective attitude toward the woman who was three times her size. I tried not to stare at Rascal's enormous arms, which reminded me of Paul Bunyan's.

The titanic Rascal ate her breakfast in a dainty, lady-like fashion.

She had a very pretty face with sharp features that were softened by her kind brown eyes. She looked up from her oatmeal for a second, smiled, and exposed deep dimples in her fleshy olive cheeks. I could see that she was even taller than the big fat Mexican who had followed me into the showers. Little Bastard ordered her, "Say hi to Jesse."

I was taken aback as Rascal spoke in a squeaky, high-pitched voice that sounded like Minnie Mouse. "Hi, Jesse."

Of course, I answered her most respectfully, "Hi, Rascal." She wasn't much of a conversationalist, but at her size, she really didn't need to be.

Smiling at my new friends, I felt safe for the first time and took a bite of my stale toast. Just then, a big black hand grabbed the side of my tray. My eyes slowly followed the large arm inch by inch up to a face. Much to my dismay, the face belonged to the lanky, six-foot black girl from the showers. She had my breakfast tray in one of her hands and a large pointed black Afro pick in the other. She definitely got my attention, since the comb looked like a weapon to me.

The girl said to me in a mean, cocky voice, "You don't want your fuckin' breakfast, do you, bitch? I think I'll take it off your hands."

I hesitated for a second, not knowing how to reply. I didn't have to because Little Bastard said, "She's hungry! Get your fuckin' hands off her tray!"

The tall bully jerked my tray up. She looked down at the short butch and said, "You've got to be fuckin' kidding me."

Little Bastard grinned harshly and nodded her head. "Rascal."

In an instant, the ton of muscle jumped off the bench. Rascal's fist, the size of a bowling ball, slugged the tall black girl in the chest, knocking the wind out of her. As she gasped and sputtered, Rascal grabbed the bitch's Afro and slammed her head down on the table. Twisting her arm behind her back, Rascal picked her up by the hair and threw all six feet of her into the wall like a rag doll.

My oatmeal, coffee and toast spattered all over the wall and linoleum floor next to the unconscious Afro-head. Rascal calmly sat down next to Little Bastard, picked up her spoon and resumed eating her cereal, as if nothing had happened.

The black girl slowly got up off the floor, mumbling under her breath, "Just fuck it, fuck it, I wasn't that hungry anyhow."

Grinning at Little Bastard, who hadn't moved through this entire explosion, I said, "Thanks, I really appreciate it. You know what? I happen to have a little cash on me. I would be honored to buy you both anything you like. Candy bars, cigarettes, sandwiches, Coca-Colas—you name it and you got it."

Rascal smiled in delight. She replied in her squeaky voice, "Cool, man."

I asked Little Bastard, "What are you in here for?"

"Armed robbery," she said, bored. "The fuzz caught me and Rascal leaving a jewelry store. We threw the merchandise into a gutter just before they busted our asses, though, and they can't prove shit. How 'bout you?"

"Felony, pimping and pandering and they caught my ass with some grass and a few Bennies too."

A light went on in her head. "You guys must have an ace lawyer, right?" she asked enthusiastically. "I would do anything to have decent representation. I got some sap public defender."

I studied Little Bastard and her partner Rascal. They both would come in mighty handy. After my run-in with the Fillmore boys, I needed more bodyguards.

"I might be able to help get you out of here. How would you guys like to work for me?" I offered.

"For real, Jesse?" Little Bastard inquired.

"Yeah, I got a good feeling about you."

She looked like salvation had arrived. "Rascal and I would be honored to be on your crew."

"You're both officially on my payroll, starting now," I told them.

"Thanks, Jesse," Little Bastard said. "This robbing shit isn't a steady gig."

"Cool," Rascal squeaked.

I shook Rascal's hand and, to my dismay, felt my fingers crushed.

The approaching matron yelled at us, "Get your sorry asses back to your cells. Breakfast is over!"

Back in my cell, I saw an opened, censored telegram on my bed from some guy named "George." On my bunk, I read the message. "Jesse, I love you. I'll see you at arraignment. I'm out and have paid for your attorney fees. I'll see you in Chinatown. Don't worry. Love, George."

"Who the fuck is George?" I wondered.

I read the Chinatown part again and realized that it was Bunny. I knew she couldn't take a chance at the letter reading gay or I would have never gotten it. "What a smart girl," I thought.

Hearing the snack cart rolling through the cell block, I got up to buy myself some cigarettes. Rascal was leaving the cart with an armful of candy bars, Twinkies, Coca-Colas and cigarettes. I was happy to see my new employee taking advantage of the company's fringe benefits. I bought myself a pack of cigarettes and said hi to a very attractive, slick-looking young black woman standing near the snack cart.

As she flashed me a broad smile, I was instantly impressed with her style. The woman's gold, diamond-studded front tooth sparkled like her mischievous brown eyes. In a thick New Orleans drawl, she said, "I'm Lovey Lupree. My skin looks like coffee and cream, smooth as my name, and pimpin's my game."

After singing her little ditty, she added, "How do you do? I am pleased to meet you," as she extended her light brown hand.

"I'm pleased to meet you too," I replied. Lovey's shiny processed James Brown-pompadour crowned her like a huge Hawaiian wave. Defiantly, a single curlicue sprang down her forehead. The slick dandy's Southern voice transported me to another age.

I introduced myself, "Hello, my name is Jesse Rawlson. Hey Lovey, I just asked my new friends, Little Bastard and Rascal, to join me in my cell for a poker game. You're more than welcome to join us."

Lovey Lupree graciously replied, "I don't mind if I do."

I headed down the corridor back to my cell. The bleakness of the place was beginning to get to me. The Daddy Tank was a special cell block that housed only butch lesbians. All the masculine girls were completely cut off without any recreation or entertainment privileges. The girls doing hard time had been stuck in this basement for years. It was quickly making sense why a girl had hung herself in here last month.

The only time a "daddy" saw sunlight was when the matrons led them through the open courtyard to the church. For that reason, my cellmates always went to church twice on Sundays.

Rescuing me from my dark mood, Little Bastard and Rascal entered my cell carrying their pillows. They dropped them on the floor as they entered. I cheerfully greeted them. "Welcome to the Rawlson Casino. Sorry, the topless waitresses are off tonight but the poker table is open."

Gallantly, I gestured with a wave of my arm toward the bed to Rascal, "Please sit down." I realized that it would be very hard to get her massive body up if she sat down on the floor.

Rascal replied in her high little voice, "Okay."

As she sat on my bunk, I watched it sink several inches. Little Bastard then sat on her pillow on the floor and shuffled the cards with the speed of a Las Vegas dealer.

Lovey Lupree arrived and I welcomed my sister in trade. "Hello Lovey, welcome to my cell. Glad you could make it."

Lovey spoke in a cultured voice. "I am pleased to join ya'll. I took the liberty of bringing you all some chocolates for refreshments."

"Wow," I thought, "this girl obviously has class."

Lovey informed us that she was the best-dressed pimp mac daddy in the French Quarter. While visiting San Francisco, she had been busted on a chump change charge called the "Three Articles of Clothing Law," stopped as she was leaving Finnochio's nightclub.

Lovey laughed as she told the story. "The only reason I got busted was because I'm black and that cop was envious of my nice clothes. That dumb white boy thought I was a man until I spoke. I was dressed so fine that night! I had on my best black Stetson, a burgundy pinstriped suit and matching alligators.

"I asked that dumb white boy, 'Don't you have anything better to do than to bust butches?' The pig gave me a lecture on the "Three Articles of Clothing Law," telling me I was in violation because I wasn't wearing three articles of women's clothing."

"The fucking doorman at Finnochio's didn't even let me in when I went there dressed in hard drag," I responded. "Those sissy bouncers are as bad as the pigs. They're always afraid of being shut down for letting anyone in who's dressed like the opposite sex. They said you can only dress in drag if you're going on stage." At this, Little Bastard and Rascal laughed, apparently from experience.

Little Bastard chimed in, "I think it's a bogus anti-gay law. I bet it's not even on the books. Man, it's just another excuse for the pigs to crack our heads."

Lovey continued her saga with an expression of innocence. "I told the cop I had a woman's belt on. I showed him my fine alligator belt. He informed me, 'Belts don't count. The next time you leave the house, young lady, you need to be dressed as a girl, because that's what you are.'"

Little Bastard and I laughed at the cop's last remark.

"Lovey, so where are you pimping now?" I asked as we played our hands.

"I was working Columbus Street, but the cops weren't very sweet. I was caught up in their sweep, so it's here I sleep," Lovey sang in her heavenly New Orleans drawl.

We all chuckled. I inquired further.

"How many girls do you have working for you, Lovey?"

"Just one at the moment and she's my girlfriend too," Lovey said with a twinkle in her eyes.

Laughing, I said, "If you'd like, your girl can work some of our tricks. We'll split the profits. We have more johns that we can handle."

Lovey smiled like a cherub. Her gold tooth moved with the beat as she sang with a wide grin, "My bitch is pretty, that is true. But she's nothing like the girls on Jesse's crew. Jesse's known around the world for the green-eyed girl and the Asian Pearl." She ended her ditty with a little soft shoe. "I'd be happy to be of service."

"Lovey," I replied. "Your singing talent alone would brighten up my crew. I must warn you ladies, though; it's been getting a little chilly in the Tenderloin lately. The Fillmore boys are throwing their weight around. It could get pretty rough."

"Good!" Little Bastard said excitedly. "We'll feel right at home. Rascal and I grew up together in Salinas. Nothing's rougher than Friday night when those grape- pickin' boys get paid."

"Great," I replied. "I need strong enforcers on my posse. I have a really good feeling about all of you. I'll pay your bail, your lawyer fees and put you up. It's a fair investment, because I need you to hit the streets running."

Lakesha interrupted the poker game. "Let's go, Jessica. Follow me. The bus is leaving for the courthouse now!"

I told my new recruits, "I'll call my lawyer today. He'll start working on getting you three out of here."

Little Bastard informed me, "Jesse, I'm booked under Kimberly Myers, and Rascal is Rosa Maria Vasquez."

"You got it," I said as I prepared to leave. "We'll all party at Chuckkers when you get out."

Lovey hugged me goodbye. She said in a low voice, "It's nice to meet another mac daddy."

"You got that right, Lovey. I'll see you on the outside."

"Sounds sublime!"

Lakesha called me in a loud, irritated voice, "Come on, Romeo, we don't have all day!"

Chapter 20

RED DEVILS

*S*MOKING A JOINT, I WAITED IN THE DARK ALLEY behind Chuckers. Loud pulsating music escaped from the red windowless building. I watched the patrons swish by me down the sidewalk. Drunken gay boys dressed as bikers called out to each other in the tribal language of queers. Shouts of, "Oh Mary!" "Girl!" and "She's too much!" floated by my space near the trash cans.

Anxiety lay beneath my grass-induced serenity. Deadly Chang the Chink was not happy with being stood up, and my blue-eyed bitch was pissed. I removed a small tinfoil wrapped roll of Red Devils from my hat lining. Opening my flask, I dropped three reds and washed them down with a swig of whiskey. I took another deep toke and tried to mellow out. I was dreading this confrontation with Bunny.

Entering the club, the music's bass beat engulfed me as the Red Devils kicked in. I checked myself out in the mirrored wall. Looking good in fine rags, my stoned eyes revealed an invincible cockiness. I adjusted my vest so it rested neatly over my beautiful charcoal gray sharkskin slacks. Tonight, I was packing a .38 and a dick. Carmen liked the feel of my dildo as it pressed against her when we slow danced. She also enjoyed knowing that I packed a revolver. As Carmen liked to say, "Nothing's sexier than a double packin' gangster butch."

As my eyes adjusted to the darkness, I spotted Bunny through the haze. At the bar, sitting between an adoring straight couple, was my tits n' pearl girl holding court.

Psychedelic lights swirled, shooting streams of light from the glittering ball hanging above the dance floor. The music was fast, but my friends were dancing slowly. They were too loaded and too cool to keep up with the beat.

The red walls of Chuckkers were decorated with the twelve signs of the Zodiac, painted in glittering gold and black lacquer. Above each booth was one of the heavenly constellations. Each star's logo could be seen from anywhere within the after-hours club. As the pulsing lights reflected off the symbols, they acted as beacons, making it easy for people to find each other in the darkness. I saw Carmen sitting at our favorite booth at the back of the club.

I maneuvered through the crowded club toward the bar. As I slowly made my way, I felt Carmen's eyes on me. I knew she got an inward tickle from watching my grand entrance through the club. My girl admired my arrogant strut. She'd often say to me, "Your attitude matches your walk. I am proud of the fact that you won't take any shit from any bitch, including myself."

Money was king, but it was chump change as far as motivators were concerned. The greatest intoxicator—what made selling your body and the price of the streets worth it—was that feeling of being cool. I believed the emotional drug of feeling hip was by far the best, badass dope.

As I sauntered up to the long bar, I passed the wannabe players who were terrified of me. I acknowledged the straight perverts who came down from the "Avenues" hunting for sex on a safari of lust.

The straight bitches at the bar put their tits in my face like stop signs to get my attention. Carmen watched as the wet bitches drooled, rubbing up against me. I stopped for a moment to say hi to the regular johns, greeting each one with a warm smile and an upbeat remark.

Coming up behind Bunny, my sexy CEO, I said, "I'm surprised to see you here tonight."

Bunny's dazzling platinum hair fell softly over her bare shoulders. She looked stunning in a bare-backed, low-cut short red dress. Dangling over her voluptuous breasts was a strand of pearls, milky-white like her soft skin. She was sipping a martini and smoking a cigarette in a long black cigarette holder. I interrupted her chat with a well-dressed man and woman sitting on either side of her. I could tell from the lustful look in their eyes that they would prefer her sandwiched between them in bed.

"Jesse honey, how fun it is to see you. I dropped by to chat with you for a second. I know Carmen's waiting for you and that you're still making your rounds, so I won't keep you. I must say, you look beautiful tonight," With a mischievous look in her brilliant baby blues, she grabbed her red rhinestone clutch and said to the couple at the bar, "I'm calling it a night. I just want a word with Jesse before I go."

Politely, the lustful perverts excused themselves to go dance, giving us a moment of privacy. With a look over her shoulder, the well-heeled lady said, "We would love to get together with you and Jesse later."

Bunny smiled sweetly at both of them as they merged into the crowded dance floor.

"Okay, girl, what's up?" I sat on the stool next to her. I lit up a smoke and waved off the approaching bartender saying, "No thanks, I'm going upstairs."

Bunny took the last sip of her martini and said breathlessly, "I hope you don't mind, but I've arranged something special; a show date for Carmen and Phyllis. Chang requested them specifically," she added, nodding to nail home the point. "His nephew is coming to San Francisco for a few days and he wants only the best. I guess the young man's a big fan of lesbian sex. Their being sisters would make it more delicious for him."

Still in the doghouse, I didn't tell her to fuck off immediately.

Bunny hurried on, not waiting for my response. "I'm sure you'll handle it, Jesse. Chang's such a dear. He doesn't ask for much."

Hearing the ice-cold edge behind her words, I panicked, knowing my jewelry store and business could be pulled out from under me.

"You can call me tomorrow and I'll fill you in on the details," she continued. Bunny popped off her stool, kissed me on the cheek and whispered, "Maybe you can come by my place later."

I was already angry because of her brazen request, but calmly, I met Bunny's seductive gaze. "Not tonight, honey. I'm not working. I'm taking the rest of the night off."

Bunny ignored the slap and replied, "Okay, I'll see you tomorrow."

As Bunny walked away, I looked for Carmen at our booth in the back. She was no longer there. She had probably gone ahead to our private meeting room upstairs to hang out with Rosie and Pearl. Carla, the owner of Chuckkers, let me use a private pool room upstairs for a small monthly fee. I headed upstairs, feeling trapped by my partner with the iron ovaries. Her non-jealous sexually-sharing femme act was wearing thin.

It seemed of late that Bunny, Little Rosie and Carmen had all caught the same jealousy bug. The previously well-defined emotional hierarchy among my whores was deteriorating. Bunny had just thrown me under the bus. Carmen would hate me if I asked her to have sex with her sister. The thought disgusted me as well.

"Femmes," I thought, "playing their catty games with each other." How could I say no? I was fucked if I did and fucked if I didn't. I reminded myself, pimps don't ask, they tell. Bunny had me by the balls. I would have to treat my girl Carmen like any other whore. It was too risky to say no to Bunny and her mob boss, not if Carmen and I were going to survive.

On the landing, I opened a door with a "Private Do Not Enter," sign and entered the small, sparsely furnished room. Little Rosie and Asian Pearl sat at the bar in front of the pool table. They were both dressed in tight miniskirts and low-cut blouses. The dolled-up ladies of the night were enjoying a drink and a doobie as they relaxed after work. Bottles of booze and half-filled glasses lined the counter.

Carmen stood next to the pool table, looking sexy. She was wearing a tight, forest-green blouse and a black micro-miniskirt. Her pool cue and four-inch stiletto heels gave her a hot, slutty look. Carmen's firm breasts pushed out against her skintight top as she leaned over the pool table to make a shot. She pointedly ignored me and focused on her solitary pool game.

Little Rosie lit up as I entered. "Hi Jesse, baby! I poured you a shot of Jack and a water back. This little girl is tired, baby. Pearl and I got every dime out of them fucking tricks tonight."

"Thanks, girls," I said as I caught a nod hello from Asian Pearl. I walked up to the small bar and downed my shot. Asian Pearl and Little Rosie's cash-filled matchbooks had been placed next to their drinks. I slid them both toward me and put them in my pocket.

Irritated by Carmen's cold reception, I walked over and snatched the pool stick out of her hand. Carmen's green eyes locked on me. Her voice was laced with contempt. "Nice of you to make it."

"I had business to take care of. I booked a show date for you and Phyllis to turn together," I said matter-of-factly, holding her stare.

Carmen looked confused for a moment, then quickly turned away.

"Fuck you!" she hissed through her red lips.

Suddenly, I slapped her. It came out of nowhere. The slap was hard enough to sting, but not to bruise. Thank God I was smart enough not to damage her face. Like everyone else on the street, we both knew you never damaged the merchandise.

"I'm not doing it!" she defiantly shouted, throwing her head back.

"What did you say, bitch?" I demanded intent on saving face in front of my other whores.

"You turn it, motherfucker!" she yelled at me.

Carmen spat in my face. Stunned, then furious, I grabbed her by the hair and pulled her toward me.

"Fuck you, bitch," I whispered in a cold rage.

Lust darted across Carmen's hostile stare, betraying a strong sexual jolt.

To teach her a lesson, I slapped her again, grabbed her and bent her over the pool table. Pinning her face down against the green felt of the pool table, I lifted up her skirt and ripped off her panties. I unzipped my trousers and pulled out my dildo, secure in its strap. I rammed my dick up into her, slamming it into her pussy.

With each forceful thrust I said, "I'm going to teach you a lesson, bitch, a good lesson bitch!" As I pushed her head down, I stuck my cock deep in her. I arched her back by pulling her long hair wrapped in my hand. I fucked her hard, fast and deep, slamming her face down with each thrust.

Pinned down, Carmen looked at the other whores through the strands of her hair. We both saw the envy and lust in their eyes as they stared. Carmen knew I wanted to humiliate her by raping her in front of my whores.

Defiantly, she glared up at me and grinned. She turned to Little Rosie and Pearl with a small smile on her face. "Eat your heart out, bitches! This is a real butch you're watching, honeys! She can fuck me in the ass if she feels like it. I'll take it because she loves me. Look closely, Rosie, because this is the only time you'll see passion from Jesse. She services your tired ass by fucking you. It's just business, bitch!"

Furious, I grabbed her shoulders and slammed her hard. As I pressed her face harder into the table, Carmen continued, "Watch closely, cunts! I own this daddy!"

I bent down and whispered into Carmen's ear, "What did you say?"

Carmen repeated, "Watch closely, cunts! This whore owns this daddy. Ladies, the real whore on the streets is the pimp!"

I was slapped by the truth. Carmen intuitively knew that the power I possessed over her was just an illusion. Like any woman, a prostitute or not, she was the real power broker in our relationship. Carmen was the realtor of our emotional property and her femininity owned the deed. The dominance that I displayed as her pimp didn't bother her in the slightest.

My moment of clarity deflated my rage. Straightening myself up, I stood silent in disgrace. Carmen got off the pool table and calmly adjusted her skirt. She brushed her hair back and faced me.

Without a word, she reached for my hand. Surprised a second time, I looked at her. Lending me her strength, she led me toward the door. She stopped in front of Little Rosie and Asian Pearl.

"What the fuck are you looking at!" Carmen demanded.

Our mutual embarrassment fused us as we fled down the steps. Loud music and psychedelic lights met us on Chuckkers dance floor. Letting go of my hand, she warned, "Don't fucking talk to me!" Carmen darted into the ladies' room.

That did it. I was on a mission. My sole aim was to get Bunny to rescind the request for the sisters' show date. I hurried out of the

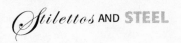

club. Running down Sixth Street, I made my way to Mission and flagged a cab.

As sanity slowly returned, I realized that my rage had been born from my fear of loss. I couldn't let Carmen walk all over me because I couldn't bear her inevitable rejection. My life and my lover would not tolerate weakness. I understood the trap we were both in. Power trumped love in this underbelly.

The downside of prostitution had reared its ugly head with Chang's perverted request. Bunny was in an awkward position too. Chang wasn't your everyday john. Risking his disapproval could be the last mistake anyone ever made. Beneath Bunny's cool demeanor was a genuine fear of the mob boss. I imagined it must have been difficult for her to ask me to inform Carmen of the booking. Bunny must have been aware that it would drive a wedge between Carmen and me.

The cab pulled up to Bunny's hilltop Victorian. The majestic view spanned the Golden Gate Bridge to the Coit Tower. Like a lawyer fighting the case of the century, I would ask Bunny to release Carmen and Phyllis from their obligation. Now was the opportune time to plead my case.

Chapter 21

FROM HERE TO NEXT SUNDAY

*L*ACE FROM **BUNNY'S BLACK NEGLIGEE TRAILED** over my face as my tongue played with her nipple. Bunny's milky soft breast filled my hand as my cock filled her pussy. The scent of Jungle Gardenia perfume lingered on her warm body as she whispered, "Don't stop, Jesse."

Bunny's breath matched the rhythm of her body as she rode me with passion. My nude body lay back on satin pillowcases in a womb of luxury. The evening sea breeze drifted through the open bay window.

In between Bunny's breathless soft moans, I said, "I'm a little concerned that Carmen and Phyllis might blow their show date. Those two are always arguing," I pointed out. "How can they convince those johns that they're enjoying hot sex with each other when they can't stop fighting for five minutes?"

"Jesse, Jesse, harder, harder," Bunny breathlessly begged. Rhythmically, she pushed into me, closing her eyes as I kissed her flushed face. Slight beads of perspiration dampened her forehead under her loose strands of platinum hair. Her flat stomach, under voluptuous firm breasts, made my attempt at persuasion a pleasurable task.

I started up again. I'd been working Bunny all weekend to set up this pitch. "Bunny, we can easily switch Phyllis with Linda from Missouri. They're both brunettes and the Chinese can't tell us apart anyhow."

Bunny's wet pink lips parted as she kissed my face and stretched up with me still inside her. She looked down with baby blues filled with rapture. "Did you say something, Jesse?"

Unsure of how to proceed, I tried a different approach. Remembering one of my mother's Ophelia's little life lessons—Flattery will get you everywhere—I said, "God, you have great tits."

She smiled down at me.

"Girl, you sure have that mob boss whipped. You could talk him into anything."

Holding her waist, I steadied her as she rose and fell, lost in lust. Her hands tightly grasped mine as she moved her body up and down on my dildo's shaft.

"I'm surprised that Chang came up with an incest act. That's so passé," I said casually.

"What?" she moaned as she pushed deeply into me. Her small hands grasped mine like rails.

With a whimper, as Bunny was reaching the height of her passion, she said between gasping breaths, "It's not passé." She leaned over me whispering, "You can still get top dollar for it."

I whispered sweet words of business into her ear, "Really? I didn't know there was still a strong market for it."

"Yes… yes…Jesse…fuck me, fuck me."

Bunny frantically rode me. Lost in ecstasy as she neared her finale, the truth slipped out, "I thought it was one of my better ideas."

"What did you say, Bunny?" I asked in disbelief.

Bunny's body ignored me as she fought to finish.

"Did you say it was your idea?" I demanded.

"Yes." She was bucking like a bronco. "Don't stop, don't stop," she moaned.

"Fuck you!" I said as I pushed her off, seconds before she came. I bounced her on her back and rudely pulled out. "You bitch! You played me!"

"Jesse, don't be upset with me," Bunny pleaded, desperately needing to get back on.

"I was a fucking chump! And to think, I was worried about your game-playin' ass!" I said in disgust. "I'm not a trick, bitch!"

I got dressed quickly, picked up my Zippo and snugged it in its pocket. Snatching my .38 off the nightstand, I rammed it in my holster.

Realizing I really was walking out, Bunny jumped up and grasped my shoulder. "Come back to bed. We can work this out."

I coolly put on my Stetson and said, "Don't play me ever again."

She sat silent and stunned on the side of the bed with blue balls.

I walked out and slammed the door. I left Bunny's pricey pad and headed back to the TL. I needed to make up with Carmen. I knew Bunny's possessiveness had gotten the better of her. I wasn't going to let her insecurities destroy my relationship with Carmen. Fury fueled my steps as I thought, "What a waste of good sex."

I caught a cab on Van Ness and in a few minutes I was walking into the Grapevine. Tuttle looked up from wiping the mahogany counter and grinned. Having recovered by this time, I gave a friendly nod to a couple of old guys sitting at the end of the bar. The two half-tanked neighborhood regulars were real diehard guzzlers. They were the only life in the joint at this late Sunday night hour. I asked old man Tuttle as I got up on my favorite stool, "Hey Tuttle, where's Rosie? I thought she'd be dancing."

Tuttle proceeded to set up my shooters with a water back. "Rosie has her panties all up in a wad about something. She told me she was too nervous to dance. Said she was lookin' for you."

I imagined Rosie was a little freaked out about my bizarre behavior the other evening with Carmen. Quickly downing a shooter, I hoped the whiskey would ease my aching head.

"She might as well be upset," I said. "The rest of my girls aren't that thrilled with me either. It's not easy having more than one woman to make happy."

Tuttle's eyes shined with childlike delight as he quipped, "Could be worse. At least your headaches come with matchbooks of cash."

Chuckling, I picked up my second shooter. "Bunny's a full-time job all by herself. I spent the weekend with her playing nice…had to get my balls out of a vice." I heard myself rhyming like Lovey Lupree as I downed another shot.

Tuttle didn't laugh with me this time. Instead, he turned serious. "I hate to bring this up, Jesse, but Carmen was in here last night smooching with the D.A."

"What! Oh, my God! All I wanna do is be able to work! These women are driving me crazy!"

"Yep, and Rosie said she really needs to talk with you. She was cussing in Spanish faster than Ricky Ricardo. That girl's acting more Puerto Rican than usual tonight. Rosie told me to tell you that if you show up while she's gone, to wait. She'll be coming right back."

"I don't think so, Tuttle. I'm not up for one more temperamental femme right now. I'm on my way to Chuckkers to meet Carmen. Tell Rosie I'll stop by before closing."

As I got up to leave, Tuttle went back to wiping the counter and gave me an encouraging word. "Carmen likes you in the doghouse. That way she knows where to find you. Have fun, Jesse." He gave me a broad smile goodbye. I dropped a bill on the bar and headed for the door.

Chapter 22

SWEET TALKIN' MAC DADDY

*A*FTER A BRISK, UNEVENTFUL WALK, I hit Club Chuckkers. Above the doorway loomed a large, new bright yellow sign: "ENTER AT YOUR OWN RISK, SUBJECT TO FREQUENT POLICE RAIDS."

"This is my kind of club," I thought. "I love this place; it's a real armpit." Sitting in front of me was Red the Biker, Chuckkers' doorman and part-time bouncer. Red sat at his post, enforcing the club's protocol of searching its patrons for weapons before they entered. I tripped on his ugly, pockmarked face, whose centerpiece was a purple-veined bulbous nose. Red asked me to raise my arms so he could search me.

"Sorry, Jesse, I mean no disrespect, but I'm going to have to search you."

"Hey Red, don't worry about it, I know the drill."

His frisking didn't bother me. It felt good not to be completely trusted. The person searching you was letting you know they were afraid of you.

Miss Carla, a drag queen and the gay club's owner, was not about to trust a bad actor like me in this unpredictable world of the Tenderloin. The last thing Carla needed was a shooting in her joint. Since Red was secretly on my payroll, he went through the motions simply for appearances. Red proceeded with his bogus pat-down, ignoring my gun.

"Hey, Jesse, watch your back. The pigs are having a field day busting you dykes. If you don't believe me, go ask Two Bits how she liked touring the alley on her face last night. The cops raided us and snatched Two Bits. They took her in the back and handcuffed her to their bumper. Then they went for a joy ride, dragging her down the alley. When they cut her loose, I hardly recognized that kid. Her face looked like a used dartboard!"

When he said that, even though I felt for Two Bits, I couldn't help but laugh. She was a pissed-off cop's dream; a hippie and a dyke.

"You better get your ass moving. Your old lady is in the back waiting for you and she doesn't look too happy."

"Thanks, Red." Appreciating the warning, I slipped him a twenty-dollar bonus. As he grabbed the money, I saw his dirty fingernails and just shook my head, thinking, "Poor Red, what's up with bikers? Are they allergic to soap and water?"

Aloud, I said, "Thanks for the heads-up about Carmen. Look Red, Little Rosie might show up tonight. If she does, don't let her in. Whatever you do, don't let her get her little Puerto Rican ass past you."

Red answered with an intense, "Righteous, righteous, right on, you got it man, no problem!"

I pulled out the Saint Christopher medal from around my neck and said a silent prayer for courage. Sitting directly beneath the glistening hooves of the powerful black bull on the wall was my favorite little Taurus. Carmen was nursing a drink and by the expression on her face, keen resentment as well.

Keeping my eyes focused on the last booth in the back, I crossed the dance floor. I felt a twinge of guilt for my Marquis de Sade behavior toward Carmen but was careful not to let my face show my feelings. I knew all too well that in this neighborhood, looking soft would be the equivalent of signing my own death warrant.

I looked right into her eyes and said in the sweetest, softest voice, "You sure look beautiful tonight. I have a little something for you." I fumbled like a blind man searching his pockets, looking for the gift.

With a desperate attempt to charm her I said, "My mind isn't functioning very well right now. I can't think, I can't even see! I am blinded by your beauty, young lady…hold on a minute, I think found it, honey…" And with that, I pulled out a small golden box.

Carmen didn't even look at it. I could see she was still furious with me. So quickly, I put the box back in my pocket.

"Jesse, you think your little song and dance is going to wash away the self-righteous looks on those dumb whores' faces?" Carmen asked sullenly. "I can still see those gawking cunts." In a mock Puerto Rican accent, she imitated Little Rosie, "I'd never say no to a show date for thousands of dollars, that's for sure! Uh-huh, baby!" Carmen snapped her fingers.

Nervously, I laughed at Carmen's dead-on imitation.

"Jesse, how the hell could you expect me to fuck my own sister?" Carmen asked with hurt in her voice.

I tried to explain. "At first I didn't know how I'd say no to Chang."

"You mean say no to your mommy, don't you Jesse?" Carmen sniped back.

Her dig about Bunny was right-on, and I came clean. "I am sorry. I really am. I wasn't thinking clearly. What I asked of you was wrong."

Carmen betrayed a small smile as she slowly turned her eyes toward me.

Encouraged by her response, I continued. "Believe me; I won't let it happen again. The bottom line is…you don't have to turn the date. I took care of it."

Carmen didn't reply but at least now she was looking at me. I took the opportunity to say something that I knew would shock her. "Carmen, please forgive me. I was wrong."

Carmen started to choke on her drink. Putting her glass down, she wheezed and shook her head. "I can't believe it," she laughed as she moved over toward me and put her hand right between my legs. She squeezed the top of my inner thigh as she rested her face on my shoulder and innocently said, "Okay honey, let me see what you're hiding in your pocket."

Smiling at Carmen's sexual suggestion, I put my arm around her and felt the closeness of her body. I let out a small sigh of relief as I kissed the side of her neck and breathed in her intoxicating scent.

I gently set the small golden box on the table. She didn't move. She just said, "You open it for me, honey."

I held her hand and slowly opened the box, exposing two exquisite emerald earrings. Each earring was a full four carats of dazzling dark green radiance encased in a stunning gold setting. They sparkled brilliantly, seducing Carmen to pick them up and put them on. The stones looked like perfect companions for Carmen's petite, beautiful ears.

Instead of taking them, Carmen shot me a skeptical look. "Jesse, where in the hell did you get these earrings from? I know you didn't take them from your shop. You'd never take jewels from your own inventory. They're beautiful all right, but what? Did some straight bitch you fucked give them to you?"

"I didn't fuck any straight bitch for these! Carmen, you wound me deeply. Of course no other girl ever wore these earrings. I went to my man, John Chow. I told that dude, 'Give me the best stones we got. Bury my ass. Here's a shovel. I'll pay any price.'" I threw my hands up in the air to impress Carmen. "I told him, 'Rob me, man! Treat me like a trick. These are for my girl.'"

Carmen started laughing as she took the earrings out of the box, tilted her head and put one on. She pulled her hair behind her ear so I could get a good look at the sparkling peace offering. Giggling, she asked, "Does it look good on me?"

"Wait a minute, let me get a really good look," I replied. Leaning over, I began to softly kiss her beautifully adorned ear.

At that moment Kitty, the barmaid, came up to us, carrying a tray of drinks and appearing flustered.

"Jesse, sorry I was late getting to your table. I got tied up outside in front of the club helping Red deal with Little Rosie. She's been raising hell out there. She says that she needs to talk to you and won't take no for an answer. Red is having one hell of a time. Here's your drinks, baby, two shots of Jack Daniel's with a water back, just as you like it. And Carmen, honey, here's another Tom Collins for you."

"That Rosie can sure be a handful," I told Kitty. "Thanks for letting me know."

I knew Kitty loved serving me because she loved my big tips. I figured she earned them, due to the fact that she was able to keep her balance, carrying a tray of drinks on those come-fuck-me high heels she wore.

I downed a shooter and asked Kitty, "Baby, how do you keep those lovelocks of yours piled up on that pretty head? I think you're in the wrong occupation. You should be teaching those queens how to do their hair."

Kitty lit up like a sparkler on the fourth of July. "Jesse, you're so bad. If Carmen wasn't sitting next to you, this old bitch might be throwing you her panties."

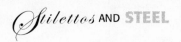

Carmen smiled. "What do you think of Jesse's little something for me?" She pulled back her hair and touched her ear to show off the emerald earrings.

When Kitty saw them, her mouth fell open. I thought she was going to drop her tray. She nearly lost her balance as she leaned forward with those big tits of hers.

"Girl, let me see them. Oh my God, they're absolutely beautiful! If Rosie hears about them, we're going to have to get more bouncers."

I was enjoying their bantering back and forth, but I was concerned about Little Rosie outside. I took out my money clip, handed Kitty a twenty and said to her, "Would you do me a favor and go call Junior at Compton's? Tell her to come over here and escort Rosie back to the Grapevine." Irritated, I added, "Tell Rosie I'll talk with her later tonight if she gets her ass back to work. You got that, Kitty?"

Kitty chuckled as she took the twenty and stuffed it between her breasts. "I'll take care of it right away, Jesse."

As Kitty started to walk away, she turned and said to Carmen, "By the way girl, those earrings are drop-dead gorgeous. Jesse must really love you."

Carmen looked happy and relaxed as she took another sip of her drink. The rhythm of the music pulsed through my body, and the Jack Daniel's found its way to my head. I was happy to have won my lover's heart once again. Bathed in Carmen's femininity, I rested my hand on my girl's thigh as I slowly leaned over toward her. Our soft lips met. We had survived another test.

Chapter 23

MISSING IN ACTION

USTY TOBACCO HAZE FILLED THE CAVE-LIKE LOUNGE of the Grapevine. Red flickering candles on the tables looked like landing strip lights leading to the stage. A small group of men at a center table sang along in off-key voices to Tom Jones' "What's New Pussycat?"

Like a cheap production of a Puccini opera, Little Rosie dramatically acted out each lyric as she danced. The dangling black pasties which covered her nipples swayed with passion as she sang back to the men. "You're so thrilling and I'm so willing to care for you…" Every time Little Rosie wailed, "Whoa, whoa," with a swish of her hips, she got a tip.

I was happy to see that Little Rosie had calmed down enough to hit the stage. Junior was sitting at the bar. Her white Stetson was sitting next to an amber-colored glass filled with scotch and soda.

Junior turned around as if she could sense me approach. I greeted her with genuine warmth, happy to see her smiling face. "Thanks, Junior. I heard Rosie has been a real piece of work tonight."

Taking the tall barstool next to Junior, I tapped the wooden counter. I gave a welcome wink and smile to the cheerful old bartender as I pulled out my Pall Malls and enjoyed a cig. Tuttle set up my usual with a smile and moved to the end of the bar to serve another customer.

My soft-spoken henchman started speaking. "Jesse, I think Rosie is pissed off at you for showing Carmen so much attention over the pool table." Junior's otherwise stoic face lit up with a mischievous grin. I could detect a spark of admiration in her eyes.

Junior continued, "I think she's jealous and just tripping. She's dying to talk to you."

"I don't know what's up," I said.

"Fuckin' femmes," Junior sighed. "Rosie said she'll only tell you what's up."

Replying with a like-minded nod, I drank one of my shooters.

The booze went down my throat and the warmth slowly spread through my chest as I listened to Junior run on about femmes.

My irate Puerto Rican mama suddenly interrupted us, wearing a cheetah skin-halter top and black skintight pants. Her verbal assault nearly knocked me off my stool.

"Thank God you're here. Why wouldn't you see me? Shit's coming down, baby."

"Calm down, girl. Tell me what's happening."

"My mink! Poof, it's gone! Those limp-dick bastards boosted my sisters! They snatched their asses! Deep shit is coming down! Where you been, baby? They could be chopped up by now!"

I grabbed Rosie by the shoulders and shook her. Sternly, I ordered Rosie, "Breathe! Slow down! Just tell me what's up!"

Rosie sniveled, took a deep breath and said, "They kidnapped Pearl…they got the hick too. We've gotta get Asian Pearl back!"

"Hold on, girl. Who got who?" I asked anxiously.

"Prince and his crank-head, loco brother Giuseppe," Rosie exclaimed. "I saw their ugly purple Caddy prowling around. Asian

Pearl and Linda from Missouri blew the gig at the Hilton last night. They never showed up. Get me a drink, would ya? I'm scared. I don't know what's going on, but we've got to find them."

"Come sit your pretty little ass down next to me. I'll get you a drink. Baby, calm down. Everything is going to be okay."

"Oh, *papi*, I'm so scared. I don't want to go missing next," cried Rosie. I watched her struggle, trying to get on the tall stool, even though she had on four-inch stiletto heels. She had to grab my arm to pull herself up.

I jerked my head back, downing another shot and trying to drown a sudden jolt of fear. "Pearl is a top-notch professional. She never blows a good date," I said to Junior.

"Jesse, Little Rosie seems to really believe that Prince kidnapped them!" exclaimed Junior. "Boss, do you think he would be loco enough to do that?"

I flashed back to the confrontation we had with Prince on Taylor Street. "I'm going to put some runners on the street and we're going to find out."

Junior nodded with an anxious look in her black eyes.

"I have to get over to the house right away," I told her. "I'm not taking any chances. I need to alert Bunny and Marie to the situation. Get everybody over to the house in an hour. It's Sunday, so it's empty.

"Have the bikers hit the streets. Offer a five-hundred-dollar reward for information about the whores' whereabouts. I'll see you in Chinatown. Got it?"

"I got it!"

The thought of needing extra muscle sparked another one. "By the way, Junior, tell Red to bring that one-eyed Indian who wants a job with him."

"I'm on it, it's done!"

"Don't shoot your mouth off to the other girls," I cautioned Rosie. "I will handle this."

"Okay, baby. I'm gonna go backstage and find a sweater," Rosie replied as she got up and headed towards the back.

Leaving the bar, I stepped off the curb into the gutter, edgily looking for Nick, who had dropped me off. The Buick pulled up and violently lurched to a stop in front of me. Through the windshield I saw the rattling spiritual paraphernalia on his dashboard recover from Nick hitting the brakes.

I hopped into the back seat and said, "Shit, are you trying to take me out, man?"

The Greek chuckled. "Sorry, boss."

I leaned against the warm cracked vinyl seats, so relieved to get out of the cold and my head.

The always cheerful Nick turned halfway over the front seat and asked, "What's your pleasure, Jesse?"

"Take me over to the house, right away."

"You got it, boss."

Nick rubbed his Saint Christopher, patted Jesus, threw down the meter and slammed on the gas. The tires screeched as the big V-8 roared away from the curb. We shot down Geary Street toward Chinatown. Nick glanced at my reflection while he adjusted his rearview mirror. "Jesse, are you okay?"

"You didn't happen to see Asian Pearl and Linda from Missouri tonight did you?"

"No, I haven't seen either one of them since I dropped both of them off in front of the Booker T. Washington Hotel yesterday night. I remember hearing Linda from Missouri arguing with Asian Pearl. Linda wanted to meet some guy at the bar, but Pearl said they didn't have time to fuck around."

"Did she say who the guy was?"

"No, Jesse, I don't know who the dude was. I just know that Linda from Missouri was very excited. The guy had extra tickets for the Jefferson Airplane concert at the Fillmore Auditorium. Traffic was a nightmare!"

"Linda from Missouri is a wannabe hippie," I said. "She loves the Jefferson Airplane."

My fifty-five-year-old street racer replied, "Asian Pearl didn't sound like she liked the group. She screamed at Linda, saying that they were just a bunch of acid heads that talk to rabbits." Looking genuinely confused, he asked, "How do they talk to rabbits? Is it some kind of a magic show?"

"No," I said, laughing. "They do sing about magic in a way, though... magic mushrooms, that is."

Nick scratched his head as he continued, "To shut Linda up, Pearl finally agreed to go with her to pick up the tickets. Pearl told me not to wait for them. She said she would be getting a ride. Hope that was cool, Jesse."

I started praying to Saint Christopher, the patron saint of travelers, for Pearl and Linda's safe return.

When I was done, I said, "It's cool, Nick. But if you see either one of them, bring them to me, okay?"

"You got it, boss!"

***

The eyes of the white polar bear stared at me, glazed and glassy. The once majestic creature was spread out in front of the fireplace. It probably never occurred to him while loping across the white arctic ice that he would end up in a Chinatown bordello.

I realized how clever Marie was to place the beautiful white bear rug here. It must have acquired untold revenue for the house, as the johns' dicks got harder and harder from their sense of power as they stood on the dead beast. The primal drive was connected to man's genetic memory from his Neanderthal days. The caveman had to go out and kill the bear, drag it into the cave, grab the woman by the hair and then pull her in and fuck her. Nowadays, all he needed was cash and a cab so he could stand on the bear and negotiate a fuck. There was a lot to be said for progress.

Jujubees fluttered into the parlor and interrupted my private musing on the bear.

"What's up, Jujubees?"

Appearing exasperated, Jujubees replied, "Miss Jesse, I have everything ready for the meeting. I don't want to complain, but I have nothing to serve but Southern Comfort. The whole bar has been stripped. The Jack Daniel's, the scotch, the liqueurs, everything is hidden in the kitchen. Marie said nothing's better on a cold night than Southern Comfort. I don't want you getting upset, Miss Jesse, but this southern bit is too much."

"Jujubees, Marie gets in a rut a little, but she's a great madam. I appreciate your input and I might bring it up to her. In the meantime, would you go into the kitchen and sneak me some Jack?"

Jujubees smiled, grateful for the acknowledgment. "Right away, Miss Jesse."

Taking a sip of my drink, I thought about my troops. We were a well-organized machine of society's castaways. My Tenderloin army was an elect division of women engaging our enemies. Like young brave soldiers, we were a seasoned group of skilled street fighters. Banding together, we avoided capture while living in an occupied territory of the straight world. In spite of petty bickering amongst my girls, we were united like a family. We would fight the male pimps for the same cause: individual freedom.

I heard a knock at the front door.

Marie asked, "What's your code?"

"My code, my dear, is four, five, six, seven. I can send you to heaven," sang Lovey Lupree.

Marie greeted the Creole pimp. "Hello, Lovey."

"I asked the cab driver to take me to Chinatown, but he must've dropped me off at heaven's door. Marie, you look like an angel."

"May I put away your umbrella, you charmer?"

"No, my dear, I prefer to keep it by my side," Lovey replied in her eloquent New Orleans drawl.

Lovey always carried a camel-colored umbrella. Hidden in the tip was a razor-sharp retractable knife blade. When pressure was applied, it poked out quickly and cut whatever had induced its release.

Lovey entered the parlor. "Jesse, are you okay? Where's Carmen tonight?"

Jujubees obliviously interrupted Lovey's serious inquiry. "Miss Lovey, why don't you give Jujubees your umbrella? Let me bring you a little Southern Comfort."

Lovey quickly transformed to a smoldering Mount St. Helens volcano. Lovey whispered back through gritted teeth, "I don't drink Southern Comfort. Do I look like a redneck to you? I only drink scotch and soda."

Not to be intimidated by a pissed-off pimp with a knife in her umbrella, Jujubees swirled out of the room, shouting over his shoulder, "Scotch and soda, coming up!"

We heard Marie call out, "Who's there? I can't hear you. Speak up."

Bunny shouted, "It's Bunny!"

"What's your code?"

"Six, nine, two…, you know I'll take care of you!"

Bunny's hushed tones floated into the parlor, as she breathlessly asked Marie, "Is Jesse here?"

Marie whispered protectively, "She's in the parlor."

I stood as the little lady entered the parlor. My spirit rose the moment I saw her. Cheerful energy followed her like the train of a happy bride. She projected a calm, take-charge attitude.

"I heard the girls are missing. Don't worry, we'll figure this out. Hi Jesse, glad to see you." She hugged me and kissed my awaiting lips. Then seductively, she whispered into my ear, "You left in such a hurry the other night... you forgot your coat."

I replied softly, "Yeah, I was a little hot under the collar."

Pacified by my sincerity, she replied, "Yes, I thought so. I have your coat in the car. I'll give it to you when I drive you home."

Satisfied that we were back on track, she reached over and hugged Lovey in greeting. She stepped back to take in the full view of Lovey's suit. "My, Lovey, don't you look handsome. Love your suit, child. Your shirt is almost the same shade of pink as my cashmere sweater."

Lovey gave a low, gallant, Sir Walter Raleigh bow and said genteelly, "You humble me, lady." Her tooth, like a beacon, shone as she smiled. "Please forgive me, but it pales in comparison to the beauty of your attire. I feel like a peasant in a field dressed in rags next to your stylish self."

Bunny kissed her lovingly on the cheek as she breathlessly replied, "You are a charmer."

A loud ruckus erupted in the hall. Jujubees cried, "Drop the Spanish inquisition act or we'll be in this hallway all night, Miss Marie. It's Red and those other dumb bikers."

In a steely tone laced with venom, Marie reminded Jujubees that she was the lady of the house. "If you don't want to find your faggoty, prima donna ass outside the door, I would suggest you concentrate on your job. In case you forgot what that is, it's being a houseboy."

Jujubees flew by, hands on his hips, muttering, "Just no respect, no respect."

Bunny, Lovey and I laughed in unison at Jujubees as we heard a pounding on the door.

Marie's voice adamantly asked, "Who's there?"

Red's whiskey-soaked voice grunted through the peephole. "It's Red. I'm here with Animal and Joe Gomez, the dude from the rock. It's okay, Jesse wants to see him."

"What's your code?"

"A hundred-and-one and you're done."

A breeze rippled into the parlor as the door opened. We listened to the heavy clamoring of chained boots as they stomped over the wooden floor. In nervous anticipation, we awaited the entrance of the "Gomez Rexsaurus."

Flanking the notorious gangster were Red and Animal. I found it amazing that those two bikers, as ferocious as they were, had been reduced to meek biker escorts. I greeted the trio of muscle warmly. "Hello, boys, glad you could make it."

Red said proudly, "Hi, Jesse, thought you'd like that I brought Joe Gomez with me. Junior said you wanted to interview him for a job."

"You're right, Red. I'm glad to see you, Gomez. I have wanted to talk to you." I then acknowledged Red's brother, Animal, the leader of the TL biker gang.

Joe Gomez said to me, "I'm happy to be of service. All the boys on the yard spoke very highly of you."

One look at Joe revealed why he inspired such fear in everyone. He moved and spoke with the precision of a short, stocky tank. His gaze in his one visible eye was unflinching. The other was covered with a large, black V-shaped patch.

The intensity of the one eye glared at you as he spoke in a voice that you knew camouflaged pure violence. The black eye-patch strap wrapped around his wide head over slick black hair that was pulled into a ponytail. Under Joe's patch was a huge, thick scar that caressed his brown cheek, running from his lip to the bottom of his ear.

Legend had it that when he was really pissed, the flat wide nostrils in his bull-like nose would flare open, and the hippies swore that they had seen smoke come out of them. Many a night, the hippies as well as other street people had seen Joe in action, when he would take out half the guys in a biker bar, bare-handed, just for exercise.

I admiringly viewed the tattooed monster in front of me and then spontaneously slugged him in the arm. I felt my fist hit pure brick, as if I were a gnat flying into Godzilla. The one-eyed halfbreed just as spontaneously punched me back in the arm with a short, soft blow and said, "Fuckin'-A. You are one fuckin' crazy bitch! Pure balls! No wonder why you run the TL."

In my childhood, I would playfully spar with my dad and older brother, and I felt at home with this maniac. Maybe it was also my inherent respect for mean Yaqui Indians. I grew up listening to my Spanish grandmother telling stories about Yaquis, who would attack a train and kill everyone on board for their jewels. My grandmother's sister barely escaped with her life in the early 1920s in Durango, Mexico, when Yaquis attacked the first-class compartment of her train. Joe was half Yaqui, and I thought how fortunate I would be to have him in my army.

Like a group of guests at a festive party, Bunny, Lovey, the bikers and I stood outside the dining room. Jujubees, not to miss any of the action, excitedly eyed Joe up and down. I recognized a hint of lust in the Filipino's gleaming eyes as he flirtatiously addressed the ex-con. "Mr. Gomez, welcome to the Tara of the West." He seductively touched his gardenia and continued, "Please follow me to the dining room."

With his best Barbara Stanwyck turn and a sexy shaking of his ass, he led the trio of denim-clad, long-haired, burly bearded bikers to the table. Bunny and Lovey followed them and sat at the mahogany table. Within moments the rest of my army had assembled.

Rascal walked in wearing a burgundy pinstriped-suit. Adorning her head was an umbrella-sized black fedora. Her sidekick sported a conservative three-piece suit. From under a pushed-back hat, Little Bastard's smile lit up the room.

"Boss, look at my new shoes!" Rascal proudly lifted up her foot. Her deeply polished burgundy alligator shoe was actually the size of a small alligator.

"You're tabbed back, dressed to kill," I replied with a wink.

Walking to the head of the table, I pulled out the heavy, cushioned mahogany armchair and sat down. I asked Marie to sit next to me.

The southern belle floated on her feet as if waltzing in a grand ballroom. She took her place and gazed up at me like a woman in church listening to the preacher for her salvation.

Bunny, in her hot pink cashmere sweater and tight little black miniskirt, walked like a queen to the opposite end of the table and sat down. The noisy, heavy-booted, leather and chain-clad men pulled back their chairs and I patiently allowed everyone to settle in under the large glittering chandelier.

"I want to thank all of you for coming tonight on such short notice. Rosie alerted me that Asian Pearl and Linda from Missouri are missing. As you know, there are a lot of rumors going around that Prince and his boys are trying to take over the Tenderloin. It's too soon to know if our girls are in trouble or if they're just flaking out. Either way, they're MIA."

Little Rosie said excitedly, "That's scary. That's why I warned Jesse!"

"That's cold," said Red, growling to the group. "Fuck them punks!"

Animal shouted, "My boys will kill the motherfuckers!"

I waited for the uproar to die down. "I want you to find them. Get the word out on the streets that I'm offering a five-hundred-dollar reward for information leading to their whereabouts. This is top priority! Lovey, you cover the Fillmore district, and Junior, you handle North Beach."

"I'll get the word out, Jesse. Five Bennies is the score for finding missing whores," Lovey rhymed.

"You got it, boss," Junior replied.

"Because of our success, the lowlife, wannabe lightweight chump-change pimps are envious of us," I continued. "When we were broke, no one was upset. Now that we're stylin', Prince wants to fuckin' tax our asses!"

I waited for the wails of indignation around the table to fade.

"As you all know," I said, "Prince and his crank-head, pimple-faced brother Giuseppe, are trying to push us out of the Tenderloin. They're not gonna put their fat-ass whores on our streets!"

There was a spontaneous burst of applause. I took my drink and said, "We'll drink to that."

I took a sip of my drink and watched my motley band sip theirs.

"Animal, why don't you give us your two-cents' worth?"

"I'm the leader of the bikers. We're Jesse's enforcers. My job is to break anyone's skull who fucks with us. I keep the peace so no one hassles Jesse and her girls."

Joe Gomez, in a low, coarse voice said, "I don't break skulls. I tear their fuckin' heads off! I cram them up their asses! I cut their balls off and shove them down their throats! I skin them alive and feed their flesh to my dogs!"

All eyes fixed on him as we held our breath, terrified. The room fell dead silent. The ferocious Indian's eye squinted as he snarled, spitting across the table.

"Don't even think of fuckin' with me or one of my people! I'm from the old school. That's why they call me a dinosaur. If I take a vow of loyalty, I guard my boss with my life!"

Joe suddenly jumped up and backed away from the table. He dramatically grabbed the bottom of his shirt and jerked it above his waist, showing a massive muscular abdomen covered in deep scars and crude prison-style tattoos.

He stuck his forefinger into a deep hole under his rib cage and said, "See this fuckin' hole here? Some dumb-ass poked me with a knife. I pulled the knife out myself and skinned the chump alive with it."

Marie, Little Rosie, Junior and I quickly made the sign of the cross as Little Bastard's mouth fell open. Even Rascal, who was quietly nibbling on cheese, stopped chewing.

Joe solemnly announced, "I took my time skinning him and made my ancestors proud." Then he sat down again, crossed his huge arms over his massive chest and frowned from his bitter memories.

In hopes of soothing my anxious crew's frayed nerves, I gave Joe a warm smile of approval. "Mr. Gomez, you are a pride to your race, your family and your ancestors. I have never seen such beautiful scars on any human being. I'd much rather have you work for us than against us. You'll find I don't like violence. I only use it as a last resort, but without respect in the Tenderloin, you're dead." That reminded me of something I wanted to ask him. "Do you mind if I ask you a question?"

Joe studied me with his one eye like the jury wasn't in yet. "Go ahead and ask."

"How do you feel about working for a woman?"

He waved off that problem with the chop of his hand. "I'm here because women are smarter than men. I don't want to do any more time. I need a legitimate job with a boss that has the clout to keep me out of the joint."

That made sense to me, so I assured my new bodyguard, "I can hire you as a driver for our jewelry store so your parole officer will know you're working. Can you drive with one eye? Do you have a license?"

Joe laughed. "Sure, I have a fuckin' license, and when I drive, people stay out of my way."

"I believe you, Joe," I said sincerely. "I was also wondering if you'd be comfortable working for a gay woman."

He shook his head rapidly. "Jesse, my sister is a queer and she raised me. I love her. Some horny Pachuco in our barrio didn't treat her right, though. The bastard beat and raped my sister when he found out she was queer. I tied him to the same bed he raped her on and I fed him each of his balls, one at a time. I washed them down his throat with his own blood."

I gently responded, "I understand."

Joe continued, "That's why I did the time on the rock. I don't like dudes who fuck with queers."

"That's very cool, Joe," I said, becoming aware that my foot was tapping the floor double-time. Silently, my crew waited as I contemplated my decision. An association with Joe would open the door to a sewer of humanity. I'd be waist-deep with an evil sadist.

But Tenderloin history was heavy with tales of murdered women, shot in the head and dumped like trash. If we were to survive, I had to act decisively.

I asked Joe, "Will you pledge your loyalty and join my troops?"

"I'm at your service, man. Respect...respect," Joe solemnly swore.

"I want to welcome Joe to the family!" I announced. As the convict nodded like a pleased bear, everyone clapped. Right-ons and far-outs rippled down the table.

I held my glass high and said, "Let's toast to Joe!"

Chapter 24

SUTTER STREET

*T*HE HALL THAT LED TO MY APARTMENT in the graceful Victorian on Sutter Street was long, dark and empty. I walked in the silence of the sleeping building feeling as empty as the corridors. I was engulfed in the same loneliness that I often felt when I walked through the cold streets of the Tenderloin at night. The hole in my gut felt like the wind could howl through it. The subtle, elusive ache floated under the booze and drugs, ever reminding me that I was on my own.

I couldn't shake the emptiness as I thought about recent events. I knew the meeting had gone well and that I was lucky to have an army at my command. Yet I also knew that playacting like a gangster was ending. It was becoming the real deal.

At the elevator, I pressed the round white button. I patiently waited for the cranky old machine to groan down from the top floor. After a muffled thump, the ornate brass cage door appeared in front of me. I pulled it open and stepped inside the gaudy 1940s-style elevator, so uniquely San Francisco, and pressed the bold black number three on the brass plate. My humanity was getting as rusty as the gears in the elevator that brought me to the third floor.

Walking into the apartment, I was hit with the scent of fresh flowers. Daisies and tulips accented my place from room to room.

Like gentle little friends, the green vases and brilliant flowers welcomed me home.

My spirits lifted as I thought about what my witty younger brother, Max always said, "If you take a nice piece of cheesecake and put it in the refrigerator next to a pastrami sandwich, in the morning it's going to smell like pastrami." I guess you could say that I had been thoroughly "pastrami-ized". The thought of Max lightened my mood.

Removing my Stetson, I hung it on a wooden peg beside the front door. Taking off my coat, I struggled with the large, pearl buttons, forcing them through the tight slits in my camel-hair coat. I felt restrained in the heavy jacket in the warm entrance hall, trying to get free of it and keep my balance at the same time. I steadied myself by grabbing the coat rack, closing my eyes and feeling like a drunken cartoon character hanging onto a lamppost.

Starting my strip act, I fought with the buttons on my French-cuffed shirt. I shook my head, took a deep breath and gave myself a pep talk so I could handle the daunting task of removing the tight Ace bandage wrapped around my chest. I followed the tips of my alligator shoes like a compass guiding me to my bedroom.

I closed one eye to steady myself, an old trick I had learned driving as a drunken teenager through the streets of Woodland Hills. I had become a master at eliminating the double line in the single-line highway by using my hand as a patch over my eye. I smiled inwardly as I realized I was now exactly like my new employee, Joe Gomez, with the one eye.

Dropping my sharkskin suit jacket on the floor, I struggled with my onyx and gold cufflinks. I realized I was not up to the task as I saw my bed beckoning to me like a welcoming lover with outstretched arms.

I zeroed in on the four-poster canopy bed and made a dive like a high jumper, gauging my perfect flight up and over the footboard. I was enjoying this act of defiance, knowing I could never do this if Carmen were in the bed. She was always concerned I would mess up the beautiful silk canopy. The pattern displayed images of voluptuous Renaissance women. I landed safely between the plump pillows which lay like mountains on the bed.

Carmen and I had argued about the need for ten pillows for one fuckin' bed. I had lost that battle and so found myself sitting partially upright. This was a good thing because I needed to pull off the makeshift elastic girdle around my chest.

The tight binder flattened my breasts so my chest looked like a young man's and enabled my beautiful shirts to fit well. Still struggling with my cufflinks, which now felt like handcuffs, I finally dislodged them. Like Houdini, I ripped off my shirt and threw it on the floor.

Pulling off my binder, I tossed it across the room. It hit my statue of St. Francis of Assisi on top of my dresser. The Ace bandage bounced off the poor saint's face and landed perfectly on a little gold trophy Carmen had given me. The plaque read: "World's Greatest Lover."

I admired my excellent marksmanship as my suppressed breasts popped to attention with their liberation. I lay on my back as my nipples pointed up, feeling the cool breeze of fresh air. Gazing up, I studied the nipples of the nude lady above me on the canopy. With a final act of exertion, I kicked off my shoes. I closed my eyes and drifted into an intoxicated sleep.

I woke from my drunken snooze at the sound of Asian Pearl yelling, "Jesse! Jesse!" I opened my eyes and saw a pair of nipples painted on the canopy above me. Doubting my senses, I closed my eyes and wondered if I was dreaming, if I was hearing things, or if it really was Asian Pearl doing the yelling. Whatever it was, all I knew for sure was that I wanted to go back to my pleasant sleep.

Just as I started to escape back into my slumber, I heard a noisy knock at the door, chased by the screams of an irate Asian whore who demanded, "Jesse, let me in!"

I yelled back, "Hold on!" Stumbling out of bed, I went over to the dresser to get my gun. Shaking my head in an attempt to clear my foggy brain, I leaned against the door and listened. With my heart pounding, I bravely asked, "Is that you, Pearl?"

Pearl answered anxiously, "Yes, Jesse! It's Pearl. Linda from Missouri is with me."

I shouted back through the door, "Wait a minute! I'll be right with you!" I scrambled towards the closet. My bare chest made me feel caught, nude and vulnerable as I stood there without my binder on. I threw open the closet door, grabbed a bad boy, "James Dean-type" dark blue shirt, streaked with red flames, and put it on in a hurry. I was not about to be caught in a crisis with my tits out.

Feeling the weight of the .38 in my hand, I wrapped my finger around the trigger, in case the bitches had company. I rested my cheek against the front door and looked through the peephole at the distorted-looking figures waiting to get in.

I cracked open the door, leaving the chain on, and looked down the hallway, searching for the enemy. I felt Asian Pearl's hot breath in my face as she leaned through the crack and shouted, "Jesse, hurry, let us in!"

Reaching up, I unlatched the little gold chain and released it. I tucked my .38 into my belt, feeling the cold, hard edge of the muzzle against my groin. The two lost girls both looked disheveled and haggard. The fear on Pearl's hardened face set off an alarm in my gut.

Pearl hurried into the living room. "That fucking Giuseppe had our asses trapped for days! We've been in hell!"

Linda from Missouri followed in step and sang out the word, "Hell!"

I found myself trailing behind the tall, plump hooker who hobbled bowleggedly. As usual, Asian Pearl's high-teased bouffant of curly lovelocks had red dragon chopsticks sticking out of them, but the normally calculating ice princess was clearly distraught. Linda, the naïve untainted child of the Midwest, seemed traumatized as she obediently trailed after Pearl. The look on Linda's face made me think of a scene in an old Western movie in which the hollow-eyed children come out of hiding after an Indian attack.

I let my shell-shocked troops roam through my apartment. Pearl crossed the living room and stopped in front of the cherry wood English-styled bar whose glass top was covered in bottles of expensive liquor and crystal barware. She poured herself and her sister in prostitution a tall glass of scotch.

I watched in amazement as this Asian woman downed the scotch like a truck driver in one long chug-a-lug. Linda followed suit. After refilling their glasses, the two disheveled whores plopped down on my cocoa-brown leather couch.

Like a visitor in my own home, I politely waited for them to settle in before I went to the bar and poured myself a drink. I went over to the dark green Queen Anne chair across from them and took a sip of Jack Daniel's. I was relieved to see the color start to come back into Linda's angelic face.

Pearl, with venom in her voice, related what had happened. "That mother fuckin' son of a bitch Giuseppe kidnapped us and burnt Linda!" The way she said the word "burnt" made my skin crawl.

Pearl grabbed Linda from Missouri's skirt in an attempt to pull it up. Linda quickly yanked it down, clutching the hem of the skirt tightly in her fist. That's when I saw it was stained with blood.

Hate filled Linda's previously lifeless eyes, and she said with anger and shame, "Stop it, stop it, you fuckin' chink bitch. I don't want Jesse seeing my legs, they're fat."

Asian Pearl kept her temper. "I am not a chink, sweetheart. I am Chinese bitch, with Japanese blood on my mother's side. Now, Jesse has to see your legs. You're not fat, you're just Midwestern. You're very American looking. You are making a fortune with that girl-next-door look of yours. Now relax, I have to pull your skirt up."

Pearl's hand reached between Linda from Missouri's legs, but again Linda refused to let her lift it up. The tug-of-war continued for a few moments before

Asian Pearl angrily dropped the charade of concern. "Pull your fuckin' skirt up, bitch. Let Jesse see Giuseppe's handiwork."

Coming to the traumatized girl's rescue, I told Pearl, "Let her alone. Take your hands off her."

I reached over to put my arm around Linda and she flinched. Giving a tender smile, I gingerly sat down beside her on the sofa. I patted her gently on the back, like a mother burping her newborn. Linda's frightened eyes were quickly pooling with tears. Gently, I placed my hand on the back of her head as I softly brushed her forehead with a kiss. Snuggling close, I put my arm around her, holding her tightly as I reached over and placed my hand on top of hers. I smelled a hint of urine and body odor.

I whispered in her ear in a soft but strong fatherly tone, "Everything is going to be all right. You're a really beautiful girl and you're safe now. I just want to take care of you and see what happened. Linda honey, I promise not to look at anything you do not want me to see, okay?"

With a sniffle and a small nod of her head, she answered, "Okay."

"And by the way," I continued, "I think you have a beautiful body."

I felt her clenched fingers relax under my hand as we jointly, slowly hiked her skirt up until it reached above her knee. Just a few inches above the knee on the inside of her thigh, I could see a red trail of pain step-laddering toward her genitals.

Pearl's slim finger hovered above, marking the way with her long curled red fingernail, stopping for a second in front of each gaping and open red sore. The whore pointed to each perfectly round small wound, exposing the layers of burnt subcutaneous skin, encircled by a bright red rim around the white oozing flesh. Pearl stopped following the trail an inch from her burnt pussy.

"Those fuckin' sons-of-bitches, Prince's brother Giuseppe and his running buddy, Bubblegum Guppy, thought she was a fuckin' ashtray! Jesse, you'll find the initials 'PP' branded into her ass for 'Prince's Property.' His brother is a chain-smoking, sick meth-addicted chump that took his sweet time putting his cigarettes out on her. He kept telling her that's what she gets for not being his old lady and working for a freak."

Pearl's eyes were void of compassion—cold, dark and flat like a shark's. She suddenly grabbed the skirt, yanked it out of our hands and spread it over Linda's knees. A moment later she jumped up, pulled off her mink in one quick motion and threw it over the arm of the couch. "I am so fuckin' sick of living in that mink! That half-pint Puerto Rican chi-chi mama can have her fucking rent-a-coat back! It stinks! Just like that hick bitch of yours does!" She pointed an accusing finger at her. "That bitch got us into this mess by flirting with that black lovesick bastard Giuseppe at the Fillmore. She played him to score concert tickets." She sneered as she recalled the scene. "All this shit just for a few fucking tabs of acid and front-row seats at the Fillmore Auditorium. Linda had to see the Jefferson Airplane like the "real hippies" do, high on LSD."

Pearl glared at Linda. "Well, go ask Alice how to dump a pimp with a hard-on! Giuseppe's now jonesing for white Midwest pussy!"

Feeling more like a reprimanded child than a gangster pimp, I let her rave on. She needed to get the horror out of her, at any rate.

Pointing at the fur coat, she said, "This mink stinks like a rat. I stink from sleeping in this bad luck coat, locked up for days in that asshole's basement. I don't care if I ever see a motherfuckin' mink again. I was so happy to see that ugly horse face of Prince as he came into his lowlife brother Giuseppe's cellar and rescued our asses." She took a long pull on her drink. "I was getting sick from the smell of Linda's burning flesh and I haven't slept for days! Giuseppe kept bad-rapping Linda all night, and she would yell every time that punk raped her. Bubble Gum Guppy would pop his Bazooka bubble every time Giuseppe rubbed his cigarette out on Linda. He'd sit there jacking off while his boss amused himself," Pearl angrily reported.

I felt bile rise in my throat as rage and disbelief simmered in me. Asian Pearl asked, "Fuckin'-A, Jesse, what took you so long to scare those motherfuckers into letting us go?"

I was jarred from my shock of picturing Linda's tortured body, trying to comprehend what had happened. "What did you say?"

"Jesse, what took so long to get the word out on the street that you had hired the Gomez Rexsaurus? Didn't you know we were in trouble? We always show up for a good date." As Asian Pearl continued talking, I started putting the pieces together. "When Prince showed up, he told Giuseppe, 'There's been a change in plans. Let the bitches go. I don't want to swallow my balls with my own blood. Rumor has it that the chick with a dick is hiring Joe Gomez on her crew.'

"Prince couldn't wait to get his sorry ass over to Giuseppe's crib. That phony wannabe player acted like he didn't know we had been kidnapped. Prince threw his brother under the bus, coming into the basement like the cavalry yelling, 'You let these bitches go! Why did you go against my orders? Never fuck with Jesse's bitches!' Then he slapped his punk brother alongside his head."

Pearl picked up my Zippo off the table and lit a cigarette. She inhaled deeply and, as if exhausted from telling the story, gave out a sigh as she exhaled. She raised her glass high in a toasting gesture and said, "Here's to Joe."

I was irritated with the hard-eyed whore who I knew did not really respect me. Pearl was a low-button snob, the kind of person who had contempt for the privileged. She thought someone was weak simply because they did not assault their enemies. I told Pearl, "I had my troops out looking for you. I would have freed you soon. He will pay for this, trust me."

She merely replied, "Thank God for Joe Gomez. It's about time you finally hired somebody with balls."

"I'm calling Little Bastard and Rascal to come over and take you both back to the house."

Pearl without argument said, "Okay."

"Linda, honey," I said, "I want you to take a nice warm shower. You can put on my terry cloth robe that you'll find hanging on the back of the door when you get out. Just give me your old clothes and I'll throw them away for you. I'm calling Junior to pick you up some underwear and a nice new dress. Go get cleaned up and make yourself at home, okay? Are you hungry? I can fix you something to eat." I studied the girl, who was now silently crying. As I wiped away a tear, her pretty bottom lip quivered.

Childlike, she asked me, "What do you have to eat?"

"Good question. I don't know what I have to eat, but Carmen always stocks my refrigerator up with all kinds of goodies in case we get the munchies. When Junior gets here, I'll have her fix you a little something."

Impatiently, I said to her, "But first things first. Go take your shower. I want you to be nice and clean for when the doctor visits you. I'm sending Dr. Elena over to Tara of the West to take care of you. I don't want those burns getting infected. Don't worry; she'll give you something for the pain."

Then, shooing her off the couch like a mother hen, I said, "Go on now. Do what I say."

I lit up a Pall Mall, took a deep drag and started to think of a game plan. A heavy weight lifted from my chest as I picked up the phone and called Junior to tell her our girls were home and safe. I heard her groggy voice answer, "Hello, is that you, boss?"

"Yeah, Junior. I got some business for you to take care of."

Chapter 25

THE CONTRACT

*L*ITTLE ROSIE SAT CURLED UP IN A CHAIR with her red-painted toes sticking out from under her black mink coat. Humming along, she was as mellow as the Nina Simone music playing in the background.

A tarnished silver roach clip sat on the table in front of Junior, a stub clamped between its teeth. Next to it, casually lying out, was a large round wad of cash wrapped in a thick rubber band. Junior's soft face caught the light of a flickering candle on the coffee table.

The room felt like a warm safe cocoon, draped in a pink haze from the dim lights and the tint of my rose-colored shades. I listened to the soulful singer and sat on the couch with my feet up, resting next to an open shoebox filled with weed. My lighter was inside the box's lid, along with a small amount of cleaned grass and a pack of Zig-Zag papers for easy access.

A large gallon of Red Mountain wine, a favorite throwback brand from my days of poverty as a runaway, dominated the center of the table. Tonight, the nostalgic bottle was encircled by long-stemmed crystal glasses that proudly displayed the nasty-tasting cheap wine. Just like my old days on the streets, we talked trash, laid back and passed the grass.

Junior was slouched in the brown leather recliner until a hot loose grass seed burned her crumpled white dress shirt. Her serenity disrupted, she quickly brushed off the front of her shirt. "Oh, shit," she said as she sat up, "I like this fuckin' shirt. Damn it, now I got a seed hole."

Amused by Junior's mishap, Little Rosie giggled. "You butches are all alike. You can't keep a shirt clean to save your life. What would you do without us femmes? Who would take care of you dumb dykes, hm?"

"That reminds me Junior, where the fuck's Carmen? Maybe I should send you to the Drake to make sure she didn't marry that motherfucking D.A."

Rosie laughed at that last remark and said, "Jesse, that femme's not going to marry any rich john. Carmen wants to tie your ass down. She doesn't like sharing you with me. Carmen doesn't realize that you and I got an understanding. She's probably getting herself all dolled up so she can walk in here like the Queen of Sheba."

As soon as she said that, we heard a knock on the front door.

"Thank God she's here," I said. I jumped up and walked across the room in my stocking feet, excited to see Carmen. As I swung the door open, I said, "Hey baby doll, what took you so long." To my amazement, I looked directly at a large black hand holding a big red velvet pouch. I heard a male voice say, "Didn't know you cared, baby."

Startled sober, I looked up and saw Prince's pockmarked, ugly horse face. It had an unusually friendly expression on it. Prince smiled, exposing crooked stained teeth and a gold cap that color-coordinated with his neck chain. Chuckling, he started toward me. Like a lady being led in a dance, I was forced to step backward so as not to have the six-foot-five giant step on my feet.

Prince strutted through my hall with the attitude of my long-lost brother coming over for Thanksgiving dinner. Loudly, as if making an announcement, he said, "I brought you girls a little gift. I've come to join the party and I've left my brother Giuseppe at home. I brought you bitches a six-hundred-dollar bottle of scotch!"

Rosie and Junior shifted in their chairs, trying to conceal the fear and rage they were feeling toward our intruder. The energy in the room went from mellow heaven to terror-ridden hell as we were all caught with our weapons down.

I regained my cool first, falling back on years of training, and remembered my manners. I gave Prince the traditional street greeting, "What's happening, man?"

I took the bottle of scotch that was obviously a peace offering. Junior, like a dutiful wife, got up and took it from my hand. The tension in the room was as thick as the fog on a cold morning in the bay.

Prince arrogantly tossed his black Afro-head back and gave a sneer, looking nastier than usual. In a hushed voice wrapped in contempt he said, "I've come to make amends for my brother snatching two of your bitches. That fool thought the corn-fed country girl was in love with him. He's whacked on speed. Giuseppe wanted to make Linda his old lady. The ho said no, so he burnt her pussy."

"What the fuck did you say, Prince?" I asked in disbelief.

"Let's not fuck with each other," he retorted. "I've come to talk business. Shit, bitch, enjoy this bottle of top-shelf scotch. Consider it payment for the damages done to your bitch."

The cobra of rage asleep in its basket rose within me. In a heartbeat the cobra erupted and struck Prince. "Take your fuckin' bottle of scotch and cram it up your ugly ass! Fuck you and the horse you rode in on!"

In a flash, a shiny long blade appeared beneath my eyes, as it pierced my t-shirt between my breasts. I felt the cold steel tip as it rested against my skin. Breathless, too terrified to move, my friends looked on.

I fixed Prince with an evil stare. "Try it motherfucker!" I yelled. The force of my words shook him. Prince stumbled backwards. He looked like he knew I was crazy. He checked to see if Junior or Little Rosie had drawn their guns.

Stepping backward in retreat, he held his knife tightly in his hand. Like a cornered lion he roared, "You're dead, motherfucker! You're dead, motherfucker!" Prince kept pronouncing my death warrant as he steadily retreated to the front door, continuing to yell his threat in the hall as he fled.

The three of us rushed to the door like football players heading for a tackle. Little Rosie and Junior's bodies pressed behind mine as the three of us slammed the door closed and bolted it as if we were trying to prevent a break-in, after the fact.

Rosie ran through the hall back into the living room as fast as her short little legs could take her. Out of her purse she pulled her Derringer. Following suit, Junior leaped to the coat rack, pulling her .38 out of the waiting holster.

My shaking hand grabbed the cold closet doorknob in a death grip as I turned the handle, desperate to get my gun. My hand embraced the cold steel. The adrenaline running through my body like an electrical current, slowed down enough for me to breathe. The three of us huddled in the hall, guns drawn and hammers cocked. We all stood there and shook. As I turned around, I realized, "Oops, I fucked up."

Rosie had her pearl-handled Derringer in one hand and the other on my arm. Her sharp nails pressed into my flesh. "*Aye, aye, aye,*

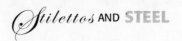

you got the Fillmore boys' mark on you! He'll put a contract on your head! 'You're dead, motherfucker' means you're gonna get whacked! Are you okay?" she asked.

Junior echoed her, "Jesse, are you okay?"

I heard their voices over the rushing whoosh filling my ears, like an ocean of fear making me immobile and unable to respond.

Junior tried to get my attention. "Boss, are you okay?"

Finally, I snapped out of my paralysis. I replied to my terrified crew, "I'm fine. Fuck 'em if he can't take a joke." For all my brave words, though, I knew the struggle for control had escalated. I should have realized after Linda was burned that I had to answer back.

I was a lover, not a fighter, but I sure had a fight on my hands now.

Chapter 26

G-STRING CHEETAH

*P*RINCE DIDN'T TAKE LONG TO BACK UP HIS THREAT. Joe Gomez took the first bullet and fortunately survived. He, Rascal and I had walked out the back door of Chuckkers, when out of nowhere, a black Lincoln pulled up. The doors flew open and bullets rained out. At the time, I hadn't really taken Prince's threat seriously. As the bullets ricocheted off of the dumpsters, however, I realized that I did truly have a contract on my head. Gomez bravely took a bullet in the shoulder, rushing in front of me to protect my ass.

After winging Joe, Mutton Chop tried to jump back into the passenger side of the Lincoln. Like a raging bull, though, Rascal picked up a trash can lid and smashed it over the chump's head. The clang on his head echoed through the alley. In a thump, he hit the ground. Enraged, Rascal then picked him up by the throat and smashed his head right through the passenger window of the Lincoln. The car tore down the alley with the Mutton Chop Chump stuck in the window, his limp, dangling body scraping the ground.

For the past week, my crew and I had been under siege. Our fortresses were the now heavily guarded Chinatown bordello and my apartment.

Security demanded that my crew stay off the streets until we could launch an offensive. My soldiers bunked together and kept off the streets. Guards were posted at the Chinatown bordello, my apartment and at each key crew member's residence.

My ladies and I were dealing with the hardest part of siege warfare; confinement. We were all sick of being cooped up.

The grumblings of Little Bastard as she talked to her restless sidekick, Rascal, faintly drifted into the living room. They were standing guard in the hallway, and my crew of bikers stood outside the building keeping watch. All of my bodyguards were armed with sawed-off shotguns, .45s, blades and chains.

I had issued an order to the street hookers to hide while we were under siege. They bunked with their sisters in trade, the bordello girls, at the house in Chinatown. To prevent further kidnapping, it was safer for them to wait out the battle there.

My dreary boredom was interrupted by my phone ringing. I picked it up and heard Carmen's voice at the other end.

"What are you up to?" Carmen inquired.

"Hi, baby doll," I said, relieved to hear her voice. "I'm doing nothing but watching the clock go by. Just playing gangster and hiding out."

"Poor baby. What's a pimp to do?" Carmen teased.

"Tough it up, girl," I answered.

Carmen's alluring voice continued, "I can come over and keep you company. We can play gangster together."

Fighting back temptation, I said, "It's best for you to stay at Phyllis's. I'm a target, and I don't want you to get hit by being too close."

"Junior and Animal can escort me… we're all bored to death," Carmen whined. "How about I drop by and have dinner with you later on?"

"That'll work," I said. "Until then, I'll just suffer alone without you, baby." I hung up and got back to my morbid musing.

My unhappy whores were behind the walls of Tara of the West. Heavy-hearted and restless, the ladies realized that if they left the house, they would leave with their old escort; fear.

The only hooker who seemed unaffected was, oddly enough, Linda from Missouri. Marie had informed me that she would disappear mysteriously for hours. She seemed restless and excessively withdrawn. Marie wanted me to talk to her, and Animal was bringing her over any minute.

I heard Animal's deep voice as he greeted my butch enforcers outside. I quickly went to the door to let Linda in.

The wholesome whore looked solemn as she greeted me, "Hi, Jesse, Marie said you wanted to talk with me?"

"How are you feeling?" I asked. "Come sit down. Let's chat for a minute."

"All right, Jesse,"

Her plump face radiated a youthful freshness. Glossy jet black hair was piled high in perfect lovelocks. Her clear blue eyes stood out against her flawless skin. She wore a simple blue dress that complimented her slightly full figure.

"I would offer you a drink, but as you know, we're all on the wagon."

She sat down across from me as I relaxed into the couch.

"Linda, I'm concerned about you taking off. It's dangerous as hell. What's going on with you?"

Linda instantly broke into tears. Her voice had a petulant tone as she said, "Why are you on my ass? I'm still bringing in money."

"This has nothing to do with money, Linda. It has to do with your security and our resources right now. I don't want you leaving the house."

"Since when do you care what happens to me?" she asked, evading my eyes.

I snapped back, "I don't know what you mean by that comment. Just fucking follow orders."

Her tears dried up and she gave me a hateful glare. "You're just on my ass because I'm fucking straight. Pearl said if I was gay and you were banging me, I would have never gotten kidnapped in the first place. We didn't have any protection like your other girls."

This was the first I'd heard of this. "I don't need to explain myself to you, Linda. Pearl is a streetwise warrior bitch who didn't want security. So next time if you have a problem, talk to me."

"All right Jesse," she said as she got up.

"Good, I'm glad we have an understanding," I said softening. "Promise me you won't go anywhere without letting Marie know. You've been through hell and I don't want you to hurt yourself."

The hollowness in Linda's eyes disturbed me. Considering what she had been through, I assumed she was still recovering from it. I walked her to the door and told Animal to take her back to the house.

I was jonesin' for a stiff drink and a joint. Yet, I had to follow my own orders. I put an Otis Redding LP on the stereo and settled back into my vapid ennui.

Soon, Rascal's high-pitched voice resonated through the door, interrupting my reverie. "What are you doing running around unguarded, you *pinche loca!*"

"Don't fuck with me, Rascal! I have something important to show Jesse," my Puerto Rican spitfire spat back.

Opening the door, I said, "Come on in, Rosie."

The mammoth dyke shot Rosie an evil glare.

Rosie smugly said, "*Mira cabron*, I'm special." She strutted through the door of my apartment, wearing her mink.

I said to my bodyguards, "What the hell. Crazy femmes... by the way, Carmen will be over later."

Rosie laughed at my dutiful-husband remark. "Carmen, Carmen, Carmen! You need to spend a little time with your favorite chi-chi mama."

Her impish look made me smile. "I could use some entertainment," I replied truthfully.

"*Aye, papi.* I was gonna shoot that faggot Jujubees if I had to stay five more minutes."

She placed a large bottle of champagne, which had a large gold bow on it, down on the coffee table. Throwing her hands to her chest, Rosie proclaimed, "My art is suffering. My dancing is going to hell. Use it or lose it, baby!" Like an elegant Flamenco dancer, Rosie clapped her hands and stamped her feet.

She headed to the bar and poured herself a water glass full of rum. Just as quickly, she filled a glass with Jack and handed it to me.

"Here, let's drink to my new routine," Rosie toasted. "We'll pop the bubbly later to celebrate."

I gave her a disapproving look as I took the drink. "We can't get fucked up. It's dangerous."

"*Papi*, don't be silly. We're safe. There's an army out there."

Rosie chug-a-lugged her rum. Not to be impolite, I joined her.

She pulled a bomber out of her purse, fired it up, and passed me the joint.

Rosie said coquettishly, "I can't wait for you to see my new routine. Sit down, baby."

I took a hit, obeyed the lady, and passed back the grass. She picked up a record she had brought and pranced over to the stereo.

"I'm gonna come out of the hallway. Keep your eyes closed and count to ten. Promise, *papi*, you won't look! Count slowly," Rosie instructed excitedly.

I chuckled when I heard blaring from the stereo, 'Wild thing, you make my heart sing.' After counting to ten, I opened my eyes to find Rosie clinging to the hall doorway like a leopard scratching a tree. She wore a long black feather boa, a short see-through nightie and a cheetah g-string.

Her lips sang with the lyrics as she seductively growled at me. "Wild thing, you know that I love you."

She arched her back and pulled away from the door like a stripper in heat. The sexy Puerto Rican crouched down on all fours. Lust filled her eyes and hot lips as her brown face flushed with heat. She prowled across the floor. Like a tail, the feather boa flowed behind. Her full breasts pointed the way to her prey. I watched the lioness of seductress slowly stand up. She danced backward and threw off her skimpy nightie.

Rosie's soft brown velvet flesh and firm tits were bared. Black swirling pasties sparkled above her g-string. Dancing towards me, Rosie shimmied out of her g-string, which clung to one stilettoed foot. I chuckled with delight as Rosie flung the g-string across the room with a firm kick. It landed perfectly on top of a lamp shade. She turned her back to me, wrapped her fingers around her shoulders, spread her legs wide, and bent over firmly.

I whistled, admiring her flexibility and enthusiasm. Dramatically, she rose up and slinked forward. She encircled my neck with her feather boa and straddled me. Her breasts greeted my face as she lowered herself onto my lap.

The sex kitten purred, "This is the special part of my act. You take off the pasties."

As my mouth kissed her breasts between giggles and a growing lust in my groin, Rosie unzipped my zipper, winked, and ground into me. She wrapped her arms around my neck and pressed her boobs into my face.

"Bite off my pasties, daddy!"

I gripped a pasty between my teeth, yanked it off, and spat it out over her shoulder. Quickly I nibbled the other pasty off her nipple. I blew it over her shoulder—and stared right into the eyes of Carmen.

"What the fuck!" I shouted as Rosie pulsated on my lap.

Carmen stood transfixed.

"I wanted to surprise you," she said testily. "Little Bastard said you were expecting me."

Rosie stopped her performance and gave Carmen a catty glance over her shoulder.

With controlled fury, Carmen said, "Enjoy your suffering, Jesse."

"Wait a minute, Carmen!" I cried. "I was just helping Rosie with her new routine."

Carmen picked up the champagne and hurled it at the bay window behind us. The sound of shattering glass blasted through the room as my window rained down to the sidewalk below. Grinning, Carmen quipped back, "I have a new routine too. I'm spending the weekend with the D.A. It might be nice to try the real thing for a change."

Alarmed by the crash, Rascal lumbered into the living room with a cocked shotgun. She surveyed naked Rosie on my lap, then the expression on Carmen's face. Letting out a long sigh, Rascal uncocked the rifle and went back to her post. My girl left as quietly as she had entered.

"Carmen, wait!"

Chapter 27

CAMELOT HOTEL

*T*HE **TEMPTATIONS' TIGHTLY ORCHESTRATED CHORUS** serenaded my apartment. Fighting the urge to call Carmen once again, I brooded despondently. She hadn't taken any of my calls. Worse, she had been seen hanging all over the D.A. They were spotted like a couple of love birds leaving Carmen's apartment. The frightening thought entered my mind that maybe he was becoming more than a trick.

Asian Pearl stood in my living room discussing her game plan. She had just arranged for me to meet with an assassin named Scope. She was hoping I would hire him to resolve the Prince problem once and for all. Pearl was eagerly explaining the benefits of having Prince and his twisted brother killed.

On the other side of the coffee table sat Junior, jacketless with her shirt sleeves rolled up. The silver butt of her .38 rested against her chest in her shoulder holster. Across from her sat Little Rosie in the Queen Anne chair with her pearl-handled Derringer sticking out of her black bustier.

Asian Pearl stood with a beer in one hand and the other on the back of Rosie's chair. "Listen, Jesse, you know you can't fucking flatter your way out of this one. We're going broke. We can't work. We can't even fucking party! I'm going to get a beer belly drinking this shit," she said, holding up her bottle of Schlitz. "Who wants a geisha with a beer belly?"

I had to hand it to Pearl. That was a strong selling point. Like prisoners desperately in need of a jail break, we all listened intently to her plan.

"Gomez is lucky to be alive," Pearl went on. "What more is it going to take until you kill those sons-of-bitches? Jesse, are you listening?"

"Pearl, Rascal gave Mutton Chop a new trash can lid hat. She smashed that dude's head so hard the trash can lid looked like a Jiffy Pop crown!"

"That's chump-change payback!" said Pearl. "Do you think that's going to scare Prince?"

I stood up likewise and stated my reservations to the group. "If I have Prince and Giuseppe killed, I would fall to their level. That's not cool. Things would snowball into a huge bullshit war between all the Fillmore players and everyone in the Tenderloin. It would spread like an incurable disease. With all the carnage in the streets, no john would ever feel safe doing business with any of us."

Pearl sneered ay my objections. "I've arranged a meeting with the best assassin on the West Coast, Jesse. His name is Scope. Of course, a real street person would hire him, but it's your call. Do what you want."

The Asian bitch was crossing the line with the "real street person" comment, but I held my temper. Instead of kicking her ass for her disrespect, I said, "Pearl, I appreciate your efforts. I'll meet with your referral and I may end up hiring him. You were smart to act so quickly. It took a real street person like you to be able to acquire such resources, but unfortunately," I added, "other street people may end up dead from not thinking things through."

In a voice that let them know the discussion was over, I said,

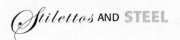

"Pearl, you and Little Rosie are going back into hiding at the house with Marie. Got it?"

The girls simply nodded in response.

I called out, "Rascal, come in here for a minute."

My stoic warrior walked in cradling a sawed-off shotgun against her chest and squeaked, "What's up, boss?"

"Rascal, take Pearl and Rosie downstairs. Have Animal and Red escort them back to the house in Chinatown."

"Yes, boss," answered the big girl.

"I am sick of being cooped up with trashy house whores!" Pearl complained.

"I am a call girl. If I wanted to live in Chinatown, I would have got married!"

***

The mission of interviewing a killer required the darkness of the seedy Camelot Hotel. The building was a haven for degradation and immorality, including murder. I asked myself, "What spiritual force governs the place and the time of the major events of our lives?" I wondered if we have an inner compass that guides us to a particular town, street or restaurant.

Street lore had it that our beautiful city by the sea became a gay mecca back in World War I. The navy would drop off dishonorably discharged faggot servicemen at the San Francisco harbor. The crime-ridden Tenderloin district quickly became a gay ghetto filled with queers from all over the United States. Like the ones before me, my personal journey of independence was born at the intersection of Turk and Taylor.

This corner was the place where the major events of my life had come together. My reconciliation with Carmen and many of my business dealings transpired here. It was the crossroads of my life, and I had come here now to protect my girls' and my new position.

We walked through the tacky lobby, passing the nodding manager, Ted Summer. He was sitting slouched over in a little office chair on wheels, his big body stuffed between its arms. Behind him were little wooden boxes which held the room keys.

His sunglasses dangled at the bottom of his nose beneath his big Panama hat and his loud Hawaiian shirt. Ted was oblivious to the fact that it was late fall and that he was a smack-head manager living in a dirty, flea-bitten hotel. In his mind, it was always summertime. His passion used to be golf trips to Miami, but the only trips he took now were in his head. We silently filed past him, careful not to wake him as we dashed into the stairwell.

The gray wooden stairs creaked and the peeling paint flaked under my black wingtips as we ascended toward the assassin's room. I checked my piece under my jacket and felt the top of the cold steel handle.

I heard Junior take her piece out of her leather holster, checking it as we continued our climb.

Slipping my hand into my trouser pocket, I caressed my lighter and felt reassured by its weight and familiarity. I quickened my pace, taking two stairs at a time, excited at the prospect of finally dealing with this fucking shit.

I began to think that this might actually turn out okay and I spoke to Junior in hushed tones. "Asian Pearl said that he'll be by himself. We're supposed to meet him in Room 412. Guess what…I think that's the first place I ever fucked Carmen."

I heard Junior chuckle behind me. Once again, my one track mind had broken the tension.

Within moments we reached the fourth-floor landing. I cracked the stairwell door and looked down the hall. The coast looked clear, so we walked to Room 412 and quietly rapped on the door three times. Junior stood at my side with her hand inside her jacket over her piece. The door cracked open. I leaned in close and felt a blast of hot breath. In a husky whisper, a woman asked, "What's your code?" I replied through the crack, "Twelve, twelve."

The door opened slowly into a dimly lit room exposing one bare light bulb suspended from the ceiling, casting shadows against the wall. A statuesque Asian drag queen stood before us. I felt shivers go up my spine at her unexpected presence. I was expecting just a military man who was an active-duty sniper. Pearl had assured me that I would be meeting with the assassin alone.

Sensing my apprehension, the Asian queen told me, "I'm Asian Pearl's cousin, Joy Luck. You'll be meeting with my old man, Scope. Come in."

I believed the drag queen because she was wearing chopsticks, painted with dragons that were identical to Asian Pearl's. She was also adorned with lovelocks. They must have shared the same hairdresser too. The dead cold glint in her eyes also resembled her kin, looking like shark eyes about an inch under the water.

The queen was older and much harder, though. She was wearing a tight leather miniskirt and a leather halter top which held up a fortune in hormone shots. Inked into her high cheekbone was a small tattooed dot, which revealed her affiliation to a convict tribe.

She said in a husky, cigarette-strained voice, "My cousin's told me all about you. I'll introduce you to Scope."

The room was small, yet it was considered deluxe for the Camelot because it had a bathroom and a bedroom. On a white coffee-stained sink in the corner rested a hot plate next to four little blue-and-white Chinese teacups. On the other side of the room was a small daybed placed against the wall. Lying on cheap leopard velvet pillows and a tattered beige bedspread was a slinky young man. Across his lap lay a high-powered rifle with a long barrel and a large scope at the top.

He did not acknowledge our presence as he methodically stroked the barrel between his fingers. He was cleaning the steel shaft with a small white cloth, caressing it as gently as his lover's penis. His rapt attention on his task had the energy of a sexual moment, and I felt like a voyeur as I waited to be introduced.

The Asian companion said in a gentle voice, "Honey, I'd like you to meet Jesse, the young lady my cousin Pearl told you about."

I hesitated to greet him, as I didn't know the proper protocol for meeting a professional killer. Not knowing what else to do, I stood politely with Junior at my side, waiting for him to finish his task.

After a long, awkward moment, his eyes rose from his tool of destruction to look up at me. He said in a lifeless monotone, "Hello, Jesse. Respect, man, I've heard nothing but good things about you."

"Respect, man. I'm pleased to meet you too. Pearl is the main lady in my crew, and she tells me you're in special ops and a top-notch sniper in 'Nam, freelancing while on leave here." I made sure to mention, "My brother's over there. I gotta hand it to you."

The young soldier, with small beads of sweat on his high fore-head, peered over his John Lennon glasses. "That's cool. I'm not happy with those mother fuckin' peaceniks over at Golden Gate Park. They have been burning our beautiful flag. They've been having orgies all weekend in the name of peace. Those love freaks! I hate acidhead traitors. I'd love to give them all a gift from 'Nam!"

Scope lifted up his rifle, pointed it above our heads and pulled the trigger. With a terrific roar, he shot a fucking hole in the wall and calmly said, "Bang!"

Junior and I ducked. I shouted, "Peace, brother, peace!" sounding like Two Bits the hippie. Plaster fell from the wall to the floor. Joy Luck casually grabbed a broom and began to sweep up the mess.

Scope continued as he laid his rifle back onto his lap, "Glad to hear your brother's doing the deal, that's cool."

Having found common ground, Scope had responded to the first rule of sales; rapport building. The emaciated warrior gave us a faint smile as he waited for me to speak.

Still nervous from the gunshot, I decided to add another dash of flattery. "My brother tells me tree jockeys like you live up there for days. You guys are famous for not disturbing a twig." I piled it on a little. "Pearl told me you volunteered for that duty. I'm impressed. I have to admire your endurance."

Scope then said to us in a relaxed tone, like a commanding officer ordering his men, "At ease. Why don't you girls sit down?"

"Thank you, Scope, I think I will." I gestured for Junior to sit and we took the two white wooden chairs in front of a milk crate coffee table. Scope nervously licked the open cracks in his dry bottom lip like a lizard. His flat gray eyes stayed focused, unlike his tongue, which due to some nervous disorder, had a life of its own. His creepy tongue action made it difficult for me to concentrate.

I started right in. "What's your asking price and is it negotiable?"

Before he had an opportunity to answer, I put my hand up in a halting gesture, risking the disapproval of the man with a high-powered rifle in his lap. "No offense, but I was under the impression that Junior and I would be talking business with you alone."

Scope gave a measured nod of his head as if to acknowledge my concern. "Jesse, this is Asian Pearl's first cousin, and believe me, you can trust her because she's real street, just like Pearl." I nodded okay, and he continued, "I got to go back to Fort Ord in a few days, so I'd like to handle our business tonight. I'm just like any other soldier," he said, cracking a grin. "I needed to see my old lady while I'm on leave. From what I hear about you and the ladies, I thought you could appreciate that."

I considered his reply and thought, "It takes all kinds. A horny death-addicted soldier and a female impersonator, they definitely made an interesting couple." I asked again in a straightforward manner, "What are your terms?"

For the first time that morning, Scope came alive. "I'll take fifty percent up front and the rest when the job is done. To kill Prince it will cost you sixty-five-hundred, and if you want me to dispose of his body that's another grand."

I paused, remembering my father's words, "When negotiating, whoever speaks first loses."

I waited until Scope went for the close and offered me a deal. "I can throw in his brother, Giuseppe. I'll dispose of both of them for ten grand, total."

He gave me a smile like a used car salesman. "I understand it's been a little tight for you lately. My old lady's cousin hasn't been able to work much. Guess your whores are off the streets until this blows over. I want you to pay what's in your comfort zone."

"Thanks man, I appreciate it. A break would help."

Scope then made me another offer. "If I nest up above the Booker T. Washington Hotel and knock them both off as they leave their apartment, I'll just let them lie where they drop. For that I'll charge you only seven grand. I'm easy and I'd appreciate referrals. So what do you think?"

Scope's soft-spoken remarks caused my skin to crawl. I replied, "Scope, you're a professional and I believe that you can do the job. I need to discuss this privately with my crime partner Junior in the other room for a minute." I rushed to explain. "I told Pearl to inform you before our meeting that I was still considering some other options. I wanted to meet you in person because I always make decisions based on my gut reaction to people."

I then removed my hat so as to appear extra comfortable, like I was going to stay a while. I didn't want the trigger-happy young man to think I was gonna bolt before I gave him an answer. Politely I asked, "Where can I chat with Junior privately?"

By way of a reply, Scope yelled, "Joy Luck, is the bedroom clean or do you have all of your girly-girl shit in there?"

The dragon lady raised one pencil-thin eyebrow and replied like a bored, haughty queen, "Those gowns are part of my craft, honey."

"Joy Luck, one of these days…. Pow! Right to the moon!" Scope gave an order with a flying finger, "Show Jesse and Junior to the bedroom."

The geisha wannabe, with a deadpan expression on her face, said, "Follow me."

As if following a hostess to our table, Junior and I followed the buxom beauty to the other end of the room. The bedroom was tiny with a twin-size mattress on the floor. On the mattress lay a pair of silver, sequin-studded gowns and a rhinestone tiara. The royal head-dress rested on top of a large red, open suitcase-style makeup box.

As soon as the Asian queen left and shut the door, I sighed in relief. I whispered to Junior, "I can't believe Scope fired off his rifle right in the middle of the living room. He's fuckin' crazy." I nervously huddled closer to Junior, making sure we weren't overheard. "There's something wrong with this whole fucked-up picture. This place looks like a set out of a bad Fellini movie with these tacky-ass wigs, dresses and bras piled high on this filthy, zebra-striped bedspread."

Junior whispered back, "You got that right, boss."

"Shit, Junior, Scope's creepy dick of steel and his cold ice queen are giving me the willies. I think I saw Joy Luck in the drag show over at Finocchio's the night they performed acts from *Madame Butterfly*. This is not a fucking professional environment. I expected a little more class for ten grand. I'm making a life-and-death decision here. You know and everyone on the streets knows, I'm a lover, not a killer."

Junior echoed, "Me too, boss."

"I don't believe in hurting people, let alone killing them. I just like to make money, man. I'm a good Catholic girl, dammit!"

Junior echoed again, "Me too, boss."

I was glad my henchman was backing me up. "This is some serious shit here. We're talking hell…forever! I got to figure out who I'm dealing with." I paused to gain my composure and said to Junior, "We all know that to understand anybody on the street, you got to know what they're hooked on."

Junior nodded and said like a true street veteran, "That's for real, boss. You don't know the drug, you don't know the person."

I got real quiet and said, softer than a whisper, "That dude's hooked on blood." Junior and I immediately made the sign of the cross.

Junior, wide-eyed and breathless, said, "Yeah, what's up with the bloody lips?"

I replied, "I know by the way he caresses the barrel of his gun, he kills for enjoyment. Plus, he dropped his price too fast and too easy. That tells me that the dude's addicted to killing."

Junior got quiet and said what all street people say when they're confused. "Cool."

"He would knock both of our asses off, just for fun. Then he wouldn't have to worry about witnesses. If I'm going to hell for killing someone, it won't be to feed a blood-jonesing tree jockey." That made up my mind. "I'm not killing anyone and I'm not hiring his white ass," I decided aloud. "I'm just not sure how I can get us out of here without pissing him off, though."

"I don't know Jesse, but I do know you can talk your way out of any situation." Nervously, she added, "Boss, I'll back your play. Should I take out my piece?"

Before I could answer I jumped, along with Junior, at the bellowing voice of Ted Summer in the hallway. "Joy Luck! You dickless bastard, get your ass downstairs with the rent! The owner is on her way over! You're a week fucking late, bitch!"

Junior and I held our breath, expecting Ted, who obviously had shot some bad smack, to get an unexpected gift, courtesy of 'Nam. Grateful for Ted's interruption, we looked at each other and like firemen at a fire drill dashed out of the bedroom, through the living room and toward the front door. We both stopped for a moment in full flight as I turned around to graciously excuse myself to the young man who was hurriedly disassembling his large rifle and placing it in an aluminum briefcase.

I caught the assassin's obviously displeased metallic eyes staring at me. I felt like he was speaking to me from behind the cross hairs of his rifle scope as he said, "Catch you later, Jesse."

I replied with a tip of my hat, "Respect, man. You got that right. I'll get back with you tonight. I don't want fuckin' Ted to put us together in here."

He gave me an all-knowing nod as if embarrassed by the intrusion.

The stoic dragon lady opened the door with the enthusiasm of a Chinese restaurant hostess and let Junior and I depart.

The musty smell of the hallway was a welcome relief from the heavy incense-laden room with the two whack jobs enjoying their romantic rendezvous. I made a beeline for the stairwell with Junior, anxious to get back to the safety of the Tenderloin streets.

Chapter 28

THE BOOKKEEPER

*W*ITH JUNIOR AT MY HEELS we arrived at Nick's cab. He seemed relieved to see us returning without a gang of shooting pimps chasing us.

"Take me to the flower stand on Powell and Market," I said as we jumped in.

"You got it," replied Nick.

He threw down the meter and slammed on the gas. Within moments we arrived at the cable car turnaround at the bottom of Powell. Nick pulled up to the little open-air flower stand.

I grabbed the cold chrome door handle and told my cabbie, "Pick me up at my bookkeeper's apartment an hour from now."

Junior began to follow me, ready to jump out. I touched her shoulder and said firmly, "Junior, hold it. I want you to go back to the house. Call my bookkeeper and let her know I'm stopping by this morning."

Junior raised an eyebrow in surprise. "Jesse, you're not thinking of walking through the Tenderloin by yourself, are you?"

"Junior, lighten up. No one or their brother is going to be out at this God-forsaken hour. It's ten o'clock in the morning."

I took out my piece, feeling the cool butt of the mother-of-pearl handle in my hand. I quickly passed it behind the front seat to

Junior. She reluctantly took the snub-nosed .38 from me. "The last thing I need," I explained, "is to get hassled by a pig on the morning beat who doesn't know me."

Junior, who knew what I was like, just shook her head. In a tone of resignation she said, "You got it, boss."

I flashed Junior a big grin. With a short wave goodbye, I said, "Its cool man, I'll be fine."

When I exited the cab, the scent of the flowers hit me before my feet hit the cement. The radiant jewels of nature stood in silver tin buckets on the sidewalk. Dainty white-petalled carnations and bold yellow sunflowers waited to be chosen. Their brilliant joyfulness shouted to the world, "Life is good!"

A pang of sadness came over me as I stood admiring the fresh flowers. I remembered happier times when I would pick each flower with care for all my ladies before making my rounds. Walking through the Tenderloin, I would visit my girls, carrying their favorite flowers like a route salesman. I would drop by to pick up the cash and talk a little trash.

We'd share a drink to celebrate surviving one more night without getting busted. It was a good routine and I enjoyed listening as my girls gave their report on each trick turned. We'd smoke a joint and laugh over some of the strange-ass shit that came down while working. One thing was certain; weird shit always happened when you were out hookin'.

As I approached the flower stand, the lively hustle and bustle of the mid-morning crowds lifted my spirits. I listened to the happy cling-clang of the cable car as it rumbled down the track. Above me, screeching sea gulls swooped through the air between the tall buildings.

I arrived at the little sidewalk flower stand and was greeted by Feather, the cheerful hippie florist. "Hello, Jesse."

The pretty girl's light blue eyes were upstaged by the bright purple and blue, tie-dyed headband wrapped around her forehead. Sprouting out of her wild mane of frizzy blond hair, a single beaded braid fell down the side of her face. At the end of it, a roach clip dangled, adorned with a vibrant feather. Instantly, my eyes where drawn to her long, colorful peacock earrings that danced in the sunlight. She always wore them in honor of her idol, Janis Joplin, who she believed was a wild beautiful bird. Feather's bold earrings gave birth to her street handle.

I replied with a broad, warm smile, "Good to see you, young lady. You're prettier than the flowers in your hand. If you got any better looking, you could get arrested, child!"

The hippie chick giggled the same little giggle of any lady who receives a sweet little spoonful of a woman's favorite drug; flattery.

"Fix me up a dozen of those crimson roses, would you sweetie?"

"Jesse, did you get yourself into the dog house?"

"Nope," I answered.

"You're not here to buy supplies for your flowers and flattery formula?"

I laughed as she made reference to my "Jesse love formula."

Though she'd heard it before, Feather asked, "Tell me how that formula works again?"

Proudly, I recited my own personal tonic for the occupational hazards that went along with pimping. "Fuck-ups are followed by flowers and flattery, which always lead to a makeup fuck. Unfortunately, I have been so busy dealing with that pockmarked, wannabe pimp and his limp-dicked brother; I haven't had time to fuck anybody."

Feather gave a deep belly laugh. "That's a shame. I'm sure your girls miss fighting with you."

Flowers were my favorite weapon in my raid of hearts. My

clean-up formula was a tried-and-true method for reinstatement of my lover's strained feelings of affection. I knew that enough flowers and flattery followed by a powerful make-up fuck made my women beg me to fuck up again.

In my mind's eye, I pictured my old Taft High math teacher writing on the blackboard in heavy chalk:

Jesse's Love Formula: $FU \times FF = MF$.

Handing her a twenty, I said, "Catch you later, you flowery fox."

I heard her giggling as I turned and strutted away. The sound of, "Hey Jude" from Feather's transistor radio carried down the sidewalk. I smiled at a businessman in his sharp, dark blue suit and thin tie who walked toward the flower stand. I was so happy to be outside, even the Brooks Brother dude looked like a human being instead of just a trick.

I weaved in and out of the stream of well-dressed perfectly coiffed retail mamas, avoiding stuffed Saks Fifth Avenue shopping bags. Even the sated look of contentment on the ladies' faces, as they clutched their expensive fixes of instant gratification, was a pleasant sight to behold.

As I made my way down toward the TL, the vibrant city scenes of normalcy helped cleanse my memories of the sewer of humanity I had just visited up at the Camelot. I noticed Linda from Missouri winding up the sidewalk. She was dressed like a full-blown hippie. Linda had traded in her lacquered bouffant for soft, long locks that ran down her back. Flowers weaved throughout her hair. Her hooker dress had been replaced with patched Levi's and a peasant blouse. When she saw me, the Missourian stopped dead in her tracks. Like a child playing hooky, she looked surprised to see me.

I suppressed the desire to tear into her. "What the hell are you doing out here, Linda?"

"I was protesting the war. All my hippie friends are in Union Square and I was helping out," Linda replied.

Compassion suppressed my anger as I replied to the spaced-out, shell shocked hooker. "We had a talk about this, Linda. I'll let it go this time. Come walk with me, I'm on my way to my bookkeeper's. You can just wait and we'll go back to the house together."

Her face filled with dismay. "How far away is it? I'm so tired from walking all day. We marched halfway to Chinatown."

"It's just around the corner," I assured her. "You can rest at the coffee shop next to Harriet's building. It's right on Eddy and Taylor."

"All right Jesse," she said, "but I'd rather go home. I'm really tired."

Not wanting to be saddled with the corn-fed wannabe hippie, I flagged an approaching cab. "Now get in this fucking car and stay put in the house. You're off duty until we talk again." I handed Linda a twenty as she hopped into the back of the taxi.

I walked on, holding the bundle of roses wrapped in green cellophane snugly under my arm. Meandering through the TL was the most pleasurable way of taking care of my business. I wondered if Jackson the shoeshine man would be at his stand on Eddy Street at this pre-noon hour. He was the unofficial gossip columnist, the Rona Barrett of the Tenderloin. Jackson was also on my payroll, so any information that came to him would come to me.

It worked the other way too. A bit of trivial gossip strategically placed in the right person's ear could be very profitable. They listened to Jackson's seemingly harmless, casual chitchat between the rhythmic snaps of his shoeshine rag. He was a very helpful spy and the perfect transmitter of street news.

Jackson's job description also included sales, because his stand was a referral base for johns. The man had an understated demeanor, making him an artist at instant intimacy. When he was shining a man's shoes, his relaxed attentiveness had the same effect as a hairdresser has on a woman.

As I approached, I noticed him fiddling with the little transistor radio inside the shoe stand. The small silver radio rested on a cigar box and was softly playing next to three large, elevated, stuffed-brown leather seats. As he adjusted the volume on the radio, the harmonized voices of the Four Tops grew louder.

I could hear Jackson singing with them, "Sugar pie, honey bunch…" and I caught myself singing along with him. "You know that I love you…"

I felt as slick as Stax as I glided up behind him. I interrupted our duet by giving Jackson an enthusiastic traditional street greeting, "Hey man, what's happening?"

The old black man turned around to see who the backup singer was, and his face broke into a warm smile. His friendly glow caressed me like the sun's rays rising in the east as they flood across the waiting earth. I felt a sense of peace that dispersed the last dregs of tackiness from my meeting at the Camelot.

"Hey, Jackson, how 'bout a shine?" I cheerfully inquired.

Stepping up onto the raised platform, I sat in the middle seat, placing my feet in the stirrups beneath me. Up high in my chair, I looked down Eddy Street from my perch and felt like a fucking high roller. I pulled my pant legs up just a little bit, to protect the crease in my slacks and to expose my shoes.

Settling my beautiful black wingtips firmly in the stirrups, I bent down to watch Jackson work on them. He opened the can of polish and as fast as a Las Vegas dealer, applied the black wax in a fast circular motion with his fingers.

"I didn't expect to see you, child," he said as he worked. "I thought you'd have enough sense not to show your face on the streets."

"These are my streets," I replied, "and if I have to spend another fuckin' day cooped up in my crib, baby-sat by a mammoth Amazon and her half-pint sidekick, I'll kill myself and collect Prince's bounty for my parents."

A wide grin spread across the freckles on his high Cherokee cheekbones. He replied seriously, "Prince's fucking people drop by daily trying to bribe me. They want me to set your ass up. That dude has a real hard-on for you."

I nodded in agreement. "You got that right. The Fillmore boys have never cared about running the TL business before."

Jackson continued, "Prince obviously can't handle a woman showing him up. Word has it that you wouldn't accept his amends. I heard it was good Scotch too. That's what he's really pissed off about, 'cause he's a cheap motherfucker!"

"Maybe."

Jackson went on elaborating on the situation. "Prince thinks that if the fuckin' cops can run the TL and collect their fairy and dyke chump change, so can he."

"I don't care what the bastard thinks. He thinks just like the rest of America, that we're not supposed to have any fuckin' queers and if they do exist, they better be invisible. Jackson, this is 1969…we don't have gays in America… hell, we're just now discovering blacks!"

Jackson gave an extra sharp snap of the rag on my shoe. "A full-fledged turf war is not good for anybody. We'd all go broke. The heat is hip to this bullshit. Just the other day, Clancy gave me a twenty-dollar tip. I've shined that pig's shoes for twenty years and never got a tip from him before. But then, he asked me how the relations between the gay girls and the Fillmore pimps were coming along."

"Why would that cop give a shit?"

"Jesse, Rascal slamming Mutton Chop was one thing, but a turf war with dead bodies all over the news is another. Mayor Alioto and his city planners are trying to clean up the city and bring in new business dollars. The last thing they want is more bullshit coming out of the TL."

Sarcastically I asked, "Since when is it news when a fucking queer gets killed?"

"Dead queers are one thing, but gay on black is different because it's all about money. The city's image is real important right now, especially since everybody wants President Johnson's war on poverty dollars. Poor districts like the Tenderloin can get dollars along with other poor areas like Fillmore. Uncle Sam gives big bucks. That equals a lot of building contracts. The city fathers need all us poor folk to look like one big, happy family. They want to prove that each district is worthy of receiving funds."

I understood his logic and I said, "This is not going to turn into a full-on war if I can help it."

The shoeshine man nodded his head, approving. "Jesse, it's best if we black folk, queers and mental cases just get along."

"Jackson, I didn't know you were so political."

Jackson looked up at me. "If you weren't so busy fucking so many women you'd keep up with the news."

I chuckled and thought he was right, so I listened to what he had to say.

"There is so much fucking heat already coming down in this city with all of the Vietnam peace protests. The last thing they want is more fireworks. We've become a city of troublemakers. Did you know that San Francisco is thought of as this country's number one bad child? Folks are mad 'cause we just don't behave."

I thought about the many recent "love-ins" at Golden Gate Park, where the half-clothed, love-making hippies burned the flag. Images from San Francisco flashed across the United States on the news showing weed-smoking, acid-dropping, long-hair freaks burning their draft cards.

After reflecting on this, I said to Jackson, "You got a point there."

I pulled a bill out of my money clip. Jackson snatched the Benny out of my hand quicker than he could spit on the tip of my shoes.

"Young man," I said, "your company has lifted my spirits. I have been floating on a raft of psychic turds in a sewer of humanity. At least I was captain of my own ship."

Jackson grinned, "Jesse you're sounding like a poetic beatnik. I don't know what psychic sewer you're talking about but I know that I appreciate the hundred and it's good to see you. You'd better catch a cab quick and watch your back."

I jumped off the stand, turned around, and did a little dance. "Sugar pie, honey bunch…you know that I love you."

Jackson just laughed as I split down the street. "Catch ya later, man," I yelled back over my shoulder.

Within moments, I was at Harriet's building, excited to see Fritzy and cheer her up. Poor Fritzy had been staying with her sister ever since her husband, Ed died. I skipped up the steps to the front door and rang the buzzer which read, "Harriet Stinner, Bookkeeper." Being a mellow hippie, Harriet liked working from home. I stood waiting to hear the door buzz so I could go in, but instead there was dead silence.

I started to feel exposed standing outside on her step. Some runner might spot me and alert Prince's people. Each second I stood there, I felt more like a rabbit running across open ground with a hawk circling above me. I was anxious to get into the shelter of Harriet's apartment.

Trying to get their attention, I rang Harriet's doorbell again for at least a minute. With my luck, those two hippie sisters had dropped a tab of acid and were in full flight from reality on the cosmic strings of Jimi Hendrix's guitar.

I started thinking I would have to walk down to the liquor store to call them. As I was about to leave, I noticed a big fat guy through the glass door. I watched the dude dressed in blue overalls climb up a stepladder in the foyer. He placed a toolbox by the bottom of the stairs and took out a large pair of orange pliers. The man began to remove a light fixture from the ceiling. I took the opportunity to pound on the door to get the workman's attention so he would let me in.

The glass shook under my aching knuckles as I rapped on the door and yelled, "Hey man, let me in!" The huge dude ignored my pounding and stayed up on his stepladder, determined to finish his task. I started to feel the stir of my rageful cobra that had been pleasantly resting through the charming, morning walk.

Again, I pounded on the glass, completely irritated by the fat bastard who wouldn't open the door. I pounded the door with my fist and kicked it with my newly shined shoes. Finally I got the asshole's attention. He lumbered down the steel steps of the ladder and angrily walked to the front door with sweat dripping down his brow.

"It's about time," I thought. I put my hand on the door, ready to open it. His fleshy jowls anchored his face with the expression of a bulldog, giving him the look of Winston Churchill in workman's clothes. He huffed and puffed in an exasperated manner, emphasizing his annoyance at being interrupted. With a fleshy paw he pulled back the door. As soon as it cracked open, I was hit by a fierce breath of booze and tobacco.

He gruffly barked, "Don't ring the buzzer, you fucking whore," slamming the door shut in my face before I could stick the point of my wingtip in it. As I heard the violent bang and rattle of the glass door, I thought, "It's a good thing my foot wasn't in it."

As he turned around and walked toward the ladder, I yelled to his back, "Let me in, dude, my bookkeeper works here!" The burly dude turned around, charging the door like a bull. Opening the door, he yelled, "Fuck you, whore!" Spitting in my face, he slammed the door shut again.

I felt his hot saliva on my cheek and exploded. "Fuck you, motherfucker!" Fueled with rage, my fists pounded the glass like a hammer and I kicked the door. "Fuck you! I'm not a whore, asshole!" I wiped the oozy spit that felt like thin rice pudding off my cheek, rubbed my hand clean on my trousers and reached for my piece. I was determined to blow his fuckin' head off.

My verbal tirade of "fuck you's" was halted with the sudden awareness that I had left my gun with Junior. I quickly attempted to compose myself and try a new strategy.

In a firm, calm voice I said, "Listen man, I'll give you a twenty to let me in. Just open the door dude and I'll give you twenty bucks!"

The offer got the gentleman's attention. He looked directly at me through the glass and studied me for a second. I saw in his eyes a hint of recognition as he said to me, "Oh, you're Jesse the pimp." I felt myself relax and I took a deep breath, relieved that he would now let me in. The dude looked familiar. He was probably one of my girls' johns.

The man pulled the door open widely and I heard him greet me, "Hey, Jesse the pimp." I stepped through the archway and heard a loud crunch. I felt a powerful blow on top of my head. The dude had cracked my skull with his orange pliers.

Blinded by a gush of warm blood that trickled down my face, I fell on one knee and raised my arm above my head in defense. I saw the pliers fly down and felt another crack. A large fist hit my jaw as I fell to the side. Dazed and dizzy, I looked up at the bastard. I saw

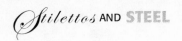

my older brother's face flash in front of me. When we were kids, he had knocked me down more than once.

I focused on this fat guy's crotch. Cocking my fist, I flew up off the carpet, giving him a direct blow to his balls with every ounce of my being. The hit stunned him for a second as he continued to whale on me with his pliers. I danced and weaved with the speed that I had fought with as a child. I jumped up and threw him a blow to his plump face: two hard fast jabs to his nose, drawing his blood for the first time.

I raised my left arm to block his arm and punched him with everything I had in the middle of his solar plexus, knocking the wind out of him. He clipped my nose with the end of his pliers and I heard it crack. I tasted the blood as it gushed over my lips into my mouth.

Knowing my fists were no match for his strength, I took a quick two-step back. I grabbed the cold steel handle of my buck knife and pulled the razor-sharp blade open. It felt like slow-motion as I plunged the blade into his huge belly. The sharp knife pierced his overalls and body like a warm knife cutting through soft butter. Repeatedly, the blade easily sliced through the layers of his flesh. I felt my fist pressing against his blood-soaked belly as he continued to whale on me. I shifted gears and changed the position of the knife. Like a flying swing my closed hand flew upward, time after time, trying to jab his balls with my blade.

I protected my head as he kept trying to split my skull with the pliers, while he backed up from the deep cuts I was inflicting on him. The dude finally stopped to look down at his stomach. It was oozing blood like crazy, soaking through the denim. I grabbed his arm and slashed it open with my knife. He finally dropped his orange pliers. The startled look on his face when he stared at his gaping arm and the pliers at his feet gave me a second to change my grip on the blade.

Holding the bloody knife in my closed fist like a hammer, I thrust at his chest over and over again. I didn't stop until he dropped to his knees. After the last jab, I pulled my blade out of his flesh and felt it retract like a knife from a melon. My left hand grabbed the hair on the back of his head, and I yanked his skull back, feeling his greasy hair through my fingers.

I held my knife up to his jugular, putting pressure on the blade. I stared directly into his eyes, two inches from his face. I looked down at his bloody face as his pale blue, milky eyes started to roll back in his head. I whispered to him, in a pleading tone, "Please don't make me kill you."

A flicker of understanding crossed his eyes as he gave up and collapsed. He lay at my feet like a beached whale with his blood seeping all over the cheap gray carpet.

Standing over him, I dropped my arm, letting my knife rest at my side. I wiped dripping blood from my eyes and pressed my palm over the open gashes on the top of my head, trying to stop the bleeding. I looked down at the huge man at my feet. I saw a trickle of blood drip out of the side of his mouth, like a small red stream running down his shiny, fat chin. Panic overtook me as I watched his labored breathing.

A loud buzzing erupted in my ears and I felt my heart bursting in my chest. I swallowed back vomit and started to gag. I swung the glass door open and ran out to the sidewalk, throwing my knife underneath a parked car.

The fresh air startled me. I heard someone yelling behind me. I looked back up the steps and saw Harriet and Fritzy flying down the steps shouting, "Oh, my God, Jesse, are you all right, what's happened?"

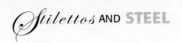

Seeing Harriet's terror-stricken eyes startled me into calmness.

I heard my voice, like a stranger's, say in a matter-of-fact tone, "The dude wouldn't let me in."

Suddenly I got a moment of clarity and reached underneath the car, retrieving my knife. I wiped the blade off on my pants, closed the handle, and clasped it affectionately, enjoying the weight in my palm. I thought to myself with gratitude how fortunate that my younger brother had always given me just the right gift.

I said to them with confidence, "Let's call the heat. This is pure self-defense. I'm going upstairs to clean up and review my books."

I put the buck knife in my trouser pocket next to my cold hard Zippo lighter. My friends stood dazed on the steps in front of me, like children watching a scene out of a horror film.

Harriet cautiously approached me, took me by the arm gently, like a nurse leading a patient and said softly, "Let's get you upstairs and put some ice on those cuts. We will go over your books after we call an ambulance, I promise."

Harriet led the way up the stairs to my delayed appointment. As we crossed the foyer, we carefully stepped around the workman's splayed body.

Chapter 29

THE BLACK MARIAH

I SAT AT **HARRIET'S KITCHEN TABLE,** leaning over a large, red leather-bound ledger, pressing an ice pack to the top of my head. I saw the black numbers, written in my bookkeeper's hand, blur as I fought to stay conscious. I called to Harriet, who was in the living room talking to Junior on the telephone, "Make sure she calls Norman right away. My luck the pigs will bring me in!"

Harriet was talking to Junior like a nurse reporting to the doctor on the condition of her incorrigible patient. "Jesse won't listen to us. We've called an ambulance and we wanted to take her to the emergency room right away. She said she came here to review her books and that's what she's going to do. Junior, she wants you to call her attorney and will you please bring her a clean shirt—the one she's wearing is covered in blood."

Their hysteria interrupted my thoughts as I tried to review my accounts. Finally I got up and took the phone out of Harriet's hand. "Let me talk to Junior."

Before I could tell Junior what I wanted her to do, she asked, "Should I call Carmen? How bad is it? Joe's back. We're coming over there right now!"

"Hold on," I replied. "I'm fine, man. It's a fucking little cut on my head. A few cuts, I guess. Some fat bastard wanted to pick up Prince's chump change. Call Norman, the heat's on the way over here. They'll probably bring me in."

"Okay, boss."

As I hung up the phone, Harriet was staring at me like I had just lost my mind. "What made you and Fritzy finally come downstairs? I was ringing your bell forever!"

My hippie number-crunching friend—who looked as dazed as I felt—replied, "Fritzy and I were going to get some Ripple wine from the liquor store. We were up on the roof meditating, trying to make contact with Ed's spirit, but the brownies we ate made us thirsty."

I just knew those damn hippies had been up on the roof tripping. My head was killing me and my blood-soaked shirt was stuck to my body. I wanted to change into something clean, but I couldn't borrow anything to wear from my stoned accountant and her sister. The two straight hippie chicks only wore the latest flower-child garb.

I folded my arms on the table and rested my head. Closing my eyes, I saw the face of the fat assailant. In the heat of battle, I hadn't had time to think about where I knew the guy from. Picturing his large, well-stocked toolbox, I finally recalled where I had seen the dude before. He had installed some extra door locks for Marie over at the bordello. I wondered if his being here was coincidental or if someone had tipped him off.

There was a pounding on the door. "Open up! It's the police!"

I got up and flashed Harriet a cocky grin. "Let's hope they're on our payroll."

"If not, they are the only cops in the Tenderloin that aren't," Harriet sighed. "I wanted to talk to you about that, Jesse. The cops' payoffs were higher this month than our referral fees."

The cops yelled again. "Open up, police!"

Harriet, not fazed by the posse at the door and determined to discuss business with me, said, "Our payroll cops might help us get rid of the Prince problem. Jesse, they certainly don't want to see you suffer a cash-flow crisis."

As she took her sweet time getting to the door, I replied, "Yeah, Bunny and I were thinking the same thing. This contract on my ass is costing everybody a lot of money."

Harriet announced just before she opened the door, "I hear you officers! I'll be right there in just a minute!"

Harriet unbolted the four locks on the door, letting the two officers enter the room. One cop was young and baby-faced, smartly dressed in his pressed, dark blue, shiny-buttoned uniform. The badge on his breast stated, "Officer Shawn O'Reilly," a befitting name for a beat cop. His older partner smelled of booze and looked like he had spent the night sleeping in the backseat of a car in his disheveled, wrinkled uniform. The black leather belt, hung low around his waist, acted like a girdle holding up his pillowed stomach. On his wide chest, a silver crooked badge read, "Officer James O'Malley," a fine name for a veteran cop.

O'Malley's holstered gun and billy club jiggled at his sides with his rolls of flesh as he walked. His puffy red face lost its mask of indifference when he saw me sitting at the table. His jaw dropped in surprise as he blurted out, "Holy shit, Jesse! That dude was twice your size!"

Officer O'Reilly looked befuddled as he rubbed his clean-shaven chin. "Did you take that dude down? It's not like you to be violent. Jesse, what the fuck happened?"

Taking a clean white, wet towel out of Harriet's attentive hand, I wiped my forehead as I explained myself. "That asshole charged me like a bull, hitting me on the head with a pair of orange pliers. He thought I was a fucking coconut and was trying to crack my fucking head open. I had no choice but to drop the dude."

Officer O'Reilly, the handsome young cop, asked with genuine sincerity, "What did you use on him, Jesse? He looks like a sponge he has so many holes in him."

The older cop said, "I saw the paramedics downstairs wrapping him up in bandages. He looks like a big mummy. The ambulance driver says it's a good thing he's so fat or he'd be dead for sure." He chuckled in admiration.

I had bought O'Malley a few drinks, more than once, as we sat and admired Little Rosie's titty-tassel pasties swirl down at the Grapevine.

"Why don't you just write this up as self-defense and let it slide?" I nicely asked him.

His face screwed up in concern. "Jesse, I'd like to be able to do that. I would, if I had it my way. I'm sorry I can't. If the guy dies, we could catch a lot of heat. We'll have to call our captain and see how he would like us to handle this."

I knew what that meant, and sure enough, when they called in, I could hear Clancy's exuberant voice boom from the receiver. The cop had to hold it far away from his ear.

"Thank God! Bring that pretty little smart-ass in! Book her for attempted murder!"

Officer O'Reilly timidly answered, "Yes sir," and hung up the phone.

With the sound of the click I said, "Oh shit! I need a drink before I take this ride." Harriet poured a glass full of Jack and handed it to me. I shot down the whiskey and told her, "Give the officers a drink."

O'Reilly politely passed. Thirsty O'Malley stood closely behind Harriet in the kitchen, like an impatient patron in a cafeteria line.

I told the young officer, taking handcuffs from his belt, "Your captain and I are old friends."

He answered, "Perhaps, but it sure seems like he doesn't care much for you right now. What's up with that?"

Officer O'Malley looked up from his drink and joked, "Damn! Jesse, you didn't fuck his wife, did you?"

Chuckling, I shook my hurting head and took a deep drag of my cigarette. Officer O'Malley gently took my arm and walked me out the door.

The young cop put a firm grip under my elbow when we reached the stairway and assisted me as we descended towards the lobby. I glanced over the rail and saw in the foyer, two hefty paramedics lifting my attacker onto a stretcher. Layers of thick gauze had been wrapped around his stomach and chest. His eyes were closed and he was unconscious. We reached the bottom of the stairs and followed the stretcher out to the street. I heard the paramedics groan under the strain of their new passenger as they gave a, "Heave-ho!" and pushed him into the back of the ambulance.

The bright noon sunshine no longer felt invigorating as it did merely an hour ago. My joyous basking in freedom while I visited with Feather and Jackson seemed a lifetime away now. The doors of the Black Mariah opened. I walked up the rear steps like a guest at the guillotine and entered the darkness of the cage on wheels.

My eyes adjusted to the lack of light as I held my breath against the stench of urine, vomit and booze. I sidestepped a pool of puke and sat down on the narrow side bench. I lowered my aching head into my cuffed hands, using them like a filter, and took a small breath. I tasted my own blood that continued to seep down my face onto my fingers. I was not concerned about my head wounds or the blood I was losing. I knew my wounds would heal. What disturbed me was that I was losing myself. It had never occurred to me to walk away from the fight. Surrender was no longer an option. Winning and staying on top was now at the core of my nature, regardless of its price.

I heard the engine start and felt the jolt of the wagon as we started down the street. I spread my feet far apart on the filthy floor to keep my balance. If Prince were in front of me, I'd kill him with my bare hands. I was trapped alone in a container built for human waste because of a jealous punk and his kid brother. My life was a living nightmare, and the most terrifying part of the dream was the sweet taste of hate after I plunged my knife into the fat belly of Prince's flunky. I now understood the gut-level rage of war and felt compassion for my older brother fighting in 'Nam.

The small mesh window in the back door allowed a little light to stream through. All alone, I mused on the dark detour my life had taken of late. Realizing that I had hit the lowest point in my life, I felt utterly exhausted. I closed my eyes and rested as we lumbered through the streets.

I was jarred by the lurching stop of the paddy wagon. The door handle squeaked as I got up and walked to the rear of the truck. The welcoming sun greeted my shame as the doors flew open.

Officer O'Reilly said in a fatherly tone, "Are you ready, young lady?"

I nodded my head and said, "Yeah."

"Okay, let's get you stitched up."

Wounded by his kindness, I mumbled, "Right on," quickly forcing my voice to match the stoic mask that fell over my face like a hood.

I was covered in blood, and my suit and shirt were ruined. My clothes smelled like the interior of the paddy wagon, and my own body odor assaulted my nostrils like cheap cologne.

I put my foot down on the ribbed steel steps as I descended from the back of the Black Mariah. Seeing the caked blood spots on the tips of my newly shined black shoes hurt me worse than my head. My wrists were killing me, and the open gashes decorating my crown were clamoring for attention. Officer O'Reilly held my arm to help me keep my balance as he escorted me through the emergency entrance's electric doors.

The faces of the distressed brightened as they saw me enter the waiting room. I was sure they were thinking that whatever their diagnosis might be, it beat going to jail. I avoided their stares of morbid curiosity and self-righteous contempt.

Just as I thought it couldn't get any worse, a portly, middle-aged male pig named Charlie walked into the emergency room. He said to Officer O'Reilly, "I'll take her from here."

Officer O'Reilly released me to the changing of the guards.

"Come on, high roller," said Charlie roughly as he jerked my arm, causing my wrists to hurt and a sharp pain to streak across my head.

My new escort was sporting a three-day old beard and a tire-sized belly, wrapped in a bad attitude. His whole deportment spoke of self-importance. Charlie's slovenly uniform harnessed his watermelon belly that swung like a wrecking-ball as he led the way.

We entered an examination room at the end of the hall. Dressed in green surgical scrubs there stood a wafer-thin nurse with mousy-brown hair. "Hey, Charlie, looks like you'll have to uncuff this one." The nurse spoke to the cop in a harsh voice like I didn't exist. "Get her up on the table. Make sure she's lying on her stomach!"

"All right Sally. I'll uncuff her, but make it quick. She's a live one. And be careful that this dyke doesn't hit on you." Charlie pointed his finger at me in warning and said, "Behave, you fucking queer!" Then he turned around and left the room.

After Charlie's last remark, I studied the nurse's wrinkled face which held a perpetual scowl and thought, "Yeah, right. I can't wait to fuck Sally. Like all gay people, my secret mission in life is to turn all heteros into queers."

Disgusted, I jumped up on the exam table and lay on my stomach. I wondered, "Where the fuck is my lawyer?"

Sally angrily barked orders through pursed lips. "Hang onto the rails! The doctor is very busy. He doesn't have time to numb your head."

As I answered, "Okay," I heard the doctor come in. He barked a few medical orders to the nurse. He vigorously examined my head and then cursed. "I thought this was a woman! More filthy Tenderloin trash…disgusting!"

I closed my eyes and waited for the pain. A teardrop sneaked silently down my cheek. Like a friend it hid from their view. Slowly the tear crossed my face before it fell to the floor without a sound. I swallowed the sobs wailing inside, so as not to give the contemptuous voices above me any satisfaction.

Their contempt wounded deeper than the orange pliers.

Chapter 30

CARMEN POR VIDA

*M*Y ESCORT COP CHARLIE STAYED BY MY SIDE as we exited the elevator and went to the property room. I was handcuffed again, having gotten a few moments' reprieve from having to wear the bracelets during the fingerprinting.

The bright fluorescent lights of the lobby gave the room before me a surreal, cold look. The furniture and the posters on the walls had the same ambiance of every institution catering to the unfortunates of the world. Like a county hospital or the welfare department, the room had a starkness that let you know that nothing pleasant happens here.

The walking-dead pigs, bored to death by the routine of receiving criminals, greeted us with indifference. As they crossed the room, the cops bantered with each other, smug in their superiority to the lowlifes in their care. Shadowed by the tall, straight-as-an-arrow, spit-and-shine man, I felt powerless and tired. The tower of license-to-kill muscle made one more sly remark as he opened the door for me to the small property room. "Jesse, the captain of homicide said to put you in the drunk tank. Guess he doesn't like chicks with dicks," he chuckled as he uncuffed me.

I shot him a "Fuck You" glare and rubbed my wrists, relieved to be free of the police jewelry. A thin, emaciated cop with a limp shuffled up to the window and said from behind the counter, "Take everything out of your pockets and any jewelry you have on and put it in this tray."

I replied in a low defiant voice, "I got the drill." I felt my Zippo in my hand and was reluctant to leave it with the weasel-faced, pale cop. I removed my gold money clip that held a large wad of Bennies from my pocket. I held it with my lighter, along with some loose change and put everything inside the wooden tray. I reached behind my neck and unclasped my silver Saint Christopher medal with its unique little square face and gently placed it in the container. Then I took off my gold cross with the diamond in its center and caressed it between my fingers. I read the inscription on the back: "Carmen Por Vida." The cross was a gift from Carmen and she told me it had been blessed by the Pope. Carmen had purchased it at a secondhand store in Oakland, but I still believed her.

After I signed for my belongings I was given a small handwritten pink receipt. Charlie then took me by the elbow, guided me out the door and we walked side by side down the stark corridor.

We came upon an open office with a tiny desk and a large matron sitting at it. She reluctantly levered her burdensome body out of the chair and said to me, "Well, if it isn't Jesse the pimp. Welcome to HELL!" After emphasizing the word "hell," she grinned.

"Thank you," I said, pleasantly smiling back. When I heard her voice, it occurred to me that I had met her somewhere before, but I just couldn't place where it was.

She then said to Charlie, "I'll take her from here," as she opened the door to the cellblock.

I left my date for the day and followed the older woman with the short, stiff hairdo. The brunette had streaks of silver in her hair at the temples, making her head look like a football helmet with racing stripes.

The matron's practical black, thick-rubber-soled shoes squeaked as she led the way with a key in her hand. I avoided the eyes of the cellmates as I made my way through a gauntlet of misery. Still, I was curious to find out who the matron was, so I asked her, "Excuse me, ma'am, do I know you?"

The gruff woman replied, "We both admire the same lady, Little Rosie. God only knows why she likes you."

Then I realized she was Little Rosie's woman trick who always sat at the end of the bar, drowning her frustration in beer and pretzels. She shook her head in disgust and opened the cell door.

I heard an excited, "Jesse!" come from the cell's back, bottom bunk. I recognized the Afro-headed youngster, whose street name was, "Nikki the Grape." She sat up in excitement, overjoyed to see me. "Jesse the pimp! How cool! It's you, man. Is it really you, man?"

I entered my cell and heard the dreaded, "clank" as the jealous matron blew me a little kiss from her plump lips. "Have fun, Jesse."

I had been reduced to the lowest accommodations with the bottom of the street hierarchy. Much to my disgust, I was sharing a cell with Nikki, a notorious teenage winette. Thrilled with my arrival, she started talking a mile a minute as I sat down on the lower bunk across from her, holding my head in my hands. I heard her chattering faster than a chicken pickin' corn. "Damn, Jesse, I can't believe you're in the drunk tank. Good to see you, man, I'm honored. But you're a VIP. Why aren't you in the felony tank?"

I reluctantly replied, "The head dick doesn't like me. I'm not very popular with the matron either. She's a trick of Little Rosie's and probably resents paying for what I get for free."

A flicker of compassion entered her warbly voice. "Did Prince's boys crunch your head? You look like shit. Damn, they chopped your fine-ass-hair off! I can see your skull!"

I pleaded to my excited cellmate, "Can you cool it for a minute? My head is killing me."

She then slowed down to take a breath. In the moment of blessed silence, I asked my bunk buddy a question. "Do you have a smoke?"

She moved faster than her chatter as she reached under her pillow and pulled out a small pouch of Bull Durham, a cheap-shit tobacco, along with a pack of Zig-Zags. Nikki licked, talked, twisted and rolled the tobacco in a blur. She looked at me wide-eyed. "Damn, Jesse, your shirt's covered in blood. What the fuck happened?"

I took the wet, hand-rolled cigarette from her and gave her the rundown. "I had a disagreement with a gentleman. I've been booked for attempted murder. I hope the son-of-a-bitch lives. I had to stab him at least a dozen times before he dropped."

Nikki lit my cigarette with trembling hands, holding the wooden match in her pencil-thin fingers. The tremors in her hands were pre-views of coming attractions if she didn't get a drink in her soon. The young girl sitting across from me, who never had a legal drink, was slowly backing into the DTs.

"Jessica Rawlson, you have a visitor!" shouted the matron.

That was quick. Gladly, I followed the guard to the visiting room. The small enclave housed a black phone on top of a wooden counter. Pulling out the chair, I sat down in front of the security glass.

Carmen approached the other side of the glass, looking like a pop star. Her hair, styled in a flip, fell under a hot pink mod cap. Knee high, leather go-go boots added to her self-assured stride.

We each picked up the telephone receivers in front of us.

"You look really beautiful, especially in this joint, baby doll," I said to the unexpected visitor as she sat down in front of me.

"Well, I can't say the same for you Jesse," Carmen replied.

"Oh, this is nothing," I said, trying to hold my aching head high. "You should see the other guy."

"That's what I heard," Carmen commented with admiration.

"I'm surprised to see you, girl," I said sardonically. Hope I didn't pull you away from your favorite john."

"There's no such thing as a favorite john, silly," Carmen assured me with a warm smile. She glanced up to the top of my head. "Whoa! You look like Friar Tuck after a bad day."

I gave her a wry smile and just nodded. Studying my girl, who sat dolled up, rich in rags and freedom, I realized the tables had turned.

"Jesse, it seems like you could use a little assistance," Carmen said softly. "Bunny's called Norman and they're working on getting your bail lowered. But your lawyer's not certain he's gonna be able to get you out of here."

"Great. Fifteen years over my head for my last bust and now this," I groaned.

"Bunny is doing what she can, but I think I'm the one who holds the keys," Carmen said with a sly smile. She dangled her influence with the D.A. in front of me like a huge carrot.

If the walrus died, bail might not even be an option. "If that's the case, let's get me released," I said impatiently.

"Well, now that I think about it, maybe it won't be so easy to pull off." Obviously, my girl was holding out. She wanted me to apologize.

"All right, baby doll. I've been a complete asshole," I confessed. Carmen remained silent, as if in deep thought.

"You're the only girl for me. I need your help." My squirming was accented with a true sincerity. I definitely needed her help.

"How long do you think it will take your D.A. boy to get my ass out of here?"

"About as long as it will take for you to respect me, Jesse," Carmen quipped back.

I was at a loss for words. Regrouping, I assumed she wanted to hear some girly-girl shit. Maybe talk about my innermost feelings.

Carmen demanded that she was number one emotionally with me. Women came with the pimping game. But she would not share my heart.

"Oh yeah, I got it. We've been having a hard time lately. Like Liz Taylor and Richard Burton, right?"

Carmen finally smiled, watching me work so hard.

"You're the first lady of my heart. I just get crazy because I got too much passion for ya," I told her.

"We're in a love-hate relationship, Jesse. I read about a couple like us in *Dear Abby*."

"Oh, really?" I shot back. "What was the article's title? TWO QUEERS WALKED DOWN ROCKY ROMANTIC ROAD?"

Carmen's eyes grew misty—she had been thinking while we were parted. "Jesse, we could leave the Tenderloin. My parents will take us in."

"Are you jonesin' for the square life? Like the weekend queers do? Is that what you're saying, Carmen?" I inquired softly.

"Maybe you could go to barber school," Carmen mused out loud.

"I'm working on something, but it sure isn't barber school."

Carmen looked like she was going to break down crying. "You look awful, Jesse. It hurts me to see you like this. Phillip's waiting on my call. I'm gonna ask him to help us."

The crinkles in her face cleared as something suddenly caught her attention. "Jesse, slide the base of your telephone aside. I want you to see something."

Pushing the phone, I read, "JESSE AND CARMEN POR VIDA," carved into the wooden counter.

"My feelings are still the same, Jesse."

"When did you do this, girl?" I asked with a broad smile. "I didn't know you were a jailbird."

"Three years ago I got busted for panhandling. How do you

think I got the bus fare to come and see you from Oakland? You didn't know it, but I was still in high school."

"I should have been too," I said admiring the carved letters. "We've come a long way, baby doll."

"Yeah, but we're still in the TL."

"It might be fun to play house in the suburbs," I suggested. "After all, that's where I'm from."

"Jesse, I know that no one ever leaves the Tenderloin," Carmen said with resignation in her voice. "This is the only place they'll let us be together. But I love knowing that you've thought of leaving with me."

I wondered if outside of the Tenderloin, our love would die from having to live in the shadows. The fantasy of a happy ending was too good to trust.

"I love you, Carmen." I gently put down the phone as she turned and walked away.

The matron escorted me back to the slovenly day room. I passed women sleeping on newspapers, strewn across the cement floor. A couple of inmates, playing cards and talking shit, looked up at me with respect.

I found an empty bench, sat down and smoked a cigarette. My head was pounding, but my mood was better. Carmen and I had a bond that couldn't be explained. It ran through me like the cells of my body. Comforted by that thought, I put my head down on the table and fell asleep.

My nap was rudely interrupted by a rough slap on the back. The coarse voice of Helmet Head cried, "Wake up bitch! Captain Clancy would like to have a chat with you!"

I was led to a dimly lit, cluttered cubbyhole directly behind the glass-partitioned day room, where I could still hear the chatter of the confined ladies. The big man in a white shirt, with rolled-up sleeves and a cheap pen sticking out of his pocket, smiled tightly at me. "Well, Jessica, how are you enjoying your accommodations? I'm sure you're hard at work trying to recruit a new stable."

Remembering my lawyer's advice, I said nothing. Clancy took a short stubby pencil indented with teeth marks in his paw. His thick fingers, with curly black hair between the knuckles, scribbled my name on top of a yellow legal pad. The hair on his fingers matched his wiry, black Brillo-Pad toupee. He tossed the legal pad at me, like a ball to a dog, expecting me to catch it as he barked, "Write your own fuckin' statement down!"

He leaned forward and intently stared at me. "Let me help you. Just write you stabbed an innocent man twelve times and that you're sorry. How about that? And just for the record, Jessica, it looks like he is going to die. So guess what? You'll be looking at manslaughter or murder in the second degree instead of assault with a deadly weapon."

Captain Clancy sat back, enjoying his revenge. He wasn't counting on my defiance.

"I have nothing to say."

He jumped up and pounded his large fist on his desk, making a glass jar filled with pencils crash to the floor and shatter. "Damn you, Jessica! You motherfuckin' bull-dyke!"

In response, the girls in the day room started yelling at the top of their lungs. Their wails of indignation penetrated the glass. "Stop it, stop it! You motherfuckin' pig! Show her some respect. She's a woman, you lame ass!"

Helmet Head popped into the room like the riot police preventing a full-fledged revolt. "Captain, this woman is to be released immediately."

Captain Clancy whirled about, his face bright red. "What did you say?"

"Sir, the D.A.'s office just called and informed us that the man Jesse stabbed had just been released from Camarillo State Mental Hospital. He has a long history of assault. Sir, we don't have a case, and the powers that be at the D.A.'s office believe this was self-defense. They took a statement from the whack job when he came to after surgery. Unfortunately, he is not fit to stand trial, and he does not wish to press charges."

Seething, Captain Clancy glared at me and said, "Okay, Jessica...you're free to go." As I got up to leave he added, "I'm having a little barbecue in my backyard next weekend. I've invited all the rookies to come over and clean up my dog's shit. Maybe you would like to join them? You are more than welcome to come to the party, but of course you have to wear a dress. It is the appropriate attire for a woman. You can't come to my house unless you dress like a lady. And put some makeup on too while you're at it."

Helmet Head beckoned to escort me out. Before I exited, I smiled and said, "I'd be happy to wear a dress and makeup, Clancy. Do you mind if I borrow yours?" Then I blew him a kiss and left the room.

In no time at all, I had called Nick, gotten my belongings from the property room and left Hotel Hell. I viewed the vista of the city before me from the jailhouse doors, elated to be free.

I ran down each step, skipping and dancing. I dashed toward Nick's waiting cab, which was parked across the street under the lamppost. I wanted to run all the way home, shouting to the world, "Look at me, motherfuckers! I'm still here on the streets! It's all about who's left standing! I'm still standing, motherfuckers!"

The chrome door handle of the big yellow chariot looked like an old friend welcoming me to safety. I grabbed it and jumped in. I slid across the backseat and sat behind Nick. He gave me his cabbie half-turn.

"What's your pleasure, Jesse?"

"Take me home!"

He quickly rubbed his Saint Christopher medal, patted Jesus on the head, threw the black meter down and spun off toward Sutter Street.

My head was pounding, but I took comfort in the hum of the tires. I listened to the sound of the pavement disappearing behind us. I yearned for a drink.

The first thing I would do when I got home would be to have a shot of Jack and a chat with Joe Gomez. Nick interrupted my thoughts and asked, "Are you okay, Jesse?"

"Yeah, just tired and I need a bath."

"Boss, would you like me to drive you over to Marie's? Maybe you should let her take care of you."

"No, Nick. Just get me home."

I drifted into a sweet fantasy of revenge, passing the time thinking of a way I could pay Prince back. In my mind's eye, I saw Prince on a fishing boat out at sea. It was late at night, and he was lying strapped atop a bait tank. Prince looked up at Joe Gomez, who stood over him solemnly holding his long glinting knife...."What the— " was all that the doomed pimp managed to blurt out before Joe put his rock-hard hand over Prince's mouth. Like his tribal cousins, the Aztecs, the Yaqui ceremonial priest raised the shiny steel blade before Prince's eyes.

The scarred, dark-faced avenger pledged into the empty night like an Indian chief, "I will take your flesh. I will stuff your mouth with your own skin. Then I will feed you to the hungry sharks."

As Joe proceeded to keep his word, I looked away. The stoic Yaqui performed his task mercilessly under the watchful eyes of his ancestors, my crew and the starlit heavens…

My thoughts were interrupted by Nick's voice. "Jesse, you are awful quiet. Are you sure you're alright?"

I opened my eyes to the sight of my apartment building as we pulled up to the curb. "Yeah, Nick, I'm okay."

I was startled by my fantasy of revenge and asked God to forgive me. I prayed for my sanity. Yet as I stepped out of the taxi, I was greeted by Joe Gomez.

The bull of a man charged the cab. I raised my hand up in self-defense, expecting a lecture from my one-eyed baby-sitter. Instead, Joe greeted me like a long-lost sister as he threw his gigantic muscled arms around me. As the gangster squeezed me hello, the scent of Brylcreem reminded me of why I preferred women.

"Jesse girl, let me get you in the house! I want you off the sidewalk." Joe put his arm around my shoulder, pushing me towards my front door.

Joe's large frame was sheathed in a baby-blue suit, which only a one-eyed Yaqui Indian would be brave enough to wear. The hem of his slacks rested on top of his new black-and-white spectator shoes.

"Joe, it's good to see you back on your feet again. Don't start in on me. I know I was wrong to split on Junior. I promise it won't happen again if you promise not to wear baby blue in the winter."

Joe laughed and gave a snort through his flat, bull-sized nose, "*Chingado*! You're one crazy bitch! Who did this to you, boss? Tell me so I can go and cut off his balls."

"I wouldn't worry about him. He was just a fool that thought he had a good idea. I want you to leave him alone. He won't be out of the hospital for a long time at any rate. We won't have any trouble with him again. Trust me, we have bigger fish to fry."

We got into the cramped elevator with Joe's big body taking up more space than is dignified. He looked curiously at my head as we silently rode upward.

To escape his scrutiny, I yanked the ornate, gold accordion doors open as we reached the third floor and made a beeline to my pad. Junior, with a smile on her face and a drink in her hand, opened my front door before I even reached it. The relief on her face was as welcoming as the crystal glass filled with Jack.

"*Oralé* Jesse! I am so happy to see you, man! There is a hot tub waiting for you. Bunny is on her way over." Her voice dropped. "I hate to tell you, boss, but Little Rosie's in the living room. She's been here all day crying. If I was you, I'd take a bath now 'cause it's the only peace you're going to have for a while."

I just nodded my aching head and took a good swig of the whiskey. I felt the warm liquid burn down my throat, like an elixir of peace, fortifying me for the chi-chi mama who barreled down the hall toward me like a roller-derby chick.

I could hear her exclaim as I dashed into the bathroom and slammed the door, "Jesse baby! It's a miracle! Thank God, the Virgin Mary and all the saints heard our prayers. Come out of the bathroom, honey. Let me hug you a little!"

Her words were mercifully drowned out by the gushing water that I turned on to reheat the tub. I heard Junior shoo her away like a mother protecting a tired father assaulted by excited children the moment he walks through the front door after work. "Rosie, not now!"

Their voices kept me company in the bathroom as I regarded the stranger in the mirror. My brown eyes now had a hint of a different spirit behind them. I leaned into the mirror over the clean sink and admired the doctor's handiwork. Large cords and black sutures stuck out of my flesh like thread sewn through a Thanksgiving turkey breast.

As I washed my face, getting the specks of blood off my forehead, I really appreciated old Dr. Rath now. When I had my appendix out at age twelve, he had used extra-small stitches so that I wouldn't scar badly. He said that I was a beautiful girl and that the last thing I needed was an ugly pelvic scar. The stitches on my head and my shaved crown made me look like a Franciscan friar who had been sewn up by a butcher. My rage at Prince for doing this to me boiled a little higher.

I hurriedly unbuttoned my shirt and stepped out of my filthy slacks, throwing them both in the trash bucket beneath the sink. I never wanted to see that bad luck clothing again. I yelled through the door as I hopped into the tub, "Junior, tell Rosie I'll talk to her and Bunny after I'm cleaned up. Get everyone over here in twenty minutes. We're going to have an emergency meeting."

Junior shouted back through the door, "Okay boss, but do you think it's safe?"

"Yeah, Prince's crew thinks my ass is still in jail. Tell them to be careful but to get over here right away. Call Animal and his bikers and tell them to pick up my people and escort them over here."

"Okay boss, you got it."

As I closed my eyes and slipped into the tub, the warm, soothing water flowed over my half-bald head. I was grateful I had so many Stetson hats. The hat that was knocked off of my head during the fight had definitely bit the dust. Within moments I was dressed in the clean clothes that Junior had laid out for me in the bathroom. Another thoughtful touch waited on the sink: a glass filled with Jack Daniel's next to two Darvocet pain pills and a clean Ace bandage binder.

When I saw the Darvocet pills, I realized that Bunny must have been at my house earlier that day. She was the only one who carried those wonderful pills. She always said that she was a good Jewish girl and believed in being prepared for health problems. I started to comb my chopped-up hair and thought it was a good thing hair grows fast.

I took the pills and swallowed them. I splashed my neck with Aramis and then removed the gold cross. Not accustomed to wearing so much religious jewelry around my neck, I was beginning to feel like Nick's dashboard.

As I held the cross in my hand, I was captivated by its glistening diamond and the irony of the gift. I reread the inscription on the back, "Carmen Por Vida." I studied it, feeling the edges in my fingers. I slipped the cross in my slacks pocket to keep my Zippo lighter company.

Suddenly, a stab of pain pierced my chest. I gasped for breath as I leaned on the sink and clutched the faucet handles, waiting for the pain to pass. I was too young for a heart attack.

I gasped in rapid breaths as I fought the panic that was overtaking me. I sank to my knees, put my head down between them and clutched my hands behind my neck like a child in a drop drill.

With my eyes closed, I felt terror encroaching and struggled to overcome its titanic wave. My blind fear told me that each panting breath was my last. Yet the other side of my mind urged me to breathe slowly as I rested on my knees on the cold tiled floor.

From my innermost self, I heard a voice of reason. "Jesse, you're having a panic attack. It will pass. You almost died today."

Each fully drawn breath slowed my fear down. I envisioned the floating pale blue eyes of the man that I had stabbed today rolling back in his head. I knew then that the terror I felt was not from my brush with death, but from almost taking the life of another human being.

I feared more for my soul than my body as I prayed quietly on my knees. As I curled into a fetal position, I whispered to myself, "God help me. I can't do this. I don't know how to do this, Father."

I wanted to lie prostrate on the cold floor, but I had to get up. I fought off the self-righteous voices that repeated in my head. "God doesn't love you. You are a queer and you will go to Hell. You will not die in God's presence because you are different!"

Junior rapped on the door, saving me from my tortured thoughts. "Hey boss, are you okay? Can I come in? Do you need anything?"

I grabbed onto the sink counter and pulled myself up. In a shaky voice, I told myself, "Get up, Jesse. You can do this. In the Tenderloin, it's all about who's left standing!" More loudly, I told my concerned henchman, "I'm fine. I'll be out in a minute."

Junior shot back, happily, "Cool! Everyone's here. Prince or the U.S. Army couldn't keep them away."

I managed a smile and said to my reflection in the mirror, "A rat-a-tat-tat, Jesse's back! It's show time!"

Chapter 31

DORIS AND THE DYKETTES

*T*HE LAST FEW DAYS SINCE MY ENCOUNTER with the fat, pliers-wielding bastard had passed uneventfully. Tonight I had issued the order to charge. No longer on my knees, I looked forward to giving Prince a taste of his own medicine. After careful calculation, I decided to implement an old military tool of deception. My crew and I were dressed in full-fledged camouflage.

The big van rumbled down the alley behind Chuckkers with Rascal at the wheel. The radio was blaring, "Chain of Fools," which my crew was enthusiastically singing along with. I sat in the backseat squished between Junior and Little Rosie, thinking, "This is a *van* of fools."

I had a sudden twinge of fear that our reverse-drag camouflage would be detected and that this mission might fail. I was afraid that Prince's henchmen, parked outside surveying Chuckkers, would recognize members of my crew, even though we were in disguise. Rascal, Junior and I were wearing dresses, wigs, makeup and stiletto heels. We were all dolled up like showgirls. Asian Pearl and Little Rosie were dressed like butches. Little Rosie looked like Elvis and Asian Pearl like John Lennon. My concern about being recognized was reinforced when the van went over a big pothole in the alley, jolting us all and tilting Rascal's sleek black, pageboy wig.

We were impersonating a singing group and performing at Chuckkers nightclub tonight. I wanted my crew on stage in front of a club full of witnesses who could attest to our whereabouts. We just had to get safely past Prince's men into the nightclub. Before our performance, my troops would attend a secret meeting upstairs in Carla's office.

Rascal, the muscular bull-dyke, daintily adjusted her wig. She turned to Doris, our choreographer, who was sitting next to her, and asked in a high, squeaky voice, "Do I look okay?"

Rascal's big hands grasped the wheel of the passenger van that displayed "Doris & the Dykettes," freshly painted in large letters on the side. Doris, sitting shotgun, was warming up her voice, preparing for her, "Proud Mary" solo. She was a good friend and neighbor who lived across the hall from me. She had joined us in this masquerade to help us out of a jam.

The pretty-faced black woman was straight, but she was as blind to sexual preference as I was to color. The past year we had become very close friends. I would often attend Glide Memorial Church on Eddy Street to hear Doris sing. Her voice was as pleasant as she was.

Tonight, Doris was all dolled up in a sequined black dress and long rhinestone earrings that matched her jeweled, black satin pumps. She had organized our make-believe group of entertainers and helped get the butches dressed as femmes and the femmes as butches. She was aided by Miss Zada and Miss Penny in transforming my crew. I could barely recognize them by the time the gender-deception experts had finished applying the theatrical costuming.

The only thing that gave my crew members away was their distinct personalities, which could not be hidden under the wigs, makeup and strap-on dongs. I had issued the order that, under no circumstances, was anyone to smoke grass tonight, knowing that if a bullet didn't kill us, our own laughter would for sure.

Like a nervous Broadway choreographer, Doris lovingly turned around to address her troupe of wandering minstrels. "Now remember, girls, just keep smiling onstage! Breathe, keep moving and keep smiling! Just follow my dance-steps and BREATHE!"

Little Rosie had been practicing speaking like Elvis Presley, in hopes her voice would match her sideburns and wig. She drawled in a low southern voice, "How can I fucking breathe with this tight-ass, titty-killing binder wrapped around my chi-chis? Uh-huh!"

Asian Pearl dropped her British accent as quickly as she could pierce her pointed chopsticks into someone's balls. She yelled at Rosie from the second row, "Quit whining, bitch! At least you're a fucking brunette. I've got a blond Beatles' wig on! I look like a rice bowl with hair. Plus, I can't see through these fucking round-rimmed, John Lennon glasses. I look like a freak. Whoever saw a blond Asian on the *Ed Sullivan Show*?"

I ordered them both to cool it. Their stage fright was starting to make them unruly. My main concern was that the stage wouldn't withstand Rascal's gigantic body in motion. It was one thing for the platform to support the band, but it was another for it to hold Rascal and all the other girls dancing and performing our act. As a preventative measure, I had split my crew into two acts.

I told Rascal to drive around Chuckkers a few times to get a handle on how many of Prince's boys were staking out the club.

"Okay, Jesse," Rascal replied in a high voice, more appropriate coming from a lady dressed in a basic black dress and white pearls.

I stared at Rascal, the muscle-bulging migrant farm worker, praying that she could actually walk in her high heels. The bull-dyke's defined forearms showed every flat of grapes she ever carried.

Our van drove alongside the '68 purple El Dorado. It was the same color as Prince's favorite suit. Inside, two of his men were dozing in the front seat on their stake-out.

I ordered Rascal, "Hurry up and pull us around back. Lovey Lupree should be hooking up with us upstairs in a few minutes. Let's get into the club now before those boys wake up from their nap."

Rascal nodded her big head, careful not to tilt her wig. The butch in pearls then politely squeaked, "My pleasure, Jesse!"

Passing the club's marquis, I read:

"CHUCKKERS PROUDLY PRESENTS: DORIS & THE DYKETTES MUSICAL REVIEW…AND SURPRISE GUEST ARTIST."

Within seconds, the Doris & the Dykettes tour van came to a screeching halt behind the club next to the trash cans. Rascal grunted as she got out of the driver's seat and turned the handle of the sliding passenger door. I heard the door open. My crew got quiet, preparing to disembark. Like paratroopers over Normandy, they jumped out the side of the van as if it were a military transport.

I hit the wet pavement running and yelled, "Charge!" I stumbled in my four-inch stiletto heels. Picking myself up, I hiked the satin midnight blue gown up above my knees and sprinted again with my troops behind me.

As we made our way to the back door of Chuckkers, my first lieutenant, Junior, passed me with long strides. She looked marvelous, revealing a firm thigh in the split of her red Flamenco dress. My henchman pushed the door open, dropping the Spanish fan that was wrapped around her wrist. She held the door as we filed in.

The barmaid Kitty, holding a huge tray of drinks above her head, stepped aside to avoid being knocked down by the passing troop of strange entertainers. We marched up the narrow stairway to Carla's office.

I heard Kitty's lust-filled voice behind me. Like a cat in heat, she whined to Asian Pearl, "Love the Lennon glasses, you Brit bad boy."

Asian Pearl shot back, "Nice tits, bitch!"

Kitty moaned, "I'm off at two."

I tossed my long hair over my bare shoulder and yelled, "Move it, Beatle boy!" as I rescued Miss Kitty from death by chopstick.

We ascended to the top of the stairs and rushed into the office. Carla, the drag queen owner of Chuckkers, usually shied away from violence in her club. Tonight, however, she fully supported us in this momentous battle defending our gay turf.

The room was arranged with rows of little brown leopard-skin chairs, placed neatly in front of a large blackboard in her spacious, gaudy office. The walls were covered with expensive fuchsia fabric, and a zebra-print chaise lounge occupied the corner. From the ceiling hung a glittering chandelier spotlighting a nude Greek Adonis statue with a laurel leaf crown on its head and a pronounced penis. The walls displayed huge blown-up photographs and oil paintings of Carla, the queen herself, in poses of her favorite idols: Marilyn Monroe, Judy Garland, Betty Davis, Barbara Streisand, Diana Ross and Mae West.

In the corner was a fabulous wet bar stocked with a plethora of top-shelf liquor and fresh ice, awaiting our clandestine assembly. As we filled the room, I told the girls to help themselves to a drink and take a seat.

I filled a water glass full of Jack Daniel's straight up and downed it like a shot. Growing more and more annoyed, I peeled the partially attached false eyelash off my eyelid and stuck it onto the side of my glass. I searched for my lighter and pack of Pall Malls from their new home in my cleavage, which was supported by an awful wired push-up bra. I took out a cig, threw open my lighter and carefully lit up so as to not burn my wig.

Standing in front of the chairs, I called the meeting to attention. I turned for a moment, bent over, and adjusted my tits. My girls settled into the chairs behind me. I found it challenging to get into the mindset of a commanding officer while in heels and a dress.

I saw waves of apprehension running through my troops. Sensing the stage fright as the amateur hour grew near, I told them, "Calm down, ladies. You all look great. Just think of it as playing army and Halloween all on the same night. If you can face fuckin' tricks, gangsters, pigs and squares, you can certainly get through this meeting. We're gonna keep it short and simple."

I heard a knock at the door. Rascal extracted a small silver pistol from her garter belt and leaned her massive body against the door. In her squeaky voice she demanded, "Who the fuck's there?"

A rough voice bellowed through the door, "It's Red. Lovey Lupree is here with me. One-hundred-and-one and you're done."

I picked up a piece of thick chalk from the blackboard and said, "Let 'em in."

As Rascal opened the door, a breeze from the South fluttered in, with the smell of fragrant magnolias surrounding her. The room gasped, enchanted with the gorgeous Creole as she sauntered in, twirling a large parasol. She wore a sea-foam green, spaghetti-strapped dress, revealing voluptuous breasts. On her ears were teardrop diamonds that matched her diamond-studded front tooth.

Lovey smiled as she sashayed toward the front row of seats and said in a singsong upbeat tone, "Lovey Lupree's here, as you can see. I wanna be part of history. We're gonna fight and make it right. It's time for them to pay for that hooker heist!" She gave the room a broad smile and added, "The pigs can't get us 'cause we'll be in plain sight!"

Little Rosie was adjusting the huge rubbery dildo that was strapped to the side of her leg and poking her thigh under her pants. Lovey held her parasol over her shoulder, refusing to set it down.

I imagined that it had a retractable blade on the end, just like her deadly umbrella.

With a commanding voice I took control of my crew. "Okay, everybody calm down! Let's get back to business. You look lovely, Lovey. I'm sure our southern friend agrees that all of this bullshit has hurt every one of us in the pocketbook."

Lovey Lupree quipped, "How do you make a whore moan? You don't pay her!" She laughed out loud and the rest of my crew followed suit. For the first time this evening, everyone appeared relaxed.

"Now girls," I continued, "I grew up watching gangster movies and learned a thing or two from them. If a mob boss wanted someone whacked or worked over, they always brought in thugs from another town to do the job. Usually that unknown muscle came from a small town in Italy, but in our case, it's Mexico."

My crew chuckled as I continued. "Knocking off a head boss like Prince would threaten the other Fillmore pimps. That could bring us more enemies and a bloody battle we don't want to fight." I paused to emphasize that point. "The Prince problem can be handled in more creative ways. We'll take his crew out quietly, one kneecap at a time. I'm going to try and keep it civilized."

My crew was captivated by all the planning. "As the war escalates between us, it will put all the other Fillmore bosses under the spotlight. The mayor doesn't want violence in the city. The powers that be are trying to hustle war on poverty dollars from the Feds. The pigs will start hassling every pimp in San Francisco. Luckily, we have an advantage the men don't have to survive the heat. Thankfully, we have friends in high places. The disruption to the Fillmore pimps' business will persuade them to pressure Prince to call a truce." Several girls nodded, understanding the reference to Carmen.

"Tonight, we will do things the old-fashioned way and apply a little muscle. We'll be on stage in full view of the Tenderloin, so when the shit hits the fan it can't be traced back to us."

I checked my watch and gave my battle orders like a general. "Ladies! On stage right now! Break a leg!" I led the way through the door and down the stairs. My tits bounced to the sound of my girls' giggles.

The brass of the Motown band at the rear of the stage glistened under the stage lights. Miss Carla held a silver microphone in her hand. She was dressed in a long, black-sequined gown and glittered with excitement. Her Marie Antoinette-styled hair rose like a skyscraper toward the ceiling. Strutting onto the stage, dangling the mic cord behind her like a train, she announced, "Ladies and gentlemen, Chuckkers proudly presents, Doris and the Dykettes!"

The crowd erupted in thunderous applause. Junior, Lovey, Rascal and I stood in the wings. We watched Doris march on stage with Little Rosie. Asian Pearl followed closely behind, angrily cussing in Chinese as she fixed her wig. The pounding beat of the Motown rhythm band lit up the stage with the music of "Proud Mary." Doris hiked up her dress up like Tina Turner, revealing plump legs as she flew onto the stage dancing.

She grabbed the mic, pranced down the stage and sang, "Left a good job in the city...." Asian Pearl and Little Rosie spun their arms to the beat, shouting out, "Rolling, rolling, rolling on the river!"

Little Rosie added a few moves of her own, swishing her hips with a Latin flair from left to right. Her tight trousers disclosed an unwelcome bulge that she self-consciously kept pushing down against her thigh. Asian Pearl pushed Little Rosie, who bumped her while shaking her ass in Pearl's dance space. Pearl kept swirling her arms as she shouted, "Move it, bitch!" Miraculously, the femmes finished the number without killing each other. The packed house cheered. Doris & The Dykettes were a hit!

Doris, Rosie and Pearl bowed and ran offstage. Doris passed me and said, "Break a leg, Jesse!" Miss Carla took to the stage again, blowing kisses to the singers as they exited. The glittering queen walked to center stage and dramatically paused until the crowd was quiet. "Ladies and gentlemen, now the surprise act you've all been waiting for. I present to you, the sexiest, hottest, badass bitches this side of the Golden Gate." Excitedly Carla shouted into the microphone, "The Tenderloin's very own…Jesse and Her Outlaws!"

As a thunderous wave of applause burst over the stage, terror jolted through me. I felt nude in my low-cut dress, panty hose and g-string. I looked at the clumsy butches in heels behind me and prayed. Waves of catcalls and roars of applause shook the room.

"Ladies!" I shouted to my butch enforcers. "Tits up!"

"Stop in the Name of Love" started up. "Follow me!" I ordered as I ran on stage. Using flamboyant gestures I picked up from Miss Zada, I sang lead while my butch buddies moved behind me like synchronized swimmers. I dramatically thrust my hand forward like a diva as I pleaded, "Stop in the name of love!"

I pushed my wig out of my eyes and looked behind me. I cringed as I witnessed the botched choreography of my backup singers. Rascal stumbled about, totally off the beat in tight shoes that tortured her toes. I made it to the finale, exhausted from balancing in my stilettos. As our left hands shot up like stop signs, we all shouted, "Stop!"

The audience roared as we took our final bow. Flashbulbs flickered before us as I caught sight of Doris enjoying a cocktail at the bar. She was sitting next to Captain Clancy and a couple of his undercover cops. The shocked expression on Clancy's face was probably due to finally seeing me in a dress.

As we took a deep formal bow, we heard Rascal's dress tear up her buttocks. Much to my dismay it was followed by the loud sound of her gun clanking to her feet on the stage. Rascal, looking like a wide-eyed Buckwheat, stood and gasped. I prayed that the distraction of Rascal's huge bosom would divert Clancy's attention.

Like alert soldiers, Junior stood close and acted like a shield while Lovey began to spin her parasol low to the floor. Behind the spinning cover, Rascal picked up her piece and daintily stuffed it between her huge tits. The quick maneuver worked.

As we left the stage, we heard shouts of, "Encore, encore!" Unable to escape Miss Carla, who blocked my retreat with an insistent push, I returned to the stage. I turned around and told my backup singers, "Let's do 'My Guy.'"

Junior answered, "You got it, boss," as Rascal and Lovey nodded in agreement.

The band leader looked toward me for my cue. Over the wails of, "More!" I told him, "Play Mary Wells', 'My Guy'," as my high-heeled dyke buddies loyally stumbled behind me.

Leading the way, I sang, "Nothing you can say can tear me away from my guy."

Stunned, Captain Clancy watched from the audience as my back-up chorus chimed in, "My guy."

I leaned forward, exposing my pushed-up cleavage. Gazing sexily at Clancy, I sang, "Nothing you can do 'cause I'm stuck like glue to my guy." Slowly, while emphasizing the lyrics, "I'm sticking to my guy like a stamp to a letter," I pantomimed licking a postage stamp and a long envelope.

Playfully, I taunted the beet-faced captain as the audience sang along with laughter. Happily, I sang out, "No muscle-bound man could take my hand from my guy."

Rascal, Junior and Lovey flexed their muscles to the beat in sleeveless gowns as they echoed, "My guy." We finished our big finale. I blew a kiss to Clancy before bowing to our adoring fans. They crowded around us as my crew hustled back upstairs to reconvene our meeting.

Once in Carla's office, we all grabbed a drink and celebrated our performances, congratulating each other and reliving the moment.

"All right ladies, good job. Let's sit down and finish up our business." I ordered. "I want to get the fuck out of these clothes."

Everyone took a seat and quieted down. I knocked off a shooter of Jack and lit up a fat joint which I'd stashed in my pushup bra. After a long drag, I passed the bomber around the room. "Enjoy, ladies… you've earned it," I said. A mellow hush fell over my exhausted crew as we unwound.

Just then, we were startled by an unexpected pounding on the door. Everybody jumped from their seats. Rascal rushed to the door again and squeaked, "Who's there? What's your code?"

When there was no reply or sound of Red's coarse voice outside, I ran to the door and pulled out my gun from my garter belt. I demanded, "What's your code, dude?"

Drowning out Red's reply was the voice of Two Bits the hippie. Hysterically shouting like the house was on fire, she exclaimed, "Jesse! Boss, it's me! I got an important message. Let me in!"

I put my .38 back in my garter belt holster. I instinctively turned around and waited for my troops to put their weapons down so I wouldn't be hit by friendly fire.

I opened the door. Red's denim jacket brushed my shoulder with his huge red beard. He was just a blur as he jolted past me. I stepped aside making room for his hyper companion. My nerve-shattered butches, relieved at seeing it was Two Bits, plopped down like tired old men. With their legs spread wide, they returned their guns to their garter belts and purses. The femmes, breathless from breast binders and fear, put their pieces in their suit jacket pockets and sat down alongside them.

Two Bits was speechless. Her eyes were wide open at the sight of Rascal in basic black with pearls. She looked like she was having an acid flashback.

"It's camouflage," I assured her. "Its cool man, you're not fucked up. I'm really in a fuckin' dress and yes, you're right, that is Little Rosie with a dick."

Red replied in his gravelly whiskey-soaked voice, "You look hot, boss."

I tried to regain my dignity and look like a commanding officer in my dress and push-up bra. Remembering my manners, I tossed the bangs of my long, blond feathered wig off my forehead.

I watched the color come back into their faces and said, "Go help yourselves to a drink and then tell me what was so important that you had to interrupt our meeting."

Two Bits walked down the aisle, looking like a flower child in a garden of glamour. The scent of pot and incense, dried watermelon seeds and wilted daisies wafted with her to the front of the room.

Glowing from her position of honor, Two Bits spoke in an out-of-breath, excited voice. "Some shit came down in Fillmore boss! It all started when Giuseppe walked out the back door of the pork shop shack—where the old, evil-eyed bitch cooks. When he went to his car, the Gomez Rexsauras jumped out from behind some trash cans. Bang! Bang!" she shouted ferociously.

"Joe shot Giuseppe's kneecaps out, one at a time. Boom! Boom!" Two Bits used her hand like a make-believe gun and pointed down toward the knees of my troops. She shouted again, "Boom! Boom! Boom! Boom!" Everybody in the room jumped to the rhythm of her beat.

"Giuseppe was down on his knees, in a pool of blood, begging, 'Don't kill me, man, don't kill me, man!' Joe went up to him and pistol-whipped him, smashing his jaw into a thousand pieces! Giuseppe went down hard, man."

Two Bits paused, turned and looked me in the eye before she continued, "Joe kicked him onto his back and all his broken teeth fell out. Then the crazy Yaqui ripped open Giuseppe's shirt and put his cigar out on his chest!"

Exhausted, Two Bits told us the rest. "Gomez burned Giuseppe's chest over and over again. He kept saying, "This is for Linda from Missouri!" Then, he stuffed bags of heroin in Giuseppe's pockets. I took off 'cause I heard the heat coming. I don't know where Joe is now, boss."

Instantly, I put on a game face, though my stomach was roiling with a sickening awareness that I had just become "real street." A ruthless gangster was born with the news. I became acutely aware of a new power I was feeling in my gut. It was wrapped in a sensation of calm strength. Being a gangster pimp was no longer an act. The crippling of a man was a direct result of my order. Joe had just carried my request out to the ultimate extreme.

Everyone in the room was stunned at the news. Asian Pearl looked at me with a smile of satisfaction. The ice princess said with pride, "Jesse finally got that Fillmore pussy's attention. Now we're real Tenderloin bitches, and they're in the wrong neighborhood!"

Fucked-up Giuseppe had been punished for his mutilation of Linda gang-land style.

Junior chimed in, "Joe Gomez is one crazy Mexican! Who's standing now, *Vato*!"

Little Rosie jumped up and announced, "Giuseppe has bad karma! Now he's the hostage! The pigs own his ass!" She gave a loud snap of her fingers and then said in true Elvis style, "Uh-huh-huh, thank you very much."

I waited for the laughter in the room to die down. Rosie's two-cents' worth had given me an idea. "Ladies, this could be exactly what we needed. I am a student of the art of war, and there are some basic guidelines. It's all about carrot and stick. We now are dealing with a classic hostage exchange. County Jail has Giuseppe, and we have the key to get him out."

Junior's eyes came alive with awareness as she excitedly joined in, "Boss, the cops and the D.A. dude can really help you this time!"

"You got that right, Junior."

My Puerto Rican Elvis had unknowingly identified our leverage, and my loyal henchman had reassured me that we had the clout to ask for a very big favor. The dirty cops that worked booking in County Jail would be our trump card.

With newfound confidence, I addressed my troops. "Prince knows we have people in our pocket that he needs. His brother's only hope of getting out is for the evidence to magically disappear. And there isn't a judge in San Francisco that will let Giuseppe out on bail."

Lovey spoke up, "I know, as a black sister, that brother is in a world of shit! It would take a miracle to change a white judge's mind!" Then Lovey smiled like a cherub and added, "Or a word from above from the D.A.'s office."

I smiled at Lovey's wisdom. "I'll offer Prince a very simple deal. He gets Giuseppe, and we get a truce and the contract off my head."

"He'll agree to your truce, Jesse," commented Asian Pearl. "If he doesn't, we can always call Scope to finish the job."

"I believe the other Fillmore pimps will want Prince to concede so we can all get back to work. Pearl, if Prince persists we will have to get more persuasive."

Doris frantically ran into the room. Breathless, she said, "Jesse, you better get back on stage. Joe's here! He wants to make an entrance while Clancy is still in the audience."

"Oh, shit!" I said. "Wait for me, I'll be right back," I told my crew. Quickly, I ran down the stairs adjusting my tits.

In a moment I was back on stage. Carla had just informed me and the audience that I would be performing in a duet from *West Side Story*. The band on stage jumped into the tune, "Somewhere."

I grabbed my mic and followed the spotlight. It landed on Joe Gomez in a sequined blue velvet jacket. His jacket sparkled like crushed diamonds as he walked with a huge saxophone toward the stage. Out of the darkness, Carmen's voice magically rang out as the spotlight found her. "There's a place for us …."

Slowly she walked, encircled in the light. Her auburn hair flowed as her hands reached out toward me. Like an angel in a white peasant dress, she called to me, "We'll find a new way of living…"

Our eyes met as we sang to each other. As the crowd rose to their feet with tears in their eyes, Carmen ascended the stage. Joe hovered behind with his saxophone, mournfully keeping her company.

I stood in my blue gown, holding Carmen's hand as we serenaded each other:

"Somehow, someday, somewhere!"

Chapter 32

PINK ROSES

*T*UTTLE HAD THE JACK DANIEL'S WAITING FOR ME before I sat down on the bar stool at the Grapevine. The shot glasses sat back-to-back, filled with the dark amber liquid, a water glass behind them. A small glass ashtray was placed in front of me by tan, weathered hands. Tuttle's eyes, illuminated by the large Schlitz Beer sign behind the bar, danced in the soft light.

"Jesse, it's great to see you," Tuttle said. "The word on the street is that the truce between you and Prince is holding. Thank God because business is good again. Nothing is worse for business than a turf war."

I reflected on the wise old man's words as he wiped the mahogany counter. "Yeah, Tuttle, that's for sure. We're celebrating tonight."

"I can see," Tuttle laughed. "Are the roses and the pretty little bag for me?"

I smiled back at the old booze pusher. "In your dreams. Can you put this behind the bar for me?"

"Sure, Jesse," the old man said as he took a large bouquet of pink roses and a small, lavender gift bag and placed them under the counter. I took a drag off my cig, watching the smoke drift into the darkness.

The cease-fire between the Tenderloin queers and the Fillmore pimps had been earned in blood. Prince, a man of reason and limited capital, had agreed to a truce brokered by Bunny. She visited Giuseppe in the County Jail infirmary and had him contact Prince to negotiate a truce.

Prince had agreed to meet with me and work out the details of the cease-fire. We were to meet at the Why Not cocktail lounge. I would be accompanied by Joe Gomez and Junior. Prince would bring Blondie the Swede and Bubble Gum Guppy along for the parley. The terms of the truce would be discussed over a couple of drinks.

Every pimp, cop and hooker, along with Mayor Alioto, welcomed an end to the hostilities. The pigs were tired of working overtime. The terms of the truce were plain and simple. Giuseppe would beat the sales and distribution of heroin charges. The solid case would never make it to trial. Much to the embarrassment of the city, all the evidence would mysteriously disappear from the property room. The inquiry into why Giuseppe was found with two blown-out knee caps and a ton of dope would be dropped.

Tuttle interrupted my thoughts by asking, "How's Carmen doin'?"

"Good, Tuttle. We're both relieved all this bullshit is over."

"I bet. I know I'm glad you girls are all in one piece."

"This war scared the hell out of Carmen. She asked me if I would like to go to barber school. My girl thinks I would make a cute barber."

Tuttle's sparkling blue eyes squinted as he gave me a deadly serious look. "She might have a point. It's better to be a broke live barber than a rich dead pimp."

"Well, Tuttle, a thousand-dollar-a-night whore might find trying to live on a barbershop jockey's salary a serious bummer."

"That's true," Tuttle agreed.

"It's a nice fantasy, old man, but I'm not dressing like a girl to cut guys' hair. I've never been a weekend queer. Carmen knows I'd rather die from a bullet, free on the streets than from shame, hiding in the straight world." I downed the shot of whiskey.

Tuttle hit the wooden bar with a closed fist. "Don't let any fucking straight person judge you ever. When we're drunk enough, we'd fuck a snake if it would hold still."

Letting go a gut-busting laugh, I stood up and put a twenty on the bar. I was interrupted in the middle of my exit by Little Rosie rushing up to me with the corn-fed hooker in tow.

"Where the hell have you girls been?" I asked the exhausted looking Linda from Missouri and my dancing-eyed Puerto Rican vixen.

"We've been out shopping," Rosie said, beaming. "We ripped through Macy's. Them retail white broads are still spinning. They never seen two surviving turf war hookers shop. Uh-huh!" Rosie patted Linda's ass as she ordered Tuttle, "Give my big sister a beer. Isn't that what you big girls drink?" She asked Linda with a sassy leer.

"Rosie, you're such a bitch," answered the sullen call girl.

"Now girls, stop bickering. We have a lot to celebrate. In fact, we're all goin' dancing at Chuckkers later tonight! Why don't you join us, Linda?" I asked the solemn Missourian.

"No thanks, Jesse, I think I'll just relax with my beer. Rosie wore me out. We couldn't find one g-string in my size. Jesse... I really hate dancing. My legs are way too fat. I'm ready to go back on the escort circuit. I'm okay now."

I contemplated Linda's request, a reasonable one at any other time. I had taken her off of the escort list after the kidnapping. She had been staying in the bordello with Marie during the hostilities. Her usual amiable temperament, though, had been interrupted by frequent bouts of rage. I had paired her up with Little Rosie, and she had started working at the Grapevine. I had hoped that the dancing and being free of Asian Pearl would help in her recovery. I considered it disability leave.

Bunny and I had been concerned about her since the rape and torture she had experienced. Most disturbing was her mysterious disappearances from the house at all hours. Looking at Linda, I could see our rehab plan was not working.

Little Rosie, irritated with my lack of attention toward her, dumped a shopping bag full of sequined g-strings onto the bar.

"Have a drink with your baby girl, Jesse. I haven't even seen you since the cease-fire. You don't love me no more? Come on; pick a new g-string for me." She leaned in close. "Maybe this one will be luckier and we won't get caught."

"God knows I love your g-strings, Rosie, and I've missed you. I'll have a drink with you and a dance at Chuckkers later. Right now, though, I'm going to Compton's for dinner. Hey, old man, can you get me my stuff?"

Tuttle—who was standing safely at the other end of the bar—said, "Sure Jesse."

As the phone rang, he reached under the counter and pulled out the dozen pink roses, my gift bag and placed them next to the g-strings. He walked back to the wall phone.

Rosie excitedly grabbed the roses. "Oh, *papi*, they're beautiful," she said, inhaling the fragrance with an intoxicated glaze in her eyes. "What's in the little bag for me?"

Linda from Missouri sipped her beer and, too bored for words, sighed, "What makes you think it's for you?"

Before I answered Rosie, I weighed my two choices. Either I could tell Rosie the truth and risk hurting her feelings, or I could give her my gifts for Carmen.

"Well, Rosie, I got Carmen the flowers and a little gift because it's her birthday," I lied.

Rosie grabbed my arm, pulled herself up to the bar stool, and shot daggers at me. "*Mentirosa! Bastardo!* Carmen's a fucking Taurus! You think I'm stupid?"

"Rosie!" Tuttle called. "It's the phone!"

Unwilling to relinquish her death glare at me, Rosie shouted over her shoulder, "Who the fuck is it?"

Tuttle dropped the receiver and it dangled from a cord on the wall phone. Shuffling past Linda from Missouri, he whispered to Little Rosie, "It's your woman trick, the matron. She says she has to talk to you."

I nudged Rosie and said, "Don't be rude. Helmet Head is one of your best johns."

Rosie grabbed the shot of rum Tuttle had just poured for her. She downed the shot and defiantly told me, "Fuck that pussy-jonesin' dyke! She takes too long. If she gets any fatter, I'll have to roll her in flour to find the wet spot."

We all watched as Tuttle turned an unusual shade of red.

I extended my hand toward the flowers. "Listen, my little chi-chi mama, I just bought a house in South Sausalito, and me and Carmen are going to celebrate. Plus, we'll all have a little getaway in case we have another turf war."

Rosie jumped off the stool and threw the bouquet of roses onto the floor. She put her hands on her hips and started yelling in Spanish, "*Soy rosas roja!* You think I'm not as good as Miss Flat White Bread!" She stamped her heel a few times. "Fuck pink roses!" she declared. "I know what's in the bag, it's a fucking ring!"

"I don't know what the fuck you're talking about. I said I just bought a house."

"You're gonna play house?" Rosie hauled off and slapped me. "I can't believe you're marrying that bitch!"

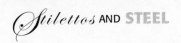

She took the tip of her shoe and ground a fresh pink rose into the cement floor. She looked at me with scorching eyes, "Don't forget, I was your first girl."

I said wearily, "I'm late. I have to get to Compton's. We'll talk about this later."

Tuttle patted Rosie's back and poured her rum. She downed her shot as the phone rang. Tuttle implored, "Rosie, it's probably the Matron again. Talk to her!"

"Tell the bitch to call me later!" Rosie demanded.

"Get the phone, Linda." Tuttle said, exasperated.

Linda did as she was told. I hugged Rosie and said, "I'll be at Compton's in an hour. You can come and talk to me then."

Rosie burst into tears and took my handkerchief. She patted her eyes, smearing thick black mascara.

"You never communicate with me, Jesse. You think I'm just a girl to party with. You should take me more seriously." Rosie spoke with a strange malice in her voice. I tried to kiss her forehead goodbye, but Rosie pulled away. Her eyes bore into mine with a malevolent darkness.

I looked away and called to Linda, "I'll be over at Compton's in an hour. You girls are welcome to join Carmen and me for dinner. Hey, Missouri, bring your little straight ass over to Chuckkers. We're all going dancing tonight!"

Linda lowered the receiver and shot me a huge smile.

Chapter 33

COMPTON'S

*S*KIPPING UP THE WET STEPS, I entered Carmen's building with my key and I headed down the elegant hallway. As I approached her apartment door, I heard the stereo playing. Aretha Franklin was singing Carmen's favorite song, "Natural Woman." I gave three fast raps. "Hi, baby doll," I said with a smile as she opened the door.

She stood before me in a cream-colored, Asian silk dress that draped the curves of her body like a gentle waterfall. The short sleeves barely covered her narrow shoulders. The Mandarin collar was closed at the base of her neck and red silk threads attached the chic golden buttons. Embroidered Asian fans with shimmering emerald tassels ran down the ridges of her breasts.

Her gaze held a smoldering heat as she waited for me to enter. At that moment I realized that Carmen was the only girl for me. Carmen threw her arms over my shoulders, pulled me close and kissed me.

She tugged me into the apartment and I set the gift bag down on the coffee table en route. She jumped on me, kissing my open mouth, her stilettos off the ground, her legs wrapped around my waist. She moaned in desire as she felt my strap-on press against her.

I slipped my hands into the slits of her dress and felt her smooth, inviting bare ass in my hands.

While her mouth stayed locked on mine, sucking my tongue, I carried her to the bedroom. I threw her down on the bed and ripped off my jacket. As she seductively lay there, Carmen teased me with her legs and freshly painted red toenails. Slowly she curled one leg up, bending at the knee as she slowly traced the side of her defined calf with her Italian stiletto.

Unhurriedly, I unbuckled my gun holster and hung it on the bedpost. I flung my black Stetson across the room onto her dresser and crawled onto the bed like a panther stalking its prey. With a giggle she squirmed on the bed, moaned and whispered, "No."

"Don't say no to me, young lady," I whispered back like a playful daddy. "I'm gonna get you!"

She pulled me down and wrapped her arms and legs around me. Lying on top of her, I felt her breasts press against mine. She frantically undid my belt, reached into my pants and grabbed my cock. With a moan and a thrust of her pelvis she slipped me inside her.

I became lost in the rhythm of our bodies fucking. I kissed Carmen hard as she shuddered and whimpered in burning spasms of ecstasy.

When her breathing slowed to normal, she whispered into my ear, "I love you, Jesse."

She kissed me and held my face in her hands. I ran my fingers through her hair and tenderly kissed the top of her closed eyelids. I pulled back, looked into the now serene, glazed eyes that had burned with lust a few minutes earlier and asked with a gentle smile, "Why were you so hungry for me tonight?"

She let out a deep sigh as she played with my hair. I leaned on my elbow and searched her green eyes.

Carmen confessed, "I've been so afraid. Every day I expected to get a phone call from Junior telling me you were dead. I'm glad it's all over, that it's just you and me now."

I slowly rocked her in my arms. As I held her, I felt her hand reach, moving up my inner thigh.

I stopped her hand in its tracks. "We'll come home early. We have all night to make love."

Carmen giggled and said, "I'm holding you to it."

I got up from the bed, grabbed my jacket off the floor and said, "I'm sorry we had to go through this bullshit. We're safe now."

"I guess…as safe as anyone can be in the Tenderloin," said Carmen.

"That's true. We might have to wade through a little more bullshit. But I think the worst is over. Now it's back to taking care of business."

Carmen got herself together and went into the bathroom.

I was pouring myself a shot of Jack when I heard her ask coquettishly, "What did you get me, honey?"

I swallowed the shot and responded, "Guess!"

Carmen entered the living room and sat on the couch waiting for me to join her. I decided to pour myself another shot of Jack.

Carmen watched me. "That looks good. It's so chilly outside. I'm in the mood for a little whiskey too. Pour me one, okay?"

I was surprised that she would have Jack and not her usual Tom Collins. I poured the shot and sat next to her on the couch.

We toasted as I said, "Here's to the truce! Let's enjoy it!"

We downed the Jack and Carmen looked towards the lavender bag as she began to guess what was in it. "Is it a ring, Jesse?"

"No."

"Is it an emerald bracelet?"

"No."

"Is it a strand of white pearls? Huh?"

"No."

"Let me see what's in there!" Carmen got up and opened the bag, pulling out a gold business card holder. Stunned, she read the words, "Baby Doll" on the face of the card holder, spelled out with inlaid emeralds.

She hesitantly opened the card holder.

I mischievously said, "What's it say? Read it to me!"

She pulled out a lavender-colored business card and read, "Carmen's Fine Jewelry of Sausalito." Once she understood its meaning, a teardrop streaked across her face.

"Does this mean what I think it does?"

"Well, I know you wanna leave the life. It's fine with me. I kind of like the idea of visiting my old lady in the suburbs. I'm not quitting, but you can. I bought you a jewelry store."

In a soft, faraway voice she said, "I never thought I'd get out. I never thought I would live to get out of the TL."

She looked up at me and searched my eyes. "Are you sure about this, Jesse? Are you really saying that I am owner of a jewelry store and that I can give up my johns?"

I kissed her hand and smiled. "This is a good investment. I'm kinda getting hooked on the legit business crap anyway. It's a nice sideline." Pulling away, I snapped my fingers. "This is a good gig. You're the front and I'm your silent, invisible dyke partner. It's about time the burbs got a taste of the TL."

Carmen gave an excited giggle and said, "You are a bad boy."

"Come on, retail momma. I'll tell you all about it at Compton's. I'm hungry. We'll be meeting up with the gang at Chuckkers later. Let's go, baby doll."

"It's gonna be fun. It's been a long time since we could all party together," said Carmen. I began to walk to the door when Carmen gently touched my arm. I turned back to her as she said, "Hold me, Jesse!"

I wanted to get going, but in that moment I conceded and held her as she dropped her head onto my chest.

"I had no idea you were planning this store for me."

"Why the hell do you think I was so anxious to go and see my bookkeeper? I've had this game plan for a long time. I don't tell everybody my shit, bitch. Now grab your mink, it's chilly outside."

As if she hadn't heard a word I said, she said to me tenderly, "Kiss me,"

"We'll never get out of here," I growled. I grabbed her and kissed her long and passionately.

Caught in the moment, I whispered, "I love you." She melted in my arms.

I regained my composure and said "Now, let's get the fuck out of here!"

Carmen grabbed her arctic white fox wrap and we were out the door. After a brisk walk through a light drizzle and impending fog we arrived at Compton's.

Our arrival caused a stir in the crowded restaurant. Half the queens of the Tenderloin were there in their long gowns, fake furs and cheap wigs. Their happy chatter flew across the tables. Each synthetic bitch tried to verbally beat back her opponent's volley of cheap-talkin', witty trash.

Carmen and I were greeted from the back booth in the corner by the warm smiles of Joe and Junior. My shadows were having a cup of coffee and shootin' the shit in Spanish. While covering my back they were watching the restaurant's entertaining floor show.

Across from them sat a few queens that were notorious for causing a riot in Compton's. All hell broke loose in August 1966 when one of them quietly refused to go to jail for impersonating a lady. As she was being dragged out to the Black Mariah, she threw a cup of coffee in the cop's face. Warrior queens started beating the pigs with their purses and high heels all the way down Turk Street. Lesbian commandos threw sugar shakers through windows, and burned down Tommy's newspaper stand for good measure. We made headlines that night because it was the first time queers fought back in San Francisco's history. I tipped my Stetson to the ladies as we passed.

Carmen and I went over to our favorite table by the window, which the regulars knew not to occupy. Just as we were sitting down, Miss Zada stumbled over to us. She adjusted her falsies in her red halter top as she spoke.

"Carmen, you look beautiful! I would die for that coat."

Miss Penny came over and pulled Zada away slurring, "Come on, queen. Let's get out of here before they pour us into a Black Mariah."

"You tell her, Penny. It's a hassle getting you ladies out of the tank!" I playfully reminded the inebriated party girls as they left Compton's.

Karen came over to take our order. "You girls want your usual?"

"That sounds good, Karen," I replied.

"You got it, ladies." She set two cups of coffee down in front of us. They nestled on clean white paper doilies in beige ceramic saucers. Karen gave us a smile and marched off toward the kitchen.

Carmen and I sat quietly. Her fingers were intertwined with mine as she rubbed the rim of her coffee cup absentmindedly. We contentedly waited for our meal.

All of a sudden, I was distracted by a shiny object that caught my eye outside the window. The dark night and the reflection on the window cast a large shadow above Carmen. I saw the Star of David with a glint of diamond, then a red spark fly out of the barrel of the gun. I heard glass shatter and felt a spray across my face as a burning pain bore into my chest. I fell back, seeing Prince shooting at me through the glass as I collapsed to the floor. My hands were in front of me and all I could see were red flames.

Lying on the floor, I heard screams, gunshots and Carmen's labored breathing. She lay next to me, her face covered in blood. Her blank stare was lifeless, I realized.

Desperately I grabbed her wet, blood-soaked hair. I pleaded into her ear and felt the cold emerald earrings touch my lips. "Wake up! Wake up, Carmen! Wake up!" I tasted her blood on my mouth. A wild groan poured out of my soul.

I saw black-and-white spectator shoes before me. Suddenly, I was pulled from the floor and cradled in Joe Gomez's big arms. My voice screamed into the still-frozen restaurant. Fighting to break loose of Joe's grasp, I yelled woozily, "Let go! Let me go! Carmen! Carmen!"

Junior ran ahead of us. I saw her weapon drawn as she shouted to Joe, "Get her in the car!" Around me, I noticed vaguely, everybody remained pinned to the floor. Joe followed her out the door as Junior fired at the fleeing purple El Dorado.

My face hit the cold leather seat and I heard the door slam shut. I couldn't understand why all this warm blood covered my chest. As the car roared away, I fell into darkness.

Chapter 34

THE RUSE

I SAT IN THE SOLITUDE OF BUNNY'S LIBRARY, awash in memories of Carmen. Holding Carmen's childhood catechism book of prayers, I leafed through the pages. Her mother had Phyllis deliver it to me to help comfort me in my grief.

Fresh bouquets filled the room along with cards of well wishers. The rest of Bunny's home was decorated in modern sixties décor, accented by an excess of femininity. Wisely, she had left the library in its original Victorian elegance.

Her home had served as my hospital for the past two weeks as I recovered. Like an angel of mercy, Bunny attended to my every need while allowing me to mourn. As I set Carmen's prayer book aside, a nuclear rage bellowed in my gut. I asked God to forgive me. Turning the other cheek was not an option for me or my crew.

Prince's bullet had missed my heart by an inch that night at Compton's. My body was healing, but my soul lingered in a black abyss. Fortunately, my enemies believed that I had died with Carmen. Soon my troops and I were going into battle, using my false demise to spring a trap.

My plans for a truce certainly hadn't worked out. But no one could have seen it coming. Giuseppe's release, our bargaining chip, had failed. He had been discovered hanging in the shower room with his pants dangling around his ankles. He'd been slit from his belly to his sternum.

Prince immediately assumed that I had ordered his brother's murder. His reasoning I could understand. What baffled me is how Prince knew I would be at Compton's. It had been my first night out after weeks of hiding. Only my people knew where I was going. Like flipping through a Rolodex, my mind searched for the rat in my crew.

In my analysis, I utilized the detective's tried and true trinity; motive, means and opportunity. Only my inner circle had been aware that Carmen and I would be at Compton's that night: Joe, Junior, Marie, Bunny and Rosie. They all had the means. Any one of them could have contacted Prince by a runner or by dropping a dime. Prince provided the opportunity since he could and would do the killing.

Joe could have taken me out at any time if he were after the hit money. But if he didn't stay steadily employed, he'd go back to the joint. Junior also could have made fast cash, but I knew she'd never work with Prince. Marie and Bunny not only loved me, but for them, I was more valuable alive. Rosie believed that I was retiring from pimping and moving to the burbs with Carmen. That pointed the finger at her. I hadn't forgotten Rosie's jealous tantrum and glare of death which still haunted me.

We would take no prisoners. My coveted humanity had died with Carmen on the cold floor of Comptons. Mercy had been strangled out of me by the hands of necessity.

Bunny's soft voice interrupted my thoughts as she entered the room.

"Honey, I want you to take your antibiotics. Even Al Capone was not immune to infection."

My little Florence Nightingale was right. I took my antibiotics and washed them down with a shot of Jack.

Bunny reminded me, "Don't forget to drink water, like the doctor said."

"Okay." I replied as I sipped some water too.

I lit up a Pall Mall. I took a deep drag, expanding my chest muscles. They pulled tight, painfully stretching the recently formed scar above my heart.

While I had been under emergency surgery, Bunny had been at work securing my future safety. Bunny assured Captain Clancy that we would offer the police our full cooperation. She had convinced Clancy to tell the public that I had died en route to the hospital. Like all cowards, the killer would brag and hang himself. Clancy agreed and told the newspapers to report:

"TWO HOMOS FATALLY SHOT AT COMPTON'S GUN BATTLE."

The runners and whores who spread the word did a great job. The pimp parasites believed that Animal, Red and the rest of my bikers had fled.

Prince and his boys had been rippin' and runnin' through the Tenderloin, talking trash about how none of my crew had the balls to return. Those sick, limp-dick chumps were drunk on the bullshit dope we fed them. Clancy's investigation, however, was not going as he'd expected. Like every other murder in the TL, no one had heard or seen anything.

Carmen's revenge would be my private task. We lived by our own code and would handle this street style.

"Jesse, Captain Clancy called earlier to see how you were doing. I thought that was very sweet of him," Bunny informed me.

"That's nice of him," I replied, distracted by my recent obsession.

"Jesse, do you feel you're ready for taking care of business? You seem a little preoccupied."

"Yeah, I'm looking forward to it. What's bugging the hell out of me is who the fuck dropped the dime?"

Bunny sighed and said, "Little Rosie's been distraught, insisting she's innocent. She appears to be genuinely sad."

"I don't know," I said. Bunny hadn't been there that night. "I wish I could find out before she gets on that boat with Prince tomorrow night. No matter how painful it is for me, I'll order Joe to take her out if she's the guilty one."

The doorbell rang. "It's probably Pearl," Bunny said and got up to answer the door.

I had come up with a plan of how to kill Prince and his crew without leaving a trace. This time he would feel the sting of a woman's revenge. This was personal, and I had to show the boys I could run the Tenderloin.

Asian Pearl and Little Rosie had infiltrated the enemy's camp easily. They had convinced Prince that they were now his whores. A few days ago they had started to work for Prince, setting the stage for tomorrow's mission.

Prince believed he was the new King Pimp of the Tenderloin. He thought that all the lezzy whores who had worked for me now desired his big dick. He was willing to expand his business with the cured queers. Asian Pearl had gone so far as to convince him that she had brokered a lucrative deal on their behalf by purchasing kidnapped, virgin sex slaves from China.

Soon the undercover hookers, Pearl and Rosie, would be escorting my enemies onto the *Floating Dragon*. Asian Pearl's father's boat was often used in smuggling operations. Prince and his men believed they were in for a festive night at sea. While cruising, they would enjoy cocktails and a seafood buffet. They would rendezvous with a Chinese cargo ship holding the sex slaves. What he didn't know was that the *Floating Dragon*'s friendly crewmen were my hired assassins.

Asian Pearl entered the library, dressed in a black leather trench coat and dark sunglasses. The shades in this late evening hour made her look like a genuine Mata Hari. Bunny fixed Pearl a scotch on the rocks.

Pearl greeted me with, "Respect, Jesse." Surprisingly she asked, "How you feeling?"

I viewed the Asian ice princess with a new perspective. The hardened street bitch was right. If I had hired Scope, Carmen would be alive today.

"Hey, how are you doing, Pearl? Dealing with Prince must be some kind of experience."

Asian Pearl took a cigarette from a crystal cigarette holder on the coffee table. She lit it with the heavy matching table lighter. She removed her shades and looked me in the eye. "He's easy next to dealing with Rosie twenty-four seven."

In spite of myself I chuckled. "I can imagine. A pain in the ass is one thing, but a dime dropper is another. I hope for her sake she's not. How's your mission coming along?"

"I just left the Booker T. Washington bar. Everything is good to go. Prince, the dumb limp-dick, bought the story hook, line and sinker," Pearl said with a sly smile. "He has no idea he'll be shark bait by this time tomorrow night."

"That's good. At least he'll die with his friends after they're used as chum."

Bunny reached over and took my hand. Her soft fingers reminded me to be civilized. "Jesse, the sharks will seem merciful after Joe deals with him. Just the thought of it sends shivers down my spine."

"Prince handed me this." Pearl dropped an envelope of cash on the table. "It's his half of the deposit for the sex slaves. The bastard said something interesting when we were having a drink."

"What's that?" I asked.

"He said it was about time Rosie and I joined his stable, since Linda from Missouri had jumped ship weeks ago."

Bunny's voice expressed the shock that I felt. "So that's where the bitch has been!" Venom seeped through her lips she continued, "I wonder if the bitch collected the five grand on Jesse's head as well!"

"Now I can't trust that Missouri bitch or Rosie," I said, dismayed.

"Jesse, I'm gonna get to the bottom of this! I'm going to visit the Why Not bar," Bunny exclaimed.

Pearl and I looked over at her in surprise. I asked, "Why are you going to that cop bar?"

Bunny replied calmly, "In detective movies, they always say, 'return to the scene of the crime.' This all started with Giuseppe's death. I'll go talk to the guards that were on duty when he got shanked."

"Hopefully we'll find out who the rat is before my crew leaves shore. You don't have much time," I said.

"You'll be surprised what I can find out in just a few minutes," Bunny replied.

Pearl and I didn't respond, knowing that we had just heard the truth.

"Bunny, do you mind if I talk to Pearl alone for a moment?"

"Not at all, honey, I'm excited about all this." She kissed me on the cheek and exited the room.

"Pearl, would you like another scotch?" I asked.

Pearl gave me a suspicious look. "No, thanks, I'm cool."

I took a sip of my Jack. "Pearl, I've had time to think. You were right and I was wrong. I should have hired Scope like you suggested. I didn't want to carry the weight of that sin. Later I realized not killing my enemy was suicide. I've always been told that suicide is the greatest sin."

Pearl took a drag of her cigarette as I indulged in my musing. "You've turned out to be my best soldier in the trenches."

Pearl's eyes moistened, startling me, for I'd never seen a trace of emotion in them before.

"Pearl, I'm promoting you to the rank of captain. I'll let my soldiers know that you're in charge of the Prince assignment."

"Jesse, I think I'll take that other scotch now."

I got up and poured my geisha a drink.

Chapter 35

BABY DOLL

*T*HE POWERFUL ENGINE OF THE LINCOLN TOWN CAR rumbled as we neared the dockyard. I watched the lights of San Francisco pass with Bunny by my side. Deadly Chang the Chink's wheelman manned the helm and one of Chang's bodyguards sat shotgun. The stoic escorts kept their eyes on the road. Under each of their right ears was a large, black orchid tattoo. The hired muscle wore the logo of their mob boss with pride.

My high-powered rifle was stashed in the trunk. It had been a gift from Scope. The Vietnam special ops soldier had also supplied my crew members with miniature walkie-talkies. He had personally wired Asian Pearl's bosom with the assistance of his lover Joy Luck, Pearl's cousin.

My post would be on top of a cargo container, overlooking the *Floating Dragon*. Bunny had insisted I wear a heavy overcoat with a fur collar due to the seasonally cold weather. She was dressed for the occasion, wearing skin-tight, black leather pants and stiletto-heeled boots. On her head she donned a tilted, black mink beret.

Placing her hand on my knee, Bunny slid closer to me.

"Jesse, I had a very interesting chat with a few cops earlier today." Mysteriously she opened her purse and pulled out a folded piece of paper.

Intrigued, I asked, "What did you find out?"

"Well, it so happens that Giuseppe had a violent argument with a fellow inmate a week before he was stabbed. The most helpful guard told me that man is under suspicion for his murder. He also informed me that the gentlemen's name was Calvert. It rang a bell."

"Calvert," I replied. "That does sound familiar."

"The reason it sounds familiar, honey, is because we've both heard it before. Calvert Lee Tucker is Linda from Missouri's husband!"

"That fucking bitch!" I cried.

"Yes, and it so happens that Giuseppe and Calvert had the same brunette visiting them. So I asked the sweet officer to let me take a peek at the visitors' log."

Bunny slipped the folded piece of paper into my hand. I switched on the overhead light and read. Linda Sue Tucker's name appeared twice on the roster the day before Giuseppe had been killed.

Bunny looked at me intensely. "Linda is twisted Jesse. She loves cruel men. That's why she married Calvert." Her lips pressed together tightly. "It's always the ones who swim sideways that you can't see coming."

It all made sense to me. I remembered seeing Linda talking on the phone at the Grapevine the night Carmen was killed. I also saw Linda the morning I was attacked outside my bookkeeper's. The truth hit me hard. I had been so focused on Little Rosie that it never occurred to me to even suspect Linda.

"Oh my God. Do you think she had anything to do with that fat ass hitting me over the head with the pliers? I thought he might be one of our johns, since I remembered seeing him working over at the house one day."

"After I found about Linda, Marie and I had a talk. We discussed that episode and the man who attacked you. Marie informed me that he was a regular john of Linda's. She could have easily called him so they could split Prince's hit money."

Picturing Linda from Missouri in her hippie drag, I flashed back on her getting in the cab that day. Motivated by five grand, she probably had jumped right out and went to a phone booth. She could have called her trick. It takes five minutes to get anywhere in the TL. When I was getting my shoes shined, Linda was trying to get me knocked off.

"Bunny, thank God I was always taught to give people the benefit of the doubt. Otherwise, I could have made a rash decision," I thought out loud.

"You were wise to wait, Jesse. The matron dyke also had a chat with me today. She told me she's been frantically trying to reach Rosie for weeks. The night you and Carmen were shot, she had called the Grapevine. She asked Linda to warn Rosie that Giuseppe had been killed. She didn't want Rosie to get hurt in the crossfire.

"Helmet Head has been calling the house. Poor thing never got through Jujubees. His message was always the same, 'Little Rosie is inconsolable and incognito.'"

"This will be the last game that farmer's daughter ever runs," I said in simmering rage.

"Jesse, Pearl told me Linda is with them. It's your decision."

Our Town Car cruised through the dockyard and pulled up behind a huge cargo container. Bunny squeezed my hand and said, "I'll be waiting right here."

Chang's henchman opened the trunk to retrieve my rifle. I stepped out after him. Pulling out my trusted Zippo, I lit the paper in my hand. I watched it burn as if it were Linda's funeral pyre.

He handed me the rifle and I slung it over my shoulder. Checking the miniature two-way radio tucked next to my .38, I climbed up the ladder. Looking over the edge, I saw that the makeshift fort offered me a perfect view of the *Floating Dragon* resting in the slip below. The deck was decorated with glowing strings of colorful oriental paper lanterns.

The ridges of the cold steel beneath me chilled my body as I awaited Junior's arrival. Gazing out at San Francisco Bay, I listened to the soft squeaking of the gently rocking boats. Pulling out my silver whiskey flask, I unscrewed the cap, attached with a small silver chain, and took a sip.

Blanketed in darkness under the canopy of stars, I longed for Carmen. My lonely soul bled as I waited to avenge her death. Suddenly a shooting star streaked across the skyline behind Alcatraz Island. As it disappeared into the darkness it left a vast emptiness that reminded me of our short-lived time together.

My mind flooded with memories of Carmen. Her image flickered through my brain like a silent film in a penny arcade. A barrage of precious moments flashed before me: the touch of her warm hand resting on mine, her auburn hair and dancing green eyes as she smiled, her voice saying, "I love you, Jesse," the last time we made love. She was gone before I really knew what happened. All I knew was that her life had run out before my very eyes.

Junior's voice crackled from the walkie-talkie, startling me. "Boss, I'm coming up. Don't shoot my ass!"

"I won't shoot you. Come on up, *Vato*," I answered.

Junior crawled over to me. In silent grief, with Junior by my side, I looked out at the dark ocean water.

"Boss, looks like this will all be over soon," she said reassuringly.

"You got that right. Well, I finally found out who dropped the dime. It was Linda from Missouri."

Junior's jaw dropped. "No shit!"

"Yeah, guess she had the hots for Giuseppe. Every time she went missing, she was at County Jail visiting the sick fuck."

"Thank God it wasn't Rosie," Junior commented. "I would have missed that Puerto Rican bitch."

"Yeah, me too," I said with a sigh. "The whole situation is sad. It breaks my heart. Linda is so young."

Junior stiffened at my side. "This is war and, like you said, boss, we gotta do the job ourselves this time."

"Carmen died because I wasn't respected," I said darkly. "Fear is what the TL respects. Rumors of our enemy's gruesome demise will run through the TL like a river of blood."

"That's cool, boss."

"Rumors are a powerful tool on the streets, Junior."

"Boss, I checked everything out on the boat. I met Deadly Chang's son, the ninja dude. He was so excited to show me his father's gift, a new sword from Guangdong. *Aye Chingao!*"

Bunny's love struck mob boss had rented a floor of suites at the Drake Hotel for him and his entourage. Tara of the West's finest were keeping them company. The suites down the hall from the partying mobsters served as a barracks for the rest of my crew—Lovey Lupree, Marie and her sidekick Jujubees.

"Junior, I hope my soldiers are gonna be as professional as Chang's."

"Boss, since Carmen's death, everyone's got their shit together."

"You got that right, Junior. Even butt-fucking Scope and his hormone-heavy bitch surprised me with their professionalism. I'm glad I listened to my father's business advice to never burn bridges."

Junior and my conversation ended as we suddenly heard crackling voices over our walkie-talkies. The voices of Prince and my crew alerted us that our enemies were approaching. The partying passengers must be cruising through the docks.

I studied the *Floating Dragon* through the high powered scope of my rifle. It had a red dragon painted above its name on the stern. I smiled, realizing it matched the dragons on Asian Pearl's chopsticks.

Little Rosie's voice excitedly piped in over our walkie-talkies, "Oh, Prince, baby! Thank God, I see the *Dragon* yacht. I'm starved."

We heard Linda say, "I love seafood buffets! Pearl honey, did you order fresh cracked crab?"

"Yes, Linda. We are gonna have a real feast tonight," purred back my geisha captain.

Prince's baritone voice chimed in, "Oh good. I can't wait to have me some shrimps!"

The sound of popping Bazooka bubble gum signaled Bubble Gum Guppy's enthusiasm.

I radioed for the captain of the *Floating Dragon*, "Come in, Captain Scope. Come in…over."

"Yes sir, Jesse…Captain Scope here. Over."

"Heads up, Scope. The target is entering the docks. Is everyone in their positions?"

"Affirmative. All systems are go!"

"Scope," I said, "I want you to inform the crew that we have a new party guest. Make sure you give Linda from Missouri the same royal treatment as our VIPs. Is Joy Luck with you?"

"Yes, she's right here, commander," Scope replied.

"Put her on the radio, will ya?"

The haughty queen asked in an indifferent tone of voice, "What can I do for you, Jesse?"

"Please speak to your cousin Pearl in Mandarin and tell her that Linda is the dime dropper. Make sure Pearl introduces her to Chang's boy."

"Of course, Jesse."

I called for Joe on the radio. He was hiding in the closet of the captain's quarters. "Joe, come in."

There was silence.

I called again, "Come in, Joe. Do you read me, Joe?"

"Yeah, boss. I'm here," Joe finally responded in muffled tones.

"Joe, what took you so long? Are we good to go?"

"I was sharpening my skinning knives…I'll make my ancestors proud tonight."

I grimaced at Joe's comments and felt a chill run up my spine.

"Joe, by the way, Linda has been assigned to the ninja guy. Rosie's in the clear."

"Got it, boss," Joe replied.

I contacted our lookouts with my walkie-talkie. "Little Bastard… heads up. Our guests have arrived." Little Bastard and Rascal were perched at their post lying on top of a cargo container across from the gangplank. They were armed with high-powered rifles, covering our backs in the event of any glitches.

Little Bastard responded, "Boss, they're in our sights."

We watched the headlights flood the cement of the parking lot below as the big V-8 pulled up. The beams shot out from the chrome-toothed grille of the Lincoln and illuminated the gangplank leading to the *Floating Dragon*. Like an Indian scout high on a cliff, I watched my game plan unfold.

Prince's voice punched through the static on the walkie-talkie. "It's a shame I killed both them bitches. That Carmen would have been a sweet dessert…"

His vile words made me want to pull the trigger now.

Junior tried to adjust the frequency so we could hear him more clearly.

"...oh well....daddy had to teach Jesse a little respect. What dumb bitches!"

As the loud-mouthed, loose-lipped parasite rapped crap to my girls, I caressed my gun.

Little Rosie's excited musical voice came in over the speaker and flooded the night air. "That's right, big daddy! Uh-huh, baby!" She punctuated each lie with the loud snap of her fingers.

Asian Pearl's voice chimed in, "We're going to make a fortune off those peasant bitches. We won't pay them a dime!" With a sleazy hiss, she added, "With sex slaves, there's no overhead."

"Pearl sounds real cold, boss," Junior remarked.

"She is...and very dangerous."

Prince bragged, "Pearl, my little fortune cookie, too bad I blew Carmen away. The green-eyed bitch was fine! Once she got a taste of my big cock, she would be cured!" Prince grabbed his cock to emphasize his point.

"She was an amateur, daddy. Now you're dealing with a pro," Asian Pearl stated arrogantly. "Tonight, I'm gonna give your balls a real special treatment!"

"They're all yours, baby!" Prince answered.

Junior and I saw the stretch limo pull up to our dock and watched the passengers unload. Bubble Gum Guppy got out first and opened the door for Prince and the ladies. Next, out stepped the tall, stunning henchman, Blondie the Swede in a fine Italian, three-piece, royal blue suit. The gorgeous blond, like a Hollywood movie star going to a premiere, looked out of place at the desolate docks. Linda, acting like an actress before adoring fans, held onto Blondie's arm as she exited the car.

I said to Junior, "Looks like Linda got herself all dolled up. Guess she thinks she's a movie star now."

Asian Pearl was glittering with diamonds. She wore a black cocktail dress with a white sealskin fur coat. Her lovelocks concealed deluxe razor-sharp chopsticks with the extra long blades.

Prince, the VIP guest, stepped out of the vehicle. His towering height was magnified by a mammoth afro-puff. He wore a loud-ass, purple leather coat.

Little Rosie emerged from the car and carefully placed her four-inch, diamond-studded stilettos onto the ground. She hugged her long black mink with her elegant, black-gloved hands. Rosie's foot-high, ratted beehive was crowned with a ruby and diamond-encrusted tiara that glittered under the wharf's fog lights.

Junior and I heard the low voices of the passengers over the walkie-talkie clearly coming through Pearl's wire, nestled snugly between her tits. We listened to their footsteps on the wooden dock. Their words drifted through patches of broken fog floating up to us.

We listened to the lowlife pimp's lame impersonation of a pirate as the group ascended the gangplank. Acting like a wannabe Captain Hook, he yelled orders to his motley crew of pirates. "ARRRG-GGHHH! Listen up, wench bitches! ARRRGGGHHH! When we pick up them China dolls, I want you pros to suck my dick! Teach those little chop-suey sex slaves how it's done in America! ARRRGGGHHH!"

Little Rosie threw her arm up in the air, attempted to snap her gloved fingers and responded to Prince, "You got it, big daddy. I'll teach them real good!" Rosie exclaimed in her thick Puerto Rican accent. "Before you know it, those slave bitches will be sucking as good as an Electrolux."

Prince and his entourage chuckled and guffawed.

Like a ghost out of the stillness, on the deck of the *Floating Dragon*, the evening's hostess, Joy Luck, mysteriously appeared at the top of the gangplank. Her face painted with heavy, stark white Madame Butterfly makeup. The queen stood elegantly erect, dressed like a sultry geisha. She wore a loosely wrapped, brilliant red-silk kimono decorated with beautiful white cranes. The garment's pattern framed her overexposed, cavernous cleavage. Joy Luck's nipples protruded through the silk like welcome buttons. Like a royal headdress, her towering love-locked hairdo matched Asian Pearl's right down to the chopstick hairpins.

The Asian hormone junkie held a tray of martinis out to the ascending guests. She greeted them in a husky, seductive tone, "Welcome to the *Floating Dragon.*" Joy Luck smiled demurely and bowed her head.

Prince swaggered up to the ship's deck toward Joy Luck but seemed oddly intimidated by the haunting dragon lady. He performed a full bow to her and said, "Thank you." Eyeing the drinks on the tray, he grabbed one of the martinis and downed it.

One by one, Prince's entourage walked up the plank. Each passenger was greeted by an elegant bow from Joy Luck as they took a drink from her tray. Pearl gave her cousin a subtle bow as the party procession passed under the oriental lanterns onto the deck.

Junior and I saw Captain Scope, dressed in his crisp white captain's uniform, walk briskly onto the deck. He welcomed the guests with a toothy grin.

"Welcome, friends. We're going to rendezvous with the Chinese merchant ship in international waters off the Farallon Islands. The weather is clear tonight. It should be a smooth ride."

Scope then barked, "Joy Luck, take care of these folks!"

The diesel engines kicked in and an inconspicuous deckhand deftly released the ropes. This sailor was none other than Deadly Chang the Chink's own son, *Hei An Tian Shi*, a.k.a. "Dom the Dark Angel," his father's most proficient assassin. This recruited master of

martial arts was a notorious ninja warrior who had delivered countless souls to the Pure Land.

Joy Luck chatted briefly with Pearl. Taking Linda by the arm,
Pearl walked her casually over to the Asian deck hand. He gave a
formal low bow to Linda. The beat of the diesel engine matched my
heart as I offered up a silent prayer asking God for forgiveness. The
Floating Dragon took my enemies to Hell. Growing silent, the boat
disappeared under the Golden Gate Bridge.

Once the ship faded from view, Rascal and Little Bastard moved
like shadows toward Prince's vacant limo. The duo of professional ex-
burglars quickly hot-wired the car and took off toward their favorite
chop shop in Oakland.

"Junior," I said, "between the great whites and the burial at sea,
Captain Clancy won't find a trace of Prince. He'll be really pissed
when he hears that we've all been partying at the Drake tonight. I
hope he enjoys looking through all our room service receipts."

"Yeah, boss. We've all been spiffing the hotel staff a lot of cash."

"Money talks and it buys silence," I mused aloud.

The San Francisco skyline and the harbor lights caught my
attention as the *Floating Dragon* motored farther from the mainland.
"Junior, I'm gonna catch a few minutes alone. Thanks for everything.
I'll meet you back at the Drake."

"Oh sure, boss," she replied, understanding. Junior proceeded to
climb down the rear of the cargo container.

Looking up at the North Star, I could feel Carmen's presence
envelop me. A wisp of Chanel and a hint of soap seemed to hover in
the breeze and flooded my senses. I yearned to hold her.

A full yellow harvest moon hung over the Golden Gate Bridge
and the glimmering black sea. High in the heavens like a diamond,
the North Star anchored the darkness. The jewel of the heavens
reminded me of Carmen, who I knew was watching over me.

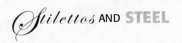

Memories of my girl gave me courage. We had spoken as young lovers in sacred hushed tones. The warmth of her young body soothed me as we held each other close. I remembered her words as she whispered into my ear, "You can't fool me with your player's act. I can see your beautiful soul."

Carmen gazed into my eyes, captivating me. I took in her words as she whispered, "I understand the need to keep up a front, Jesse. In the TL, it's all about who's left standing."

The chilly night air and the salty sea mist briskly welcomed me as I got to my feet. I stood and faced the dark. Yielding to the soft wind, I leaned back. A salty tear crossed my lips as I said quietly, "Thanks, baby doll."

Acknowledgments

FIRST OF ALL, I would like to thank my beautiful parents, Bill and Ofelia Estes. Knowing them, they're at a cocktail party, reading my book in Heaven, sharing their witty humor and compassion with my ancestors, exclaiming, "Did she really say that?"

I believe it should be customary to award Purple Hearts to the friends and family at the completion of a novel, for enduring the barrage of insufferable updates on, "the book." Since I am devoid of medals, I can only offer my sincere gratitude for those who stayed on the battlefield and my understanding to those who deserted.

DEEPEST GRATITUDE

Suzanne Gagnier, my first fan whose mantra was, "Keep writing." Now, my Personal Manager, who took me down the Yellow Brick Road and introduced me to David Guillod.

David Guillod of Paradigm Talent Agency of Beverly Hills. David's enthusiasm and insightful expertise are the pillars of *STILETTOS AND STEEL*.

Howard Sanders of United Talent Agency, for being the liaison to Fletcher and Company of New York.

Swanna MacNair, Literary Agent of Fletcher and Company. She has the voice of Sunday morning and the drive of Monday morning. Swanna's undefeatable, contemporary vision is a gift that made this book possible.

Eric Feig, of Rosen Feig & Golland, LLP, in Beverly Hills. Eric, my Entertainment Attorney slew a dragon for me on Fifth Avenue. Heads roll as he sips lattes and taps a laptop.

John Paine, Editor of *STILETTOS AND STEEL*. John cut a clear path through jungles of pages, while nudging my pen in the right direction.

Bayard Storey, Studio Script Analyst. Hails from Harvard and is my classy, literary henchman. He has my back.

Isabel Storey, Literary Consultant. She had the heavy task of analyzing the first draft. After that, she climbed Mount Whitney.

Dorris Hall, Typist and number one cheerleader. Like the Calvary, her keys galloped to meet deadlines.

Jeanne Ardito, "Editor in Chief of Weed Pulling," who copy edited the first draft.

Javier Ramirez, Writing Assistant. A talented young man who comes to the rescue when I'm stuck for the right word.

Joyce Fetty, Actress. She pedaled up to me and suggested that I also do a graphic novel. Hollywood power broker on a bicycle.

Darrell Fetty, Screenwriter / Actor, brought my work to Howard Chaykin, the world renowned graphic artist. A gallant gesture.

Howard Chaykin, Author and Graphic Artist. The energy of Howard's noir art will be magnificent for my story. Our artistic collaboration is the perfect marriage for STILETTOS AND STEEL.

APPRECIATION

April Muffoletto—Consultant

Barbara Gottlieb—Graphic Artist

Brian McKinney—Personal Stylist and Digital Media Consultant

Christopher Larsen—Web Master

David Blattel—Photographer

Dotti Albertine—Award winning book cover artist

Greg Shay—Henchman

Holly Gagnier—Actress/Consultant

James Dybas—Actor

James Will—Graphic Artist

John Goodman—Actor

Katherine Starr—Film Director: Material Lies

Kim Boten—Production Manager

Linda-Marie Martinez—Consultant- Multi-Media and Public Relations

Melinda Spencer—Publicist for Jeri Estes

Mike Milo—Artist/Emmy Award Winning Animator: Pinky and the Brain

Rene Sanchez—Graphic Artist

Richard Zelniker—Screenwriter/Director: Vinyl

Sean Lewis—Actor

Suzanne Gagnier—Project Photographer

Bravo! To the professional actors, models and technicians who have tirelessly worked on the STILETTOS AND STEEL platform. I proudly call them, "My Crew." To meet these talented young people, visit: **www.stilettosandsteel.com**

TRAIL GUIDES

If I were to be specific about everyone's contribution, it would make Ulysses by James Joyce a fast read.

Amy Schiffman

Ann Hadsell

Angela Hunt

Arthur Spector

Bobby Harvey

Billy Million

Dan Cullinane

Dave Blaker

Debra Steinbaugh

Denise Nagy

Diana Gould

Harriett Savedra

Jim Strzalkowski

Joe Gomez

Karen Tang

Katherine Segal

Kay Ostrenko

Lilli Ungar

Lovey Curry

Sue Nagy

Wendy Chisholm

GRACIOUS FRIENDS

Bobbi Constantine, Operations Manager of Western Costume

Ella Matthes—Owner/Publisher of the LN Magazine

Gary Boettcher—Good friend

ACKNOWLEDGMENTS

Mariah Hanson—Club Skirts
Ruel Gunnell—My handsome manly man in Utah
Russell Bowmen—Thunderbolt Spiritual Books in
    Santa Monica, California
Susan Stryker—Historian and Emmy Award
    Winning Producer: Screaming Queens
Tom Adler—The Essential Gay & Lesbian Directory
    and GayYellowBook.com

Gail Wilson
Joy Gere
Larry Tuttle
Liz March
Marie Stinner
Richie Kellog
Terry Graham
Uncle Danny

CENTER STONES
My Entire Family
Uncle Henry, Aunt Elisa and my loving cousins
Silvia Memminger—my cousin—and her
    running buddy, Aunt Mary
Ala-Nesters, Radford tribe, Valley Club and
    trudging buddies, world-wide
Back to Basics family on Crenshaw
Ted Summers—Numero Uno, Head Honcho of
    Patience, Love and Guidance
Fran Summers—for sharing Ted
Master Sun-Don Lee, the third Patriarch of
    Forshang Buddhism
Professor Yi-Hung Su of Forshang Buddhism
Sister Helena Chou of Forshang Buddhism
Brother John Chou of Forshang Buddhism
Dr. Huy Hoang and staff of Natural Health Medical
    Center, in Lawndale, California
Saint Charles Borromeo Church of North
    Hollywood
Pacific Palisades Writer's Meeting

LAST BUT NOT LEAST
Immeasurable thanks to Giselle Nagy, my special
    lady who gently rocked my words to sleep at
    night, then ran a comb through their hair in the
    morning, sending them off to the world, clean
    and neat.

MY INDEBTEDNESS
To friends who walked with me in the darkness
    and to those who carried the light.
Alabam Corruthers
Chuck Chamberlin
Ed Wade
Frankie Fergusen